lo. e

CW00351160

McNALLY'S EMPIRE is a spellbinding story of
a remarkable family whose founder creates an
enormous, successful magazine empire.

Terence McNally the First came to America a
poor Irish immigrant. From the bitterest of
beginnings he rose to command a vast empire.
Yet no amount of success could rid him of the
heritage which his grandfather had left him, a
heritage which would haunt his dreams and
claim as victim his beloved son.

Terence McNally the Second was a driven man,
following unwillingly in his father's footsteps
along a path of dangerous, destructive passion.

Megan McNally saw the empire there for the
taking and vowed to have it for her own, even
at the risk and condemnation of those who
cared about her most. Soaring from the slums of
1880s New York where Terence McNally the
First lived, to the gleaming towers of twentieth
century Fifth Avenue, McNALLY'S EMPIRE is
a dramatic and passionate saga.

Gertrude Schweitzer

McNally's Empire

CORGI BOOKS

McNALLY'S EMPIRE

A CORGI BOOK 0 552 12437 0

Originally published in Great Britain
by Judy Piatkus (Publishers) Limited of Loughton, Essex

PRINTING HISTORY
Judy Piatkus edition published 1984
Corgi edition published 1984

This book is set in 9 on 11pt Times

Corgi Books are published by Transworld Publishers Ltd.,
Century House, 61-63 Uxbridge Road,
Ealing, London W5 5SA.

Made and printed in Great Britain by
Hunt Barnard Printing Ltd., Aylesbury, Bucks.

To my husband

Seest thou a man diligent in his business? he shall stand before kings; he shall not stand before mean men.

Proverbs 22:29

Prologue

The first Terrence McNally was born on a farm in Lisdoornoo, in the south of Ireland. The size of those poor Irish farms was so pitiful – tiny plots separated from neighboring plots by a border of stones – that there was no question of dividing them. By the custom of primogeniture the eldest son inherited what little there was. The others got nothing, had no hope of anything. Many of them drank their lives away. Some, crazed by alcohol and frustration, struck out in terrible ways.

The first Terrence McNally was a younger son. His survivors did not acknowledge him. His son, born after his death, was not named for him but called Padraic. No one ever spoke of the father at all or of what he had done to have his existence denied.

At the request of Padraic's mother his youngest boy was named Terrence McNally the First. It was not known whether she thought that in this way her husband, the true first Terrence McNally, would be memorialized, or whether she meant to complete his obliteration. In any case, the second Terrence McNally, this son of Padraic's was the first to be born in America.

Padraic McNally, a big bull of a man with a soft voice and peaceable ways, had brought his wife from the old country to a tenement in an Irish slum in New York City. He got a job as a hod carrier. The tenement on Little Water Street was a filthy ruin, full of rats and cockroaches, and the job, carrying a trough of bricks and mortar on his shoulder fourteen hours a day, six days a week, paid barely enough to keep the two of them alive, but Paddy thought he was lucky. He was in America, where everyone sooner or later got rich.

Paddy was a man who liked what he knew and distrusted change. Left to himself, he would have been one of the last to give up on his blighted homeland and set out for a strange country across thousands of miles of ocean. But his mother had persuaded him to go. Those who left for America, which the Lord had blessed, would flourish like the palm tree.

'Ye'll need a wife along,' she told him. She had married off her four daughters. He was her only son. 'Take Aggie Reilly. She'll make ye a good one.'

Paddy had not thought of marrying yet. He could always find girls for his needs, and the other comforts were provided by his mother. Still, he would have to have a wife someday, and his mother was right. It would be better to take a girl from home than wait till he got over there and then have to marry a foreigner. His mother was right about most things.

'Aggie's no beauty,' he said.

'That she's not, but beauty is vain, and a woman who feareth the Lord is to be praised.'

When Paddy got to know Aggie better, he wondered whether she did fear the Lord. She surely feared nothing and no one else.

'She might not have me,' he said to his mother.

'She'll have ye. It's not every man will see her virtues like you do.'

Aggie had been there all of Paddy's conscious life, like the scraggly bush that jutted out of the flat green land between his farm and her father's, two farms away, but he did not know, until his mother told him, that he saw her virtues. She was a tall, rawboned girl, almost as tall as Paddy himself, with freckles and wild orange hair and a great beak of an Irish nose. Her mother had died when she was eleven, and she had kept house for the eight years since, feeding her six brothers and her father and washing their dirt-stiff clothes on a board with its ridges half worn away from her scrubbing. Ah, yes, a girl like that would handle America with her left hand and keep a husband well fed and clean with her right.

'But how will her da let her go?' Paddy asked his mother. 'Her being the only woman in the house and all?'

'Never you mind that,' she said. 'He'll have another woman soon enough.'

'You don't know he will.'

'I do know, because it's myself will be the woman.'

'Yourself?' Paddy gaped at her. He thought she could be only his mother, not somebody's wife. 'Has he asked you, then?'

'Not yet, but he'll see the sense of it as soon as you ask Aggie. He's got a brother already in America, in a village with a name I can't get my tongue around – Massasomething. We'll all go there when the time comes. His brother will find us a place to live and work for the men as well.'

'But how was that agreed, then, if you've not so much as been asked yet?'

'It wasn't agreed, but it will be,' she said. 'I'll see to it.'

Paddy knew she would have seen to all of it, given the chance. She did see to his marrying Aggie and herself marrying Aggie's father. What she could not see to was the course of the lightning that struck the older newlyweds as they rode back from the church through the storm, their wagon the highest spot on that treeless stretch and themselves, close together on the wagon seat, higher still. The charge went through their bodies, uniting them in death before they had a chance to be united in life. The same week of their nuptial mass they were returned to the same priest in the same Lisdoornoo church for the funeral mass.

Paddy was bewildered by grief. 'I'll not go to America now,' he said.

'You will,' Aggie said. 'If you stay, you'll starve, and myself with you.'

'I'll not go without her.'

'You will, for she's in no state to be taken along,' Aggie said. 'We'll go on Friday week, as planned.'

11

Paddy looked carefully at his new wife. 'You sound like herself. I do believe you're cut from the same bolt of cloth.'

'That's as may be, Paddy McNally, but it's not after mothering you I am.' She looked him straight in the face, scarcely needing to tilt up her chin. 'This is a wife you married.'

'It is that.' His arm circled her waist. She was sharp-boned there, but not everywhere. In the night he had found her soft places, her roundnesses. In the dark she was as seductive as any beauty. 'I'm not likely to be forgetting,' he said.

They left for America on Friday week, Aggie and Paddy and Aggie's brothers. It was a long, rough crossing. All eight of them were sick in the hot, jammed, stinking, lurching steerage, but Aggie managed to stagger among them to wipe up their vomit and put wet cloths on their foreheads. She waited until the day they were to land before telling Paddy that he and she would not be going to Massachusetts with the others.

'Uncle says nephews is one thing but he can't be looking out for the whole of Lisdoornoo,' she told him. 'There's no blame on the man. I'm only his niece, and you're no true blood relative of him at all. But he says New York City is a grand place, with plenty of work for a great strong man like yourself. He says so many Irish are settled there already it's just like home.'

It was nothing like home, and for a long time Paddy yearned to be back farming his green land, blighted or not. But he got used to it. In time the New York slum was his home, and hod carrying his work, and it was as if he had never known anything else. He stopped expecting to get rich. Some men were not cut out for riches, even in America.

If Aggie expected something different, she never mentioned it. She battled the dirt and the vermin and made soups and stews out of bones coaxed from the butcher and half-rotten vegetables that sold for pennies and were, with the worst parts cut away, tasty enough. She was enthusiastic in bed, delighting Paddy and also embarrassing him a little. A good wife was supposed to be compliant, but he had never heard of one who was eager. He had made no mistake, though, in listening to his mother and marrying her, homely as she was and her looks not improving with time. The only trouble he ever had with her was after their fourth boy was born.

'That's the end of it,' she told him. 'We'll not be making another one to feed.'

'You don't know that,' he said.

'I do.' She had the new baby at her breast, the milk running out of the corners of his greedy mouth. 'There's something I've heard of in the street. You put it on yourself and it keeps the juice from getting in me and making a baby.'

'It's filth you're talking, woman!' Paddy said in rare anger. 'I never thought to hear such talk from me own wife.'

'There's no filth about it.' She plopped her breast out of the mouth of the baby, who was suckling in his sleep. 'I'm only saying we have no need to keep on with it when there's a way we can stop it.'

'Well, it's filth it sounds like,' Paddy muttered. 'And a sin it is for certain to stop a baby if the Lord is wanting us to have another.'

'If the Lord is wanting us to have another, when likely it would starve, or one of us would, He's got no sense.'

Paddy stared up at the ceiling, as though expecting a massive fist to ram through it and strike Aggie dead. But when he looked at her again, she was still alive, calmly laying the infant in the wooden crate that was serving its fourth stint as a cradle.

'So you'll go out then, Paddy, won't you, and get that thing?' she said.

'I will not.'

'If it's shy you are, I can ask where and get it for you.'

Paddy, who seldom raised his voice, roared, 'I'm

13

thinking this wife I married is no decent woman, but a hoor!'

'Shush, Paddy McNally,' Aggie said. 'You'll be waking Terrence.'

'Terrence? Who, might I ask is Terrence?'

Aggie indicated the sleeping infant, who had not yet been christened. 'Terrence McNally the First. It was your ma told me to name the last boy that. "How will I know which is the last?" I asked her. "Ye'll know," she said, and she was right.'

'Terrence McNally,' Paddy said. 'It's a nice sound it has.'

'Terrence McNally the First. She was particular that should be in it.'

'Why?'

'I don't know. Your ma didn't say. But isn't it grand?'

Paddy grinned down at the rudimentary features of the milk-drugged creature in the crate. 'It's not very grand he looks yet. Maybe he'll grow up to it.'

But Paddy did not see his sons grow up. One of his fellow workers slipped on a wet board nine feet above the spot where Paddy was working. The whole trough full of killing bricks crashed down on Paddy's head.

'It's a hard thing to get hold of, Father,' Aggie said to the priest. 'My da riding by just that very minute when the lightning came out of the sky. And now my man just on that spot where the bricks fell down.'

The priest said it was the will of the Lord.

'I'll not believe that, Father,' Aggie said. 'Because if it's the will of the Lord to kill a good man with a wife and four small boys, then I'd have to be hating Him for a cruel one.'

The priest made the sign of the cross over her. He asked the Lord to forgive her, for in her grief she knew not what she said. Aggie spoke to no one else about Paddy's death. She did not go to church again.

14

PART ONE

Terrence McNally the First

1868–1880

1

Terrence went to work when he was ten, four years after his father died. He also killed a man that year.

The job was in Jimmy O'Brien's saloon after school. O'Brien was the ward leader. When people wanted things, they came to him. They treated him with respect and paid him money. He was so rich he wore silk shirts and had two gold teeth. Terrence thought about it while he swept the sawdust. He decided to become a politician like his boss.

The slum was all he knew. Its sights and sounds and smells were no more noticeable to him than his own fingers. But he saw, as Paddy never had, how Aggie hated it.

He was the only one of the four boys she had been able to keep with her. After Paddy was killed, his boss had sent a clerk to convey his condolences and fifteen dollars to tide her over. He had also given her work, doing his family laundry at almost half what he had paid Paddy. Aggie was grateful for his generosity, but however hard she tried, she could not feed and clothe the five of them on what he paid her. Finally she sent the three older boys to three of her married brothers, all of whom were working in their uncle's shoe factory in Boston. With only Terrence and herself to fend for, she managed.

Terrence scarcely remembered Paddy. He did not miss having a father. Aggie fought the devil in him as Paddy never would have, beating it out of him whenever she thought it necessary. Sometimes she punished him unjustly, thinking it better to be sure than just. He never resented it. Some of his misdeeds went undiscovered and unpunished. All in all, it balanced out.

'I'll teach you not to be so free with your fists,' she told him, 'if I have to take the skin off your back.'

'Ma, you want me to stand there when some kid comes after me because I'm Irish and—'

'It's not some kid coming after you I'm speaking about, Terrence McNally the First, and you know it. It's not standing there I mean. It's you starting it I'm speaking about. It's you wanting something and punching to get it.'

What he punched to get was respect, though it was not a word he would have used or a clear concept in his mind. He knew only that without it he would be victimized, preyed upon, laughed at. It was necessary to fight, but he took no pleasure in it for its own sake. He won because he was big and because he was artful and not hampered by fury.

Neither of the two boys who were fighting the day the Irish haters came had any of these advantages. They were puny and pugnacious, wildly thrashing and battering each other while an audience of other boys and a number of men egged them on. Both their faces were cut and bloody. They kept slipping in the garbage that overflowed into the street, falling against the ring of spectators, who pushed them eagerly back to each other.

Terrence was just coming home from work. He would have been inside by the time the mob came swarming down Little Water Street, but he could not easily get by the fight. The Irish haters came while he was trying to push through. Before anybody noticed, they were there, swinging fists and clubs and bottles, cursing the dirty Irish, raging to rid the city of them, and wipe them out, the dirty foreigners, or send them back to their own dirty, potato-eating country where they belonged.

Everybody who was out in the street was caught in the melee, even a few women sitting peaceably with their small children on the steps of their tenement buildings. The Irish haters were on the steps, too. They were everywhere. They were the only ones with weapons. One young Irish boy found a bottle in the garbage, but before he could straighten up with it, he was knocked down, left to moan in the gutter with his ribs kicked in.

Terrence had a cut on his arm from flying glass. He smeared himself all over with the blood, worked his way to a lamppost, and slumped behind it, looking close enough to death to be left alone. Through slitted eyelids he saw men and boys he knew beaten up, trampled on, lying face down in rotting garbage mixed with their own blood.

He saw a burly man in paint-stained overalls take fourteen-year-old Frank Moore's skinny arm between his hands and snap the bone as if it were a twig. The man smiled while he did it – and smiled wider when Frank screamed. Then the man, still smiling, bent down to where Timmy Conroy, who was four years old, was standing on the steps of Terrence's building, pressed hard and frightened against his mother's knees. When Timmy began to cry, the man called him a sniveling Irish puppy, hit him hard across the face, and started to pull him away from his shrieking mother.

Terrence dove. He chose, without conscious decision, the exact moment when the burly man, bending and pulling at Timmy, was off-balance. He dove for the man's legs and butted him behind the knee joints. The man fell heavily. Terrence heard the crack of his head on the stone step. He did not wait to wonder why the steps were suddenly clear of people or to notice that all over the street both Irish and Irish haters began to melt away. He leaped over the burly man, lying still against the steps, and raced inside and upstairs to his flat. The only thing on his mind at that moment was to wash away all traces of blood before Aggie came home and thought he had been fighting.

'There's a dead man laying in front of the house,' she said when she got there. 'Nobody at all in the street but him. Do you know what it is happened?'

'I heard a lot of shouting and screaming,' he said, not

lying. 'I think maybe it was the Irish haters.'

Dead? he thought. *Killed?* He went outside later to see. The man was still smiling, as if he had got the better of the dirty Irish after all. His face had turned greenish white, and his eyes were open and staring, uninvolved.

Terrence had seen dead men before, killed in accidents and fires, in workmen's riots, by rat bites and starvation, but he had forgotten how they looked. He never forgot the dead face of the man he had killed. Not that he was sorry or felt guilt. He just never forgot the man's dead face.

The police came and asked questions, though they knew it was useless. Nobody on Little Water Street ever told the police anything. The burly dead man was taken away and Frank Moore's arm mended and Timmy Conroy played on the steps, rolling a rotten potato he found in the garbage on the street.

'It don't matter where you live just so you live decent,' Aggie said. 'Just so you don't waste what's born in you. You've got a head on you, Terrence McNally the First. I'll teach you to use it if I have to beat you black and blue.'

Though she never touched him with affection or spoke a tender word to him, he knew what he meant to her. She had let his brothers go and kept only him. They were good-looking boys (the uncles had sent daguerreotypes), but he had Aggie's outsized nose and little sharp blue eyes, her orange hair and ungainly body.

'The Lord must love the great ugly likes of us to make two,' she told him once.

She was all scrawn by then, the resilient young flesh dried to a tough tegument over the large, sharp bones, but he saw no lack of beauty in her. He had no notion she was worn-out, three-quarters finished at thirty-three. He thought she could lick anybody, and would if she had to.

'Couldn't you be a ward leader, Ma?' he asked her.

'There's an idea now. A woman ward leader. Or will I dress up in trousers so they think I'm a man?'

'Ain't there no woman ward leaders then?'

20

She shook her head. 'It's a man's job.'

'Why? Couldn't you do it?'

'Get out with your questions, Terrence McNally the First! There's no matter if I could or couldn't. They don't allow it. If it's ward leader you want, you'll have to be it yourself.'

'How?'

'Don't be asking me how. Find out. You've got a head on you, and with a mouth in it as well.'

He thought Jimmy O'Brien might laugh at him. Terrence permitted nobody to laugh at him, but he could neither beat up O'Brien nor get at him in any of the ways he had devised for those bigger and stronger than himself. O'Brien was too powerful.

Terrence studied him while wiping the tables and emptying the spittoons. 'You're the biggest man in New York, almost, ain't you, Mr O'Brien?'

O'Brien was a short, muscular man with minimal black hair and a jowly Santa Claus face. 'Well, there's a few bigger,' he said, showing the gold teeth.

'Could I ever get to be like you, Mr O'Brien? Not as big. I know I couldn't never be as big. But someplace maybe near half?' The blue gaze upward from under the heavy lids was pure and worshipful. 'If you told me how and I did just like you told me?'

O'Brien cleared his throat. 'How old are you, kid?'

'Thirteen,' Terrence lied.

'Well, you got a couple years. Just stick around and work hard. Keep your mouth shut and your ears open, and I'll see.' He gave Terrence's shoulder a playful punch. 'I like a kid with ambition.'

Terrence learned to listen to beer-loose tongues and to select out what was worth repeating to O'Brien. Sometimes O'Brien rewarded him with an extra nickel or even a dime. Terrence could see there was money to be made as an informant, but ward leader was what he was after. He was unclear as to the function or purpose of a ward leader. But he knew it meant money to release his mother, and something else that he had come to want for himself. Something that he had no words for. Something Jimmy O'Brien had and Terrence needed. He felt he had only to stay close to O'Brien and wait a couple of years.

When O'Brien's cashier left to work in a bank, O'Brien offered Terrence the job.

'Now that you're fourteen,' he said (Terrence was not yet twelve), 'you can quit school and work for me full time. I'll pay you twice what you're getting now.'

Terrence raced home to tell his mother. Twice what he was getting was five dollars a week. With the seven she earned, washing clothes for four different families, maybe they could afford to move to a cleaner flat on a better block.

'You're daft,' Aggie said. 'They won't be after letting you quit school, and if they would be, I wouldn't.' She was peeling potatoes, carefully saving the peelings for the next day's soup. 'You're going to get all the learning you can, Terrence McNally the First. With that, and the head you've got on you, someday you'll be somebody.'

He knew better than to argue with her. Besides, he was not completely cast down. Although he admitted it to no one, he liked school and learned quickly. Facts fascinated him – all kinds of facts. While his classmates struggled with *McGuffey's Eclectic Reader*, he devoured abandoned newspapers and read Henry James in discarded copies of the *North American Review*.

'My ma won't let me quit school,' he told Jimmy O'Brien, 'but I could be your cashier the same hours I'm working now, and you wouldn't have to pay me only a dollar more a week.'

'Fifty cents,' O'Brien said. 'I gotta figure on paying somebody to be here when you ain't.'

Terrence was pleasant to the customers; he made change fast and accurately; he could be trusted. O'Brien had what he told his wife was the 'bargain of the century'. Terrence knew he was a bargain, but he thought it might work to his advantage later on.

22

The following year O'Brien got in trouble with the party. Terrence did not know what the trouble was. He did not even know O'Brien was no longer ward leader until he noticed people were not coming into the saloon to give him money anymore or to hang on his favor.

'I got to cut your pay, kid,' O'Brien said to him one day. 'I can't keep open Sundays no more, so that's less time you'll be working, which means you get less money.'

'How much less?'

'Seeing as how you're a good worker and I like you, only fifty cents.'

'That's more than one day's pay, Mr O'Brien. One-seventh of three dollars is forty-two and eight-tenths.'

'Listen, kid, you're lucky I'm even keeping you on. You got any idea how much business I'll lose, the cops calling the Sunday law on me and shutting their eyes to it for every other saloon around?' His thick lower lip trembled. 'Anyhow, there ain't no such thing as eight-tenths of a cent.'

'Leave that off then,' Terrence said quickly. 'Pay me two fifty-eight, and it's a deal.'

Terrence was too pleased with himself for putting this over on O'Brien to realize until later that he would be earning only eight cents more than when he first started working in the saloon. He probably could have found another job, but he did not try. He felt he had to stick with O'Brien. Besides, he thought things would get better. O'Brien knew how to finagle.

Though Terrence was only thirteen, he looked nearly like a man. He had grown most of the way to his eventual six feet one inch and his voice had changed. If his beard had been darker than its peculiar pale orange, he would have had to shave every day instead of every two. A few months after his pay had been cut, he spoke to O'Brien again. 'Soon as business picks up, you got to give me more money, Mr O'Brien. Two fifty-eight is kid's pay, and I ain't a kid no more.'

'You ain't as old as you said you was neither. Did you

23

think you could fool Jimmy O'Brien?'

O'Brien's good teeth still flashed, but they were flanked by empty spaces now. His fleshy face had a grayish cast. He looked fifteen years older than his forty-six years.

'Anyway, business ain't gonna pick up,' he said. 'They're doing me in, kid.'

Terrence sat down on a stool, facing O'Brien behind the bar. It was four o'clock in the afternoon. The only customer in the place was a derelict at the other end of the bar.

'Who's doing you in, Mr O'Brien?'

'You seen that feller was in here before? Little feller, dressed natty?

Terrence nodded. 'He didn't buy no drink.'

'He wasn't in here to buy no drink. Know who he was? Mr Charles Cornell, the water register.'

'What's a water register?'

'He's the feller collects the money for using water. Never seen him around here before, have you? Good reason, too. Where's my water faucet?'

'You ain't got none. You bring water from where you live.'

'One hundred percent! I ain't got no faucet. I don't use no city water here. You think that makes any difference to Mr Charles Water Register Cornell? I got to pay anyhow. And not no reasonable bill, like I oughta get if I *was* using the water. I got to pay for enough water to damn near drown the whole ward. If I don't, they'll shut off the water at my home. And you want more money soon as business picks up!' O'Brien made a soft, sneering sound. 'Between none of the Tammany boys coming around no more, and the Sunday closing, and now these here crazy water bills, there ain't going to be no business at all.'

'Is it Mr Cornell that's . . . ?' Terrence began, but O'Brien had not finished.

'Putting me out of business is what they been aiming at. One little thing they don't like, and they don't want to let me live.'

24

'Who, Mr O'Brien? The party?'

O'Brien walked away from him. He wiped the top of the bar with a dirty cloth that hung from his apron. He plunged some glasses into a basin of gray water and stood them upside down on the counter under the bar. After a while he came back to Terrence.

'You want to stick with me, kid?'

'Sure, Mr O'Brien, but I got to be paid.'

'You'll be paid. I ain't sunk yet.' He leaned his arms on the bar and lowered his voice to a confidential murmur. 'I got a proposition I been thinking about since it started looking like they wanted to shut me down. Now with this water thing, I don't see no reason to wait. We'll close the place, sell it. Then what we'll do, we'll operate private. I know a supplier who'll take care of us, no questions asked. We'll take orders to deliver liquor to party meetings and conventions and such, cheaper than they're getting it now. There'd be good money in it.'

We. Terrence tried the pronoun silently on his tongue and liked the taste of it. 'How would we get the orders?'

'That's where you come in. We can't let anybody know I'm in it at all. You tell them you got an uncle or somebody in the business, and he'll make a very special price for members of the party, but you got to keep it secret who he is on account of his other customers who have to pay the regular price. Or whatever you want to say. You got the gift of the gab. Just so they don't have no idea it's me. That'd finish me good.'

'What's anybody want to put you out of business for?'

'Listen to the rest of it, kid. It's not only the price that's the come-on, but you'll personally deliver any order, big or small, anyplace. They'll go for that.' His gold teeth glinted. 'What do you say?'

'Is it the party wants to put you out of business, Mr O'Brien? Did you do something the party didn't like?'

'I don't see as that's got anything to do with you, kid.'

Terrence looked straight at him. He spoke at half his ordinary rattling speed, thinking the words out carefully.

25

'You need me for this, Mr O'Brien. You can't do it without me, and I can't do it without you. So that makes us like partners, don't it? A partner's got to know what's going on.'

O'Brien stared at Terrence as if he had never seen him before. Suddenly he began pounding so hard on the bar that the derelict at the end jumped in fright.

'Kid, you're cute! You got more twist to your tongue than a pretzel. Partners!' He shook his head. 'Jimmy O'Brien, partners with a kid who ain't dry yet behind the ears!'

'My age don't matter. You need me,' Terrence said quietly. 'So tell me what they want to put you out of business for.'

O'Brien wiped his hands on his stained apron. He pushed his lips in and out. 'You know who Tweed is, kid? Boss Tweed?'

'Sure. The boss of Tammany Hall.'

'The boss of the whole damn city,' O'Brien said. 'I had a little business going with the cops in the ward, but I wanted to spread out. I was ambitious. A man has a right to be ambitious, don't he? Only I got into a few other fellers' territory.' He paused. 'You know what I'm talking about, kid?'

'Graft,' Terrence said.

O'Brien blinked. 'Well, that's the way of politics. One hand feeds the other. I'd've been all right if I hadn't tried to get too big. In this city, if you're big, you got to feed the Boss, too. The other fellers put the Boss onto me, and I was finished. Lack of loyalty, he called it. He said he'd be lenient on account of the wife and kids, but I don't know what he calls lenient. Not shooting me?'

Terrence knew politicians made deals with the police and got paid for using their influence to help people who had to get around the law or were in trouble with it. Maybe O'Brien should have stayed in his own territory, but Terrence thought they could have just told him so, warned him, instead of trying to ruin him. He was sorry

26

for O'Brien.

'How you going to afford to pay me for this new job, Mr O'Brien?' he inquired. 'There's a lot to it. I think it ought to pay pretty good.'

'You said we was partners, didn't you? Well, partners share the profits, don't they? So every order you get, I will give you a percentage of what we make on it.'

Terrence considered this. 'What percentage?'

'Well, you got to remember I'm supplying the merchandise. That's the biggest part of it. Twenty percent would be about right, but I like you, kid. I got a soft heart. I'm going to make it thirty.'

'Forty-five, Mr O'Brien. Like I said, you can't do it without me.'

'Listen, kid, I been good to you. I kept you on and paid you regular, when I didn't have hardly no money to do it. Thirty-five.'

'I could've worked at Flaherty's anytime. Mr Flaherty told me if I ever needed a job, he'd take me on. Forty percent, Mr O'Brien, and I won't take no less.'

O'Brien sighed. 'Blackmail, that's what it is.'

2

Terrence was so full of himself on the way home that he could hardly handle it. Exuberance was not within his ordinary experience. He patted the junkman's emaciated horse, which was standing at the curb. He greeted the lamplighter, a half-demented old man who muttered endearments to each gas flame as he lit it. He pushed his cap back a little on his head and took off his frayed and outgrown jacket, feeling too warm for it in the chilly November evening.

A girl was huddled on the bottom step of the dark hallway of the tenement. He could not see who she was until, as he passed her to go upstairs, she lifted her head and looked at him.

'What's your hurry?'

She had a hoarse, not unpleasant voice. Her features were thick, and her hair was drab and tangled but reasonably clean.

'I got to get home, Maureen,' Terrence said, making no move to go.

Her name was Maureen Conroy. She lived on the third floor, one below the McNallys', with her mother, grand-mother, four younger sisters and brothers, and a father who never went out except to panhandle for whiskey. Terrence had sometimes seen three or four boys waiting for her to come out of the girls' entrance after school, but he had not given it much thought. She had left school two years before, when she was fourteen.

'What's the matter then?' The hoarse voice rose to a baby squeak. 'Scared you'll be late, little boy? Scared Mama'll spank?'

If she had been bigger and a boy, he would have handled her, but he did not know how to get at a girl.

'I'm not scared of nothing,' he said. 'I can get home anytime it suits me.'

'Yeah? Well, let's go sit on the back stairs then. It's more privatelike.' She held out her hand. 'Help me up.'

Her hand was small and dry, with soft-feeling little bones. A girl's hand. He had never held one before. He thought he would have to let it go when she was on her feet, but it clung to his.

They sat down in the musty darkness of the back stairs, impervious to the perpetual mingled smells of grease, cabbage, garbage, and human waste. Maureen's thigh slid against Terrence's leg. He sat paralyzed with rapture.

'Come on,' she whispered.

He bent stiffly and pressed his closed lips to her mouth. It opened. Her teeth clicked against his teeth. Her tongue joined his, whether in his mouth or hers he could not tell. He felt her fingers fumbling at his trouser buttons, and then his dick was in her hand, growing and growing as it had surely never done in his own, until he thought it would burst.

'Put it in me,' she ordered.

He was not sure he could find the place. To his relief she took charge and guided him. For an instant he was aware of an exquisite warmth and wetness closing around him. Then he exploded inside her. At almost the same moment a shoe like a spike of concrete kicked his rump, and he rolled off her with a yelp.

'Get up, ye lousy, stinkin' bastard! Never let it be said Fergus Conroy killed a man while he lay on his back. And as for you, ye little—' The voice broke off. 'Where is she? Where'd she get to?' it roared. 'Whaddye do with my Maureen, the dirty little hoor?'

Terrence lay where he was, moving his head just enough to make sure Maureen had indeed disappeared. He could barely see the man bending over him in the darkness.

'Maureen?' Terrence said. 'There wasn't no Maureen here.'

'Wasn't, huh? Ye're a stinkin' liar,' Conroy said, but with a trace of uncertainty. He leaned closer, peering into Terrence's face, exuding waves of stale whiskey. 'Who the hell are ye anyhow? Whyn't ye get to yer feet like a man?'

Terrence groped for his jacket, which he had dropped somewhere on the floor. He meant to swing it at Conroy, distract him, and escape up the back stairs as Maureen must have done. But the flame of a match flared close to his face, and before it went out, before he could move, his arm was in a horny, unyielding grip.

'Ain't no use trying to get away, boyo,' Conroy said with sudden mildness. 'One, I got ye, so ye can't. Two, I know ye. I'd know that ugly mug anywhere.' He chuckled. 'Mrs McNally's kid, ain't ye? Not hardly old enough to stop pissin' yer pants, and yer stickin' it in some bitch's.' The import of his own words appeared to revive his anger. 'Get up, ye little bastard! When I'm done with ye, ye'll wish ye'd never got no nearer Maureen than Connemara.'

Terrence squirmed experimentally, but the bony fingers

only tightened, digging painfully into his flesh. 'It wasn't Maureen, Mr Conroy. It was a girl in my class in school. She don't even live in this buiding. What would Maureen want with a kid my age?'

'Ha! That little hoor wouldn't care if ye was in diapers, just so ye had a big enough thing to shove in her.' Conroy had hold of Terrence's other arm now. He hauled the boy to his feet. 'Come ahead then.'

Terrence tried to dig his feet into the crumbling cement floor, but Conroy dragged him along as if he were a reluctant puppy on a leash.

'Where you taking me, Mr Conroy?'

'Ye'll know soon enough.'

Terrence did not think Maureen's father really meant to kill him, but he could not be sure. Jimmy Donovan's father had stuck a knife in Jimmy's mother and the man he caught her with, and nothing had happened to him. Everybody said it was what any husband would do. Probably it was the same for a father.

'Listen, Mr Conroy, it wasn't Maureen, so you got no right to do nothing to me.'

'I ain't?' Conroy released one of the boy's arms. An open hand the size of a paving stone smacked Terrence across the face. 'That's in case you're a stinkin' liar and it wasn't nobody but Maureen, which I think it wasn't. Ye wanna call a cop?'

Terrence thought his nose might be broken. He felt with his tongue for missing teeth, surprised that there were none. For a terrible moment he thought he was crying, but it was only involuntary tearing from the blow. He had not cried since babyhood.

They came out into the light of the front hallway. It was only when Conroy began yanking him up the stairs that Terrence suspected his intention, and he was not sure a violent death would not have been preferable.

Aggie opened the door. She pushed wisps of dulling orange hair back from her forehead with one arm. Barely glancing at Conroy, she examined Terrence's face with a frigid stare.

'So that's why you're late. Fighting again, is it?'

'It's not fighting did that, Mrs McNally,' Conroy said. 'It's meself.'

'Yourself?' She did not move from the doorway, but her head whipped around to him. 'And what's the meaning of it, ye great elephant, hitting my little boy? Was it so drunk ye were ye didn't know him from one of yer own? I'll have the law on ye, so I will!'

Terrence had an instant of hope. If he could get away from Conroy now, get into the flat with his mother and slam the door before anything more was said . . .

But Conroy did not loosen his hold on Terrence's arm. 'I jest now caught yer little boy,' he said, 'givin' it to a girl on the back stairs, beggin' yer pardon, Mrs McNally, like no little boy at all.'

She glanced briefly at Terrence, then stared coldly at Conroy again.

'And that's none of yer business, is it? Far as I know, it ain't yer job to go after boys that's foolin' with girls on back stairs or noplace else.'

'I didn't go after nobody, Mrs McNally,' Conroy's tone was conciliatory. 'It was lookin' for my Maureen, I was, and I found this one and a girl on the stairs in the dark. He says it wasn't Maureen, which is why I lugged him home instead of—'

'If it wasn't Maureen,' Aggie broke in, 'what were ye hitting him for?'

Conroy shifted his feet. 'In case he's lyin', which I think he is.'

'And anyhow, if it was Maureen,' Aggie said, as though the man had not spoken, 'what did ye think ye was after doing? Looking out for her virtue? Her that lifts her skirt for any trousers come down the street? If it was Maureen, it was her led him on, and my boy, here, not hardly knowin' yet what girls is for. So ye ever lay a hand on him again, ye great bully, and I'll have the law on ye double, for this time and that as well.'

31

Conroy dropped Terrence's arm as though it were hot and retreated down the stairs. Aggie pulled Terrence inside and slammed the door.

'Well,' she said, 'that's the last we'll see of that one, the drunken bum.'

Terrence grinned with relief. He touched his tender face gingerly with his fingers and went to inspect the damage in the piece of mirror over the kitchen sink. The red imprint of Conroy's hand was splayed like a huge birthmark across his cheeks and chin. His nose, outsized to begin with, was starting to swell grotesquely.

'Here.' His mother shoved a clean rag into his hand. 'Wring it out in cold water and hold it to your face awhile. Y'ain't likely to be no pretty sight tomorrow anyhow, but that might ease it some.'

The water ran cool, not cold, and had a peculiar smell that was, to Terrence, the ordinary smell of water. The kitchen sink was used to wash dishes, clothes, and themselves. When Terrence had finished with the dripping rag, he cleaned out the sink with another rag and a sliver of soap, the way his mother had made him do from the time he could reach high enough.

'Turn around now, Terrence McNally the First,' Aggie said.

The tone of her voice startled him. That day he had handled Jimmy O'Brien. He had done it to a girl as easily as any grown man and got nothing worse for it than a smack in the face. Aggie's voice broke in on his pleasure with himself. He turned slowly.

'Is what he said true?' The sharp blue of her eyes had faded, but they could still glitter, hard as marbles. 'Was ye on the stairs with Maureen, or any girl, like he said?'

Terrence thought of denying it. His mind began darting, working out reasons why Conroy might have picked on him.

'Don't try lyin' to me,' his mother said. 'I'll know if ye try, and it'll go much worse for ye.'

'It was Maureen,' he said. 'She thought it up, not me. I

32

didn't hardly know what was happening.'

Aggie kept the belt that had been his father's on a nail behind the kitchen door. The first lash cut him across the legs, through the thin, shiny long trousers she had bought him from a pushcart so he would not have to start high school in knickers.

'That's for shifting the blame,' Aggie said. 'She didn't make ye do nothing ye never heard of before and wasn't wanting to do.'

'You said she—'

'What I said to that drunken bum and what I'm after saying to you is two different things.' She swung the belt again. 'Don't you never put the blame on nobody else for something you done yerself. Turn around.'

He was as tall as she was, and twice her bulk. He could have taken the belt from her. It did not occur to him to try.

'That's for carrying on with girls, the young age of ye,' she said, flogging his back. 'It's a thing for men, not children, and don't ye be forgetting it is.' She hung the belt back on its nail. 'There's diseases they have as well, those girls the likes of Maureen, doing it with they don't care who. Catch one of them diseases, and it'll be after rotting your brain.'

He went into the windowless hole of a room where he slept now that he was too old to sleep in the kitchen with his mother. He took off the clothes he wore to school and work and put on a torn shirt and outgrown knickers that hung on a nail in the wall. Aggie had supper on the table when he returned to the kitchen, a stew of carrots and potatoes, enriched with a bone to which a little meat had clung, with stale bread (sold cheap) to dip in the thin gravy.

'I'm getting you out of here, Ma,' Terrence said. 'Soon.'

'And how will ye be doing that?'

'Me and Mr O'Brien is partners now. I'm gonna get forty percent of everything he – we make. That's almost half. Me and you'll move to a nice place, clean, with no rats or nothing. You could maybe start looking for a place

33

uptown.'

'Uptown, is it?' Aggie shook her head. 'Out of the dirt is one thing, and good riddance, but you'll never get me way up there. What would I do, I'd like to know, without an Irish face around me?'

'I think there's Irish uptown, too, Ma.'

'Not my kind.'

They ate in silence. Terrence's inclination was to lean over the plate and shovel the food in as fast as he could, but he restrained himself. He had learned that if he chewed slowly, making every mouthful last, his incessant hunger was better satisfied.

'What's it for?' she asked him then. 'Jimmy O'Brien making ye a partner and all? Don't be telling me it's his kind heart.'

He looked her full in the face. 'Mr O'Brien got treated bad by Mr Tweed, Ma, so he lost his business because Mr Tweed told his men not to go to his place no more, and closed him Sundays, and made him pay big water bills when he don't even use no water, all on account of the Boss don't like him, so what I got to do is get some business back for him, and he only wanted to give me twenty percent but I got him up to forty.'

'I don't know half what you're saying when ye go rattlin' away like that, like ye have wheels on the words. What I wish ye'd be telling me is how a kid only a couple months in long trousers will get the business back for him when he can't do it himself.'

'Mr O'Brien says I have the gift of gab.'

'Ye have that, all right!'

'The boys could come and see us,' he said quickly, before she thought of anything else to ask him. 'If we get a nice place, bigger and all, they could maybe stay.'

She spoke of them as 'the boys', and so he did too. He barely remembered them from the last time the uncles had brought the three of them down from Boston, nearly four years ago. He did remember he had not liked them, had not felt they were his brothers and had been pleased when

34

the youngest, a year older than himself. spilled tea all down the front of his fine-looking clothes.

'Are they rich?' he had asked his mother when they left.

'Next to us.' She had been standing at the window, watching them go down the street, the smallest one holding the Uncle's hand. 'I won't be having them come again to this place. Maybe I done wrong, keeping ye here,' she had said without looking around, 'when I could've sent ye off to live decent like them. At the time I thought it was a little thing to be asking, to keep one out of the four, but—'

'I like it here, Ma, with you,' he had said, moving closer to her. 'I'm glad I ain't where they are. They're snot noses.'

She had turned swiftly and smacked his cheek with her hard hand. 'Don't ye ever be letting me hear ye speak like that again. It's your brothers they are.'

He hardly ever thought about them. Aggie mentioned them rarely. They sent cards at Christmas which she stood up against the kitchen window for a while and then added to the others in a cardboard box above the stove. Terrence was relieved every time Aggie put them away. Now and then someone asked him whether he had any brothers or sisters. The answer seldom came instantly to mind.

Yet now he said, 'The boys could come and see us . . . they could maybe stay.' A moment before he said it, he did not know the thought was in his head. He did not want the boys to come. He certainly did not want them to stay. But the words were right for the purpose.

'That would be grand,' Aggie answered. 'Not to stay. They wouldn't be wanting to stay after all this long time up there, going to school, and Paddy starting in the shoe business and all. But wouldn't a visit be grand, though? Us in a nice place, and them not wishing they was away?'

'Why is Paddy quitting school, Ma, if they're such swells? Why don't he go to college?'

'Swells? Who said they was swells? They're McNallys, same as you.' She got up and took the plates to the sink.

'Anyhow, there's not everybody is cut out for it. You're the one with the head on ye, Terrence McNally the First, and ye'd better be using it instead of the other end of ye, or ye'll never be nobody.'

He did not see why she was bringing that up again, for no reason. But he was satisfied. She had said nothing more about his partnership with Jimmy O'Brien.

<h1 style="text-align:center">3</h1>

O'Brien bought a secondhand bicycle for Terrence's use and equipped it with a basket substantial enough to hold a large crate. Under the top, visible layer of groceries, the bottles nestled unseen. No one wondered about a grocer's boy, riding his bicycle around the streets to make his deliveries.

Terrence had never ridden a bicycle in his life, but he did not mention this to O'Brien. He walked the contraption until he had disposed of its cargo and then practiced riding it. By the end of the second day he could balance it without falling off until he had to make a turn. In less than a week he felt confident enough to ride with the bottles aboard. He whizzed along for blocks, leaving all the pedestrians, and even some of the carriages, behind. The closest he had ever come to such exhilaration was when he was inside Maureen, but that had been over much quicker.

O'Brien opened a small harness shop on Hudson Street as a front. Behind it was a shed where he stored his crates of liquor. The crates were well hidden under piles of junk, and the door to the shed was padlocked. Still, he never kept more on hand at a time than could be explained away as his personal supply. He and Terrence were never seen together. They transacted their business in the shed late at night, in total darkness. The groceries that concealed the bottles in Terrence's bicycle basket in the daytime were replaced by books during the hours when no grocery delivery boy would be making deliveries.

If, in spite of all this, any of their customers was shrewd enough to suspect the identity of Terrence's mysterious 'uncle', he never mentioned it. The prices were too favorable. Without a saloon to maintain or a license or excise taxes to pay for, O'Brien could sell liquor much cheaper than any legitimate purveyor.

The entire undertaking appealed to Terrence. Its illegality was of no concern to him, beyond the possibility of being caught. In his world the law was the largely corrupt police, to be paid off by those who had the means, to be outwitted by the others. The need for stealth and cunning to avoid arrest was only an added fillip.

Because he still thought she had some mystical way of knowing when he lied, he always told Aggie as much of the truth as he possibly could. He told her now that he was working with O'Brien in his new business and helping to bring in customers, leaving her to assume he meant the harness shop.

'It's a lot of money you're making for a small little place like that,' she said.

'We're good businessmen.'

'What business is it you're doing at night, though? If you're after that Maureen again, I'll have the hide off ye, Terrence McNally the First.'

'You already did.' He grinned at her. 'I ain't crazy enough to chance it again. Besides, I got no time for Maureen. What I do nights is talk to fellers in the ward that can maybe help me get to be a politician someday.

'Well, ye better not be lying. If ye are, that tongue ye got, and the Irish grin on ye, won't do ye no good at all.'

She questioned him no further, and Terrence felt not only relieved but perfectly virtuous. He had not lied about anything.

Maureen, when he happened to pass her, took no more notice of him than she had before their abbreviated coupling, but other girls were happy to relieve the besetting stiffness of his member. He had learned how to

37

protect himself against the dangers of brain rotting. He had also learned how to prolong his pleasure.

Even so, these encounters occupied only a fraction of his time. He often made evening deliveries to a club meeting or party in the ward and hung around the kitchen doorway, watching and listening. From time to time he did have a conversation with one of the men.

'You're the young feller talked us into ordering booze through you, ain't you?'

'I didn't talk you into it, Mr Flynn. I only told you how good I could do for you, on account of my uncle, and you was smart enough to take me up on it.'

Flynn laughed and clapped him on the back. He said, 'You've sure got the gift of gab, son,' which was what people always said. 'You'd make a good politician.'

Dennis Flynn was the man who had succeeded Jimmy O'Brien as ward leader. He had a long, stringy body and a long, pouch-eyed face full of broken capillaries that made him appear ruddy. His nose looked swollen and inflamed, and his eyes tended to water. Terrence had known a likely customer when he saw one.

'That's what I want to be, Mr Flynn. A politician.'

'Y'do, eh? What age are you, son?'

'Nearly eighteen,' Terrence said, recklessly adding on four years.

Flynn grinned. 'If you're more'n sixteen, I'll eat my hat, but I never blamed a feller for trying.' He clapped Terrence on the back again. 'Come around in a few years, and I'll see what I can do for you.'

'You might forget all about it by then.'

'Not a chance. A politician's got to have a good memory. Forget a face, and what goes with the face, and you lose the man.'

'I'm gonna write that down. That's my first lesson on how to be a good politician. Thanks, Mr Flynn.'

'Don't mention it. I'm always glad to help an ambitious young feller.'

'Maybe I'm too ambitious.' Terrence gave him the pure,

reverent blue gaze. 'I mean I want to be like you someday, Mr Flynn. I know I can't never be as big, but if I aim that high, do you think I got a chance of getting maybe halfway up?'

Flynn laughed again. 'Save it for the voters, son. They'll eat it up. You can't lay it that thick on an old hand like me.'

'Well, I'm only learning,' Terrence said. 'Anyhow, I wasn't laying it on much. It's true I want to be a big politician like you.'

'With that tongue of yours, and a little help from me, I've not much doubt you could be President. Terrence, your name is, ain't it?'

'Terrence McNally the First.'

He seldom told that to anyone anymore, though he invariably used it as his signature. He had no words to affirm that it was his special feature, singular and recondite, yet that was how he sensed it. Experience had taught him not to offer it loosely, but there were times when he judged, or felt, that it might be advantageous to mention it.

'Terrence McNally the First.'

'It means if there's more Terrence McNallys to come, they'll be the Second or the Third or some other number, but I'm the First.'

'Ah!' Flynn said.

He sounded as if he understood, but Terrence doubted that he did. It made no difference. Flynn, whatever he said about his memory, might forget him. Or remember vaguely that he had seen a face like that, hair that color, someplace before. Terrence McNally the First, however, was unforgettable. There was only one such name in the world.

Somewhere in his mind, dim as an old dream, was a story about his grandfather who had died in Ireland before his father was born. It was that man who would have been Terrence McNally the First. But in some way, for some terrible reason, his name and he himself were

39

erased as though they had never existed.

'There's only one Terrence McNally the First in the world, and that's yourself,' Aggie had told him. 'So see ye don't disgrace the name.'

Miss Howard, his eighth-grade teacher, had put it more affirmatively. 'You have a duty to the Terrence McNallys that come after you. *Noblesse oblige*, it's called.' She pronounced 'oblige' with a long *i*. 'It means you owe it to them to live so that they will be proud to bear your name.'

Miss Jessica Howard was in some ways a prototype of the teachers of her time: plain, awkward, largely ignorant of the world, indifferently educated, an involuntary spinster tied to an aging widowed mother. But unlike many others, she liked children. She took an interest in them and enjoyed teaching them.

Terrence thought she was all right. She took him and his name seriously. Like his mother, she expected him to become somebody. As soon as she saw him reading newspapers and magazines out of trash cans, she began supplying him with books. Sometimes she even came to the flat with something she thought he would like to read. He liked to read anything. The stabbing of King Arthur by Mordred was no less real to him than the shooting of President Lincoln by Booth. He did not discriminate between the works of George Henty and those of George Eliot. Miss Howard thought that unimportant, as long as he kept reading. She never asked him what he thought of a book, though he sometimes told her of his own accord.

'You ought to go to college,' she said to him one evening, when she stopped by with some books. 'To the free College of the City of New York.'

He did not know any politicians who had gone to college. 'I have to take care of my mother,' he said.

He had not thought of it that way before, but now that he had said it, he liked the sound of it. Miss Howard's response was not what he expected.

'You have your own life to live, Terrence.' Her pale, mild eyes looked suddenly feverish. 'Never let anybody take your life away from you. You have older brothers. Your mother is their responsibility, too. Don't let them avoid it.'

Terrence did not know how she knew about his brothers. He did not understand everything she had said, and since he saw no way to answer her, he did not try.

'We're going to move away from here,' he said. 'I make enough money now so we don't have to live like this anymore.'

She looked round at the peeling walls, the stained sink, the splintering floor, the rusty stove, the small window that was so grimy again an hour after Aggie had washed it that only a pale little light filtered through.

'It's not so bad, Terrence,' she said. 'At least there are only two of you, not six or seven. At least it's not in the cellar, and you do have a window.'

'She hates the rats. We're going to move to where it's too clean for rats. I make enough money now,' he said again. 'We can live where there's a janitor and they keep the front door locked so bums don't come in and piss in the hall.' He looked at her sitting there in her worn but neat brown bustle skirt and jacket, her small hat losing its shape but trimmed with flowers, perched high on her clean, smoothly arranged brown hair. 'There's no rats where you live, is there, Miss Howard?' he asked her.

A little color came up into her flat cheeks. 'No.' She looked down at her folded hands and then straight into his face. 'Save your money for college, Terrence. Everything else will come to you afterward. It won't matter, later on, where you started life, only how you went on with it.'

Aggie would not move. She said she had thought it over and changed her mind. What if they were paying more rent, and then he lost his job with Jimmy O'Brien and had to take another one at much lower pay? Anyhow, she was used to it here.

'What about rats?'

41

'I'm used to the rats as well. I might even be after missing them. We don't have it so bad, ye know,' she said. 'Not like when there was the six of us in two rooms and only your da's pay to feed us all.'

'What about the boys?'

'The boys is fine as they are. It's only for me own pleasure I'd have them, not theirs. And all the worse for me when they'd be leaving again.'

When he gave her the money he'd earned, she divided it into three parts, returning a small sum to him for his pocket money, keeping another sum toward household expenses, and hiding the remaining amount in the box over the stove, under the dozens of Christmas cards from the boys.

'For when ye go to college,' she said.

'You've been listening to Miss Howard. That's why you won't move.'

'I don't need Miss Howard to tell me my own mind.'

'Anyhow, who says I want to go to college?'

'Nobody's asking ye, Terrence McNally the First.'

Since the money he earned varied from week to week, she would not have known if he had held some back for his own purposes. It did not occur to him to do it or to her to think he might.

But he was not fooled into believing that she no longer minded the filthy hallways and the rats. He thought if he made more money for her to put aside, in time he could get her to move. The idea of college had begun to take hold of him, partly because of a book Miss Howard had brought him called *Tom Brown at Oxford*. He did not think he would ever be anything like Tom, and he did not believe the College of the City of New York would be like Oxford in England. Still, he thought all colleges must have something particular that other places did not have. He thought all college students must know things that ordinary people never learned. They surely did not live on Little Water Street.

In order to make more money, be began going outside

the ward for customers. It meant much more traveling and sometime he had to ride miles back and forth to make deliveries. The muscles in his legs ached and cramped and then toughened so that he could have pedaled from one end of Manhattan to the other without discomfort. He soon became well known among the Tammany members who discreetly dealt with him. The booze boy, they called him. He liked that. There was a little amusement in it, but more admiration; even a rough affection. He was the kind of quick, persistent, reliable kid they would not have minded having for a son.

He brought home twice as much as any workingman on Little Water Street; still Aggie refused to move. She would not give up the washing either, though they could have done without her minimal earnings. Her only manifest recognition of the improvement in their circumstances was in the food she put on the table, most of which she piled on Terrence's plate.

'Never mind me. There's not much of me to fill. You'll be needing it against the time ye might lose this fine job of yours.'

'Ma, I keep telling you it ain't no job. Mr O'Brien and me have a business, and we ain't going to lose it.'

'I don't trust no liquor business.' He had finally told her that was the business, while fast-talking her into confusion as to its exact nature and the need for secrecy. 'I don't trust no business at all with Jimmy O'Brien.'

'You don't hardly know him.'

'I know what people say.'

'They're against him because he got in bad with the Boss. He's all right. He always treated me all right.' But it was a waste of time to argue with her. 'I guess we'll still be living in this dump when I'm a millionaire,' he said.

She turned and smacked his face. 'Don't ye be calling it a dump, the way I clean and scrub to make it decent. It's our home, Terrence McNally the First, and I won't have ye calling it no names.'

A few weeks later Terrence was pedaling back along

Centre Street, after making a delivery in his own ward. It was about five o'clock of a hot, muggy August day, and he was sweating heavily. But he was not aware of his discomfort. He was thinking about a girl who had smiled at him earlier that day on Anthony Street. He knew it was not his appearance that attracted girls to him, but he had never wondered what else it might be.

'Hey,' someone called softly. 'Hey, booze boy!'

Terrence braked so abruptly that he almost fell over the handlebars. No one used that name except in private. No one had ever approached him in the street before. It took him a few seconds to recover, to peer with convincing bewilderment at the figure that leaned against the lamppost, almost bending into its contours.

'What d'ya say? You talking to me?'

The figure detached itself from the lamppost and became visible as a thin young man in a black suit. He stepped into the street, nimbly avoiding clusters of horse manure and came as close as possible to Terrence's bicycle. He spoke directly into Terrence's ear.

'Mr Dougherty wants to see you.'

Terrence shifted the bike a little, straddling it with his feet on the ground. 'I don't know no Mr Dougherty. I think you got the wrong feller.'

'You're the booze boy, ain't ye? Red hair, freckles, big nose, bike with a basket.' The young man pointed at each of these items with a long forefinger as he mentioned them. 'Mr Dougherty's my ward leader. Seventh Ward. He wants to see you.'

'What's he want me for? I don't know him. I don't know you,' Terrence said cautiously, suspecting a trick. He had recently acquired a few customers in the Seventh Ward. If the leader wanted to see him, he could have passed the word through them. 'I still think you got me mixed up with another feller.'

'I ain't got you mixed up. My name's Farley. Now you now me. Mr Dougherty you'll know when I take you to him at the club. What he wants to see you for is business.'

Farley's lips, which were so pale as to be almost indistinguishable from the surrounding skin, parted in a grin of overwhelming toothiness. 'Booze business.'

Terrence knew the big clubs needed steady supplies of liquor for the clambakes, picnics, balls and election day rallies they sponsored. The Seventh Ward club was said to be one of the most successful in the city, with a new clubhouse that was supposed to be like a palace. If what this Farley said was true, Terrence would get a chance to see the place and maybe do some important business. If it was not true, and Farley was part of some kind of cop's trap, he could talk his way out of it.

Farley invited himself to sit behind Terrence on the bicycle, clasping him around the waist, crowding him half off the seat over the high front wheel. Each time they went over a bump or rounded a corner, Farley tightened his arms convulsively.

'Loosen up, Farley,' Terrence said. 'We ain't going to fall unless you squeeze the breath out of me.'

By the time they arrived at the clubhouse on East Broadway Terrence was drenched in sweat. Farley, on the other hand, seemed to be shivering.

'Don't never ask me to ride with you again, booze boy,' he said. 'Nothing that don't have hooves or tracks was meant to go that fast.'

Terrence said nothing. The club's magnificence had struck him speechless. The walls were freshly papered and painted. Everything in the house was new. Red velvet upholstered the rosewood furniture in the parlor on the first floor. The chandeliers were bronze and gold. A grand piano was reflected in the huge framed mirrors, as was a glimpse of the bar and billiards room behind the parlor. Terrence had never seen such luxury. He recognized some of the objects only from descriptions he had read in books. The color of the velvet carpet on the stairway, a deep mauve, was unknown to him.

'This is a nice place,' Terrence said.

'Yeah. It ought to be. Mr Tweed himself loaned the

money for it.' Farley's head swiveled around to Terrence. 'Twenty thousand he paid to have it fixed up like this.'

He led the way to a paneled door on the third floor. He knocked, opened the door at a 'Yeah?' from inside, and stuck his head in. 'I brung the booze boy, Mr Dougherty.'

Terrence entered a large, airy, carpeted office with a massive mahogany desk at its center. Behind the desk sat a tall, smiling man with white hair, a fresh and almost unlined complexion, and hard light blue eyes that looked as though they belonged in another, less genial face. He wore a dark gray suit with a maroon cravat, and a heavy gold watch chain stretched across the waistcoat. Terrence had not been in the presence of such elegance before, but he gave no evidence of awe.

'Farley says you want to see me on business, Mr Dougherty.'

'Yeah, I do. I do. Sit down and cool off.' The smile widened, cutting creases as deep as dimples in the smooth face. 'So you're the booze boy. Terrence McNally's your name, isn't it?'

Terrence said it was. He had a feeling Dougherty would resent anybody else who was the First of anything.

'From what I hear, you must be a pretty smart young feller, Terrence. Customers all over town now, haven't you?'

'Well, not all over town yet, Mr Dougherty, but we're spreading out. We can supply you with anything you need. I guess you heard about our prices. They can't be beat. Our service neither. I deliver myself, fast, anyplace you want, as much as you want to order. If you—'

'Whoa!' Dougherty broke in. 'They told me you've got a galloping tongue, and it's no lie.' He laughed amiably. 'I'm not ready to talk about ordering, but say I was. You've got a basket that holds, what? A case? Two cases? How can you fill any kind of big order?'

'Just last week I delivered ten cases of whiskey for a committee meeting. I made a lot of trips, but it didn't take me no more'n a few hours. I'm a fast cycler.'

Dougherty leaned back in his chair and looked out the window. 'What about a barrel of whiskey? Could you handle that? Along with one hundred kegs of beer, fifty cases of champagne, twenty gallons of brandy, and ten gallons of gin?'

Terrence did not know whether he could have thought up any answer to that or not. Before he had a chance to absorb the question, Dougherty turned back to him.

'That's the amount of liquor we used in one day last year, when this club held a rally for a state senator. And you're talking about ten cases. Maybe that's big business for a kid from the Five Points, but to anybody else it's a joke. A boy on a bicycle, pedaling around the city to sell a few bottles of booze.'

Terrence stood up. He jammed his fists into his trouser pockets. 'Is that what you wanted to see me about, Mr Dougherty? To tell me I'm a joke?'

Dougherty looked at him. The smile had disappeared. 'You thinking of hitting me, booze boy? I wouldn't advise that.'

'I wasn't thinking of hitting you, Mr Dougherty.' Terrence paused. 'Only thinking I'd like to.'

Dougherty's splutter of laughter sprayed moisture all the way across the desk. 'You're all right, Terrence. You're a boy after my own heart. It isn't you I mean is a joke. It's what you're doing. Look at you.' He traced the air around Terrence's shabby jacket and outgrown trousers. 'A smart feller like you, the work you're putting into it, you ought to be living like a king.'

'You got some kind of proposition for me, Mr Dougherty?'

'Maybe I have and maybe I haven't. Don't be in such a rush. Sit down. Tell me a couple of things about yourself. You still go to school?'

The man made Terrence uneasy. He would have preferred to be away from this place, magnificent as it was. But he would not go. He could not risk missing something big. He sat down and talked, and as he talked,

Dougherty nodded.

'College? That's good. That's fine. Maybe a smart boy like you ought to go to Columbia College, or Harvard, or one of those ... Politics? You'd have a real future in politics. You could move over to my ward, get a nice place for your mother and yourself to live, and I'd take a personal interest in you . . .' He was smiling again. 'Sound good to you, Terrence?'

'Sure. Only I got to go home for supper soon, Mr Dougherty, so if you're going to tell me how to get the money for all that, please start.'

'I will, Terrence, I will. Just one question I want to ask you first. This uncle of yours. The liquor supplier. Who is he?'

'Like you said. My uncle.'

'What's his name?'

'I can't give his name. He's a big dealer. If it got back to his other customers he sells cheaper to Tammany Hall men, he'd have to sell it cheaper to them, too, and he wouldn't make hardly no profit.'

'That's a good story, but nobody believes it.'

Terrence shrugged.

'Everybody knows who your *uncle* is, booze boy. Everybody knows it's Jimmy O'Brien.'

'That's more'n I know. I worked for him once. He didn't pay me hardly enough to put in my eye.'

Dougherty opened a drawer of his desk. He took out a box of cigars, selected one, snipped off the end with a cigar cutter, and slipped off the band. He lit up and blew rings at the ceiling. 'I'm surprised, a smart boy like you getting mixed up with O'Brien,' he said then. 'He's no good. He's a no-good crook. He stole money from Boss Tweed, did you know that?'

'I only worked for him in his saloon. I don't know what he did noplace else.'

'Well, that's what he did. Stole money from Mr Tweed the same as if he took it out of his pocket. Money the Boss advanced to fix up his club, decorate it, buy new furniture, like in my club here. O'Brien got the place painted up a little, bought a couple of chairs and a secondhand rug, and kept the rest himself. You didn't know that, booze boy?'

'How should I know that? I swept out his saloon, cleaned off the tables, stuff like that. If he was going to cheat Mr Tweed out of his money, would he tell me?'

'That's not all he did. He cheated me, too. He came over here to my ward, where he didn't belong, and tried to make crooked deals with my people.' Dougherty leaned across the desk and looked into Terrence's face. 'You think a no-good crook who cheats his own boss, his own party members, is going to give a kid like you a square deal?'

'I keep telling you, Mr Dougherty. I got nothing to do with him.'

'Yeah.' Dougherty sat back again. 'Well, let's say, for the sake of argument, he was the one you're in with. Let's say his real business was liquor, not that hole-in-the-wall harness shop, and he had you getting customers for him and making deliveries. I'd lay odds, he'd be cheating you some way, paying you half what anybody else would, maybe, when you're the one bringing in all the business, or—'

'I don't get paid wages. My uncle and me's partners.'

'Yeah? Well, if O'Brien's your partner, he's making more profit than he's telling you. That or something else. Some way he's not giving you a square deal. You can bet on it.' Dougherty took his cigar out of his mouth and examined the chewed wet end. 'What would you do if you found out you had a partner that was cheating you?'

'My uncle ain't cheating me.'

'For the sake of argument. What would you do?'

'Quit.'

'Quit him? That's all? Leave him with the money he cheated you out of and the customers you got for him and walk away? Go back to sweeping saloon floors maybe?'

Terrence was silent for a moment, arranging his answer.

'Let's say, for the sake of argument, you was me and you had a partner that was cheating you,' he said then, 'what would you do, Mr Dougherty?'

Dougherty smiled. He put the cigar back in his mouth and talked around it. 'I tell you what I'd do, Terrence. I'd take his business right away from him. I'd figure it was owing me.'

'How? He's the one has the liquor. Maybe he couldn't spread out much, but he could find a boy to deliver to the customers we already got.'

'A boy he can trust? A boy who'll pedal all over the city, back and forth five times to deliver ten cases of whiskey? A boy smart enough to avoid the cops?'

'I got to get home for supper, Mr Dougherty, like I said.' Terrence moved in his chair, as if preparing to rise, and placed his thick hands squarely on his knees. 'I better hear your proposition.'

'Yeah. Well, let's just keep on talking for the sake of argument. Let's say I have a feller here in my ward that wants to set up in business like O'Brien. A ward leader takes care of his own, isn't that right?' Dougherty waited for Terrence to nod, then shifted the cigar to the other side of his mouth and talked to the wall beyond Terrence's head. 'So if I have a feller like that in my ward, I naturally would want to help him be successful. You could say there's enough business in the city for both him and some small-time dealer who thinks ten cases of whiskey is a big order, but I don't see it that way. Not when the small-time dealer is Jimmy O'Brien. When it's that cheating son of a bitch, what I want to do is wipe him out and get his customers for my feller.' Dougherty spoke without heat, with no change in the affable expression of his smooth face. His hard blue eyes still regarded the wall. 'Let's say, for the sake of argument, that's how it is. I could get rid of you, too, use a kid from my own ward, but one, I like you, I like the way you handle yourself; two, the customers have confidence in you; three, you could move into my ward.'

He paused. Terrence said, 'For the sake of argument, what would the money be?'

'Twenty per cent commission on every order. Not on the profit, on the price. No more pumping a bike with a couple of cases in a basket. You'd have a wagon to drive, enough room in it for the kind of big delivery I told you about before. You'd see more money than you ever saw in your whole life put together.'

'The cops'd notice a wagon.'

Dougherty's eyes moved to Terrence's face. 'I've got the backing of Mr Tweed. His one hundred per cent backing. The cops notice what I tell them to notice.'

Terrence was not aware of thinking through the things Dougherty had told him or of working out what he would say in response. He knew what he felt. He knew the way he felt would be relieved when he had said what he had to say to Dougherty and left.

'I'd sure like to drive a wagon and all that.' He stood up. 'I wish it wasn't only for the sake of argument.'

Dougherty's eyes narrowed. 'Don't play games with me, booze boy. I made you a generous offer. Try dickering for more and I'll withdraw it.'

'I ain't playing no games, Mr Dougherty. If it wasn't my uncle, it'd be different, but I can't do the dirty on my uncle.'

He moved toward the door. 'You're a fool,' Dougherty's voice said behind him. 'You belong in that rathole you live in. You're never going to get out of it. Leave here now and you're finished.'

Terrence left. He meant to close the heavy door quietly, but it slipped out of his hand and slammed behind him.

He pedaled home, his mind on Jimmy O'Brien. He did not completely trust O'Brien. He did not completely trust anybody but Aggie. O'Brien had always tried to take advantage of him and was probably doing it now. Terrence had only his word for what the liquor cost him. Still, O'Brien had treated him decently when he was working in the saloon, not bawled him out all the time or knocked him around, the way some bosses did. He had kept Terrence on when he had hardly any customers and could have done without him. If he lost his liquor business, he and his family would not know how to get along on the little he made from the harness shop. They were not used to it, the way Terrence and Aggie were.

4

Two nights later, half a block from the shed, with a case of whiskey and a case of brandy in his basket, Terrence was arrested. The cop was waiting in a doorway. He stepped out in front of the bicycle with his billy upraised in warning and a lantern in his other hand. He made Terrence take his books from the basket, revealing the bottles of liquor underneath. Terrence would not tell him where they had come from, but the cop knew. He made Terrence wheel the bicycle back to the shed and walked beside him, gripping his arm, with the billy handy.

O'Brien had gone. Terrence thought he must have heard him and the cop coming along and beat it fast because he had left the door open.

'What d'ya bring me here for? What's this place?' Terrence asked.

'Don't be playing the innocent with me,' the cop said, and cracked Terrence across the legs with his billy. 'You know what it is like you know the back of your hand. Your place of business. Business that you and Jimmy O'Brien have been doin' unlegal and not gettin' caught until now.'

'Listen, I'm just a kid. I couldn't be in business with nobody,' Terrence said. 'Fifteen is all I am. I couldn't have no place of business.'

'Shut up and take that case of booze inside. You're gonna show me where you keep the rest of the stuff.'

The cop poked Terrence hard in the ribs with the end of

the billy, prodding him into the shack. He shone the lantern around the junk-cluttered room.

'Go on. I ain't gonna search through all that. Show me.'

Terrence stood there. Outside the shack, outside the circle of light from the lantern, it was totally dark. He and the cop might have been alone in the world. For the first time in his conscious life he felt helpless.

'I can't show you nothing. I don't know what you want. I ain't never been here before.'

The cop hit him in the face. The blow was so hard that Terrence's head rocked back on his neck and the room tilted. He thought the cop might kill him.

'I'll look,' he said. 'Maybe I can find what you want.'

'No maybes. You better find it quick. Next time I won't treat you so gentle.'

Before Terrence could move, another cop tramped into the shed, gripping someone's arm.

'Caught him,' the second cop said. 'I see you got the kid.' He held the lantern up to Terrence's face. 'What he do? Resist arrest?'

'Yeah. You know these bums from the Five Points. Toughs from the day they're born.'

'This one did the same. If I wasn't bigger, he'd've knocked me cold and got away.'

'I'm telling you, you got the wrong man,' O'Brien said. 'I'm a respectable shop owner. That there's my harness shop. Here's where I store what I got no use for right now. I don't know what you think I done, I don't know what you hit me for.' He was talking too fast, the words blurring into each other. He sounded as if he might cry. 'What's this kid doing here? He used to work for me when I had the saloon. What's he doing here?'

'He was just going to show me where you keep your booze,' the first cop said. 'The booze you been sellin' unlegal all over the city.'

'You're talking crazy. I ain't seen this kid since he worked in my saloon. How would he know where I keep anything? I don't sell no booze. I sell harnesses. That there's my—'

'Go on, you,' the first cop said to Terrence. 'Show me where the stuff is.'

'Listen, I got four, five cases,' O'Brien said quickly. 'Not to sell. It's my own supply. I keep it here because the wife, she don't like booze around the house. She don't like me drinking. I'll show you where it is. I ain't got nothing to hide.'

The second cop held his lantern so that it spotlighted O'Brien scrabbling in the junk, shoving aside sacks and old newspapers, scraps of metal and leather. His face glistened with sweat. One of his eyes was swollen and red.

'I keep it covered like this so the wife won't see it if she comes here. See? Four cases. You ever hear of any dealer who don't keep no more than four cases in stock?'

'Ain't you missing a couple?' The first cop focused his lantern on the cases of whiskey and brandy that Terrence had brought in from his bicycle basket. The cases and the bottles were identical to those O'Brien had just uncovered. 'I caught the kid with 'em, so don't tell me the two of you ain't in business.'

'I don't know nothing about this kid since I lost the saloon. I don't know nothing about no booze business.' O'Brien's voice was beginning to squeak, as if somebody had him by the windpipe. 'I don't know nothing about those two cases.'

'You tellin' me they ain't yours? Look at 'em. Look at the cases. Look at the labels on the bottles.'

'Maybe he don't see so good outa one eye,' the other cop said. 'Maybe I might as well shut the other one for him, too.'

'No, listen, you're right. They must be mine. Only I don't know how this kid—' O'Brien stared wildly around the room. 'I got it!' he said suddenly. 'I got it! He must've stole the booze. He must've broke in here, looking for stuff he could use or sell, and found the booze and tried to sell it. He used to steal from me in the saloon, too, but I didn't say nothing. I felt sorry for him, living where he

54

did, but I wasted my sympathy. They're all thieving bums. I ain't in no booze business. This kid—'

The cop dragged Terrence and his bike out to the street again. Behind him Terrence heard the heavy footsteps of O'Brien and the other cop.

'Where are you taking me?' O'Brien gasped. 'I can't walk this fast. I ain't so young no more.'

'I'm bleedin' for you, but they ain't hitching up the paddy wagon to drive two prisoners six blocks.'

'Two prisoners? Whaddya mean, two prisoners? The kid stole the stuff. I didn't do nothing.'

The cop jerked Terrence's arm again. 'Why ain't you speakin' up? Did you steal it?'

'I never stole nothing.'

'You been in business with him, ain't you?'

'I don't know nothing about no business.'

The cop raised his billy again but lowered it without striking. 'Wait till I get you to the station house. We'll see then if you'll speak or not.'

But in the station house, a red-brick building with the jail behind it, a sleepy-looking cop behind a high desk asked Terrence nothing but his name and address. Then he locked him in a cell eight feet square. It smelled familiarly of urine, like the hallway of his tenement building. He took off his shoes and lay down on the iron cot, on top of the coarse, musty blanket. Aggie had never let him lie on the bed with his shoes on.

He wondered if anybody would let her know what had happened to him. What would she do to him if she found out? It might be better if she never did, if she believed he had just gone away or even was lying dead someplace. He thought she would rather have him dead than where he was.

O'Brien was yelling from the next cell, but Terrence did not listen. He knew that because of Dougherty, who was surely behind the arrests, O'Brien was finished, and Terrence might as well wipe him out of his mind. But he would not forget what O'Brien had done. Nobody else would ever get the chance to do anything like that to Terrence again.

He lay in his clothes all night and, for the first time in his life, did not sleep until nearly morning. He was not disturbed by the reeking, almost airless cell or the lumpy mattress. But he could not get out. That was what kept him awake. He wanted to go over and bang on the barred, locked door of the cell and yell. He saw himself doing it. But he held on to the iron sides of the cot and stayed where he was.

In the morning Aggie came to see him. She had on the faded cotton print dress she wore to go uptown to do the laundering. She had tried to screw her wild hair into a neat knot, but orange-grey wisps had escaped to spring out all over her head. The whites around her green eyes were streaked with red.

'Ye'd better be telling me the truth, Terrence McNally the First,' she said. 'Did ye do it or not?'

'It was a good business, Ma. Some of the customers were big men, ward leaders and all. The only thing was selling it without no license. That ain't so bad, Ma. It ain't stealing or nothing like that.'

'Save yer gab.' She sat down on the cot and closed her eyes. Terrence stood against the cement wall. 'I never thought to see the day. What's to become of ye now, Terrence McNally the First?' She did not wait for an answer. 'It's me own fault as well. I never liked it, you and Jimmy O'Brien, but I let it rest. The money was so grand. All that to put away for yer college. I didn't ask enough questions. I wasn't wanting to know.' She opened her eyes and looked up at him. 'It's meself should be here in the jail along with ye.'

'No, Ma.'

'It was me pride. Thinking I could make a decent man of ye myself, never mind the thieving and murdering all around us. Thinking I could keep ye with me, just the one, and ye'd turn out as good as the boys I let go, even get to college and be somebody big. Me pride. And not wanting

56

to spoil it with knowing the truth of how you got the money.'

'Ma, I ain't done nothing so bad,' he repeated desperately. 'Only not having no license.'

'It's in jail ye are. Nobody decent goes to jail.' She said that again before she left.

In the late afternoon the warder told Terrence he had another visitor. Terrence could not think who it would be. Miss Howard did not cross his mind.

'I went to your flat to bring you this book.' She held it out so he could see the title: *John Brent* by Theodore Winthrop. 'Your mother didn't want to tell me where you were at first, but she finally did.'

She sat down on the cot, pushing her bustle up behind her and laying the book carefully beside her on the blanket. She had on the same brown skirt and jacket she had worn the day she had told Terrence he ought to go to the College of the City of New York. Her flowered hat was new, but as shapeless as the old one. She sat with her hands folded over the book in her lap, as if it were natural to be sitting on a cot in the cell of a jail.

'It's an exciting book,' she said. 'It will help pass the time. Mr Winthrop, the author, was killed very early in the Civil War.'

Terrence stood away from the cement wall and looked down at his big scuffed shoes. 'Did she tell you what they pinched me for?'

'Selling liquor without a license, yes.' She spoke matter-of-factly. 'What can they do to you for that?'

'I don't know, Miss Howard. Ma thinks it's the finish of me, of college and everything.'

She shook her head vigorously. Her voice rose. 'No! You must go to college no matter what.' Her pale cheeks flushed. 'I'll talk to somebody.'

'Who you going to talk to, Miss Howard?'

'I don't know yet, but I'll find out. I'll go to the—' Her voice faltered a little. 'To the top – person.'

'The best one would be Mr Flynn.'

'Mr Flynn?'

'Mr Dennis Flynn, my ward leader. He knows me. If you say Terrence McNally the First, he'll remember. The First. Don't leave that out. Tell him Mr Dougherty of the Seventh Ward got me arrested.' He described his encounter with Dougherty, the words running off his tongue. 'Don't tell him about me wanting to go to college. Ask him won't he help me because I'm in his ward and all I did was not have a license and I still want to be a politician like him.'

Miss Howard kept nodding as he spoke, manipulating her fingers as if counting off the points to be made. At this last she stopped, her hands half raised.

'That's not true, is it? You don't really want to be a politician.' She did not say it as a question.

'A politician can get things to happen the way he wants. People look up to him and pay him money.'

'Oh, Terrence, no. Most politicians are corrupt. They gouge money out of people. They use evil means for their own ends. And they're brought down finally, Terrence. Even that terrible Mr Tweed has been brought down at last.'

'Boss Tweed?'

'It was in the newspaper this morning. The jury found him guilty of a hundred and two offences. He may have made things happen his way for a long while, but he could not stop the *Times* or the *Nation* or *Harper's Weekly* from exposing him, and now he is nothing.' She went on. 'I'll say you want to be a politician like him to Mr Flynn if you think that will dispose him to get you released. But I won't believe it. You're meant for something better.'

'What?'

'Oh, there are so many things, Terrence. With a college education, there is no limit to what you can be and do. If it's power you want, you can have that, too. Other ways than in politics. You'll learn them in college.'

After she had left, Terrence began reading about John

58

Brent, the noble adventurer, and Don Fulano, the heroic black stallion. He knew that fiction was not fact, yet it seemed no less true to him. Although the characters and their behavior were wholly outside his experience, he trusted in them as others trust in a world, a life, beyond the finite ones they know. He forgot where he was until darkness obliterated the print. It was all the worse to come back from the open plains on a galloping horse, its black mane streaming in the wind, to the airless locked cell. He lay awake as he had done the night before, gripping the sides of the cot, but this time exhaustion caught up with him long before morning.

He was released on a Sunday, two days later. No one told him anything except that he was free to go. He did not see or hear O'Brien. Later he learned that O'Brien had been tried and convicted, not of selling liquor without a license but of bribery and misappropriation of political funds while a ward leader, and sent to serve a seven-year sentence in the forbidding penitentiary on Blackwell's Island.

When Terrence got home, Aggie was waiting for him. Miss Howard had stopped by to tell her that he was getting out of jail.

'I made ye a good soup, thinking they wouldn't be feeding ye much in that place,' Aggie said. 'Eat it slow, Terrence McNally the First. When it's gone, ye won't be having soup with meat in it no more.'

'Why not?'

'And where would we be getting the money now, when ye've no work at all?'

'I'll get work.'

'Not that pays enough for putting meat in soup and saving for yer college as well. Not if it's *honest* work.' She watched him swallow the soup with greedy haste. 'Miss Howard says they'll still let you in the college. I think it's queer, a college letting in jailbirds.'

'I ain't no jailbird. They sent me home, didn't they?'

But he did not mind what she said, or what she called

59

him, as long as she didn't start telling him that it was her fault, too.

After school the next day Terrence went down to the St Patrick's Democratic Club to see if he could find Flynn. Flynn's clubhouse was old, with none of the magnificence of Dougherty's, but it served the same purpose. It was not only a political, but a social institution, a haven where men could get away from their wives and families, and enjoy themselves with their friends. At almost any hour of the day or night a man could drop in and be sure of finding companionship.

The place was familiar to Terrence. He had delivered liquor there at least once a week for nearly a year. Most of the members knew him, if not by name, by sight. A fat man shooting billiards in his undershirt told him where to find Flynn.

Terrence trudged a couple of miles in the thick, motionless heat to a building site on Broadway. Flynn was the contractor for the building, and Terrence saw him standing at the edge of the excavation where the foundation was being laid. The ward leader was in his shirt sleeves, drinking beer out of a mug while he talked to one of the workmen.

'Well, young feller,' he said to Terrence, grinning, showing his pointed teeth. 'Nice lady, that teacher. Thinks the world of you.'

'I came to thank you for getting me outta there.'

'Nothing to thank me for. Come on in the shade. It's hotter 'n hell here.' He led the way to the construction shack and sat down on some boards on the side away from the sun, motioning to Terrence to do the same. 'You wasn't meant to be in more than a couple of days. It was O'Brien Dougherty was after, not you. What were you doing when the cop arrested you? Lugging a couple of cases of booze around?' Flynn took a swig of his beer. 'A feller can't be sent to jail for that.'

'I was sent to jail.'

'Only to scare you a little. Show you it's not a good idea

60

to go up against a man like Dougherty. It coulda been much worse. What's a couple days in jail?'

'It ain't nice,' Terrence said. He squeezed his big red hands together until they turned white. 'Mr Dougherty had no right to put me there. All I did was turn down a job. That wasn't no reason to put me in there where I couldn't get out.'

'Come on, young feller, you know better than that. Dougherty is one of the most powerful ward leaders in the city. He has a right to do what he wants to do. You got off easy.'

'Well, anyway, now I need a job, Mr Flynn.' He looked over at the workmen, their perspiring faces clownlike with cement dust. 'Maybe I could lay bricks or—'

'You couldn't,' Flynn broke in. 'You just can't pick up that kind of work. You want a job in construction, you got to learn it. You got to join a union. It ain't something you can do after school, like sweeping out a saloon or delivering booze.' He squeezed Terrence's arm. 'Go on home now, young feller. If I can dig up something for you, I'll let you know.'

'You know where I live, Mr Flynn? Little Water Street?'

'Yeah, I know. Terrence McNally, Little Water Street. I don't forget anybody's name or where they live.'

'"Forget a face, and what goes with the face, and you lose the man." You told me that once, Mr Flynn.'

'I'm flattered you kept it in mind.' Flynn spoke dryly, but he looked pleased. 'Good night, young feller.'

Terrence walked home. He told himself he would hear from Flynn. He told Aggie that Flynn was going to get him a job. She said nothing. He did not know whether she believed it or not. He did not know for certain whether *he* believed it.

'It may not be real quick, though,' he said to her. 'I better do any old work while I'm waiting.'

She answered that. 'You better.'

He had not looked for work since he was ten years old and got the job in O'Brien's saloon. He tried factories and

61

shipyards, but nobody wanted an unskilled, inexperienced part-time boy. He tried grocery stores. One had a sign in the window – 'ERRAND BOY WANTED AFTER SCHOOL' – in black letters, and in green letters underneath: '*No Irish Need Apply.*' The others had no openings or maybe, without coming out and saying so, did not employ Irish either.

He kept hoping to hear from Flynn, but he was not really surprised when he didn't. Then one day, still jobless, he came home to an almost deserted street. Nobody was lounging on the steps or fighting or hurling garbage or lying with a clutched bottle in the gutter. He saw why when he reached his building. A cop was walking up and down in front of it, swinging his billy. Mrs Conroy, Maureen's mother, started out the door, carrying the bundle of dirty rags she used to simulate a baby when she was begging uptown. As soon as she saw the cop, she scooted back inside.

Before Terrence could turn back too, the cop called to him.

'McNally?'

Terrence stopped dead. He might have run, but his legs would not move. He saw himself back in that cell, locked up for some nameless crime, nobody, this time, to get him out.

'You're McNally, ain't you?' The cop approached him. 'Terrence McNally? I got a message for you.'

'A mess—' The end of the word stuck in his throat.

'From Mr Flynn. He says you should go up to the Hoffmann House and see Dick Healy behind the bar, tell him Mr Flynn sent you about the job.'

'The Hoffman House?'

The cop looked at him as if he did not have all his marbles. 'Yeah, the Hoffman House. You know where it is?'

Terrence shook his head. The cop gave him directions – over to Broadway, up to Madison Square, a few blocks north, and he'd see it. A big marble building. He couldn't

62

miss it.

Terrence tried to picture a place called the Hoffman House, but nothing he envisioned equaled what he saw when he arrived. The elegant Hoffman House was the most popular hangout for clubmen in the city. Crystal chandeliers, marble columns, and a floor of inlaid tile adorned the bar. Wealthy men in dark cutaway suits with light trousers and vests, winged collars and silk ascots sat at the marble-topped tables. For their salacious enjoyment, a floor-to-ceiling painting of nudes by Bouguereau, called 'Nymphs and Satyr', hung on one wall. The first few times Terrence looked at it he turned red with embarrassment as well as lust. For all his sexual experience he had never seen a totally nude female.

He got the job of dishwasher in the bar. That evening he went home to find the kitchen overflowing with half-mended garments. Aggie was trying to sew up the seam of a heavy coat. Her hands were knotted and swollen from the years in hot laundry water, and the needle kept slipping and jabbing her fingers, leaving little drops of blood on the coat. Although she had to bend her head right up close to the work to see what she was doing, it did not occur to her that she needed eyeglasses.

'I'll get the hang of it,' she told Terrence. 'They say over around Houston Street and Delancey there's whole families do sewing, little children and old grandmothers and all. It don't pay much, but it's something.'

She was soaked with perspiration. Her face was white, and her torn fingers shook. Terrence pulled the coat away from her.

'You don't need to do it. I've got a job.'

'Ye have, have ye? Well, there's jobs and jobs, and I'm not thinking much of your kind. At least sewing is honest.'

'Ain't washing dishes honest?'

He told her all about it. He described the Hoffman House bar in detail, leaving out only the painting. She would never know it existed anyway. Women were not

63

admitted to the Hoffman House bar at any time.

'The pay ain't bad either,' he said. 'Four dollars a week.'

'It ain't so much we can't use more. If something happens like with Jimmy O'Brien, we'll have a bit besides my washing money to be getting on with.'

She reached for the coat, but he kept it out of her grasp. 'You can't do the washing and this too. You'll get sick.' He began gathering the strewn clothes into a bundle. 'Tomorrow after school I'll take this stuff back where you got it.'

'Will ye listen to him now? Too big for his boots he's getting,' Aggie said, but she made no move to stop him. 'Since when is it you're telling me what I can and can't do, Terrence McNally the First?'

'If you ain't got sense enough to know, *somebody's* got to tell you.'

He heard himself say this, yet he could hardly believe the words had come from his mouth. Aggie did not even answer him. She sat where she was and smoothed her sore fingers. After a while she got up and started cooking their supper.

'Let's have meat tomorrow,' he said. 'A man can't do a good day's work without meat in his belly.'

'All right,' Aggie said.

5

The idea of college had appealed to Terrence, but he had not really believed in it. Not believed he would actually pass the entrance exams and sit in classrooms with students who had never hustled booze, or brained a rat, or killed a man. It had nothing to do with any fear of being looked down on or not fitting in. When he read *John Brent* in his jail cell, he had seen himself as Don Fulano, the black stallion, galloping over the plains in the wind, but he had not actually believed that he could ride a horse or that he would ever feel the wind on the plains. That was how it was with his vision of college.

The first day he went there, he felt like somebody else. He had on a good dark grey suit, polished black shoes, a white shirt with an attached hard collar, a blue bow tie, and a gray bowler hat, all purchased secondhand the week before. He knew these clothes were right because he had copied them from a magazine picture of a college student, but he had never worn such an outfit.

'It's grand ye look,' Aggie said.

'Well, it cost enough.'

'Wasn't that one thing I was after putting the money away for? So ye could go as fine and proud as any other?'

The piece of mirror over the sink showed only his head and neck. He had to peer down at himself to see how he looked. In those clothes he did not recognize his own body.

'Ye needn't be admiring yerself all day,' Aggie said. 'Grand clothes is fine for a start, but so far you're no better and ye know no more than in the old ones.'

Terrence walked the thirty-odd blocks to the college at Twenty-third Street and Lexington Avenue. He stayed well in from the street to protect his clothes from the dirt that sprayed from carriage wheels and horse's hooves. Just before he reached the college, he stopped to wipe off his shoes with a piece of newspaper he found on the sidewalk. That first day he felt it to be the action of some other person inside a college man's strange clothes, but the strangeness was soon gone.

He had always liked school and stayed easily at the head of his class, but his real life had been elsewhere. He had had no time for companionship, only for incidental contacts of the classroom and the schoolyard. He had gone straight from school to work, straight from work to supper and to study with total concentration until he had finished his assignments and could get on with the business of the evening. His sole diversions, in snatched

65

moments, had been reading and willing girls. From the time he was ten years old and went to work for O'Brien, he had never played a game. He had never in his life sat down and discussed an idea.

Yet in only a few months at City College he felt as if it were a familiar place to which he had returned after a long absence. Everything about it appeared right to him, the way a college ought to be: the red, turreted, ivy-covered Gothic building; the assembly hall with its cane settees; the cherry desks and revolving stools in the classrooms; the spacious gaslit library. All this was exactly as it seemed he had known it would be.

He made friends. He wrestled and raced with his classmates round Gramercy Park or sat with them on the grass under the trees and talked about girls, and God, and the corrupt administration of President Grant, and the meaning of life. Some of these things he had never really thought about before, but he had no trouble discussing them. With the gift of the gab a person could discuss anything.

At the start of his sophomore year he told his boss, Dick Healy at the Hoffman House, that a reliable, hardworking college man like himself deserved a better job than dishwasher. Healy began letting him work behind the bar and, when there was a rush, wait on tables. He got no increase in salary, but he was allowed to fill up on the free lunch, which saved on suppers at home. He could also keep the tips left by the men who ate in the bar. When Terrence waited on tables, he made sure to be so quick and efficient and agreeable that customers often tipped him more than the usual quarter.

No matter how late he got home Aggie was up, though sometimes he found her asleep with her head on the kitchen table. When his heavy tread woke her, she always denied having slept.

'I was only putting my head down for a minute to rest.'

If he had studying to do before he went to his room, she usually stayed up, too, mending, or washing, or cleaning and pressing the suit he wore to college every day. Sometimes she would lie down on her bed in the corner of the kitchen, saying she wanted to ease her back, and she often stayed there, asleep all night in her clothes. Her snoring disturbed him at first, but he learned to tune it out. When she was awake, she liked to listen to him talk. He had altogether dropped his street grammar, even with her.

'It's grand ye talk now,' Aggie said. 'College talk.'

One evening that spring she noticed a handsomely bound book on the table and carefully touched its morocco cover with her rough fingers. 'That's a fancy book for studying out of,' she said.

'It's not for studying. It's essays to read for enjoyment.' She did not ask him what essays were, and he did not tell her. 'Pete Littlefield lent them to me. He's a friend of mine.'

'It's no Irish name he has.'

'Ma, the world is full of people who aren't Irish.'

'And don't I know that? Ye needn't be talking to me like I'm an idiot, Terrence McNally the First. Anyhow, it's rich he must be,' she said, 'to own a book the likes of that.'

'You don't have to be rich. You can buy books secondhand, the same as a suit.'

'But a book for enjoyment ain't like—'

'Ma, I've got to study.'

He wished he had not told her about the book, not mentioned Pete Littlefield. His new friendship with Pete had nothing to do with his life on Little Water Street, in this kitchen with the grimy window and the rats in the walls.

Pete had read books Terrence had never heard of, books to which Miss Howard had been too limited to guide him. He lent some of them to Terrence so that they could discuss them afterward: Paine's *Common Sense*, Mill's *On Liberty*, novels like *A Tale of Two Cities* and *Daisy Miller*. Pete loved to talk about books, about anything. He was as great a talker as Terrence. They kept talking at the same time or interrupting each other, arguing, agreeing, both of them flushed and shining-eyed with the fun of it.

When they walked downtown together after school, people turned to look at them. They were a striking pair: Pete, thin and dark, loose-moving, with finely cut features in a bony, high-coloured face; Terrence an inch or so taller and powerfully built, homely but no longer ugly with his orange hair cut shorter than the fashion to tame it and his pale, freckled face filled out so that it accommodated the size of his nose.

One afternoon they had walked to Astor Place, discussing *Crime and Punishment* all the way. Neither of them had read it – there was no English translation – but they knew the story from their professor, who was of Russian origin and considered it the greatest work in all of literature. Each day he had dramatized an episode in the book, sprinting back and forth across the room to take the parts of the various characters, to the hilarious amusement and involuntary education of the class.

The boys were arguing about Raskolnikov's motive for murder, which Pete thought was powerful, and Terrence found implausible.

'Even if he was crazy, he wouldn't have killed her. It went against the kind of man he was.'

'That's naïve. Anybody's capable of murder in the right circumstances, even if he's not half out of his head the way Raskolnikov was.'

'I don't think so. If you've got a certain kind of nature, you can't do something against it.'

Terrence was not sure he believed this. It was not in his nature to kill a man, but he had done it. Killed by accident, though, not murdered. There surely was a difference. Anyway, it scarcely mattered whether he believed it or not. It was the arguing itself he loved, the game of using words to persuade.

They usually parted at Astor Place, but now Pete said,

'Let's finish this. Come on home with me.'

Terrence had never been to Pete's home. He did not even know exactly where Pete lived. They had not talked about their personal lives. It was as though each of them materialized each morning in the English class where they had met and dissolved each afternoon on Astor Place.

'I can't,' Terrence said. 'I've got to get home and study before I go to work at six.'

'It's only a little after three. Come on. We can study together later.'

On the way Pete asked Terrence about his job. 'It's rotten to be poor, isn't it?' he said. 'We're pretty poor, too. We lost most of our money six years ago, in the Panic. That's why I'm at City College. I was supposed to go to Columbia, but the Panic finished all that. Anyway, City's a good school. I'm glad I'm there. If I'd gone to Columbia, we wouldn't be here now, arguing about Raskolnikov.'

Terrence shrugged to cover his pleasure. 'You'd have found some other fellow to argue with. It's your nature, like it's not Raskolnikov's to murder an old woman.'

Pete lived on Lafayette Place, a wide cul-de-sac three blocks long, lined with trees and solid houses that looked like mansions to Terrence.

'Before the Panic we were going to move up to Fifth Avenue. Now I guess we're stuck here,' Pete said. 'I don't really mind, though. My mother hates it because it's not fashionable anymore, but I don't care. I like this house. I was born in it, and everything's the way I'm used to. We'll go up to my room.'

Terrence followed him into a large, dark hallway. They were about to go up a carpeted staircase when a woman's voice called out to Pete.

'That's my mother,' Pete said. 'We'll have to go in.'

They entered the parlor, a large room so crowded with heavy furniture that its size was diminished. It, too, was dark; there were four windows, but floor-length burgundy velvet draperies excluded the May sunlight. Two shadowy figures sat on the sofa. Before them was a table on which a tray held cups and saucers and a silver coffee service.

'Mother, this is Terrence McNally the First.'

Mrs Littlefield wore a dark-colored bustled dress with a tight waist and flounces. Pete had her coloring, her handsome nose and mouth, but not her hooded, remote eyes.

'McNally.' She gave Terrence a cool, limp hand. 'That's an Irish name,' she said in a flat voice. 'What does "the First" signify? I'm not acquainted with Irish customs.'

'It isn't an Irish custom. My grandmother—'

But she was not listening. 'I'm afraid there's no more coffee,' she said to Pete. 'I wasn't expecting you.'

'I'll make more. It will only take a few minutes.' The girl who said this was dressed as fashionably as the woman, but her dress was pale pink. Even in the dim light her fairness was unmistakable. Her hair was arranged so that blond curls covered her ears and lay close against her neck.

'My sister, Sylvia,' Pete said. 'Sylvie, Terrence.'

She looked down at her clasped hands and murmured something Terrence could not hear. He said nothing at all. He did not know he was staring at her. Before she turned to leave the room, her eyes flashed up to his face, and then she was gone. He thought he was supposed to understand something, but he did not know what.

Pete told him to sit down. The soft cushion of the chair sank under him. He tried to seem comfortable, in case Mrs Littlefield looked at him. But she talked to Pete and Sylvia as though he were not there.

Terrence was used to tea. He did not like coffee, but he took a cup and tried not to grimace at the bitter taste. He could tell Mrs Littlefield was watching him. He thought she was about to speak to him, but when he looked at her, he saw that her eyes were not on his face but on his big hands around the little cup. Sylvia, sitting beside her on the sofa, raised her own cup slowly, holding the handle with the thumb and two fingers of one hand, as if to show

70

him how. Terrence put his cup down and stood up.

'It's getting late. I can't stay any longer. I've got to get home. Thank you for the coffee.'

'Listen, Terrence,' Pete said to him in the hall, 'don't mind my mother.'

Terrence shrugged. 'Why should I?' He moved to the door and stopped, powerless to leave until he spoke her name. 'Sylvia. Your sister. How old is she anyhow?'

'Sixteen. Why? What do you—' Pete stopped. He put his hand on Terrence's shoulder. 'Don't think about Sylvie. She's—'

'*Think* about her? I don't have to think much to ask you how old she is, do I?' He shook off Pete's hand. 'I'm not *thinking* about her. I never saw her before, did I?'

'You don't have to get angry. I only—'

'And if I was thinking about her – why would I? But if I was, what do you care? Don't you like Irish names either?'

'Don't be a chump.'

'All right then, what's the reason? There's got to be a reason you said I shouldn't think about her. If I was doing it, which I'm not.'

Pete cleared his throat. 'The only reason is for your own sake because Sylvie's so fickle. One week she likes one fellow; the next week she likes a different one. She makes them all unhappy. I don't want a friend of mine to be unhappy.'

'Well, I won't be because I'm not thinking about her. I can get plenty of girls. What do I want to think about Sylvia for?'

He thought about her all the way home. Girls often occupied his thoughts, but not like this. He was not planning where to get her alone or wondering how quickly he could get inside her pants. It was her face that was on his mind, her hair, the little he had heard of her voice, the look he felt he was meant to understand and did not. He knew girls like her existed. He had read about them, seen pictures of them. But he had never known one, been in the same room with one. *Sylvia*. Pete's warning had not

71

lodged in his mind. He had barely heard it.

It was not until he reached Little Water Street and was kicking garbage out of the way to get to the front door that he shifted her back into the house on Lafayette Place, with the velvet draperies and the soft chairs and 'I'm not acquainted with Irish customs' and a thumb and two fingers on the handle of a coffee cup.

'Ma, we're going to move out of here,' he said to Aggie. He had said it a dozen times before, but asking, not telling. She heard enough of what was in his voice now to turn from washing his socks at the sink and look at him.

'That's an old tune, Terrence McNally the First. I'll sing another old one back. When you're done with yer college and ye have a fine job, maybe we'll be thinking about moving.'

'No, Ma, we're going to move now. We've lived in this rathole long enough. If you won't look for a place, I'll find one myself and move us in.'

Aggie put her hands on her hips. 'You will, will ye? And where will ye get the money? It's not meself will be letting you have it.'

He said, 'It's as much my money as yours. I have a right to say how we spend it. I want to live better than this.' He paused, looked away from her, and then forced his eyes back to her face. 'If you won't move, I'll go without you.'

'Are ye threatening me then, boyo?' she asked him softly.

'Ma . . .' he began, and had to stop and start again. 'Oh, Ma, you know this is no place for me, for either of us. You said it yourself, that time I was in jail. You said you should never have thought you could bring me up to be decent in a rathole like this.'

'I never said rathole. And ye did turn out decent. Ye wasn't never meant to be in that jail. Didn't they find out they made a mistake and let ye go?'

It was the first time she had admitted that he had not belonged in jail. For months after his release she had referred to him as a jailbird. When Fergus Conroy had dropped dead in the street, a bottle clasped in his arms like a beloved woman, Aggie had warned Terrence he might go the same way. Terrence never even had a glass of beer. He did not like the taste of alcohol and could see no other reason for drinking it, but once he had been in jail, Aggie had seemed to believe that no vice was alien to him. Not until now had she ever indicated that he had been released from jail with no charge or record against him.

'Anyway, that doesn't change anything,' he said. 'This is the worst neighborhood in the whole city. We don't have to stay here. We're not that bad off. I don't mean we can move to Fifth Avenue, but we can find a place without rats and garbage and men pissing in the hallway.'

She dried her hands on her apron and sat down so heavily that the rickety chair's joints groaned. Her face was gray, the-skin loose on the bones like an old woman's.

'It's worn out I am from your gabbing,' she said. 'I can't be letting you live alone, now can I? Who'd wash yer socks and iron yer suit?'

Every afternoon, when he came home, he asked her if she had found a place. She always said she had looked but had seen nothing she liked that they could afford. He began to believe it was not only a lack of money that had kept her there but an attachment to what she knew, as awful as it was. He had read about a man, imprisoned for fifteen years, who did not want to leave his familiar cell. Terrence could not imagine such a thing, but he supposed older people had different feelings. He would give her a little longer and then start looking himself.

6

Terrence had other things on his mind. Some of the happiness of his first college year was seeping away. He had thought then that he had everything he wanted for this period of his life. He did not yet know the trickery of

73

that illusion; its rabbity way of breeding other wants, and wants upon wants.

He tried out in his head different things to say to Sylvia when he saw her again. He imagined her answers. But Pete did not invite him a second time to the house on Lafayette Place. They still walked down to Astor Place together after school and separated there the way they had done before that one day. It was as though that day, with its approach to closer friendship, had never happened.

Terrence chose to believe that Pete was waiting for an invitation from him. He thought that if he said, 'We're moving soon. You'll have to come over when we're in the new place,' Pete would invite him to his house again in the meantime. But Terrence did not say that. Whatever flat they moved into would be better than where they were now, but still, he would never ask Pete to come there. Pete thought being poor was living on Lafayette Place instead of Fifth Avenue.

One Sunday Terrence went to Lafayette Place and walked back and forth for more than an hour, hoping Sylvia would appear. He considered writing her a note. He did not know exactly what he would say, but he was sure he could write something to stir her interest. By then he had created her so fully in his mind that he felt he knew her well enough and would know how to appeal to her. But he was afraid her mother might get hold of the note first and open it, and he did not want to take the risk of having her read his private words. He would have to think of something else.

Meanwhile, Aggie still had not found another place for them to live. One day, when he questioned her, she confessed that she had stopped looking.

'Ye needn't be staring at me as if I done a sin,' she said. 'It's too tired I am, after a day scrubbing clothes, to go walking all over looking at flats.'

He had never before heard her say she was tired. He had never thought of her as being tired. 'Why didn't you tell me? I'd have looked myself.'

'I thought I could take a little rest and then be getting back to it, but it don't seem to do no good.' She drew in her breath, doing it carefully, as if it were fragile. 'It's not so young I am no more.'

He did not know how old she was, and it would have meant nothing to him to hear that she was forty-four. Of course, she was not young. She was his mother. She seemed to him the same as she had always been.

'You'll have the whole summer to be looking. You'll have the time for it, with no college. I'll look at the place meself when ye think you're after finding it,' she said. 'Till then don't pester me no more, Terrence McNally the First.'

The night after classes ended for the summer, Terrence had a dream in which he was pedaling his bicycle along some dark, nameless street, with crates of liquor piled high in the basket. A voice called, 'Booze boy'. When he turned, he saw it was Sylvia. He tried to talk to her, but he had forgotten the correct grammar. Then suddenly she was in the kitchen on Little Water Street, and Aggie was pouring tea into one of their thick chipped mugs. Sylvia began pushing the mug away, saying only Irish drank tea. While she was speaking, she changed into Mrs Littlefield.

The next morning he went out to look for a flat. During the summer he worked days as well as nights at the Hoffman House, but he did not have to be on the job until eleven. He walked up Broadway, toward Fourteenth Street. When he found himself turning east on Astor Place, it was as though his feet, not his head, had directed him. He walked on to Lafayette Place, straight to the Littlefield house, and knocked on the door. It was only then that he wondered what he would say if Mrs Littlefield opened the door, or Pete, or for that matter, Sylvia herself. But he did not leave.

A gray-haired woman in a plain black dress with a cameo brooch at the neck came to the door. She was short and bosomy, and she had round pink cheeks and eyes as sharply blue as Terrence's. She looked and sounded friendly, though all she said was: 'Yes?'

'I came to see Sylvia,' he said. *Miss* Sylvia? 'Miss Sylvia.'

'Oh, I'm sorry, Sylvia and her mother are away for the summer. They won't be back until September.' The blue eyes moved over his face. 'Can I help you in any way? Would you like me to say you called when I write to them?'

'Not when you write. Her mother—' He stopped. 'I guess I'll come back in September,' he finished. bleakly.

'Were you going to say her mother doesn't approve of you?' But she did not wait for an answer. 'You'd better come in a minute. There's no sense standing on the doorstep to talk. It's all right,' she said as he hesitated. 'Nobody else is here.'

He followed her in, wondering who she was and why she was asking him into the house when she didn't know who *he* was.

'I was just going to make myself a cup of tea,' she said. 'Would you like some?'

He was reminded of the dream he had had the night before. If she had changed into Sylvia or Mrs Littlefield or Aggie – this strange woman who knew what he was going to say before he said it and offered him tea instead of coffee – he would not have been altogether startled.

'I'm sorry. You must think me very rude for not introducing myself,' she said when she returned with the tea. 'Because I know who you are, I forget you can't have any idea who I am.'

He took such a large gulp of tea that it almost scalded his throat. 'You know who I am?'

'Well, I think so. I think you must be the one. Terrence O'Malley the First?'

'McNally. How do you know—?'

'I'm happy to meet you, Terrence. I'm Nora Littlefield, Sylvie's great-aunt, her father's aunt by marriage.' She held out her hand. It felt light and papery, old, but when she smiled, she had a dimple. 'Born Nora Morgan,' she said, and giggled. 'She doesn't approve of me either, Terrence.'

'You're Irish?'

'Irish as a shamrock. Irish as your face.' She giggled again. 'That how I knew you. Sylvie told me Peter had an Irish friend, thinking it would please me, I suppose. As soon as I saw your face, I was sure it was you.'

He waited while she went on to tell him that she had come for the summer to keep house for Pete and his father. She was a widow and lived by herself, so she was glad to come here and help out. Besides, it saved her money on food and gas. She was the 'poor relation', she told him. Other Littlefield men had lost fortunes, but her husband never made a quarter of what the others still had left. He had been a good man, though, a good husband.

'Was it Sylvia,' Terrence asked her as soon as she had finished, 'who told you my name?'

'Yes, it was. The way you call yourself the First intrigued her. Peter explained the reason. Such an Irish story! Who else would start such a notion or carry it on?'

Terrence heard nothing after 'intrigued'. 'She didn't think it was silly or putting on airs? Some people do. One fellow at college even said it was un-American.'

'I don't think Sylvie thought any of that.' She leaned toward him a little, the shelf of her bosom shadowing the empty tea cups on the table. 'How long have you known her, Terrence?'

'Not long,' he said quickly, shutting out the exact truth of that one afternoon, that fraction of an afternoon, with her voice scarcely heard, her face barely seen in the dimness. His truth was something different. 'Not very long.'

'But you're in love with her, aren't you?'

Terrence looked away from the woman, fastening his eyes on the wall. He did not want to have to deal with those words. He had not applied them or any others, to Sylvia's effect on him. But without recognizing the source of Nora Littlefield's eagerness, he understood at once that it could be useful to him.

'They might never let me see her again,' he said.

'They? There's no *they* about it. What Vera, Sylvia's mother, says is what goes. My nephew never opposes her. If I wasn't a convenience to her now and then, she'd see I never set foot in this house again. He wouldn't say a word. Maybe he would have once, but when he lost his fortune, he lost his gumption along with it. She blames him, of course, and acts as if they're ready for the poorhouse, and it was all his doing. Oh, she's a mean woman! That wall you're looking at, one of the first things she did without consulting him, was sell the painting that hung there, a landscape he especially liked, saying they needed the money. They didn't need it that bad. She did it for spite. You can be sure she never sold anything *she* cared about. She—' Nora broke off, smiling and shaking her head. She was out of breath as if she had climbed a staircase. 'Excuse me, Terrence. I shouldn't be talking to you like this. I get carried away.'

He kept his head turned away from her. He sighed. 'I'm right, then. I'll never see Sylvia again. Her mother won't let me.'

'Oh, there are ways, Terrence.'

'What ways? I don't even know how to get a message to her.'

Before he left, they arranged that when Sylvia returned in September, Nora would secretly give her a message. Her answer was to be delivered to him at the Hoffman House. Meanwhile, no one was to know that he had been there, not even Pete. Sylvia and Pete did not get along well, she told him. Terrence felt that to be a reflection on Pete.

'Stop by again,' Nora said at the door. 'I'm always here alone. I'll be glad of the company.'

It was too late to look at flats that day, so Terrence went to work. He was disappointed that Sylvia would be gone until September, but as long as he believed now that he would almost certainly see her again, he could wait. He was used to waiting.

He had a good day. The weather turned unseasonably warm, and the bar was crowded with thirsty men who also ate the lavish free lunch. Terrence was frequently needed to wait on tables. He went home that evening with his pockets full of change. He decided he would spill it all out in a heap on the kitchen table and let Aggie count it.

He ran up the stairs, keeping his hands in his pockets to silence the coins, in case he met somebody on the way. As soon as he got inside the flat, he made them jingle, but Aggie had her head down on the kitchen table and for once his entrance did not rouse her. Even when he shook the coins in her ear, she did not wake.

'Ma!' he said, and took her by the arm. 'Look, Ma!'

He kept on calling her for quite some time after he knew that she was dead.

He sat up with her all night. It did not occur to him to call a doctor. Neither he nor Aggie had ever been to one. None ever came to Little Water Street. Ambulances sometimes, but not doctors.

He did not call anybody else. He was aware that things would have to be done, that she would have to be buried. But it was too late for anything that night.

He did not touch her again. He did not look at her face, which was down on her arms. She seemed hardly any different from the way she had been on other nights, asleep at the table. He thought it was a good way to leave her until morning.

After a while the lamp burned itself out. He started to refill it. Instead, he found the candle that Aggie had sometimes lit in front of a picture of the Virgin she had tacked up over the stove, and set it on the table near her head. Her hair looked soft in the candlelight, the color muted, the gray obliterated. Every so often he expected her to lift her head up and speak to him and then remembered that she would not speak again. He dozed off a few times, but only for minutes.

In the morning he washed himself at the kitchen sink, then washed the sink out and made a cup of tea. He felt like making a cup for her, too, but he knew that was crazy, and he did not do it. Then he went out, even though he did not like leaving her alone. He walked to the elementary school and waited for Miss Howard.

'I'm glad you came to me, Terrence,' she said after she had arranged to take a few hours off and they were on their way back to the flat. 'You should have let me or somebody – a neighbor – know right away. You shouldn't have been alone.'

He could not have called a neighbor. As far as he knew, Aggie had never so much as had a cup a tea with any of the women who lived there, never exchanged more than a dozen words at a time with them.

'It was all right,' he said to Miss Howard. 'I didn't mind.'

'Still . . .' She did not finish whatever she had begun to say. 'You've grown up, Terrence,' she said instead. 'College has changed you.'

He had not seen her in more than a year. He had scarcely given her a thought. Yet that morning he had known that she was the one he had to have here. She had sat in Aggie's kitchen. She had respected her. She would understand what had to be done.

Between them, they lifted Aggie from the kitchen chair and laid her on the cot. Her eyes were closed, meaning, according to Miss Howard, that she had died peacefully in her sleep.

She had known she was dying. They found a note and some bills in an envelope under her hand when they lifted her from the chair.

'The moneys wot I saved for my funril,' the note said. 'Get a preist it cant hert.'

'Her heart just gave out on her,' the doctor said.

'You must, of course, notify your brothers,' Miss Howard told Terrence.

He did not think he would have remembered about

them. As always, their cards had come at Christmas, had been on display for a time, and then had joined the others in the box over the stove. For Terrence, 'the boys' themselves were scarcely more alive than the cards. He did not want them at Aggie's funeral.

'Your mother would want them,' Miss Howard said.

Eleven of them came down to New York on a steamer of the Fall River Line: Terrence's three brothers, two of them with wives, and the three uncles, Aggie's brothers, who had each brought up one of the boys, with their wives. The uncles were partners in the Reilly Shoe Company. The boys were all executives in the company, even Sean, who was only nineteen. They were all big, dark, good-looking men. They all resembled each other and were like Terrence in nothing but size. He felt as alien to them as if they had come from Patagonia. Even their speech was strange to him, a mixture of rolling Irish consonants and flat Boston vowels that made some of their words incomprehensible.

Terrence hated the funeral. He hated the priest, who had never seen Aggie in his life but talked as if he had known her well. He hated the uncle who kept snuffling and wiping his eyes. He hated the other uncles and Sean, who tried to make their big pink faces look sad, and he hated Paddy and Michael, who showed no feeling at all. After a little while, though he stayed there in body, he absented himself. His mother's real funeral had taken place the night she died. Just he and Aggie alone together at the kitchen table.

'We tried to send her money. You know that, don't you?' the crying uncle said to him afterward. 'She sent it back, saying she didn't need it because you had a fine job and could take care of her just fine. We knew it was a lie, or you wouldn't still be living in this dump.' He shook his head. 'Stubborn pride! It doesn't make much of a meal. I hope you've got more sense.'

'Thanks, but I have enough money,' Terrence said quickly. 'I do have a good job. We were planning to move

81

as soon as we found a place.'

Miss Howard had gone home after the service at the cemetery. The others were crowded into the Little Water Street flat. The wives were in Terrence's room. One of them had looked in and said, 'My God!' and then, 'Well, at least I think it's fairly clean.' He could make her out now, sitting gingerly on the edge of his cot.

The boys and the uncles stood in a loose sort of circle around Terrence. The crying uncle did the talking. 'It wasn't money we was going to offer you,' he said. 'We want to take you back to Boston with us and give you a home and a job in the company. Don't look so surprised, boy. After all, you're the son of our poor Aggie. We can't leave you alone here to starve.'

'That's nice of you, but I'm not going to starve,' Terrence said. 'I have to stay here and do my job at the Hoffman House. That's where I work. It's a very fine place. I have to keep on with my job there, and in the fall I have to go back to college. So thank you, but of course, I can't go to Boston.'

'Yeah, I can see, looking around here, what a fine job it is. I can see what good college is doing you.' The uncle tilted his head toward the others, who made various sounds and gestures of agreement, and went on with increased volume. 'You're wasting your time, boy. A big, grown fellow like you ought to stop piddling around with books and start making a decent living. We've got a good business. With us, if you're smart and work hard, you can get someplace. In a few years you can marry a nice girl – there's lots of nice Irish girls in Boston – and forget you ever lived in a dump like this.'

'Thanks,' Terrence said again, 'but I'm used to New York. I guess I'll stay here.'

'You better think it over. Where you going to get an opportunity like—'

'I don't know what you're trying to sell him on it for,' Paddy broke in. 'If he don't see he's getting the chance of a lifetime, he don't. If he don't want to come, he don't.

We did the best we could, so now let's get out of here and go home.'

Terrence looked at the broad, handsome face of this stranger who was his eldest brother. He could see the beginning ooze of jowels above the white shirt collar.

'I have to ask you something before you go,' Terrence said. 'What's the reason you never came near us all these years?'

Paddy's eyes swiveled around to the others and back to Terrence. 'She didn't want us.'

'That's right,' Michael said.

'You mean she – Ma—' Terrence had to stop a second, the word 'Ma' echoing inside his head. 'Ma *said* she didn't because she thought, the way we lived, you'd hate coming. If you'd have done it anyway, even once – she kept waiting—'

She had never said so. He had never thought of such a thing before. But now he was sure that it was true, that she had waited.

Paddy shrugged. 'How were we supposed to know that?'

'You could have tried anyway. Just once, all these years.'

Paddy shrugged again.

They left in pairs, each uncle and each 'boy' with a wife on his arm. 'Nice funeral', one of the uncles said. 'If you change your mind,' the crying uncle said, 'let me know.'

Sean, wifeless, was the last to leave. He lingered a little behind and spoke in a thick mumble that Terrence could barely hear.

'Sorry – shoulda come – good excuse—' He started to leave and then turned back and said in a whisper, but clearly, 'I hate the shoe business.'

Terrence watched him clatter down the stairs. He thought he might have liked Sean.

His boss had given him the day and evening off because of the funeral, but Terrence decided to go to work anyway.

Alone in the flat he kept thinking that he was in a dream or that somebody had made a mistake and Aggie would walk in any minute, bringing the smell of laundry soap and something to cook for supper.

When he went home after work that evening, he saw a line of light under the door of the flat. He burst in, shaking, shouting, 'Ma!'

Miss Howard was sitting there, with her flowered hat and her black reticule on the kitchen table before her. She had lit the lamp and had been reading by it. The book lay facedown next to her hat, so that Terrence could see it was *The Temptation of St Anthony* by Flaubert.

'I'm sorry if I startled you,' she said. 'I came early this evening' – she gestured toward a pale brown loaf on a plate on the stove – 'with a cake I baked.'

'A cake?' he repeated, as if he had never heard the word before. Now he was surely in a dream, with Aggie changed into Miss Howard, sitting in their kitchen in the middle of the night.

'It's the custom, you know, to bring food when someone dies,' she said. 'I thought a cake, with tea, if your relatives were still here – but everyone had gone when I arrived. At first I thought you might have gone away with them because the door was unlocked, but I saw your things were still here, so I waited. I didn't think you'd be out so long.'

'I went to work.'

'You did? Yes, well, probably that was best. You should have locked your door, though, Terrence. Somebody could have walked in and stolen your nice suit.'

'I forgot.' He could not imagine what she was doing here now. 'Thanks for coming, and the cake, and everything.'

'Let's have some of the cake now, shall we? I'll put the water on for tea.'

He had rarely eaten cake, and never in this kitchen. Often, when Miss Howard had brought him books to read and sat here talking to Aggie, there had not even been tea.

The cake was light, flavored with lemon and flecked with bits of the rind. 'It's good,' Terrence said.

'It was my mother's favorite. She died four months ago. She was very old, you know, over eighty.' Miss Howard cut another slice of cake. Her hand on the knife trembled slightly. 'That was one of the things I wanted to talk to you about, Terrence.'

He was not sure whether she was really not making sense or he was so tired that he was not understanding her. He wished she would leave so that he could go to bed, but he could not tell her that.

'I thought one of your relatives might ask you to live with him,' she said.

'They did, but I told them I couldn't.'

'What are your plans then, Terrence?'

'Plans? Just to go on with my job and college, the same as before.'

'And stay in this flat? Alone?'

'No. Not here. I don't want to stay here. I'll find another place.'

He had not really thought about it yet, and he could tell she knew that. She smiled a little, the way she had sometimes done in the classroom when a pupil tried to fake the right answer.

'I'd be glad to have you board with me, Terrence. My mother's room is vacant now, and it's convenient to the college. I'll give you breakfast and supper,' she said. 'You can pay me whatever you can afford. I have the room in any case, and it costs very little more to cook for two than for one.'

'I don't need supper except Sundays. I eat at my job.'

He meant it as a comment, not an acceptance, but she said, 'That's settled then. I don't think you want to stay here any longer than necessary, do you? So—'

'I've been here all my life. A little longer won't matter.'

'I was thinking of the ghosts, Terrence.' She got up and brushed the crumbs off the table and put the rest of the cake back on the stove with a towel over it. 'You can move in tomorrow,' she said. 'I'll have your room ready when you get home from work.'

He was too exhausted to object or even to know whether he had objections. When he awoke in the morning, he was sure he did not want to live with Miss Howard, but he did not see how he could tell her so. While he was washing, he tried to think of some plausible reason that would not insult her. Then he stopped trying because he reached for the towel on the stove, forgetting it was covering the cake, and saw that the rats had eaten every morsel on the plate. He knew there would be no rats in Miss Howard's flat. He knew it would be nicer than any other place he could afford to live. If he didn't like it, he could always move out later on.

7

The assignment was to state a point of view on the subject of electives. Harvard had instituted the elective system some years before, but it was not in effect at City College. President Webb opposed it on the ground that the students were too immature to choose any but the easiest subjects, and many of the students agreed with him. Terrence wrote a paper in favor of the system, gathering conviction as he went along.

'This is a good paper,' the professor said. 'Very persuasive. Why don't you submit it to the *Journal* for publication?'

At the end of the day Terrence took the paper to the room where the staff of the *College Journal* worked. Pete was just leaving. They had seen almost nothing of each other since the opening of school two weeks before. Pete had joined Clionia, a literary society devoted primarily to debating, and he was on the staff of the *College Journal*. He had a new circle of friends, students who had time for after-school activities.

Terrence left his paper with another member of the staff. He and Pete walked out of the building together.

'Did you have a good summer?' Terrence asked him.

'It was all right, except we had a half-crazy old aunt keeping house for us while my mother and sister were away. She never stopped talking all summer.'

'You mean you had to *listen* for a change?' Terrence said.

Pete did not answer. When he got outside, he said, 'I'm not going home right now. I have to go across town to the printer. We'll walk downtown together some other day soon.'

'I don't live downtown anymore,' Terrence said. 'I've moved.'

He thought about Pete for a block or two and then put him out of his mind. He knew now, for certain, that Sylvia was back. Probably he would hear from her any day. Several Sunday mornings during the summer he had stopped in to see Nora Littlefield, pleasing her and at the same time reminding her to give his message to Sylvia. He had had to endure her repeated diatribes against Sylvia's mother, but he had endured much worse for other objectives. It was, after all, her resentment of Mrs Littlefield that had made her such a ready ally.

Sylvia's answer could come today. He had told Nora to have her send it to his new address instead of the Hoffman House. It might be waiting for him in his room.

The room was not, as he had supposed, part of a flat. Miss Howard lived in a house near Fourth Avenue. It was very small, with tiny bedrooms and a back parlor, and its brownstone façade was crumbling. It was, nevertheless, a house. Mrs Howard's legacy from her husband, who had left nothing else, and hers to her daughter.

Terrence's room was overwhelmed by what had once been the bed of Miss Howard's parents. There was space in addition for only a small walnut table that served as a desk, a straight chair to match, and a row of shelves on one wall to hold his clothes and other possessions. The window faced east. In the morning the sun, reflected by the brass bedposts, shone in Terrence's eyes and woke him. He loved it.

He loved the room. It was clean and quiet. He could close the door and be alone to read or study undisturbed. Miss Howard rarely bothered him. She saved what she had to say to him for the mealtimes they shared – breakfast every morning and all three meals on Sunday. He always tried to appear attentive and responsive even when he had no interest in what she was saying. The money he gave her each week was scarcely more than it cost her to feed him and pay for the gaslight he used. He wanted her to keep on enjoying his company.

Often she was still awake when he got back from his job at night. He could see the light under her door, which he had to pass on the way to his, two doors down. At first she gave no evidence of hearing him come in, but after the first few weeks she began calling out to him.

'Is that you, Terrence?... Good night, Terrence. Pleasant dreams.'

She always sounded drowsy, as if she had been asleep or fighting to keep awake. He wondered if she deliberately waited up for him. The possibility irritated him, yet at the same time it was comforting.

One night she opened the door as he went by. She was fully dressed. When she spoke, her voice shook.

'Terrence—'

She held out her hand to him and then dropped it, staggered a little, and leaned heavily against the door-jamb. She was holding a medicine bottle in the other hand.

'I'm sorry,' she said thickly. 'I'm not well.'

Alarm pierced his chest. She was going to die, like Aggie. 'Should I go for the doctor?'

'No,' she said. 'No. I have my medicine.' She showed him the bottle. Its label said 'Lydia Pinkham's Vegetable Compound.' 'Very good medicine. Don't worry.' She straightened up and went on in almost her normal clear, crisp voice. 'I get these dizzy spells. It's nothing. Good night, Terrence. Pleasant dreams.'

She seemed perfectly well at breakfast and did not mention the episode of the night before. He thought of bringing it up but then decided to let it drop. Probably it was nothing serious, just as she had said. She did not look as if she were going to die.

'You've given up the idea of going into politics, haven't you?' she asked him.

He told her he had. By then he knew that politicians were not all sleazy, treacherous saloonkeepers or corrupt manipulators, trying to stay a step ahead of jail. But Tammany Hall was still the only route to a political career in New York City, and he had left that climate behind him.

'What would you like to do, then, after college?' Miss Howard asked him. 'Have you thought of a career that might suit you?'

'Not yet. All I know is it won't be just providing some product like, well, shoes. I want to *affect* people in some way.'

Miss Howard was not yet back from school the afternoon he submitted his paper to the *College Journal*. No letters had come. Nobody ever wrote to Miss Howard. Sylvia had not written to him. Not that day, nor the next, nor the next.

She would. He could not expect her to be as eager yet as he was. He had had all summer to imagine her in his life. He had taken no real pleasure in other girls. But she could only have thought that he had put her out of his mind as soon as he had left her house that day and so had put him out of hers. Naturally it would take her time, after she got his message, to think about him in a new way.

A few days later he got a note in school asking him to come to Room 312 after classes. The note did not say what he was to come there for. It was signed 'Jacob Stern'. Terrence had never heard of him.

Room 312 was one of the small study rooms opening

out of the large assembly hall on the top floor. Seated at a desk, before a mound of papers, was a person with a long head, a long chin, a long, straight nose, and soft hazel eyes, enormously magnified by thick gold-rimmed glasses. He wore a rumpled black suit and a little round black cloth cap that sat precariously on his thick, black, curly hair. Terrence could not tell whether he was a student or a professor.

'Jacob Stern?'

'Jake. You're McNally. Sit down.' He spoke rapidly, in such a deep voice that Terrence imagined the room vibrated. 'You're staring at my skullcap. It's called a yarmulke. I wear it because I'm a male and a Jew. If that bothers you for any reason, good afternoon.'

Terrence laughed. 'Why should it bother me?'

'It bothers a lot of people. Innumerable. Many of them right here in the College of the City of New York.'

'Well, I bother a lot of people, too,' Terrence said. 'I'm Irish.' He watched Stern riffling through a stack of papers with long, deft fingers. 'What did you want to see me about?'

'Ah! Here it is.' Stern held up half a dozen attached sheets. '"Good enough for Harvard, but Not Good Enough for Us?" by Terrence McNally the First,"' he read. 'Terrible title, but I like what you have to say. What does "the First" mean? It's attention-getting, but what does it mean? The first of what?'

'The first of the Terrence McNally's. How did you get that article? I submitted it to the *College Journal*. How did you get hold of it?'

'The *Journal* didn't like it. They don't believe in the elective system. I know somebody on the staff who thought I might want to use it. I'm starting a new college magazine. A monthly, full of convincing, forward-looking articles that might light a fire under this superannuated, elephant-footed place.' He sighed and swept the stack of papers from one side of the desk to the other. 'So far yours is the only one I've got. Are there subsequent

Terrence McNally's?'

'Not yet.'

'You'll have to explain it to me someday. Right now I'm worried. I have no advertising. How can I put out a publication without advertising to pay for it? How can I put it out with one article and no staff anyway?' He looked mournfully at Terrence. 'Do you know how to sell advertising?'

'Well, I've sold booze,' Terrence said. 'But I have no time. I have a job nights, so I've got to study in the afternoon.'

Jake sighed. 'I wanted to make an impact on this college before I am graduated in June, but I may have to give up the whole idea. Do you mind leaving your article with me for a few days anyway, in case I can work something out? If I can't, I'll return it promptly.'

'Yes, sure, keep it. I hope you'll be able to publish it.'

Terrence imagined his words in print, read by President Webb, the professor, the students. 'I wish I could help you out. Maybe I can talk to some of the students.' He leaned forward. 'I'm pretty good at persuading people, Jake. Maybe I can recruit a staff for you.'

'Try. By all means, try. I'm not a recruiter myself. I have no charm.'

Terrence did not know what else there was to say, but he sat there still, drawn to something he could not name; drawn to Jake Stern.

After a moment he said slowly, 'Sundays.'

'What about Sundays?'

'We could work Sundays. That is, if you're willing.'

'Your head is not transparent. Therefore, I can't see the workings of your mind,' Jake said. 'Please elucidate.'

'If you're willing to work Sundays, I could be on your staff myself. I'm free Sundays.'

'Do you know anything about putting out a publication?'

'I learn fast,' Terrence said. 'Anyway, what can you lose? You'll have one more than nobody.'

91

Jake gathered the papers on his desk into a neat pile. 'These are just for appearance, to make me look like an editor. They're all blank. Think up a good name for the magazine between now and Sunday. Something snappy.'

When Terrence got back to his room, he found a pale blue envelope propped against a pile of books on his desk. It was addressed, in a round, firm hand, to Terrence McNally the First.

Dear Terrence McNally the First:
   You may come to my house on next Sunday at eleven o'clock. Please be prompt.

Yours truly,
Sylvia Harriman Littlefield

It took him a long time to fall asleep that night. He took the note to bed with him and slipped it under his pillow, but he could not have said why he did that. When he finally slept, he did not dream of Sylvia. He dreamed of running with rubbery legs that would not take him fast enough. Jake Stern was somewhere in the dream, and Pete, and the man he had killed when he was ten years old.

Something woke him. He never woke of his own accord when it was still dark. He heard something. Rats, he thought, before he remembered he was not in the room on Little Water Street.

'Terrence.'

The whisper brought him fully awake, his heart pounding. Miss Howard. She was sick again. Very sick, maybe really dying this time, or she would not have come to his room for help in the middle of the night. She had lied when she said it was nothing.

He sat up and said, 'Yes, Miss Howard.'

For a moment he thought that she was not there, that he had dreamed her voice. Then she said his name again and touched him. As he turned around, he jerked his arm away. He felt himself begin to burn, to choke.

Miss Howard was in bed with him. She had on a cotton

nightgown that buttoned up to the neck, but she had unbuttoned it and pulled out her breasts. Even in the dark he could see how big they were, big and flat. He looked away, nausea clawing at his throat.

'Terrence, please . . . I had to . . .'

She spoke aloud now, the same thickness in her voice as on that other night, and in disjointed phrases. He had trouble understanding her. He did not want to understand her. He wanted to leap out of bed, out of the room, out of the house, but he could not move.

'Please,' she said again. 'All these years . . . never . . . nothing.' She began stroking his bare arm again, and this time, as if it were paralyzed, he had to leave it under her hand. 'Just once . . . once . . . no harm to you . . . men aren't harmed . . . just once before I'm old . . . I had to, Terrence, because . . . who else is there?'

He said, 'Please,' too. He had to say it three times before the word would come out. 'Please go back to your room, Miss Howard.'

She stopped stroking his arm, but she did not move. She did not seem to hear him. He did not know how to make her hear him, what to tell her to make her go.

But then she said, very softly, 'Oh, my God!' and threw back the covers and rushed out of the room.

Terrence sat where she had left him. He could smell her lavender powder on the sheets. If he lay down, he had a feeling it would suffocate him. He wanted to go to sleep and wake up into a day in which it had not happened. But he could not lie down.

He had no idea how long he had been sitting there in the dark when he heard the crash. He did not know later whether he had had any suspicion of what it might be or had simply reacted to the noise, running to where it came from without thinking about it.

She had pushed a chair under the chandelier in the parlor. The chair, when she kicked it away, had knocked over a small table, and both pieces had hit the bare floor with the clatter Terrence had heard.

She was hanging from the chandelier by her bathrobe belt. Her eyes had begun to bulge, and the tip of her tongue was protruding from her mouth. Terrence thought she was dead. But when he got her down on the floor and loosened the end of the belt around her neck, she began immediately to take loud, gulping breaths.

'Go back to bed, Terrence,' she gasped as soon as she could talk. Her voice was hoarse but clear. She sounded nothing like the woman who had been in his bed. 'You need your sleep. I'm going up to my room in a minute too.'

He spoke without looking at her. 'Are you sure you're all right, Miss Howard?'

'Of course I'm all right,' she said. 'It was just a little fall. I don't believe I've even bruised anything.'

Terrence went back to his room. He could not think what to do. What he wanted to do was leave, pack his clothes and his books and just go now, in the middle of the night. But he knew that was not sensible. He was too tired anyway, exhausted, as if he had been running or lifting heavy crates. The sensible thing was to go to bed and get some sleep and figure everything out in the morning, when he was fresh.

He lay down on top of the covers, so he would not smell the lavender powder in the sheets. That way he could almost pretend that she had not been in his bed. He kept seeing her hanging from her bathroom sash with her bulging eyes and her protruding tongue, but he could stand that better than the other thing. Than her under the covers next to him, with her big, flat, floppy naked tits. *Miss Howard.*

The images merged behind his closed eyes, wavered, and swam away. He slept.

He was awakened, as he had been every morning since he had been living there, by a knock on his door.

'Yes, Miss Howard,' he answered sleepily as he always did. 'I'm up.'

She gave her usual response in her usual crisp voice. 'Breakfast in twenty minutes.'

It was only when he tried to pull back the covers and found they were under him that he remembered. He swung his legs around, sat on the edge of the bed, and rubbed his forehead with both hands. Whatever vague plans had flitted through his bewildered mind the night before had not included facing her across the breakfast table. Or facing her at all.

He should have left right away, slept on a bench in the park, in a doorway, anywhere. If he tried to sneak out now, he would have to go past the kitchen and dining room, and he was too big to be so light-footed that she would not hear him. He thought wildly of climbing out the window, but there was no way to get down without jumping and, at the least, breaking his legs.

Finally he got up, washed and shaved, put on his clothes, and went downstairs. She was sitting at the table, waiting for him. The blue china teapot, kept warm in its quilted blue cozy, stood on the white tablecloth, the matching blue sugar bowl and creamer beside it. A small wicker basket, lined with a white napkin, held hot biscuits. At Terrence's place, opposite Miss Howard's, a bowl of oatmeal gave off faint wisps of steam. Except that there were sometimes muffins instead of biscuits, or farina in place of oatmeal, everything looked the same as on any other morning.

Whether or not Miss Howard looked the same, Terrence could not have said. He managed not to look at her, first by pretending to have something in his eye and then by becoming totally occupied with his oatmeal.

'Good morning, Terrence.' She sounded the same. 'Did you sleep well?'

'Fine, thank you,' he answered, dabbing at his eye with his handkerchief.

'Let me look at your eye. If there's a speck in it, maybe I can get it out.'

Terrence imagined her close to him, her eye peering into

95

his, her breath in his nostrils. He shoved his handkerchief back in his pocket and said quickly, 'Oh, no, thank you. It's fine now.'

Though he had no appetite, he ate as heartily as always so that she would not think he was sick and try to delay him. Then he would go to school as usual. In the afternoon, before she got home, he would come back and pack his things and leave her a note that was plausible and would not make her feel bad. What the note would say he did not know. Where he would go he did not know either. But he would think of something. He could always think of something.

'I'm glad you slept well,' she was saying. 'Apparently your nightmare didn't disturb you.'

He forgot not to look at her. 'Nightmare?'

Her hair was neatly combed, drawn severely back from her pale, plain, pleasant face. Her neat brown dress, covering her to the neck, wrists, and ankles, rendered her shapeless. She looked as Terrence remembered her looking for as long as he had known her, before last night.

'You shouted my name,' she said. 'So loud it woke me. I ran to your room, thinking you were ill, but you were fast asleep, thrashing around in your bed and muttering.'

She took a sip of tea.

'Muttering?' he repeated stupidly, out of a need to fill the pause.

'I couldn't make out what you were saying, but you seemed to be in great distress. You didn't wake when I spoke to you and shook you, so I just patted you a little, patted your arm, and in a few minutes you quieted down.'

She was looking at him in her ordinary calm, objective way, yet he felt as though his eyes were locked to hers and could not shift.

'You don't remember what you were dreaming?'

'No.' He cleared his throat. 'I hardly ever remember my dreams.'

'Well, it isn't important,' she said briskly. 'I just wondered what frightened you so.' She passed him the biscuits, releasing him from her gaze. 'Perhaps you've been working too hard.'

He buttered a biscuit and ate it with no consciousness of what he was doing. 'I'm sorry I disturbed you.'

She made a gesture of dismissal. 'Oh, by the way,' she said, 'you did see the letter that came for you? I left it on your desk.'

For a moment he had no idea what she was talking about. Then, with a rush of pleasure that invaded his numbness, he remembered and did not know how he could have forgotten.

'Yes, thank you, I saw it.'

He pushed his chair away from the table, mumbling about something he had left in his room that he needed for school, and pounded up the stairs.

Sylvia's note was still under his pillow. He automatically pulled back the bedclothes to air them, as Miss Howard had trained him to do, and sat down on the mattress to read the note again. Sunday. He would see her on Sunday. In two days . . .

He sat with the note in his hand, lingering over the words, admiring the delicate, spidery handwriting, until Miss Howard's voice swam up to him from the downstairs hall.

'Terrence, you're watching the time, aren't you? I know you don't want to be late.'

He stood up, stowing the note carefully in the inside pocket of his jacket. He stood without moving for an instant, staring down at the bed. Then he bent down gingerly and sniffed the sheets. They smelled like sheets. There was no odor of lavender powder.

8

After his classes were over for the day, Terrence went to Room 312 to tell Jake Stern that he would be unable to meet him Sunday morning to work on the new publication.

Jake seemed not to have moved since the day before. He sat in the same wrinkled black suit, with the yarmulke sliding half off his curly black hair, his desk cluttered with the same blank papers.

He sighed. 'I'm not surprised,' he said. 'I'm only surprised you bothered letting me know.'

'What are you talking about?'

'Most people don't mean what they say. They say what sounds well or what they think somebody wants to hear. They promise things and then wish they hadn't and don't do what they said they would.' He spoke softly in his deep voice, with no particular expression. 'I'm not blaming you. I suppose it's the human condition. Why would anybody want to work on a college publication that exists only as a notion in some eccentric Jewish boy's head and will almost certainly come to nothing? I didn't really expect you to.'

Terrence laughed. He had planned to stay only a minute or two, but now he pulled a chair away from the wall and sat down, feeling again a warmth for this Jake Stern that he could not have explained.

'That's a pretty good speech,' he said. 'I'm not a bad hand with the words myself, but I couldn't do better. If I were backing out, the way you think, I'd feel like a worm right now.'

'You're not backing out?'

'You didn't give me a chance to tell you. I can't work Sunday morning, but I can Sunday afternoon. I'm going to visit a girl Sunday morning.'

'Ah! Well, that I understand. I have somebody myself. She's very pretty. My grandmother, who is homely, tells me beauty is only skin-deep and what I must look for is character. The trouble is, I wasn't looking for anything when I met Amelia. She simply happened to me. Now, if I find out she has no character, it's too late.' For the first time Terrence saw Jake smile. His long face spread, and his soft hazel eyes gleamed enormously behind the thick glasses. 'Is yours pretty?'

'Oh, yes.'

Terrence would have liked to say more, but for all his customary glibness no words came to him. He was not accustomed to talking this way to anyone. His friendship with Pete Littlefield, the closest in his experience, had not included personal confidences.

'However, men who succeed,' Jake said now, the smile dissolving, 'never allow women to interfere with their business. If we're going to make anything of this publication, we can't regard it as something to work on when we have nothing more appealing to do. It has to come first.' He leaned back in his chair, clasped his hand on top of the skullcap, and stared sternly at Terrence. 'If you aren't prepared for that kind of dedication, the time to say so is now.'

Terrence grinned. 'All that would sound a lot more impressive if you had a publication started and a choice of applicants to work on it. This way I don't think you can be too particular about how dedicated I am. I'm all you've got.'

Jake's face began to redden. Terrence thought he was angry, but suddenly the small room reverberated with such a deep roar of laughter that Terrence was all but lifted from his seat.

'That's right!' Jake said when he could speak. 'That's right, Terrence McNally the First! Don't let me get pompous.'

Terrence closed one eye and squinted at Jake with the other. 'I think you're implying I'm pompous myself, using that name, but you're wrong. That's a special circumstance.'

'All right. When we have time, you'll tell me about it. I have a feeling we're going to tell each other a great many things. I have a feeling we're going to be friends.' He nodded, as though confirming someone else's remarks. 'The Irisher and the Jew boy. Why not?'

'Why not?' Terrence echoed, delighted.

'Well, then, I'll see you Sunday afternoon at my house. You have the address?'

'Yes.' Terrence got halfway out of his chair and then sat down again. 'If you have another few minutes, I want to ask you something.'

Jake raised his black eyebrows and waved one hand expressively over the pile of blank papers on his desk. 'I have another few minutes. Ask.'

'Do you know anything about dreams?'

'Dreams? What is there to know about dreams?'

Terrence shifted in his chair. 'Well, have you ever had one – a dream . . . or maybe a nightmare that seemed so real you thought it actually happened? I mean, when you woke up you didn't know it was a dream, and later you kept on thinking it wasn't? Even if somebody told you you'd been dreaming?'

Jake did not seem to regard these questions as startling or peculiar. 'I don't think that's possible,' he said. 'Of course, it may be. I'm not an expert on such things. But I think you would always know once you were wide awake. No matter how vivid the dream was, I think you would be sure it hadn't been a real experience.'

'And the other way around? If it were a real experience, you'd be sure it wasn't a dream no matter what anyone said?'

'That's what I think, but how do I know? I've never had any such problem.' He looked up at the ceiling. 'Maybe it's one of those fey things that happen only to the Irish.' He paused. When Terrence said nothing, he went on, still examining the ceiling. 'I suppose this is very important to you.'

Terrence was torn between a sudden urgency to bring it all out, to purge himself of it, and an aversion to revealing his own private reactions. He was pleased with the device he thought of to resolve this, imagining it to be original.

'Not to me,' he said. 'To a friend of mine. This fellow I know asked me about it, what I thought he ought to do, and I didn't know what to tell him. You see, he boards with this woman. She's old. She could almost be his mother, and he's known her a long time, years, and she's always acted – well, he says she's always been nice to him, helped him in different ways, and all that, but the way you'd expect a woman her age would. Then the other night—' The words had rolled off his tongue, the way his words had a habit of doing, but now they slowed a little. 'Well, he said the other night he woke up, and there she was – well, in bed with him, and she wasn't – she was sort of half undressed and she wanted him to – you know – and he told her to go back to her own room. First she just lay there, and then all of a sudden – he said all of a sudden she jumped up and ran out. Then he heard something, and when he went to see what it was, he saw what it was, he saw – she tried to – hang herself.'

Jake, his eyes still on the ceiling, murmured something.

'What?' Terrence asked.

'I said, the poor woman.'

'Yes.' But pity had not occurred to Terrence before. He had felt too many other things. 'Anyway, this fellow got her down and she was all right. She acted the way she used to, as if nothing had happened, and the next morning – he said the next morning she was the same as always, too, and she said he must have had a nightmare because he yelled for her in the middle of the night, and when she went in, he was tossing around, and she patted him and stroked his arm until he was quiet again.'

Jake seemed to be waiting for something else. When it did not come, he straightened in his chair and lowered his gaze from the ceiling to Terrence's face.

'So what's the question?'

'The question? Well, the question – what this fellow is wondering is if what she said could be true. If he really could have dreamed the whole thing.'

'I've already given you my opinion about that, for what it's worth. So what if it wasn't a dream? Do – does your friend think she's going to try again? If it bothers him so much, he could lock the door. Or move out.'

'That's not it. She won't – he's sure she wouldn't try again. But he feels – if she was really there like that, in his bed, and he didn't dream it, everything's different, and every time he looks at her he feels . . .' Terrence, not knowing how to describe the feeling, trailed off.

Jake shrugged. 'What's the problem? So he moves out.'

'That's what he was going to do, until she made him think maybe it was all a dream. In case it was a dream – you said yourself, how do you know it couldn't have been? – then it would be too bad if he moved out because he has a nice room and she cooks meals for him and doesn't charge him much. If he left, he couldn't afford to live any place nearly as nice, and he doesn't even know where he'd go.'

'I'll tell you,' Jake said after a minute or two. 'If I were that fellow, I'd make it simple for myself. I'd believe it was a dream.'

'Just by wanting to?'

'Why not? Don't you believe a lot of things because you want to? When I was bar mitzvah – that's when a Jewish boy is thirteen and there's a ceremony that says now he's a man – I was a little undersized kid with a squeaky voice that hadn't changed yet and not even any hair except on my head. But they said I was a man, and I wanted to believe it, so I did. Right after that I shot up and got the deep voice and the hair. For all I know, maybe believing made it happen.'

'That's interesting,' Terrence said. 'I'll tell my friend your advice. Thanks.'

'Don't mention it. Sometime I won't know what to do, and you'll tell me what you think. It's good to get an impartial opinion.'

'My friend—' Terrence began, but Jake cut him off.

'It's also good to be candid with each other. If we're going to work together, that is, and if we're going to be friends, as it seems we are.'

'Yes, sure.'

'Yes, sure. So don't give me this other-fellow-your-friend hokum.'

'What are you talking about?'

'Don't give me this what-are-you-talking-about hokum.'

Terrence was annoyed. People usually thought what he wanted them to think. He intended to insist that it had all happened to someone else. He would make Jake believe him.

But he looked at Jake, at his mild eyes, already familiar, swimming hugely behind his glasses, and he said, instead, 'You're smart.'

'Of course. Haven't you heard? All Jews are smart.'

'That's good. It's going to take two smart fellows to make a go of this publication of ours.'

Jake shook his head in exaggerated wonder. 'A few minutes ago it was *my* publication. Suddenly it's *ours*. How did that happen?'

'Magic. Haven't you heard?' Terrence said. 'All the Irish are magicians.'

Terrence remained in Miss Howard's house. The routine of the household, and Miss Howard herself, were as they had been in the first weeks of his stay with her. She had stopped calling out to him when he came in at night. In fact, he rarely saw the light under her door at that hour. Her health had apparently improved. She no longer complained of dizzy spells, and he saw no sign of her medicine. It became easier every day to think of the events of that night as some bizarre figment. In time the episode rarely came into his mind at all, and when it did, he impatiently shook it out. He lived well at Miss Howard's. He had become accustomed to living well.

The Littlefield house on Lafayette Place was not a awesome to him as on that first day with Pete. He knew, now, how to hold a cup. He knew how to sit in an upholstered chair without alarm at its softness. In his fantasies he had gone there confidently to see Sylvia, talked to her effortlessly, charmed her as he charmed the other girls.

But that Sunday morning, as he got ready for the actual visit, all his ease dissolved. He combed his mop of red hair three different ways before it suited him. He changed from black socks to gray and back again. His fingers were so stiff and cold that he could scarcely button his shirt.

When he was finally there in the room with Sylvia, he felt wooden, wordless, a mannequin with a whirring heart. Nothing he had remembered or imagined had prepared him to deal with the reality of this fair-haired, tiny-featured girl, whose fragile little waist looked as though it would break between his hands. Even the thought sent a wave of heat from under his stiff collar up into his scalp.

'What makes you blush, Mr McNally the First?' she asked him in her high, light voice. 'Have I said something to embarrass you?'

Since all she had thus far said to him was: 'Good morning' and 'Won't you sit down?' and 'Will you have coffee?' the question answered itself, but he felt it necessary to reassure her.

'No, of course not. You haven't said anything. I'm a little warm, that's all – the coffee . . .' He set the cup down carefully on a table next to his chair. 'Coffee always makes me warm.'

'But you haven't drunk any yet, Mr McNally the First.'

'It's the steam . . .' he began, and stopped. She was making a little sound in her throat, covering her mouth with the fingers of one hand. 'You're laughing at me, aren't you, Miss Sylvia?'

She took her hand down from her mouth and looked at him with brown-eyed innocence. He had not remembered her eyes that color. They were as dark as chocolate – unexpected, startling with her fair hair and skin. In the dimness of the room that other day he had not seen her clearly at all. Today she had drawn the heavy draperies back as he came in, and she was even lovelier in the light than he had imagined.

Still, he never permitted anyone to laugh at him. If it had not been Sylvia, he would have left the house. Instead, he said, 'I didn't come here to be laughed at.'

The chocolate eyes widened. 'What did you come here for, Mr McNally the First?'

'Stop that.'

Her tiny mouth made a tiny O. 'Stop what, Mr McNally the First?'

'Stop making fun of me.' He was no longer wondering how to talk to a girl like Sylvia. He had, for the moment, forgotten about the kind of girl she was. 'Stop calling me by that name, as if you were addressing an envelope. I came to see you because I liked you that day we met, and I wanted to get to know you better, but if you're going to act like this, I might as well leave.'

She looked down at her hands, small as a child's, lying one inside the other in her lap. 'You're very crude,' she said softly. 'I noticed that when you were here before. Your loud voice, and the way you held your cup. My mother says all Irish people are crude.'

Terrence got out of his chair. She went on as though she had not noticed.

'But I liked you, too, that day. I liked you anyway.' She smiled up at him. He had never seen a girl smile like that, without showing her teeth. 'You have the bluest eyes. I was watching for you out the window this morning, and I could see the blue when you were halfway down the street.'

She liked him. She had been watching for him, eager to see him. That almost made him forget the other.

'Your Aunt Nora is Irish,' he said. 'Is she crude, too?'

'Oh, Aunt Nora!' She left it at that. 'What was it you wanted me to call you?' she asked, in a voice gone suddenly meek.

'I don't know that I want you to call me anything if you think I'm so crude.'

'Don't be silly. I said I liked you anyway. I'm tired of the boys I know. They're all the same. You're different.' Her eyelashes fluttered, settled long and silky against her cheek. 'Why do you suppose I told you to come? I even had to lie and say I had a headache so they'd all go to church without me.' She patted the cushion of his chair.

'Sit down and finish your coffee and tell me about yourself, Terrence. Is that right? Just Terrence?'

'Yes,' he said hoarsely. 'Yes – Sylvia.' He sat down. 'What do you want to know?'

'Oh, everything. The story of your life.'

Nobody had ever before asked to hear the story of his life. He started stumblingly, not sure what he should tell her. *I was born almost nineteen years ago on Little Water Street* . . . He had read autobiographies that began that way, but he didn't want to sound like a book, and he didn't want her to know about Little Water Street.

'Well, it's not much of a story. I used to live a little further downtown. Since my mother died, I've lived – well, you know where. You wrote me there. I used to work for a man – a politician. An important politician. I thought I wanted to go into politics myself, but I changed my mind . . .'

He began to warm up. Soon he was leaning forward in his chair, his eyes shining, his big, freckled, expressive face changing as he shifted scenes. He wanted the story to have a desirable effect on Sylvia. The means came automatically. He had always had a talent for enhancing the truth.

Jimmy O'Brien became an important politician; their dubious partnership, a respectable business venture that had failed because of the machinations of crooked rivals. The job at the Hoffman House, glossed over with the elegance of the decor and the encounters with wealthy, powerful men, sounded enviable. Exacting a promise of secrecy gave cachet to the new college journal . . .

'Do you go out with a lot of girls?'

She had sat without moving, only her eyes shifting, sometimes on his eyes, sometimes on his mouth. This was the first question she had asked. It broke his stride.

'Girls? Well – a few.'

'Maybe I know some of them. If they go to Normal School, I might. I know girls who meet City College boys, even though it's against the rules. President Hunter would kill them if he knew. Expel them anyway. But they meet on corners, away from the school, so it's safe enough. Do you ever meet Normal School girls on corners?'

'Not usually. What about you? I mean, you and City College boys?'

'I don't like most City College boys.'

'Would you meet me?'

'I don't know. I might. It depends.'

'On what?'

She sat without answering, a little frown creasing the perfect smoothness of her face.

'Terrence, I could help you,' she said then, and the frown disappeared. 'I could teach you how a cultivated person, a gentleman, speaks and behaves. After a while—'

'You told me just before,' he broke in harshly, 'that you liked me because I was different.'

'I didn't say *because*. I said *anyway*. I could teach you so you'd be much nicer and I'd like you much better. After a while no one would even guess you were Irish.' She clapped her child's hands together. 'You could even change your name.'

Terrence stared at her. He got to his feet again. It surprised him that he could speak because he felt as though he were choking.

'If I don't suit you as I am, good-bye.' He started for the door. 'My name will be heard from someday,' he said over his shoulder. 'Then you'll be ashamed of telling me to change it.'

'Oh, don't be so sensitive, Terrence!' She stamped her foot. 'Come back!'

'No. Why should I?'

'Come back,' she said again, but so softly this time that he could hardly hear her. 'You can kiss me if you like.'

He stood stunned, turned to stone. In his wildest fantasies he had not imagined kissing her yet, today, the first time.

'Don't you want to?' she whispered.

His blood ran again. He went to her without speaking, bent down to her chair and kissed her gently on the lips, and then was afraid she had meant him just to kiss her cheek.

But she stood up and flung her arms around him.

'That's no kind of kiss,' she said. 'Can't you kiss better than that?'

He kissed her a little more firmly and then put his arms around her, too, but he did not move his hands, and he held her carefully away from his rapidly bulging crotch. Since his encounter with Maureen Conroy when he was thirteen, he had never had to exercise this kind of control with a girl. He felt himself beginning to tremble. He thought he had better let her go before he flew apart.

Then she pressed herself hard against him and parted her closed lips a little under his, and thought melted away. He cupped her buttocks to press her closer still. He thrust his tongue between her open lips. One moment she was responding. The next she had struggled away from him with a strength so surprising, so sudden, that it dazed him.

'You *pig*!' she said in her light, high girl's voice. 'You disgusting *pig*!'

Terrence stood with his hands hanging at his sides, his breath coming in slowly subsiding gasps. He had never hit a girl. There was little natural violence in him. But he would have liked to hit Sylvia.

'You asked me to,' he said. 'It was what you wanted.'

'Don't you dare say that! Get out. Get out and never come back.'

Terrence left without a word. Halfway down the street he thought he heard her calling, but he did not look around. He kept walking at random, not knowing where he was going.

After a time, he found himself on East Eighteenth Street. He sat down on the steps of a building, not noticing that the gray September day had turned colder and that it was beginning to drizzle. He neither saw nor heard the occasional carriage that rolled by on the quiet Sunday street, bringing a family home from church.

His anger was gone. His frustration had subsided. He

108

was beginning to think with disaste of himself, rather than of Sylvia. She was an innocent girl, only sixteen years old, wanting nothing more then a little chaste kissing and hugging. He had taken advantage of her. He had acted as if she were the kind of girl who knew what she was doing, the kind of girl he was used to. She had been right to call him crude. No gentleman would have behaved as he had. She had liked him, but he had ruined everything.

Not since his arrest and his two days in jail, four years earlier, had his self-esteem been so low.

9

Terrence's enthusiasm for helping Jake Stern launch the new college monthly was greatly intensified by his unhappy experience with Sylvia. He needed something to distract him from it, to restore his conviction that he could usually find the way, the words, to get whatever results he wanted. He meant to put Sylvia out of his mind, but she kept coming into it. He had fantasies in which the magazine made such a splash that everyone talked about it, the Normal School girls were avid to get a glimpse of its brilliant editors, and Sylvia forgot his crude behavior and wished she had never let him go.

They called the journal *Pharos*. Jake had the name ready that first afternoon when Terrence arrived numbly, idealess, at his house.

'*Pharos?* What does it mean?'

'Lighthouse. Pharos was once an island near Alexandria. The lighthouse on it was one of the seven wonders of the ancient world. As soon as I read about it, I knew that was the right name. We're going to light the way so this college doesn't founder on the rocks of antiquity. That's impressive, isn't it? I think it should be in our first editorial, don't you?'

'No. It's too fancy. Where did you read about this

Pharos?'

'In history last year.'

'Last year? Then you had the name all picked out when you asked me to think one up. "Something snappy!"'

'Well, I wanted to make you feel involved in the project so you wouldn't lose interest. Anyway, who can tell? You might have produced something even better.'

Terrence, who had felt he might never laugh again, laughed at that. It was the way his own mind worked.

The division of labor on *Pharos* fell into place naturally. Terrence sold advertising space. He did not go first, as Jake had suggested, to the shops near the college that already advertised in the other City College magazines: the *Journal*, the *Microcosm*, the prestigious *Mercury*. He called on the managers of theaters and circuses and restaurants. Some cut him short as soon as they knew what he was after, but he persuaded a few that *Pharos* would have wide circulation and that it was worth a trial for the small cost ('the rates are going up soon'). The Hoffman House, where he was now a full-fledged waiter, gave him a half page ad. Edward Stokes, one of the owners of the place, who had served four years in prison for killing Jim Fisk, a rival in love, introduced him to a Dr Rengo. This gentleman gave Terrence an ad for Rengo medicine, which would improve the attractiveness of flabby college men 'by turning fat into muscle'. Armed with commitments from these substantial advertisers, Terrence had little trouble convincing the local shops to take space.

He was less successful in recruiting material and staff members. The majority of the students came from working-class families, and had to earn money in their spare time. Most of the others who might have been useful to *Pharos* had already been recruited by the established magazines or claimed to be too involved in literary societies or athletics to take on anything else. One boy said he was not interested in working on 'a Jew magazine'. Terrence did not repeat this to Jake, but since the boy said

110

it to a number of others, Jake eventually heard it.

'If he'd been talking to you,' Terrence told him, 'he'd probably have said "an Irisher magazine".'

'Don't bother trying to console me. I'm used to it. I don't even hear it.' Jake shrugged. 'Who needs any of them? We've got the money. We'll put *Pharos* out by ourselves.'

They ran two major articles in the first issue. One was Terrence's piece supporting the elective system and disputing President Webb's contention that the students were too immature to make wise choices. Jake wrote the other article. It concerned the efforts of the governor of the state, Lucius Robinson, to abolish the college on the grounds that one class of citizen should not be taxed for educating another class beyond elementary school. All that was needed for the children of the masses, according to Robinson, was sufficient commercial school education to enable them to understand their duties as citizens. Anything more, for such children, would only breed discontent. Jake denounced him at grandiloquent length.

'It's too long. It's too flowery,' Terrence said. 'Here's a paragraph I think you could leave out altogether, and here—'

Jake cut him off. 'Wait a minute. What do you know about it?' His deep voice was mild. He sounded, and looked, not so much indignant or offended as curious. 'You haven't had any experience at all. I, at least, have worked on a college journal before. What gives you the idea you know better how a piece like this should be written?'

'You wrote it. Maybe you're too close to it to see what's wrong. I don't say I know better, but I know even if I haven't had experience.' Terrence frowned a little. 'I can't tell you how I know, except I read a lot and I notice the way professionals write things like this.'

'Why don't you fix it up then? I've had enough of it.'

From then on Terrence did all the revising and cutting. Jake disliked doing it whether the material was his own or

111

someone else's. He enjoyed and had a flair for selecting subject matter, finding controversial issues, judging the best viewpoint from which an article should be written. Terrence was good at balancing the contents. It was his suggestion, when they were working on the first issue, that it needed a couple of lighter pieces. He wrote a 'human interest' story about Broas, the pieman, who for years had had a stand on the stone pavement of the lower hall of the college, where he sold indigestible concoctions, one of which he called, for no known reason, Washington pie. Jake suggested 'Washington Pie – Why?' as a headline. Thereafter the writing of headlines fell to Jake.

Terrence began taking a half hour to an hour off his study time to work with Jake in Room 312 after classes. To make it up, he sometimes had to study when he got home from his waiter's job late at night. Occasionally he fell asleep over his books, but he didn't mind. He enjoyed everything connected with publishing *Pharos*, and he was used to cramming every available hour with work and study and whatever else needed to be done.

On Sundays they worked at Jake's house. Terrence arrived there in the morning at about ten and often did not leave until late afternoon. Lengthy lunches with the family cut into their worktime, but Jake said his mother would be hurt if they stayed away from the table.

Jake had three sisters, aged twelve, fifteen, and eighteen. They all looked like Jake's father, a large, neckless man with sharp, narrow brown eyes, thick lips, and a pudgy blob of a nose. They all had dark, wiry hair with no gloss, the father's streaked with gray and spiking out springily under his skullcap. He spoke with a heavy German accent, although he had been in the country nearly thirty years.

Mrs Stern was different. She was a native American with a voice like music. Jake had her hazel eyes. Otherwise he resembled neither parent. His mother was a little dumpling of a woman whose serene face, smooth as a girl's was overpowered by a long, large-boned nose.

112

'I'm glad you're Jake's friend,' she said to Terrence the third or fourth time he came to the house. 'Jews tend to stick together, you know. They pretend it's because no one else is good enough, but that's not the real reason. It's because with each other we're shielded from ugliness. Together we're safe. Do you understand that at all?'

'Oh, yes. Where I was born, everybody was Irish. I don't think my mother knew any other people. It was for the same reason.'

'I know other people,' Mrs Stern said, 'but I have no friends who aren't Jewish. That's sad, isn't it? I'm glad Jake's experience will be a little broader.' She patted Terrence's hand. 'You'll be good for him.'

The Sterns lived way uptown in a large square house of white stone on Thirty-second Street in the Murray Hill quarter. It was a far more fashionable section than Lafayette Place, where the Littlefields lived, and the furnishings of the house were much less shabby, but Terrence thought it was the homiest place he had ever been in. Everything was large, solid, and roomy. The chairs had deep, springy cushions and wide arms. All the rooms were bright and uncluttered. It was a peaceful house.

Mrs Stern never disturbed Jake and Terrence when they were busy with *Pharos* except to call them to lunch. Mr Stern occasionally knocked softly on the door of the sewing room, where they worked on a flat table surrounded by boxes of fabric, a Singer sewing machine, and a dress form in the shape of Mrs Stern. Jake's father would come in for a few minutes, look over their shoulders, and nod approvingly at whatever he saw.

'Ya, dot's nice. Dot's a fine thing. Literachoot. From my side, it don't come. All I know is furs.' He would pat Jake's cheek and smile at Terrence. 'Dot's a smart boy, dot Jacob.'

'If he keeps telling you how remarkable you are,' Terrence said to Jake once when they were alone, 'you'll begin to believe it.'

'I'm an only son,' Jake said. 'To Papa that means I'm a

113

combination of King Solomon, Adonis, Leonardo da Vinci, and Shakespeare. Not that I'm *not* remarkable, of course.'

'Who does your mother think you're a combination of?'

'Mama? Oh, Mama just loves me. She even loves those three witches they tell me are my sisters.'

The Sterns talked a great deal about love. They did considerable kissing and touching. Even Jake and his father kissed each other now and then. It took Terrence some time not to be embarrassed by it, but after a while he took it for granted.

When the proofs for the first issue of *Pharos* came back from the printer, Jake showed Terrence how to make up the dummy. They cut the long sheets of printed material to fit blank pages that were the same size the finished pages would be. The cut sheets were finally to be pasted on the blank pages in the desired order. It looked simple, but it was not. Often, when they had a page together, they had one or two lines of an article left over – too few to continue to another page. Then they had to find something to cut out so the extra lines would fit. Another problem was distributing the ads effectively throughout the magazine, so they would be prominent enough to read, yet would not interfere with the smooth reading of the articles. Half a dozen times Jake was ready to paste up and then changed his mind and switched something around again.

'Listen, Jake, maybe it's never going to be perfect, but we've got to finish it sometime. I say we leave it this way and get it to the printer tomorrow.'

Pharos went to press with Jake listed as editor and Terrence as assistant editor. Terrence had considered arguing that they were coeditors, but he had decided against it. The whole idea of *Pharos* had originally been Jake's, after all, and he knew more about putting out a magazine. It was only fair that he have the superior title. For the time being.

The Sunday before *Pharos* went to press, Terrence

managed to get Jake's mother alone in the hall for a moment on his way out of the house. He had no trouble asking her his question. She was like no one in his experience, yet from the first she had made him feel as if he had known her all his life.

'How can I learn to talk the way you do, Mrs Stern?'

'Why do you want to talk the way I do?' She had to bend her head back to look up at him. 'What's the matter with the way you talk?'

'My voice is too loud. I don't talk like a – well, like a cultivated person. I thought maybe you could—'

'Terrence.' She took one of his large hands between her small, plump, warm ones. 'Terrence, you're a big young man with a big voice. Your voice is fine. Talk the way you want to. Be what you are. Tell anybody who doesn't like you that way to go to hell.' Her eyes twinkled at his startled expression. 'You see, sometimes I don't talk like such a cultivated person.'

He grinned at her. 'It's a girl.'

'Yes, of course it's a girl. Don't you think I guessed that? Tell her anyway.'

Terrence did not expect to have the chance. He had imagined meeting Sylvia by accident someday and amazing her with the modulated voice and cultivated speech he had learned from Mrs Stern. It was a variation on, or an addition to, the fantasy in which she was dazzled by his success with *Pharos*. But he did not really expect to see her again.

Two days before the first issue of *Pharos* appeared, she was standing on the corner of Twenty-fifth Street as he walked home from school. She had on a dark ankle-length school skirt and white blouse, and her pale hair was caught back with a large bow of stiff dark ribbon.

'Hello, Terrence McNally the First,' she said, and then clapped her hand over her mouth. 'Ooh, I forgot. I mean, hello, Terrence.'

'Hello, Sylvia.' His heart was raising such a clamor that in case she could hear it, he talked louder than ever to drown it out. 'What are you doing here?'

'What do you think? Waiting for you.'

'You said you never wanted to see me again.'

She made an impatient sound. 'Oh, for goodness sake, girls say a lot of things. You mustn't take everything I say so seriously.'

'You called me a pig,' he said. 'Don't you want me to take that seriously either?'

'I don't remember calling you a pig. You must have heard it wrong.' Her innocent chocolate brown eyes looked directly up into his face. 'Would I be here waiting for you if I thought you were a pig?'

He stood gazing at her. He did not feel the sidewalk under his feet. 'We could go to a soda fountain if you'd like to,' he said.

'Oh, no, we can't do that. Somebody might see us.'

'Somebody might see us here.'

'That's different. I can pretend I don't know you and I just happened to stop you to ask directions or the time or something. If we went to a soda fountain together, it would look as if we were friends.'

'Well, aren't we?'

Her facial expressions changed almost as often as she blinked. Terrence could scarcely decipher one before it was replaced by another. A moment before she had appeared interested, concerned. Now that look was wiped away by a kind of bored sulkiness.

'Oh, I suppose so,' she said, 'but there's no need to let everybody know it.'

'Why?' He sensed that he would not like her answer, but he had to ask. 'What difference does it make?'

'Oh, Terrence, you're so stupid! Suppose Peter found out. Suppose he told my mother ... No, there's no supposing about that. He *would* tell her, he's such a sneak. He'd like nothing better than to get me in trouble. I'd be deprived of everything I enjoy for days, maybe even months, and he'd just gloat. He'd say it serves me right for being seen with a crude Irisher.'

116

Terrence sighed. 'You're calling me those things again. I told you last time, Sylvia—'

The innocent eyes widened.

'But I'm not calling you anything,' she broke in. 'It's Peter who would, not me.'

'He wouldn't. Pete and I are good friends.'

Terrence knew as he said it that it was not true. He scarcely saw Pete anymore. They had never been good friends. He and Pete had used each other for the ideas, the arguments, they both loved to spout – each paying his fee for listening in his turn. Terrence, in his ignorance, had thought this was friendship. Because of Jake Stern, he knew better now.

'If you don't want to believe me,' Sylvia said. 'you can think what you like.'

She started to move away, but he caught her by the arm. 'Let's not argue anymore, Sylvia. We're always arguing. I know I'm not the kind of fellow you're used to, but you told me that was what you liked about me, so if you could just remember that and take me as I am, we'd get along fine.'

'My goodness! You said all that without taking a single breath.' Her lips curved in the delicious close-mouthed smile. 'You can walk me to Fifth Avenue. Nobody goes over that way, so it's safe. I'm going to ride the omnibus back uptown and down again.'

'I could ride with you,' he said recklessly, though it would cost time and money that he did not have to spare.

But she shook her head. 'I like to go alone. I'm not allowed to, but they can't stop me if they don't know. I like to look at the mansions. The Astor one is pretty, but the Stewart one – that's like a palace.' They began walking west on Twenty-fifth Street. 'Someday I'm going to live in a mansion on Fifth Avenue,' she said.

'I'll build you one.' He did not know where the words came from. He did not mean to say them. But he plunged boldly ahead. 'I'll build *us* one. When I'm rich.'

She did not laugh aloud. He did not look down at her to

117

see if she was laughing silently.

'How do you expect to get rich when all you are is a waiter?'

'Never mind that. I'm not going to stay a waiter. I have plans. You'll see.'

She was silent for several minutes. 'I'll marry a man in high society,' she said then. 'We'll be invited everywhere, like to Mrs Astor's ball every year, and I'll have the most beautiful gown there. We'll travel in Europe. Maybe I'll even be presented at court. My mother says a girl as pretty as I am can marry any man she wants to if she sets her mind to it.'

Terrence listened more to the sound of her voice than to her words. The words did not matter. She was confiding in him, telling him her secret fantasies. He took her hand, and she left it in his.

'The man you're going to want to marry,' he said calmly, 'is me.'

'Oh, you're so ridiculous! Do you think I'd ever marry an Irish waiter? You don't even look like a gentleman. I don't know why I bother with you at all.'

She pulled away from him, started to leave, and turned back. 'You can come to my house next Sunday morning while they're all at church,' she said imperiously, and then giggled. 'I'll have a headache again.'

He stood and watched her walk down the street, tentatively swaying her narrow hips. He did not move until the horses drawing the omnibus came trotting along Fifth Avenue. When Sylvia got on, he turned and walked back the way they had come.

She could say what she liked now. He knew how things were going to be. She would let him kiss her again on Sunday, but this time he would not allow himself to kiss her the way he had when she called him a pig. There was plenty of time for that. He was used to waiting.

Sylvia McNally, he murmured to himself. *Mrs Terrence McNally the First.*

*

118

The day after *Pharos* appeared, President Webb called Jake to his office.

'Maybe he wants to congratulate you on the fine magazine,' Terrence said.

'Unlikely. I don't think he ever congratulated anybody for anything. He might have heard what I said in history class last week. I said there is nothing romantic or noble about war. General Alexander Stewart Webb wouldn't like that. He has wounds and the Congressional Medal of Honor to prove how romantic and noble it is.' Jake shrugged. 'Well, all he can do is give me one of his lectures on patriotism.'

When Terrence went to Room 312 to ask Jake what had happened, he found his friend kneeling on the floor, sorting through the contents of the bottom desk drawer. He looked up as Terrence came in. His long face was white.

'What's the matter?' Terrence asked him. 'What are you doing?'

'Getting my things together.' He stood up slowly, brushed at the dusty knees of his black suit without removing the dust, and leaned against the wall. 'Webb suspended me. For a week from classes. Forever as editor of *Pharos*.'

'Jake! Why?'

'Because I published an article that took a position he opposed. Insubordination, he called it. "I will not allow insubordination in the College of the City of New York." He pointed out that a soldier in the army can be shot for it.' Jake gave a weak smile. 'I suppose he wanted me to know how lucky I am to be only suspended.'

'Jake!' Terrence said again. 'Jake, the article supporting the elective system? My article? Why are *you* suspended? You didn't write it. If anybody ought to be suspended, it's me.'

Jake shook his head. 'I'm the editor. I'm responsible for what's published.'

'But I'm the assistant editor. And I *wrote* it. If he'd

known I wrote—' Terrence patted Jake's arm. 'You wait here. He's probably still in his office. I'm going to see him right now and tell him—'

'Terrence, it's no use. Didn't you hear what I said? It doesn't matter who wrote it. I'm responsible. All that can happen is that he'll suspend you too, and that will be the end of *Pharos*.'

'It will be the end of it anyway. I can't put it out without you.'

There was a silence. 'Maybe we could still do it together,' Jake said finally. 'The only difference would be that my name wouldn't be on it and nobody would know.'

'And you'd never get any credit.'

Jake shrugged. 'Who needs credit?'

But Terrence knew he didn't mean it. That first day, when he sent for Terrence to come to his room, he had said he wanted to make an impact on the college before he was graduated in June. He would not be satisfied with an anonymous impact.

'Listen, Jake, Webb can't do a thing like this. It's—' The notion, like many of Terrence's ideas, came to him while he was talking. 'It's against the Constitution. It says right in the beginning, in the First Amendment, isn't it? – you know, you're the history major – that nobody can interfere with the freedom of the press. Doesn't it say that?'

Jake's magnified eyes looked tired. They looked like the eyes of an old man. 'In this college General Webb can do anything he wants to do. We're his troops. The laws are different for troops.'

'That's not right. We can't just let him go against the Constitution. You can give up if you want to, but I'm going to make him reinstate you!'

'Stop bellowing like a wounded bull. How do you propose to make him?'

'I don't know yet, but I'll think of something.'

In the four years Terrence had worked at the Hoffman

House bar, first as a dishwasher behind the bar and finally as a waiter, he had become as much of a feature of the place as the famous Bouguereau painting. He was, to begin with, almost as instantly visible, with his height and breadth and fiery hair. In spite of his size, he was deft and quick, and he was always courteous, good-humored, and unruffled, even with customers who were not. Many of the men who came to the bar for the first time had heard that Terrence was the best waiter there and asked to have him wait on their table. Many of the regulars liked to start him talking and found his rapid flow of words amusing.

Terrence had not hung around politicians from the age of ten without absorbing some of their skills. He never forgot a man's name or, once he had found it out, his occupation. If he heard that the man had a wife and children, he inquired after them. He was flattering without overdoing it. Ordinary men frequented the Hoffman House, but so did the rich and powerful, and sometimes the former turned into the latter. He was agreeable and attentive to everybody. There was no telling when he might need someone influential.

The man Terrence approached now, several evenings after Jake had been suspended, was neither famous nor rich. He was a young man, not much older than Terrence, named Wallace Lane. Lane had come to the Hoffman House early that past summer, when Terrence was working there full time. He had bought the one drink required to get the full lunch free and then had not had the customary quarter for the tip.

'I'm sorry, I didn't know,' he said. 'I haven't been here before. I'm accustomed to Mould's. You don't have to tip there. But I'll come by tomorrow and bring you the quarter.'

Terrence told him not to bother. When Lane came again some weeks later, Terrence would not accept a tip. He had taken an instant liking to the slight, hungry-looking young man and felt sorry for him. Probably he was one of the penniless artists or writers who went to

Billy Mould's bar on University Place to fill up on bean soup. Terrence knew what it was like to be so hungry you were glad to eat the same thing every day, as long as it was filling. Aside from that, plenty of men who became prominent and wealthy started out penniless. He told Wallace Lane to come whenever he wanted to and not to worry about the tip.

But Lane had not been in again until early September, after school had started. He had come in the evening, flushed, unsteady on his feet, and tried to persuade Terrence to share a bottle of champagne with him.

'You musht, Terrence. I'm celebrating. I came specially to celebrate with you because you were such a prinsh – prince – to me when I didn't have any money.'

Terrence had explained that he could not drink on the job, and did not drink anyway, but he would drink a glass of seltzer with Lane, and they could pretend it was champagne.

'What are we celebrating anyway?'

'My job. I've got a job. I've got the most wonderful, shtu-stupendous job.' His eyes had filled with alcoholic tears. 'I'm a reporter for *The New York Times*!'

He had not become an evening regular at the Hoffman House. The salary of a young reporter did not run to that. But he did drop in occasionally for a drink and a chat with Terrence. He was there that evening because Terrence had written to him at the *Times* office, saying he thought he might have a story for him.

'I guess I'd better tell you right away,' he said when Terrence came up to him at the bar. 'All I've reported so far is street accidents and fires, so if you have another kind of story, they may not let me do it.'

'This is what I think you call an exposey. Like the one the *Times* did on the Tweed Ring. Not that big, of course. I'm too busy to tell you about it now, but I'll be off in a few minutes, and if you could wait, I think it's something you can use. You could prove you ought to be writing exposeys instead of just accidents and fires.'

122

'Exposés. It's French,' Lane said, and shook his head. 'I'll wait, but they'll never let me do it.'

But the *Times* did let Lane do the story. With the help of a rewrite man, and without a by-line.

TYRANNY ON THE CAMPUS, the headline ran.

'Of course,' Jake said, elated. 'Of course, the *Times* would be indignant. Listen to this: "Unless we vigilantly protect the freedom of the press everywhere, it can be abused anywhere." They mean even at *The New York Times.* "We must allow no editor, whether of a small college journal or a big city newspaper, to be tyrannized as General Webb has tyrannized Jacob Stern for disagreeing with him." They mean otherwise, the editor of the *Times* could be next. Of course, they'd take up the cudgel.' Jake flung the paper down on the sewing-room table and threw his arms around Terrence. 'You're a genius to have realized it.'

Terrence wondered whether Jake was going to kiss him. He had grown accustomed to all the Stern family's touching, and even did some of it himself now, but he was relieved when Jake let him go.

'I didn't realize,' he said. 'Not the angle of it. I knew a lot about Boss Tweed and how powerful he was. I thought nobody could ever bring him down. But the exposé in the *Times* helped put him in prison. The *Times* was more powerful than even Boss Tweed, so I thought they'd be more powerful than Webb.'

Jake did not wait for official word from President Webb. He simply returned to his classes and to his editorial desk in Room 312. No communication of any kind ever came to him from the president. For a brief period, as the centre of a *cause célèbre*, he was a hero to some of the students. But Jake was an uncomfortable hero, stiff and strange, incapable of handling popularity with grace, and his fans soon drifted away.

'Now I can sink back into merciful oblivion,' he said to Terrence.

'You can't sink into oblivion. You're still the editor of

Pharos.'

'It's *Pharos* I want them interested in, not me. Let them read the magazine and leave the editor alone.'

But he was not left alone. The *Mercury*, considered the most influential publication on the campus, came out with an article that had obviously gone to press before the piece appeared in the *Times*. It was a scathing criticism of the 'member of the Semitic race' who edited a new college magazine and, 'with the effrontery of his kind,' set himself up as an authority on college administration, in conflict with professional educators. The article was full of epithets such as 'upstart' and 'ignoramus', with the strong suggestion that these qualities were directly associated with Jewishness.

Jake wanted to begin his reply by pointing out that the president of the college was no more a professional educator than he was, but only an army general who had nothing but social prestige and the ability to raise money and influence legislation favorable to the college.

'You can't put that in. You're still angry at Webb about the other business, but he didn't have anything to do with this,' Terrence said. 'Why don't you just start right in with the real issue?'

'What's the real issue? Anti-Semitism? Do you think I'm going to waste my time fighting every ninny who calls me a dirty Jew? It's his problem, not mine.'

'This isn't just some fellow calling you a name in the hall. This is different. This is in print in the *Mercury*. It's been made a public issue. *Pharos* has got to answer it publicly. If you don't want to do it, I will.'

'Do it,' Jake said. 'As long as you're impassioned about it.'

'Maybe you don't want to be responsible for it, though, the way you were for my piece on the elective system. Maybe I should put my name on it.'

'Maybe you should,' Jake said with one of his habitual shrugs.

'And after this it might be a good idea if we were on the

124

masthead as coeditors. That way we'd share the responsibility. You wouldn't have to keep taking the whole brunt of all this kind of thing.'

'That's very noble and unselfish of you, Terrence. I know the last thing you want is to be the coeditor of *Pharos*. I appreciate the sacrifice you'd be making, but it really isn't necessary.'

Terrence looked at Jake's long, solemn face for an instant and then grinned. 'All right, you sarcastic snake, maybe some of it is wanting it for myself. But you have to admit it's sensible for your sake too. I'm in this as much as you are, so if we're dividing the work and the fun, there's no reason we shouldn't divide the knocks. If there's ever any glory, I wouldn't mind dividing that as well, but right now—'

'Yes! Yes! Yes!' Jake interrupted, holding up both hands. 'I surrender, if only to shut you up.' He shook his head. 'When the time comes, I don't doubt that you'll talk yourself out of hell and into heaven.'

'You sound like my mother,' Terrence said.

He wondered what Aggie would think if she could see him now, coeditor of a college magazine, at home in a house in fashionable Murray Hill, courting a girl like Sylvia Littlefield. He was never able to shake off entirely the feeling that she could.

In the next issue of *Pharos* Terrence's name appeared on his reply to the *Mercury*'s attack as well as on the masthead as coeditor. 'This way it looks more impartial,' he told Jake, 'than if people think you may have written it yourself.'

'Fine,' Jake said. 'Fine. Do whatever you want. Drop your drop into the bucket. I'm going to write against keeping Fielding's, Smollett's, and Boccaccio's books out of the college library. That might have some effect in my lifetime, or my children's, or at least my grandchildren's. Though God forbid any of them should have to go to this college.'

Terrence wrote that the article in the *Mercury* smacked

strongly of the same kind of student persecution of Jews as in Russia and had no place in a free society or a college open to all citizens. He belabored the ignorance of the *Mercury* editor.

Who is the ignoramus? The editor of *Pharos*, who ranks 4th in his class on the merit roll, or the editor of the *Mercury*, who ranks 234th out of 235? . . .

Any ignoramus knows that there is no such thing as a 'Semitic race.' Jews are members of the Caucasian race. The Jewish editor of *Pharos* is a Caucasian American, just like the Presbyterian editor of the *Mercury* . . .

Miss Howard had a copy of *Pharos* at her place at breakfast a few days after the issue appeared. An instructor she was acquainted with at the college had given it to her, knowing Terrence roomed with her.

'I've just finished reading your article,' she said. 'I understand it's making quite a stir.' She gave him her teacher's smile of approval. 'You've learned to write very well indeed.'

He began eating his oatmeal. Usually at meals they shared, they talked about an event in the news or a course Terrence was taking, or Terrence gave her a version, edited for color with propriety, of some experience on his job at the Hoffman House. They were pleasant, comfortable conversations, and totally impersonal. He did not know how to respond to her praise.

'Of course, you're quite right to stand by your colleague,' she went on. 'I've had Jewish children in my classes, and I've found them just like the Italians or the Germans or the Irish or anybody else.'

He looked at her sharply, embarrassment forgotten. 'Some of them are Italians or Germans or Irish, Miss Howard. It's a religion, not a nationality.'

'Well, of course I know that. It was just a manner of speaking.' A little color had come up into her flat cheeks.

She took a sip of tea. 'Irish Jews, though, Terrence? An Irish person can't be Jewish.'

'Oh, yes, Miss Howard, there are Irish Jews.'

She finished her tea before she answered. 'Are there really? Ah, well, of course, you are learning things I don't know. You're a college man, and as you're aware, I never had the chance to go.'

'I didn't learn that in college. Jake – that's the other editor of *Pharos*, Jacob Stern – he lent me some books on Jewish history.'

Miss Howard did not seem to be listening. She was breaking her toast into dainty small pieces and smiling a little.

'It's really quite gratifying,' she said. 'As you may remember, it was I, Terrence, who encouraged you to go to college.'

'I know. I'm very grateful, Miss Howard.'

But it was not true in any profound sense until years later. At the time he said it, he was too young for gratitude.

He was glad, though, that she thought well of his article. Jake seemed as indifferent to praise as to revilement, but Terrence believed his lack of concern to be pretense, protective camouflage. He did not see how anyone could shrug off approbation as if it were no use, had nothing in it to give pleasure.

No more could he understand Jake's shrugging off the *Mercury* article, leaving it to Terrence to answer it. When his own turn came, Terrence reacted differently.

The article lifted him out of the anonymous company of ordinary students and made him known to boys and teachers who would not otherwise have had any particular interest in him. Most were delighted with what he had written and consequently with him. The *Mercury* editor's position had gone to his head since he had been elected to the post in September. He had become arrogant and overbearing and lost popularity with the students. With his professors he had never been popular. He sat in his classes restlessly, looking bored, and did just enough work to get by. Terrence was admired as the fellow who had properly made a fool of him.

But not everyone admired Terrence. One who did not was Professor Miles, a stiff, cold-eyed, middle-aged man who taught American history with a perpetual air of despair. He had a few favorites to whom he was reasonably courteous. To others he was abrupt and dismissive. But after Terrence's counterattack on the *Mercury* editor came out, nothing Terrence said, no paper he wrote, escaped the professor's sarcasm. Terrence believed Miles would have enjoyed giving him a failing grade and was infuriated because he was too good a student. For once Terrence's political astuteness failed him. He could think of no strategy but to curb his usual volubility in Miles's class and be as unobtrusive as he knew how.

One morning Professor Miles took immigration as his subject and spoke with apparent approval of the Know-Nothing movement of the 1850s, which had agitated for a twenty-five-year residency requirement for American citizenship and a law excluding any but native Americans from political office.

'But a law like that,' Terrence protested, on his feet before he knew it, 'would have prevented some of the men who started this country from being citizens for years – even some of the signers of the Declaration of Independence – just because they weren't—'

Miles did not let him finish. 'Your comment is totally irrelevant, Mr McNally. The movement I am discussing came into being in this century, not the last. It was not designed to prevent distinguished gentlemen from becoming citizens of a new country, but to keep ignorant, foreign riffraff from overrunning and disrupting an established one and coming out of their filthy, crime-ridden ghettos to take employment, and even political office, from native-born citizens.'

He said all this without heat, as if he were reading from

128

notes. He did not look at Terrence, who had not sat down.

'Are all immigrants riffraff, sir?' Terrence asked.

'I have just given a perfectly clear description of what the word means. Obviously there could be little objection to clean, intelligent, industrious immigrants such as the Germans. In contrast, we have, for example, the Irish – unwashed, unlettered, hard-drinking potato farmers, the dregs of their society, who came to this country in droves, corrupted whatever they touched, and—'

Now it was Terrence who would not let the professor finish. His voice, which he had lately tried to modulate, bounced off the walls.

'Professor Miles, I resent what you're saying. You're slurring a whole people. You're insulting me and any other member of this class whose parents came here from Ireland. You're insulting my dead father, who worked from the day he arrived in this country to support his family and whose job killed him. You're insulting my mother, who wore herself out providing a clean, decent home for me, encouraged me to keep learning, and lived long enough to see me go to college, but not long enough to see me become an editor of *Pharos*.'

When Terrence finished, the entire class rose, as if by prearrangement, and cheered. Then, although the session was not half over, they formed orderly files and walked out of the room. Miles tried to stop them, first by commanding them to sit down, then by standing at the door to bar the way. They paid no attention to his words and brushed past him as he stood.

'I'll have you all expelled,' he called after them, his dry voice rising out of control. 'I'll have every last one of you expelled.'

The students gathered around Terrence in the lower hall. One boy asked apprehensively whether the professor would really have them all expelled. His father, the boy said, would kill him if he were expelled.

'It won't happen,' Terrence said, 'because here's what we'll do.' He had had no plan until that moment. 'We'll

129

make the whole thing public. I'll write up a leaflet and have it printed as a sort of supplement to the last issue of *Pharos*. "More Bigotry in Our College" or something like that. We'll post notices and give out handbills, asking for a boycott of all Professor Miles's classes. They can't expel that many students.'

Some of the students did not join the boycott immediately, but all of them left their classroom after ten minutes, when only a few had showed up and Professor Miles had not arrived.

One of these was Peter Littlefield. 'I can't have a class by myself,' he told Terrence, 'but I want you to know I'm not in sympathy.'

'You mean, you agree the Irish are the dregs of society?'

'Of course I don't. Would I have gone around with you if I thought that?' He sounded, Terrence thought, like Sylvia. 'But I'm not in sympathy with all this agitation, the leaflets and posters and all that. You can't boycott every professor who says something you don't like.'

Terrence stared at Pete's dark, lively, handsome face and thought of their arguments, their disagreements about Raskolnikov, and was sad because that had been a game, and it was over, and this disagreement was no game.

'Is that how it looks to you, Pete? Just something Miles said that I don't happen to like?'

'I think you push yourself forward too much, Terrence. I'm telling you as a friend. Gentlemen don't do that.'

Terrence wondered how Pete would feel if he'd known he was going to have a brother-in-law who was no gentleman. Sylvia still insisted that the idea of marrying him was preposterous. She was still likely to say that she never wanted to see him again, and yet she kept inviting him to come to Lafayette Place on intermittent Sunday mornings, when she invariably let him kiss her and often pushed him out of the house later in apparent disgust. He paid no attention to what he had come to think of as feminine temperament. When she was old enough, and he

130

had money enough, they would be married.

Meanwhile, the executive committee of the college met to discuss the question of Professor Miles and the student boycott. Some of the members disapproved of the boycott. They thought that by allowing it to go unpunished, they would be opening the college to wholesale boycotting of anyone or anything that did not suit the students. They attempted to interpret the professor's remarks as a quotation rather than his own opinion. Both the appeal for punishment and the attempted whitewash were voted down. Professor Miles was given a two-month leave of absence 'because of ill health'. He never returned.

'Vy vould an educated man like dot, a professor,' Jake's father wanted to know at Sunday lunch, 'say such crazy things in a classroom? Risk his whole livelihood?'

'He couldn't help himself. He's an Irish hater,' Terrence said. 'I always thought he had something against me personally, but it wasn't that. He hates all the Irish, but the ones he hates the most are the ones he can't truthfully call riffraff.'

'Besides, he didn't think he was risking anything,' Jake said. 'Probably he didn't even expect to be challenged. How could he know Terrence was such a firebrand?'

Jake's oldest sister, Bertha, was gazing at Terrence as if she wanted to lap him up. 'You were very brave to say what you did to him. You could have been expelled.' Her voice was as musical as her mother's, but Terrence did not hear it that way – not from those thick lips. 'It was a noble thing to do.'

As often as Terrence had sat at the Sterns' table, he scarcely knew the sisters existed. They were quiet girls, talking and giggling a little among themselves, but rarely taking part in the general conversation. Terrence had nothing to say to them beyond polite comments. He looked at them so seldom that except for the difference in their ages, he would not have known one from the other. For all he knew, Bertha might have been mooning over

131

him like that any Sunday he was there. He was embarrassed and repelled and said the most frightening thing he could think of to upset her.

'It was nothing. It's easy to talk. When I was ten years old, I *killed* a man for being an Irish hater,' he said, and occupied himself with cutting up his chicken.

Mr Stern responded first. 'Dot's a choke, ya, Terrence? You vould nefer do such a thing, such a chentle fellow.'

'If it's a joke,' Jake said, 'it isn't a very funny one.'

The youngest sister, twelve-year-old Debbie, said, 'You couldn't have. How could a little boy kill a man?'

Bertha, for whose benefit he had told it, said calmly, 'If you really did do it, you must have had a very good reason.'

Terrence was silent. He chewed his chicken without tasting it. Bertha was not upset at all. The whole thing had fizzled out. He felt curiously uncomfortable and wished he had not tried it.

'Terrence.' Mrs Stern spoke for the first time. 'Terrence, please tell us about it. As long as you brought it up.' There was something in her voice that he had not heard before. 'Did you have a good reason?'

'Mama, it's a choke—'

'No, Abe, I don't think it is. Did you have a good reason, Terrence?'

He glanced at her across the table, saw none of the warmth with which she usually looked at him, and began speaking rapidly to the opposite wall.

'I was – they were there when I came home, the Irish haters. A mob of them, punching people, hitting them with bottles. There was blood all over. They broke a boy's arm for no reason, just broke it as if it were a – a chicken bone.' It was all there on the wall. He saw it as he had not seen it for a long time. He had come so far away. But it was there. 'The man who broke the boy's arm hit a child in the face next – Timmy Conroy – he wasn't much more than a baby, and the man hit him and tried to pull him away from his mother. I – I – you learn how to fight when

132

you live where I did – you have to. When you're small, against somebody much bigger, if you can take him by surprise and dive into the backs of his knees while he's off-balance, you can knock him down.' The quiet was so absolute that Terrence might have been alone in the room. 'When he went down, he hit his head against the steps. I didn't know, then, that I'd killed him, but later I heard he was dead.' He was there on the wall, the dead man with his smiling, greenish white face and staring eyes. 'Nobody ever knew I did it.'

The middle sister, Emma, the quietest of the three, spoke up. 'You must have been very sorry,' she said softly.

'No. I didn't mean to kill him, but I wasn't sorry.'

'Ach, no. Irish haters. I saw such men in Germany. Jew haters. Animals, not men.' Mr Stern reached across Jake to pat Terrence's cheek. 'Anyhow, it was an accident. Chust like I said, you vouldn't do it deliberate.'

Bertha looked around the table, addressing them all. 'He saved that baby's life. He was a hero.'

'Pass the mashed potatoes, hero,' Jake said.

After lunch, as the two boys headed for their 'editorial office' in the sewing room, Mrs Stern came out into the hall and said she wanted to talk to Terrence. He followed her into the library, a square room furnished with a brown leather sofa and chairs, a leather-topped desk, and bookcases with glass doors on three of the walls. It smelled of cigars.

'Sit down, Terrence,' Mrs Stern said. 'I'll only keep you a minute.

He took one of the chairs. She sat in another. There was still a lack of warmth in her face.

'That was a terrible story,' she said. 'But the worst was the first thing you said. Wanting it to sound as if you were a murderer, a ten-year-old murderer.' She sat with her plump hands folded in her lap, looking at him with Jake's hazel eyes. 'I know you haven't had an easy life. I know you've worked hard, and still do. But now everything you touch turns to gold.'

'Gold!' he said, startled.

'I mean that whatever you do comes out right for you. That can be dangerous for a boy of nineteen. You may begin to believe you can always make things happen your way. That you're not like the rest of us bumbling mortals.'

'I don't think that, Mrs Stern.' Terrence leaned forward in his chair. 'Why do you—? I've never—'

'Then erase unkindness quickly, Terrence, before you learn it too well.' Her eyes softened. 'We love you in this family. All of us love you. As you see, you couldn't horrify us when you tried.'

'I—' Terrence swallowed. 'I – love – all of you, too.'

Mrs Stern shook her head. 'Love can't be produced to order, but kindness can.' She rose. When he stood, too, she took his arms in her hands and looked up at him. 'It's heartbreaking for a girl not to be pretty, Terrence. Time helps, but for a young girl, it's heartbreaking.'

She left him quickly then. When he went out into the hall, she had disappeared.

10

By the time Jake was graduated from college in June, *Pharos* had replaced the *Mercury* as the leading periodical on the campus. Since their early success with controversial issues Terrence and Jake had had their pick of students for the staff. In the last controversy before Jake left the college, the magazine proved so influential that its status was established from then on.

The matter of the City College's right to exist, first questioned by Governor Robinson, and the subject of Jake's attack in the first issue of *Pharos*, had not gone away. In 1878, shortly before the close of the school year, Assemblyman Thomas Grady introduced a bill in the state legislature to abolish the college.

Pharos was the first of the school's periodicals to assail the bill and the only one to continue a vigorous crusade for its defeat. Terrence and Jake ran editorials and articles in every issue, calling for mass meetings and petitions. They printed hundreds of extra copies and had them distributed by student messengers to alumni all over the city. Largely through this campaign, a petition opposing the bill was sent to the legislature with more than sixty thousand signatures. The bill was tabled and never afterward revived.

After Jake's graduation Terrence remained the sole editor of *Pharos*. At first he tried to do everything he had always done, and what Jake had done besides. With his night job and his studies it was too much, even for him. His marks began to slip. He was tired all the time. When he fell so fast asleep in one of his classes that his professor had to shake him awake, he realized that he had better delegate some of the editorial work to other members of the staff. He reluctantly appointed an assistant editor and an associate editor and then supervised, checked, and rewrote everything they did so consistently that he might almost as well have done it all himself.

They came to him together in Room 312 one afternoon and told him that if he didn't think they were capable of doing any work on their own, they had better quit. They said they knew it was an honor to be on the editorial staff of *Pharos*, but there was no pleasure in it unless they were trusted to do their jobs without somebody constantly looking over their shoulders.

Terrence left them alone after that. More or less. He never did learn completely to trust anyone except himself to do a job properly.

On Sundays, he still had the use of the Sterns' sewing room for his editorial work, even though Jake was no longer part of it. He still ate Sunday dinner with the family.

'The room is there unused, except when the seamstress comes one Wednesday a month,' Jake's mother said.

'And we'd miss you if you weren't here.'

'Ya, like another son you are to us now.' Mr Stern chuckled. 'Our Irish son.'

At those Sunday dinners Terrence sampled a kind of family life he had never before experienced. No word or demonstration of affection had ever passed between Aggie and him, alone in the flat on Little Water Street. He could not recall that they had ever shared a joke. He did not know that they had missed something, until he began going regularly to the Sterns'. Now he wished he could have told Aggie he loved her. She would have thought he had gone soft in the head, but he wished he could have said it anyway.

One Sunday morning Sylvia summoned him to Lafayette Place and told him her parents and Pete were visiting friends after church so he could stay longer than usual. She was in an excellent humor, her manner closer to affectionate than it had ever been.

'My mother was telling some ladies the other day how delicate I've become, with all my headaches and vapors. Sometimes I pretend to faint.' She giggled. 'I don't do that when you're coming because they won't go and leave me alone when they think I've fainted, but if I don't want to do something, like go to school when I haven't prepared my lessons—' She was moving around the room, touching things, shifting a Meissen shepherdess an inch or so on a table, running a light finger over a rose petal in a vase on the mantelpiece. Terrence watched her with delight. He thought she was like a butterfly. 'Oh, I can't wait to be old enough to get away from here and do anything I want!' she said.

'When we're married, you can do what you want.'

'Married! You're always talking about getting married. As if I'd ever marry a big, homely Irish lummox like you!' But she had come close to him as she spoke, and there was none of the usual scorn in her voice. Then, as he reached for her, she whirled away from him. 'I may never marry anybody. I may become a – a – what do you call it? A courtesan. Stay with one man as long as he gives me everything and doesn't bore me and then go to somebody else.'

'Don't say such things, Sylvia, even in fun.'

'Oh, I've shocked you, haven't I?' She clapped her hands. 'Oh, you should see your face!'

When Terrence thought about those Sunday mornings in later years, he remembered some of the things Sylvia had said, but not how they had affected him. The first vague glimpse of her in the dark, shabbily elegant room on Lafayette Place had captivated him, and his enchantment had endured, but he could never afterward recall his youthful sense of her. He wondered whether any man could recapture his vision of a woman as he had first loved her, or ever come to know why he had fallen in love with her, and not another.

'Come here and let me kiss you,' he answered her now, 'and then you won't see my face.'

'Not now. I don't feel like kissing. Maybe later. Listen, Terrence,' she said, 'we can have a picnic. There's half a cold chicken in the icebox.' She giggled again. 'I'll say I recovered from my headache and was suddenly so ravenous that I ate it all.'

'I can't stay for a picnic,' he said regretfully. 'I almost always have Sunday dinner at the Sterns'. They're expecting me.'

She frowned. 'Who are the Sterns?'

'Jake Stern's family. You know who he is. He used to be the other editor of *Pharos*, and his name was in the *Times* last year when—'

'Oh, yes,' Sylvia broke in. 'The Jew. Why do you have Sunday dinner with Jews?'

Terrence stiffened. 'Jake's my best friend. I'm like one of the family. Being Jews has nothing to do with anything.'

'That's right, you wrote that famous article, after what was in the *Mercury*.' It was the first time she had ever mentioned the article. 'My brother said the *Mercury* editor

137

shouldn't have printed anything like that, but what he wrote about Jews was true, and your article couldn't change the facts.'

'Pete doesn't know the facts. I bet he doesn't really know any Jewish fellows. He's probably never had a conversation with one or been in his house.'

'Of course he hasn't. We don't associate with Jews. My mother thinks they're even cruder than the Irish.'

'And Pete's so obedient, he always thinks what your mother thinks, and you have no mind of your own, so you always think what Pete thinks, is that right?'

'My, how angry you are! Your face is as red as your hair.' She gave him her smile and came close to him again. 'I don't care what they think. Haven't you learned yet that half the things I say are only to see what will happen?' She put her arms around his waist. 'Don't go there for lunch today, though, Terrence. A picnic would be such fun, and we may not have another chance. They hardly ever go anywhere after church.'

If he weren't there by twelve-thirty, Jake and Mrs Stern would suspect he wasn't coming, but Mr Stern would want to wait a little longer. Mrs Stern would put the Sunday roast chicken back in the oven to keep warm, and they would all sit around waiting for him while the chicken dried out.

'They don't have a telephone yet, or I could let them know I'm not coming. I'd love to stay, but I don't see how I can just not show up. It wouldn't be a nice thing to do.'

But he knew as he said it, with Sylvia's arms around him and her head against his chest, that he was going to do it anyway.

Afterward he wondered whether what happened could have been a penalty. He had once worried about retribution from an omniscient Aggie for whatever infraction, but he no longer believed in either omniscience or retribution. Still, the thought skimmed his mind.

They had their picnic in the kitchen. First Sylvia washed the already spotless white enamel tabletop with a dishrag because it was where the Polish cook, who was off that Sunday, ate her meals. Then she took the chicken and a small wooden tub of butter out of the wooden icebox and a loaf of bread from the tin bread box. It was the first time they had eaten together. Terrence, who had expected Sylvia to pick daintily at her food, was astounded to see her eat almost as much as he did.

'Wasn't that fun?' she said when they were back in the parlor. 'Aren't you glad you stayed?'

'Of course I'm glad. I'll be even gladder if you give me a kiss for dessert.'

He was always wild to hold her and kiss her, and then not sure, when she was in his arms, that it was worth the torture of restraint. From the time he had decided that they would someday be married he had resolved to have no other girls. He had heard of a fellow with a colorful past who became engaged to a virtuous young lady and burned all his clothes and bought new ones so that he could go to her purified. Terrence might have considered following his example if he could have afforded it. He could not, of course, even keep to his resolve.

Terrence pulled her to him, feeling the resilience of her breasts against him and the curve of her pubis where it met the hardness that swelled his trousers. He agonized to reach the envisioned sweetness of her nipples and the wet softness between her legs and could not let himself try.

'Oh, Sylvia,' he groaned. 'Oh, Sylvia!'

He did not hear the front door close. He heard nothing. She pushed him away in time to be out of his arms when her parents and Pete came in, but it was too late for either of them to smooth their clothes or their hair.

Terrence, paralyzed where he stood, could not even begin to concoct one of his nimble stories before Sylvia was greeting them gaily, her light voice perfectly controlled.

'Mother, you remember Terrence McNally. I don't think you've met him, Father. He dropped in to see Peter – they're classmates – and we got to talking, and then –

well, it was silly and childish, of course, and I didn't think you'd be back so soon—' She looked at them with a smile of little-girl guilt. 'I was feeling much better, and Sunday's so boring, so we began playing hide-and-seek.'

Terrence had once heard a student, the comedian of the college, give a speech in such a persuasive voice and with such a plausible manner that he had spoken for nearly ten minutes before anyone realized he was talking meaningless nonsense and began laughing. Terrence had a sick, desperately controlled urge to laugh now.

The Littlefields had stopped dead in the doorway and still moved no further into the room. Pete leaned against the lintel, smiling at the floor. His mother looked poised to pounce, like some furious, voiceless cat. The first to speak was Mr Littlefield, a tall fair man whom Sylvia resembled except for his bland blue eyes.

'I'm surprised at you, Sylvia,' he said mildly. 'A young lady your age playing rowdy games with a strange young—'

Mrs Littlefield's voice cut through his like a machete through sugarcane. 'Games! Charles, don't talk like a fool!' She took a step toward Sylvia and looked at her with narrowed eyes. Above the neck of her dress, the cords of her throat were visibly distended and her head shook as though with some nervous disorder. 'You and your Sunday headaches. I should have been suspicious long ago, you sneaky little slut!'

'Ah, Vera—' her husband protested.

Mrs Littlefield whirled around to him. 'What else is she? Look at her. Pawed over by scum she deliberately planned to let into the house. Not once, but time after time. For all I know, she's had the scum in her bed!'

This time Terrence was quicker than Sylvia. He stepped between her and her mother and spoke as softly as he could. 'You have no right to say such things, Mrs Littlefield. I'm a college man. I'm the editor of the most important journal on the campus. I'm as good as anybody here. And I've never done anything to Sylvia but kiss her.

I've never—'

Mrs Littlefield had turned her back on him as soon as he began. Now she interrupted him by shrieking at her son, 'Peter, throw this Irish scum out of our house! Throw him out! And tell him if he ever comes within a block of this house or ever tries to communicate with Sylvia in any way, I'll have him maimed for life!'

Terrence looked at Sylvia, but she was watching her mother. There was no fear in her face, no sign of repugnance. She looked fascinated, excited, in a way that reminded him of onlookers he had seen once at a fire on Little Water Street, where people leaned, screaming, out of their flaming windows.

'Come on!' Peter had him gently by the arm. 'Come on, Terrence,' he said, almost in a whisper, 'you'd better leave.'

Terrence shook off his hand. 'Good-bye, Sylvia,' he said, but she would not look at him. Mrs Littlefield had begun shrieking again as he went to the door. Peter followed him into the hall.

'No use arguing with her when she gets like this. We all know to do what she wants, or pretend to anyhow, and stay out of her way.'

Terrence said nothing. He opened the front door. Peter stood against it for a minute.

'Don't try to see Sylvia again, though. She might be willing to take the chance – Sylvia's always liked things that are risky and against the rules – but it wouldn't ever come to anything.'

'How do you know what it would or wouldn't come to?'

Peter sighed. 'I guess I'd better be frank. I once told you I thought you pushed yourself forward too much. Well, this is another example.' He had hold of the edge of the door and was moving it gently back and forth as he spoke. 'I like you. I've always liked you. You're a good fellow. But we live in different worlds. You must know that. Sylvie knows it. When it came down to it, she would no more let you into our world than my mother would.'

Terrence had a swift image of Pete's handsome, impervious face disintegrating under his fist. He saw him falling back, hitting his head, lying greenish and staring like the Irish hater of his childhood.

'I'm telling you for your own sake,' Peter said.

Terrence wrenched the door out of his hand. Before he slammed it shut, he said, 'You're the scum.'

He walked the mile and a half or so to the Sterns'. He ran to begin with and did not know he was doing it until he began to pant and had to slow down to get his breath. The sound of a steam engine rattling above his head bewildered him. Water and oil dropped on his sleeve. He was now on Third Avenue, walking under the elevated train. It roared away uptown, spewing sparks and smoke, at what was said to be the incredible speed of thirty miles an hour. Terrence heard a frightened horse whinny. Runaway horses in the wake of the explosive trains were common along the avenue. He imagined himself falling under hooves and wheels, lying trampled and bleeding, and Sylvia flying to his side, her tears falling on his face. He had never seen her cry.

Jake was alone in the house when he got there. The rest of the family had gone for a drive in their carriage in Central Park. Jake was in the library, reading. As Terrence had expected, they had waited for him for more than half an hour, and Mrs Stern had been annoyed because of the chicken.

'She thought it was dry, but none of the rest of us did. What happened to you anyway?'

Terrence sat down in one of the brown leather chairs, put his head back, and closed his eyes. Jake did not know that his meetings with Sylvia had been in secret; he knew only Terrence's embellished version of those meetings and of Sylvia. Now Terrence had a need to tell it all quickly. He felt that this would relieve him, make him light and sure again. It was a new need, a new feeling. He had never unburdened himself to anyone before.

'What's the matter?' Jake asked him. 'You said you

were going to see Sylvia. Did something go wrong? You look as if somebody punched you in the belly.'

That made it easier to begin.

'Somebody did, in a way. Her mother – well, I think her mother's a maniac, or close to it – but it was Pete who gave me the real punch. I'm not in their world, he said. Not in the same world as Sylvia—' Terrence opened his eyes and looked at Jake. 'He said Sylvia will never let me into it. Their world, that is. I wanted to hit him when he said it. I almost wanted to kill him. But I thought about it the whole way up here. I thought about her and everything that's happened. And I believe he's right. I should have seen it for myself. She never meant to let me into it.'

Jake waited. When Terrence did not go on, he said, 'I think I understand a little of what you're saying, but you'd better start further back. You've been seeing Sylvia for months, haven't you? Why did all this happen this morning?'

'Nobody knew we were meeting. They just found out this morning.' Terrence sighed. 'I guess I made it all sound nice and smooth and romantic, but it really hasn't been.'

He told everything, then, from the beginning.

'So it's all over?' Jake asked when he had finished. 'You're convinced of that?'

It was a while before Terrence answered this. 'I don't know.' He spoke with uncharacteristic slowness. 'I was. When I came in here, and while I was telling you about it, I was. Now I feel better, and I'm not so sure.' He grinned a little. 'Maybe I'm doing it again. Fooling myself. But Pete doesn't know what's in Sylvia's mind. They're nothing alike. They don't even get along. She sometimes says things that sound as if she feels the way he does, but she told me not to take her seriously when she talked like that—' He had stopped lounging in his chair. His eyes were brightening. 'Why should I let him speak for her? Why shouldn't I see her and let her speak for herself?'

'Are those rhetorical questions, or are you asking for advice?'

143

'Do you have some advice?'

Jake shrugged. 'Not advice exactly. Misgivings. One, how can you see her without the risk that her maniac mother will have you torn limb from limb, as she promised? Two, if you manage to see her and she does speak for herself, how will you know she means what she says?'

'One, I'll think of a way to see her. Two, I might not know. Maybe I won't. But I have to listen to her anyhow. She may be expecting it. I can't just let her go without doing anything.'

They sat in silence. After a few moments, Terrence reached over and picked up the heavy volume that Jake had been reading. 'Oh, one of your law books. Is it interesting?'

'Not to me.'

Jake, since his graduation from college, had been working as a clerk in the office of his father's attorney. He had told Terrence early in their acquaintance that he was slated to become a lawyer. They had never discussed it. But something in the way he said, 'Not to me,' without inflection, made Terrence look at him sharply.

'Do you mean just this one book or—'

'I don't mean just this one book. I think I might not mind writing briefs, but it will be a long time before I get to that. The rest of it—' He gave a thin smile. 'My reactions range from mild disinterest to violent dislike.'

Terrence was astounded. He and Jake had been alone very little since they no longer worked together on *Pharos*, but Terrence thought he should have recognized Jake's unhappiness without being told. It struck him that maybe he would never understand what was going on inside anyone. Sylvia or anyone else.

'What made you think you'd like it?'

'I didn't think I would. I hoped I was wrong. I wish I were wrong.' Jake put the big book down on the floor between his feet and picked up a glass globe from the table

144

next to his chair. Enclosed in the glass was a little house surrounded by snow that whirled around when the globe was shaken. All the while Jake talked, his hands made a snowstorm inside the glass. 'Probably I'll be good at it anyway. I've got the mind for it, if not the inclination.'

'You talk as if you have to stick to it no matter what. I don't see—'

'Of course you don't. How could you? It's something that happens in a family like mine. A Jewish family. The son has to have a profession. Not a business, like his immigrant father, because even the most successful business can fail. A professional man is the master of his fate. He can go anywhere and take his profession with him.' Jake raised the glass globe above his eye level and tilted his head back to watch the snow from underneath. 'They could tell early that I wasn't cut out to be a doctor. Bertha used to get nosebleeds, and every time I saw her have one I threw up. But the law is an obvious choice for a boy with brains. I knew before I went to school that it was what they'd decided on for me.'

'Can't you tell them you've found out you don't like it?'

'No,' Jake said. 'I can't. Mama would probably get over the disappointment, but I think it would break Papa's heart. He tells everybody about his son who's going to be a lawyer. I wouldn't be surprised if he stopped strangers in the street.' Jake lowered the globe and looked at Terrence. 'Sometimes I envy you, with no family to please.'

'You don't mean that.'

'Sometimes I do. Sometimes I feel them – the way they love me and the way I love them, the whole thing – like a weight sitting on my shoulders. You're free.'

Terrence did not know what to say. The possibility of Jake's envy was disturbing to him, almost offensive.

'Well, I guess I'd better get to work,' he said. 'I have an editorial to write and some submissions I left here last week that need editing.' He stood up and then hesitated. 'Maybe when you get used to it, Jake, you'll like it better. After all, you've been at it only a few months.'

145

Jake did not answer this. 'I don't know whether I have a soul or not,' he said, 'but if I did, I'd sell it to be back working on *Pharos* with you. I think that was probably the happiest time of my life.'

Terrence tried for two weeks to find Sylvia. He waited along every route she could have taken on her way home from school. He waited on Fifth Avenue, where he had watched her get on the omnibus that day. He hid in a doorway near her house on Lafayette Place. Once he saw her parents, and another time, Pete, but he did not see Sylvia. He knew Nora Littlefield would have helped him, but he had no idea where she lived.

At the end of two weeks he got a letter from her. The pale blue envelope was propped up on his desk, like the first and only letter she had written him. He tore it open in such furious haste that he tore the notepaper and had to hold it together as he read it.

Dear Mr McNally:

By the time you receive this I will be far away at a boarding school for young ladies of good family. I am writing to tell you this so that even if you should somehow find out where it is, you would not try to see me or communicate with me in any way. You would not be welcome in a school of this class. Even if you were not turned away at the door, I would refuse to see you, and I would return any letter from you unopened.

I amused myself with you, Mr McNally, at a time when I was bored. Now I realize how foolish I was, and I want nothing more to do with you, ever.

Yours truly,
Sylvia Littlefield

The same day Terrence got this letter, the girl Jake had been going with for nearly three years announced her engagement to somebody else. The coincidence seemed awesome to Terrence and Jake, and then funny. When

Jake stopped laughing, he began to cry. Terrence did not believe men should cry and would not permit himself to do it.

Later they got drunk on some of the Sterns' Passover wine. The family was home, but Jake and Terrence locked themselves up in Jake's room and nobody bothered them. The wine was so sweet that it did not taste as terrible to Terrence as other alcoholic drinks, but he still took it like medicine.

For the first time in all his years at Hoffman House Terrence did not go to work that night. Instead, he took Jake downtown and introduced him to the roommate of a girl he knew. He thought it courteous to let Jake have the bedroom. The other room was a combination living room and kitchen, with chairs but no sofa, so Terrence and his girl used the floor. He pretended she was Sylvia and thrust into her so fiercely that she gave a yelp of pain that turned into a cry of pleasure. Since he had no wish to give Sylvia pleasure, the fantasy was not satisfactory.

Jake, on the other hand, seemed filled with a guilty elation. He kept talking all the way uptown about the wickedness of what they had done, but every little while, with apparent unconsciousness, he smiled. His eyes glowed hugely behind the thick glasses. Terrence finally realized, to his astonishment, that until that night Jake had been a virgin.

11

The summer before Terrence's senior year in college the Sterns bought a house in Long Branch. Mrs Stern and the girls spent all of July and August there, and Jake and his father went down weekends. They invited Terrence, but Saturday nights were the busiest of the week at the Hoffman House, as well as the most profitable for the waiters, and the boat trip was too long for just a Sunday visit.

Terrence began eating Sunday dinner with Miss Howard again, as he had done in the beginning. She had said nothing but 'Very well' when he first told her not to prepare for him on Sundays anymore, but she was plainly pleased to have him there again.

'I like a lively dinner after church,' she said. 'One is so sobered by the sermon. It's pleasant to talk of other things afterward.'

He missed the Sterns very much, but he was content enough at Miss Howard's table. She was like a familiar, comfortable aunt who listened with interest to whatever he told her. As with an aunt, he took her approval for granted. He rarely thought about her at all except when he was with her. Now that she was graying and wrinkling, the thing that had occurred during his first year in her house seemed more than ever a preposterous dream.

'Your education is nearly complete,' she said to him one day. 'That is, your formal education. We learn, or should learn, to the end of our lives. But now you are, of course, deciding about your future. I know you don't intend making a career of waiting on tables. And it's some time since you wanted to be a politician.' She gave a little laugh. 'Have you chosen something else?'

'I'm going to be an editor.' He had not put this into words before, not to Jake, not even to himself. Now it was all as clear to him as if written on a blackboard in front of his eyes. 'Later on I'll have my own magazine.'

Miss Howard nodded. 'You will. You've always done what you've set out to do.'

He was reminded of what Jake's mother had said to him once. That everything he touched turned to gold. She had warned him not to believe that it always would, but there was no longer any danger of that. Not since Sylvia, whom he had wanted more than he had ever wanted anything and who was lost to him.

After his first grief he had hated her. When his hatred faltered, he revived it by rereading her letter. He kept the

148

letter with him, changing it from the pocket of his suit to the pocket of the black trousers he wore to wait tables, until it began to fall apart at the crease and the writing was too smudged with dirt and sweat to read. Then he tore it up into tiny pieces and threw it away. He felt that he was throwing Sylvia away and that he would not think of her again.

But he was wrong. He thought of her constantly. He thought of the way she looked, and the way she felt in his arms, and the way her voice sounded when she said she liked him. Before long he was making excuses to himself for the cruelty of her letter, even fancying that someone else had written it and forged Sylvia's signature. In this way he kept her adorable, unique, and unforgettable.

He attracted other Normal School girls, as girls had always been attracted by his vitality, his sureness, his almost palpable sexuality – and because he was a school celebrity. They flirted with him. They contrived to meet him on street corners. Some were as pretty as Sylvia, and as cultivated, but not to Terrence. He was fond of girls in general. He liked the flirting and the hand holding, the surreptitious kissing, the imitation love talk. But no girl was special. When he had more urgent needs, he went downtown to one of half a dozen girls of a different sort. And only Sylvia, who had said she did not want him, stayed with him. Sylvia, who was not there.

The Sterns came back from Long Branch in the fall, and the Sunday dinners resumed. Terrence considered saving one Sunday a month for dinner with Miss Howard because the summer Sundays had seemed so important to her, and he remembered what Mrs Stern had said to him about kindness. But he hated to give up a dinner at the Sterns', especially after not eating with them all summer. After all, he did have breakfast with Miss Howard every day, and often Sunday supper besides. He decided she would understand if he explained how convenient it was for him to eat with the Sterns when he was working on his material for *Pharos*.

'I can work there all day, if necessary, just stop for dinner, and get right back to it.'

'Yes, of course.' Miss Howard poured her breakfast tea from the blue china teapot. 'Of course,' she said again, 'there's no reason why you couldn't work here. If your room is too small, you could use this table. It would save you all the time it takes to go back and forth.'

'I'm afraid it wouldn't be practical, Miss Howard. Up there I have a room that isn't used for anything else. I keep it full of papers, galley sheets, old copies of *Pharos*, all kinds of stuff, and when I'm finished for the day, I don't have to clear anything away. I appreciate the offer, though,' he said quickly, smiling at her. 'And I'll miss our Sunday dinners.'

She flushed a little, so he knew she was pleased. He was glad to be able to please her so easily, without giving up any Sundays with the Sterns.

Mr Stern kept him behind at the table one Sunday to speak to him alone. He asked about Terrence's plans for getting a job after college. Terrence replied more tentatively than he had to the same question from Miss Howard. Mr Stern was a businessman and would probe further than Miss Howard.

'I'd like to work on a magazine if I can find that kind of job,' he said. 'I hope my experience with *Pharos* will help.'

Mr Stern waved a pudgy, dismissive hand. 'Ach, Terrence, dot kind of experience don't count. A little collitch-boy magazine. It vas a fine thing for you and Chake in collitch, but to make a living?' He, like Jake, was a shrugger. 'Even if somebody vould count such a collitch-boy magazine and give you a chob, it vouldn't pay you good. You can't make a living from literachoor. Vot you want is a nice chob in a nice, solid business, vhere you could get ahead.'

'You may be right,' Terrence said, though he was sure he wasn't, 'but I'd like to try for a magazine job first and see how it goes.'

'A vaste of time, Terrence. A vaste of time. I know you

150

think because you're young, you got all the time in the world. But time flies. You turn around, and all of a sudden you're fifty years old. If you got nothing to show for it, you vant to kick yourself for every minute you vasted. Me, at least I got something to show for it.' He selected a cigar from three in his vest pocket, pulled out the gold cigar cutter on the end of his watch chain, and used it to slice a thin sliver from the end of the cigar. 'It's a good business, the fur business. Ven a man has a good business, he vishes he could have his son in it with him. For Chake, it's better he should be a lawyer. In a few years he'll be my lawyer, so in dot vay he'll be in the business, but it ain't exactly the same. It ain't like vorking every day right there, learning from the bottom, like I did, to be a good fur man.' He took a few puffs of the cigar and set it down in the holder on the edge of the ashtray. He gave Terrence a warm thick-lipped smile. 'It vould be nice to have my Irish son in the business.'

Terrence had seen what was coming, with no idea how to prepare for it. He felt sick. He ached as if he had the grippe. For the first time he understood what Jake had been through and why he was entering a profession for which he had no taste. He could not speak.

'Ya, I know.' Mr Stern, still smiling, nodded. 'You didn't expect such a thing. You don't believe it yet. But vy not? I told you many times. To me – to Mama, too – you're like another son.'

Terrence stood up. His throat was working so that he was not sure he could get the words out. But if he did not say what needed to be said, he would, like Jake, be swept off on a wave of feeling and obligation and never find his way back.

'Mr Stern, it's a wonderful offer. Nobody ever made me an offer like that before. I'm proud you think of me as a son and want me in your business with you. It's a great honor. But I have to try the other thing first. I have to try to get on a magazine.' Terrence saw Mr Stern's smile fade and his face grow cold, and he knew nothing he said

151

would be any good. But he went on. 'Don't you see? I love working on *Pharos*. It makes me happier than anything else. Maybe it would be different, doing it for a living. I may find out it isn't as right for me as it feels to me now or I'm only good enough for a college journal. But don't you see, Mr Stern, I have to try, or else all my life I'll think I missed the work I should be doing.'

Mr Stern looked at Terrence. He looked at the long ash on the end of his cigar. He took a deep breath.

'Vot's the sense to say anything more? If dot's how you feel, dot's how you feel.' He got up heavily and left the room.

The subject was not mentioned again. Terrence did not tell Jake about it, and if Mrs Stern knew, she gave no evidence that it affected her. Mr Stern was as welcoming and friendly as he had always been. But he never again spoke openly of his affection for Terrence. He never touched him again or referred to him as a son. For Terrence it was as though he had lost a father for the second time. But there was nothing else he could have said or done.

He planned to spend the summer after graduation making the rounds of the magazines to look for a job. He would take any job at any pay, just to break in. If necessary, he would stay on at the Hoffman House until he had a chance to show his ability in magazine work and was making enough money to give up waiting on tables. He had no doubt that he would find something. The country was overrun with magazines, a great number of them published in New York. It was only a question of what kind of work he could find on which magazine.

Nothing happened according to these plans.

One evening in June, just before graduation, he was bringing a tray of empty glasses back to the bar when a gentleman standing at the bar spoke to him. The man was taller than Terrence, about thirty-eight years old, slim and elegantly dressed, with a hawkish face and sharp blue

152

eyes. He had in his hand the current issue of *Pharos*. Each month Terrence left one somewhere in the bar.

'Good evening, young man,' the gentleman said. 'My name is Hamilton. Woodrow Hamilton. You're Terrence McNally the First?'

Terrence, who had used the name sparingly in his early college days, had begun putting it on the masthead as soon as Jake left. Woodrow Hamilton mentioned it as matter-of-factly as if he knew a dozen such numbered names.

'Yes, sir.'

'It says on the masthead that you're the editor of this publication.' Hamilton tapped the magazine with two fingers. 'How much of it are you actually responsible for?'

'All of it, Mr Hamilton. Everything that's in *Pharos* I either write myself or review and revise.' Terrence spoke at top speed, not only because this was his style but because a customer was trying to catch his eye. He sensed that this encounter could be important to him and that what he said and the way he said it would weigh with this man. Hamilton struck him as someone who would not be fooled by a pretense of modesty. 'The associate and assistant editors weed out the submitted articles they know we can't use, but I make the final decision about which ones to print. I also supervise the layout.'

Hamilton nodded. 'Yes. You've been described to me. The description seems to be accurate. Do you know anything about bicycles?'

The question was so unexpected that Terrence gulped. He had been sure the man had some connection with a magazine and might, if Terrence impressed him, offer him a job. Bicycles!

'I used to ride one.' Disappointment flattened his voice, but it was not in him to let his answer go at that. 'I once delivered merchandise all over the city by bicycle, and of course I had to know how to repair it if anything went wrong on the way.'

Hamilton was about to say something to this, but the

153

signaling customer had grown impatient and was snapping his fingers and calling out. 'Waiter! Terrence! A little service over here, please.'

'I see you're wanted. Thoughtless of me to keep you.' Hamilton took a card from his pocket and handed it to Terrence. 'Come to my office tomorrow as soon as your classes are over.'

Before he left the bar that night, Terrence asked around about Hamilton and learned that he was a wealthy and eccentric man who owned the Hamilton Manufacturing Company, one of the leading makers of bicycles in the country. The company's best-known model was the American Roadster, which had a front wheel nearly five feet high. Terrence remembered seeing a cartoon that showed a group of fashionably dressed people falling or already fallen off them. The caption had had something to do with Somebody's Folly. Hamilton's, he supposed.

Terrence did not want to work for a bicycle manufacturer any more than he wanted to work in the fur business, but it did not occur to him not to go to see Mr Hamilton and find out exactly what he was passing up.

The offices occupied a tall, narrow building on Broadway near Fourteenth Street. Terrence had expected to see a factory, but that, Hamilton told him, was in Boston. Here sample models occupied a large storeroom, otherwise bare. A middle-aged woman escorted him to an untidy office with a grimy window. Hamilton, wearing the same dove gray jacket and waistcoat as the night before, his black ascot fastened with a pearl stickpin, sat in incongruous elegance behind an overflowing battered oak desk.

'I know a great deal about you, young man,' he said. 'I made inquiries before I spoke to you last night. What I was told I liked. What I heard and saw of you in person I liked better still.' He spoke in crisp, staccato sentences, his hands folded loosely on the edge of the desk, his eyes never leaving Terrence's face. 'I've been called impulsive. I'm not. My instincts are excellent, and I act on them. But not without a solid base of information.'

Since he paused as if expecting a comment, Terrence said, 'You sound to me like a wise man, sir.'

'Wise,' Hamilton repeated. Nothing in his face or voice suggested it, but Terrence felt he was pleased. 'I daresay, young as you are, you've met a great many fools. I certainly have. In contrast, perhaps I do seem wise. Would you care to work for me?' The question came without transition. 'Bicycle riding is going to sweep the country. I know a joke's been made of my American Roadster, but right at this moment I have three men at the rink to teach dozens of people who want to learn how to ride it. Within ten years everybody who can afford to buy a bicycle will own one. All it needs is a little push. That's where you would come in. What do you say?'

Terrence, who tended to like or dislike people on sight, was taken with Hamilton. He was reluctant to say that the business for which Hamilton had such enthusiasm did not interest him. It was a little like rejecting Mr Stern, though he scarcely new this man and certainly had no obligation to him.

'I don't know, Mr Hamilton,' he said. 'I don't think I'd be very good at selling bicycles.'

'*Selling* them?' Hamilton frowned. Suddenly he squeezed out a dry three-note laugh. 'From what I've heard and what I've seen for myself, I think you could sell anything you had a mind to. But I have plenty of salesmen. Why would I need the editor of a college magazine to sell my bicycles? Have you asked yourself that, Mr McNally?'

'Well, I'm a good editor. Some people think if a person is good at one thing, he's likely to be good at another.'

'Not bad for a quick answer. There might even be something in it. Why did I say I didn't need you to sell my bicycles? Did I say that? It's exactly what I need you for.'

Again he seemed to be waiting for a comment, but this time Terrence was too bewildered to think of one. He had no idea what this peculiar man was telling him, what he wanted of him.

155

'You're young,' Hamilton went on, 'but I believe in youth. I had my own business before I was twenty. Youth, intelligence, ingenuity, boldness, and enough experience to bind them together. Yes. You qualify.'

'For what, Mr Hamilton?'

Hamilton squeezed out another three-note laugh. 'That's a fair question.' He leaned back, as though to regard Terrence at longer focus. 'I want to publish a monthly magazine for bicyclists. There already is one called the *Wheelman*, but I believe there's room for a bigger and better one. Mine would contain not only articles devoted to the special interests of cyclists but also feature stories and fine art in which bicycles are featured. It would attract those who are already bicycle enthusiasts. It would interest those who are not in becoming so, thereby selling more bicycles. Do you think you could edit a magazine like that?'

During this speech, in Hamilton's staccato delivery, Terrence had been inching farther and farther forward in his chair. Now he sat so close to the edge that he was in danger of falling off.

'Yes, Mr Hamilton,' he said.

'We'll call it *Riding the Wheel*.'

'That's not catchy enough, sir.' Terrence thought a minute. 'Why not just the *Cyclist*?'

'All right, you're the editor. The *Cyclist*. Ten dollars a week.'

'What, sir?'

'Your salary. Ten dollars a week.'

Terrence could not wait until Sunday to tell Jake and his parents the news. He rushed straight from Hamilton's office to their home. Only when he was almost there did he realize that Jake and his father would be at work. But he caught Mrs Stern as she was coming out the door and began talking before she could so much as express surprise at seeing him. She was dressed for a meeting, her plump little figure tightly corseted into a small-waisted floor-length black dress, her hat decorated with a stiff

156

ribbon that rose skyward to balance the large nose beneath it. When he had finished, she laid her gloved hand on his arm.

'I'm happy for you, Terrence. I know how much you've wanted a chance like this. You're very lucky.' She gave an almost inaudible sigh. 'Sometimes I worry that you're too lucky. I told you that once before, in another way.'

Her response disappointed him. 'I don't think this was all luck, Mrs Stern,' he said. 'It didn't just happen. Mr Hamilton was looking for somebody like me.'

'Yes, of course, Terrence. I don't mean to spoil your pleasure.' She patted his arm and smiled for the first time. 'Jews are afraid of good fortune. We're afraid it brings calamity behind it. The fear is in our blood, in our history. You needn't pay any attention to it.'

When he told Miss Howard, she said, 'I'm not surprised. I've always expected you to do exactly what you've set out to do.'

Jake's reaction was more exuberant. He threw his arm around Terrence and kissed him on the ear. 'Oh, God, I envy you!' he said.

Mr Stern said, 'I'm glad you got vot you vant. I hope you vill vant vot you get. Dot's more important.'

Terrence had no reason to be sobered by what either Mr or Mrs Stern had said or even to give it any thought. Not for a long time.

12

Hamilton hired his brother's son, Jules, as an assistant to Terrence. He paid him eight dollars a week. Jules complained about this from the start.

'He's putting all kinds of money into publishing the thing, but he pays us starvation wages. Don't you think it's an outrage?'

'I'm glad to have the opportunity,' Terrence said.

'Anyway, I don't consider it starvation wages. I've lived on a lot less.'

Jules complained not only about the wages but about the size of the small office his uncle had taken for them, a few blocks from his own. He also complained about the drudgery of whatever work Terrence gave him to do. He was about Terrence's age, pasty-faced and lanky, with arms and legs that frequently went limp, as if a puppeteer had loosened the strings that kept them in operation. Terrence detested him from the moment he looked at him.

But Jules had one asset. He could write. Of all the jobs on the magazine he hated doing, writing was the one he claimed to hate the most. Terrence had to prod him constantly to get down to it so they could go to press on time. Yet when Jules finally finished an article, Terrence could rarely find anything to change. Since writing was the only competence Jules had, Terrence began leaving most if it to him and doing nearly everything else himself.

It was in some ways a repetition of his first year as sole editor of *Pharos*, but now he had neither schoolwork nor a job at the Hoffman House. He could give all his time to the *Cyclist*. Much of it was spent outside the office. He went to see clergymen and physicians, soliciting contributions extolling the benefits of bicycle riding to soul and body. He persuaded authors to write stories in which bicycling was prominently featured. He consulted with engravers and printers.

One day he left New York for the first time in his life and traveled to Boston to ask Oliver Wendell Holmes to write a poem on bicycling for the April issue. It did not occur to him to view the sights of this strange city while he was there. What he happened to see and take note of was a group of stylishly dressed lady tricyclists gathered on Salem Street, in front of the Public Library, for the start of a four-day tour. Husbands and beaux were waiting to furnish most of the leg-power, while the ladies were ready to ride along, displaying their natty costumes and tourist caps. Terrence decided at once that when he got back to

New York, he would find a writer to do an article on fashions for cyclists.

It did not occur to him, either, that he had uncles and brothers living in the city. If he had, he would have made no effort to see them. They were unreal to him, mythical figures who had appeared out of the mist when Aggie died and disappeared behind it again afterward. He returned to New York elated, with Holmes's promise of a contribution in his pocket. If only Sylvia could have seen him, the crude Irishman, welcomed by the distinguished elderly author. Or know that he had his own editorial office. Or could read a letter on the *Cyclist* stationery, with his name on the letterhead. 'Editor, Terrence McNally the First' . . .

In spite of his limited experience and his assistant's limited ability to assist, Terrence managed to turn out a lively magazine. Hamilton's willingness to spend money on it when he had to helped. He instructed Terrence to offer an American Roadster as recompense to an unknown clergyman or doctor but set no limit on the price of a poem by Mr Holmes. He had confidence in Terrence's literary judgment and his eye for format and readily paid whatever it cost to back them up.

Within the year reviewers were praising the *Cyclist* as 'a most attractive monthly magazine'. It was not yet showing a profit, but bicycle sales had increased so substantially that Hamilton was satisfied to keep putting money into it. At Terrence's request he hired a business manager who relieved Terrence of all financial concerns, and he raised Terrence's salary to twelve dollars. Terrence could have made more elsewhere. He had attracted the attention of other publishers and had had a firm offer of a job from the editor of *Harper's Young People*. But Hamilton had believed in him and taken a chance on him while he was still a college boy, an amateur editor. Terrence stayed with him, as, so many years before, he had stayed with Jimmy O'Brien.

He still had dinner at the Sterns' almost every Sunday. They were his only family. Jake was his only close friend.

He did not have the time, or the inclination, for other intimacies. The *Cyclist* absorbed him.

'This satisfies you?' Mrs Stern asked him one day. 'This involvement with bicycles?'

'Not for the rest of my life. For the present, yes.'

Jake leaned across the table. 'You see, it doesn't matter, Mama. Bicycles, fishing, science. It's not important what the magazine's about. What matters is editing a magazine.'

Terrence saw Mr Stern give him a frowning look. Jake blinked and sat back. He said, 'It's like the law. It has all kinds of facets, but what matters is being a lawyer.'

Mr Stern stopped frowning and nodded. Terrence avoided Jake's eyes. He was the only one at the table who knew what Jake really meant.

He tried never to talk to them much about the *Cyclist*. Jake's envy, though there was no ill will in it, disturbed him. Mr Stern said little, but Terrence knew he still believed his former Irish son had passed up a magnificent opportunity for a stubborn, boyish whim. What Mrs Stern thought, he did not know. She rarely expressed outright approval, only love.

When he was brimming with talk about his work, Terrence spilled it out to Miss Howard. She was interested in everything he told her. His success seemed to please her as much as if it had been her own.

'Your mother would be so proud of you,' she said to him once. 'She used to say she knew you were going to be somebody. We both knew.'

He had dinner with her now at least once a week and occasionally on a Sunday. He also paid her more for his board, though she did not want to take it. As a boy he had regarded her with a little less indifference than he felt for other teachers because she liked him more than the others did and was nicer to him. He had essentially the same feeling for her now. But he had lived in her house a long time. She listened to him, catered to him, and made him comfortable, and what he paid her, even with the increase, was absurdly little. He had a sense of obligation to her that he had not had when he was younger.

Sometimes they stayed at the table long after they had finished eating while he told her about a conference of editors and publishers at which he had been asked to speak or described a well-known author who had given him a piece for the *Cyclist*. It was understood, however, that once they left the dining room, they would separate, like strangers who chat at a restaurant table and afterward go their own ways.

He had just left the table and gone up to his room one night, prepared to read a manuscript he had brought with him from the office, when Miss Howard knocked on the door. Why he suddenly thought of that long ago night when she had come to his room – or he had dreamed she had – he did not know. It rarely came into his mind at all, and when it did, he pushed it out. But now he stood against the door while he answered her, as though otherwise she might burst in. If this was a premonition, he thought afterward, it took a peculiar detour.

'There's someone downstairs to see you,' she said.

He opened the door, feeling foolish. 'I'll be right down.'

Jake occasionally dropped in when he was despondent, as a day in the law office often made him. He did not usually come this late, though, and as a rule he went straight up to Terrence's room without waiting for Miss Howard to announce him. Why, since she knew Jake, hadn't she said who was there? Terrence had not even thought to ask. It had to be Jake. He did not have other callers. Anyone else who wanted to see him came to his office.

He ran down to the living room. And stopped dead in the doorway. He swayed a little, as if he had been shot but had not yet fallen. For two years he had imagined her here, everywhere, anywhere in his experience or in his fancy. He had given up expecting the reality of her, a substantial being in an actual place. But he did not know that he had given it up until this moment, when her finite presence was more inconceivable to him than any phantom.

161

'You look frightened, Terrence,' she said. 'Have I changed so much?'

He said, 'Sylvia,' surprised that his voice made any sound.

She was across the room from him, standing close to the window. The curtains, which Miss Howard washed every week, were white and gauzy. Sylvia might have materialized from them, as from a cloud.

'Why are you just standing there?' she asked him. 'Are you angry with me? Are you still angry after all this time? It wasn't my fault, you know.'

He began to see her, to distinguish her from his fantasy Sylvia, who was always sixteen years old, always dressed in something soft and light-coloured, her pale hair always curling around her head.

Now her hair was up, smooth and high under her hat. Beneath her short, velvet fur-trimmed coat she wore a voluminous dress with a small bustle and a long ruffled skirt. She had filled out a little. He thought her skin was whiter, as if she had been ill.

'You *have* changed,' he said, answering her first question. 'You've grown up.' He sighed. 'I'm not angry. I'm – I guess the word is dazed. I never expected to see you again.'

'Well, you're seeing me now.' Her voice had grown fuller, too, slightly deeper, but the edge of impatience was so familiar that in his normal state he would have grinned. 'What are you waiting for?' she asked him.

'To make sure I'm not dreaming you.'

'I can think of a better way to find out than standing over there staring at me.'

Everything seemed to move in him at once – his heart, his muscles, the cadence of his voice. He said, 'Oh!' in a muted roar, and went to her with two leaping steps, and held her tight enough to feel the contours of her breasts through all the layers of her clothes and his. 'Oh, yes, you're real! Oh, yes!'

162

She had once called him a pig for thrusting his tongue into her mouth and grasping her buttocks to press her closer to him. Now her tongue explored his. Her body moved against his hardness. He could not think. He forgot Miss Howard was somewhere in the house. He could not remember Sylvia's innocence and purity, and believed she would let him take her right there, right then . . .

When she pushed him away, he was not sure for an instant where he was. He would not have been altogether astonished to find himself back in the room on Lafayette Place, with Sylvia telling him he was disgusting; with her mother calling him scum and shrieking to Pete to put him out of the house.

'It looks as if you missed me.' She smoothed her hair with her hands. Her mouth curved into the old enchanting smile. 'I missed you, too.'

Terrence pressed his hands against his temples. 'Sylvia, it's still hard to believe this is happening. Two years. That terrible letter, telling me—' He shook his head. 'Suddenly you're here – at ten o'clock at night. I don't know why, after all this time. I don't know where you've come from.'

She pulled his hands down from his face and led him to the sofa, where she sat a little away from him, straight and pale against the horsehair. He had never known her to be so gentle or to speak so softly.

'I've run away from school,' she said. 'I've done it before, but they always found me and brought me back and watched me like a prisoner. I felt like a prisoner, anyway, from the first. It was an awful place, Terrence. Bells for everything, rules for every minute of the day, sour old teachers and stupid girls. I couldn't stand it. I ran away three times.' Her voice lifted a little. 'They didn't expect it this time. It's only four months to graduation. They thought I wouldn't try it again with only four months to go, so they weren't watching me all the time. I left while we were in line for supper. There's a place where the line passes an outside door. I just slipped out. I left

163

everything there. All I have are these clothes and a little money I stuffed in my stocking.' She looked at Terrence, and he was struck again by the pallor of her face. 'They never thought I'd run away again, for the sake of four months, but I couldn't stand it another minute.'

He had many more questions, but he was not sure what to ask. If he said the wrong thing, she might leave him again. He had stood it before, but now that she had come back, and he had held her and kissed her, he did not see how he could ever go through losing her another time.

'So you came here,' he said.

Sylvia reached for his hand and pressed her small fingers tight around it. 'I have no place else to go. My parents would send me right back. I have no one but you.' She looked down at their clasped hands and said, almost in a whisper, 'You've been the only one for me, anyway, since the very beginning.'

He thought his chest might burst. He would have liked to leave her words untouched to sing in his head. But he had to speak.

'You didn't act like it, Sylvia. The things you used to say to me. The things you wrote in that letter. Two years without a word from you. How could you act that way if you really – care about me?'

'Love you, Terrence. I've always loved you.'

He shivered. He started to say something, but she went on.

'I know sometimes it didn't seem that way, but I couldn't help it. I was so young, and – well, afraid of my feelings. And my mother – she made me write that letter. She stood over me and told me what to say, and then she took it away from me and mailed it. I tried to write to you from school, but my mother told them to confiscate any letters addressed to you. I thought you'd find me.' She raised her dark eyes to his face again, and now he noticed the faint purple shadows under them. 'You're so clever I thought you'd manage it somehow.'

Indignation filtered through the haze of his joy.

164

'I didn't try. You said I'd be turned away. How could I know your mother made you?'

'You should have known I wouldn't—'

'How? You said enough awful things to me on your own, didn't you? And I always stood for them.' He saw her face begin to crumple and finished with an uneasy mutter. 'A person has to have some pride.'

Once he had imagined her weeping over him as he lay dead, killed by runaway horses on Third Avenue, but he had never actually seen her cry. Her tears might have been needles, each piercing him in a different place. He pulled her to him and tried frantically to kiss them away.

'Don't,' he groaned. 'Please don't, Sylvia.'

She sniffled like a child. 'If you're angry at me, I might as well die.'

'Ah, that's foolish talk.' As though she were a child, he held his handkerchief to her nose while she blew it. 'I'm not angry, but even if I were, you wouldn't die.'

She had stopped crying, but her voice was small and sad. 'What *would* I do?' She sat up. 'I haven't even anyplace to go tonight. I'd have to sleep on a bench in the park. It's February, Terrence. I'd freeze to death.'

He stared at her. 'Do you want to stay *here*?'

'Where else is there for me?'

He had not thought about it. He had not thought clearly about anything beyond her unbelievable presence.

'I don't know how—' He looked away from Sylvia to the stairs. 'I don't know what to tell Miss Howard. She's a teacher. I don't know what she'd think. You'd have to – there isn't an extra room—'

'You don't want me here.'

'Ah, Sylvia, I do. Of course I do. It's – it's the most wonderful thing I can think of.' He grasped one of her little hands and began chafing it, as though he had found her freezing on the bench and brought her inside to save her. 'It's just that I don't know how to explain you to Miss Howard.'

'You'll think of something. I can sleep right here on the

sofa.' She smiled, her face already clean-swept of weeping. 'I'm sure she won't mind when she knows we're going to be married right away.'

'Married? Do you—' His voice clogged. He had to stop and begin again. 'Do you really mean you want to marry me? You always said you'd never—'

'Oh, Terrence!' She stamped her foot soundlessly on the rug. 'Don't keep talking about what I always said. I told you long ago I didn't mean half of it. Of course, I want to marry you. That's what I came for.'

He sat back and closed his eyes, groped for her hands, and waited until he thought he could make sense. When his head stopped whirling, his happiness began to drain away.

'Oh, Sylvia, Sylvia darling.' He had never called her that before, even in his fantasies. 'Sylvia darling,' he said again. 'I want to marry you more than I've ever wanted anything.' He opened his eyes and looked at her miserably. 'But I can't right away. I only earn twelve dollars a week. It's enough for me because I pay Miss Howard so little for my room and board, but I couldn't support a wife. I couldn't afford the rent for the kind of place you'd want to live in. We'll have to wait.' She tried to speak, but he drowned her out in a rapid rush of words. 'It won't be long. I'm just starting out. Soon I'll be the editor of something much bigger than a bicycle magazine. I'll build you a mansion on Fifth Avenue, like I promised. You'll have everything you want, Sylvia, if you'll just wait a little while.'

While he talked, her face had grown whiter still and cold. 'Twelve dollars a week!' she said, as though she had heard nothing else. 'I thought you were an important person. Some of the girls at school who ride bicycles had your magazine. I thought—'

She stopped and sat very still, her eyes fixed on the white curtain across the room. He told himself it was the end of everything. She would leave him now, and this time she would never come back.

166

'Terrence, we can still manage it,' she said slowly. 'We don't have to rent a place. I can live here, too. That way it wouldn't cost you much more.' She turned and threw her arms around his neck. 'Oh, Terrence, I love you too much to wait. We've waited so long already.'

13

Sylvia and Terrence were married three days later in Miss Howard's church. Miss Howard, who made few demands, insisted on this when she learned that Sylvia, like herself, was Presbyterian. She seemed to suggest that the church wedding was a condition of allowing Sylvia to live with Terrence in her house.

Miss Howard gave no indication of how she felt about the arrangement or about Sylvia. Terrence had improved upon the truth, weaving her a piteous tale of star-crossed lovers, separated by Sylvia's half-mad mother and brutal father, who would beat her, perhaps kill her, if she went home. Miss Howard had been noncommittal, but she must have believed it. She had accepted, almost without comment, the proposal that they both live with her.

'Of course, I'll pay you for her room and board,' Terrence said.

'It won't amount to much. Nothing for the room since she'll be staying in yours.'

When Terrence remarked to Sylvia on this generosity, she shrugged. 'She's glad to have us here. If we'd gone to live somewhere else, she'd be all alone.'

Sylvia did not like Miss Howard – privately she called her a dried-up old stick – but she was sweet to her. After a week or two she began calling her Aunt Jessica, as Terrence, who had known her since he was twelve years old, could not have conceived of doing. Whether or not this pleased Miss Howard, it was impossible to tell.

At the wedding Miss Howard had made Terrence

uneasy, sitting stiff and straight in her pew, with no expression on her face at all. He had felt she disapproved, though nothing she said or did afterward confirmed this idea. The wedding had bothered him anyway. He was not used to churches, and this one was so large and empty that when he spoke his part of the ceremony, his voice seemed to boom and reboom in his ears.

No one had been there but Miss Howard and Jake. Mr Stern and the two younger girls had had the grippe, and Mrs Stern had had to stay home and nurse them. Bertha, who was engaged to Mr Stern's lawyer, Jake's boss, a man eighteen years older than she was, had been visiting her future in-laws.

Terrence had grown fond of Bertha. He had asked Mrs Stern how she could let a young girl like that marry a man who could almost have been her father.

'A girl who isn't pretty can't be so choosy,' Mrs Stern had told him. 'He's a good man who will always be able to keep her in comfort. A girl can learn to love a man like that. I did.'

Terrence had thought about this at the wedding, with Sylvia standing beside him in her white dress. She was so pretty he could hardly breathe when he looked at her. She could have been as choosy as she liked. And she had chosen him. She did not have to learn to love him.

He had almost bought her the bridal gown she wanted. He would have liked to give her anything she asked for, and someday he would. But the gown had cost nearly as much as the entire sum Hamilton had given him for a wedding present. He explained to Sylvia that if he bought her a simple white dress instead, he could put a good part of Hamilton's gift with the money he had saved over the years, and they would have a substantial nest egg. Aggie had taught him always to set money aside, no matter how little he made, but Sylvia did not know about such things.

'I want to be a real bride,' she said. 'For you, Terrence. A beautiful bride for you.'

He had come close to giving in, but he had not done it.

Sylvia had sulked for a while, called him a miser, and said she hated the white dress. Terrence had said nothing, just waited, and in the end she had smiled and worn the dress.

But her inability to understand about money decided him to keep his finances to himself. He did not tell her when he got Hamilton to give him a big raise in salary.

'But I just gave you a handsome wedding present,' Hamilton said. 'I'm not made of money, Terrence.'

'I appreciate your generous present very much, sir. My wife and I both do.' Terrence relished the taste of 'my wife' on his tongue. 'We've put it aside for emergencies. I'm sure you'll agree a young couple should have something to fall back on, and my wife and I are certainly grateful to you for making it possible. But it doesn't take care of our day-to-day expenses. My wife and I can't live on the same salary it took to support myself alone. Surely you can understand that, Mr Hamilton.'

'What I can't understand, and never have, is how you get the words off your tongue so fast without missing a syllable.'

Terrence grinned. 'My mother used to say they were on wheels.'

'Yes. Well, I wouldn't want you to starve.' Hamilton sighed. 'It doesn't seem quite right, in view of what I'm paying Jules, but I'll raise you to fourteen dollars.'

Terrence had never before said anything to Hamilton about his nephew. It seemed to him the time had come.

'Mr Hamilton, Jules isn't worth half as much to you as I am. He can write, and that's all. I could go out tomorrow and find a dozen men who can write just as well and would be of some use to the magazine in other ways besides. If he left, it would be no loss to you at all. If I left, I think you would have a very hard time replacing me. A salary of fourteen dollars is not satisfactory, sir. I need twenty.'

Hamilton's hawk face appeared to sharpen and harden. 'That's preposterous,' he said. 'Preposterous and arrogant. Where would you be now if I hadn't given you a chance

169

when you were just a boy, fresh out of college? You're still not much more than a youngster. Twenty dollars! You're lucky to get fourteen.'

'No, sir, I'm sorry. Believe me, I'm thankful for the chance you gave me. That's why I've stayed and worked for you for so little when others offered me much more. But now I have my wife to think of.' Terrence paused, took an audible breath and slowed down. '*Harper's Young People* has been trying to get me for a long time. I wouldn't want to leave you and go there, but I can't let sentiment stand in my way anymore.'

Hamilton glared and fidgeted in his chair. Then, unexpectedly, he gave his constricted 'Ha! Ha! Ha!' and shook his head. 'You're a case, Terrence McNally the First! I knew what I was doing when I plucked you out of the cradle. Of course, you're right about Jules. If he weren't my brother's son, I wouldn't keep him for five minutes. My guess is he'll quit of his own accord one of these days. Try to put up with him until then.'

Terrence was not to be so easily diverted from his subject. 'I've put up with him this long, sir, I guess I can go on putting up with him. If you pay me what I've asked, that is, and I stay here.'

He let Hamilton beat him down to eighteen dollars, the amount he had from the first determined he needed.

He could scarcely believe, still, that when he went home in the evening Sylvia would be there waiting for him. It all had happened so suddenly, so quickly. Once or twice he woke in the night, pierced by the familiar pain of losing her – the pain he had sometimes thought of as a hedge against the calamity Mrs Stern believed followed too much good fortune. When he felt her there beside him in the big bed, he had to restrain himself from shouting his joy to the whole sleeping city.

Why should he not be flooded with happiness now? He had paid for it in advance on perilous, garbage-strewn Little Water Street; in his dark hole of a room with its rat-infested walls; in the terrible immurement of two nights in jail. And he did not believe, anyway, in what was nothing but a Jewish superstition.

He knew Sylvia was not as happy as he was. He had no doubt that in time he would make her so, but she did not have his patience. She was restless in the small house, empty all day while Miss Howard was at school and Terrence at the magazine, and she had no interest in its upkeep. After all, it was not hers. She had cut herself off from her family, and the friends she had had in Normal School had drifted away when she went to boarding school. She did not try to make new ones.

'Not in this neighborhood,' she said. 'If we ever move uptown, I'll find friends of my own kind.'

'I've promised you we'll move uptown, and we will. Just wait a little,' Terrence told her. 'Meanwhile, it's not so bad here. It may not be the most fashionable section of the city, but it's nice enough.'

'Oh, anything's nice enough to you. You don't know the difference.'

Terrence tried taking her uptown to the Sterns' for Sunday dinner, but it was not a success. Sylvia was repelled by their expansiveness. When Mrs Stern tried to kiss her, she turned her head so sharply that the kiss landed somewhere in her hair. Otherwise, she was courteous enough, but stiff and formal, nothing like the real Sylvia, Terrence's Sylvia.

'I know how you feel. They embarrassed me a little, too, at first,' he told her, 'but you'll get used to them the way I did, and you'll see what wonderful people they are.'

'I don't want to get used to Jews,' she said, 'I've never had to, and I'm not going to start now.'

He tried not to get angry with her because he realized she was just ignorant. She had been told the wrong things by her mother, and it would take time and patience to guide her properly. He knew from his reading that many young women came to marriage with foolish ideas, or with almost no ideas at all, and that it was up to their husbands to educate them.

Sometimes, though, he was angry with her in spite of himself. Sometimes they quarreled, and she repeated all the old diatribes on his crudeness and his Irishness, and he in turn called her willful, spoiled, and empty-headed.

But they always made up and told each other they had not meant any of it. Sylvia would be so sweet and loving, then, that he did not know how he could ever speak a cross word to her. To his astonishment and delight, in the big bed where Miss Howard's parents had slept she had none of the reticences he had expected of an untaught girl. If, when they quarreled, her words made him question her love for him, the willingness and ardor of her body gave him entirely satisfactory answers.

One night, while he was still inside her, emptied, resting his heavy weight on his knees as he always did for fear of crushing her delicate bones, she whispered in his ear, 'We're going to have a baby, Terrence.'

Terrence said nothing. He did not move. They had been married two months. He had not considered babies, except to take precautions against having one.

'You're not glad,' she said.

'I don't know what I am. I haven't taken it in.'

He withdrew from her gently, got up and washed, and went back to lie beside her. He put one arm under her and drew her close against his side. Her skin was warm and moist.

'It's such a surprise, Sylvia. We didn't plan on having a baby yet.'

'But we're having one. Accidents happen.' Her voice had an edge, but almost at once it softened again. 'Please don't be sorry. You'll make a good father.'

Father. It struck him, rushed over him, left him with a catch in his breath. *Father*. *Da*. He had not thought of an Irish word since childhood, but he thought of this one now. *Da*. He could not remember ever saying it. He did not know what it was like to have a father. But his child would know. His *child*. His *son*.

He laughed. He pulled Sylvia over on top of him and

kissed her mouth and her neck and her breasts.

'Terrence McNally the Second!' he said.

He woke in the cold, drizzly April dawn and began wondering about the cost of a baby. He could not ask Mr Hamilton for another raise so soon. *Harper's Young People* might pay him a little more, but probably not enough. He did not want to go there anyway, or to another magazine where he would be just one of several editors. The *Cyclist*, except technically, was his. He would never again be in such complete control of a magazine's format and contents until he actually had his own.

He began to feel as cold as the day, and as damp.

'We'll have to move, of course,' Sylvia said while they were dressing for breakfast. 'We'll need a nursery for the baby.'

'A nursery?' He did not often let his loud voice loose anymore, but he was irritable from lack of sleep and worry. 'Where,' he roared, 'are we going to find the money for a place with a nursery?'

'Money,' she said. 'You're always talking about money. And you don't have to scream at me either!'

She was half dressed. Her corset was laced, drawing in her small waist to make it smaller still, thrusting up under her taut little breasts so that they rode high, protruding from the whalebone that encircled her. He bent and kissed the soft, firm mounds. She smelled, he thought, like rose petals. His wife.

'I'm sorry I screamed at you,' he said. 'It's only because I'm worried. But I'll think of something.'

When they went down to breakfast, Miss Howard said she had not been able to help hearing Terrence.

'I don't mean to pry. I never pry, as you know,' she said. 'But what I heard suggests you're going to have a baby.' She passed the toast to Sylvia and looked at Terrence. 'If that's so, I have something to say to you.'

'It's so,' Terrence said.

'Yes, and of course, we'll have to move,' Sylvia said. 'We'll have to have a nursery.'

173

Miss Howard still looked at Terrence. 'That's what I wanted to say. You don't have to move. My sewing room is small, but it will make an adequate nursery. I can take the sewing things into my bedroom.'

Terrence started to speak, but Sylvia said quickly, 'You don't want a baby here, right next to your room. Babies cry at night. It would wake you up. It would make extra work and be in your way.'

'I'd love to have a baby here, ' Miss Howard said. 'I've never had a chance to—' She broke off abruptly and went on in her severe teacher's voice. 'Naturally, I'd expect the mother to take care of the extra work.'

This time Terrence got in ahead of Sylvia. He spoke to Miss Howard in a way he never had before, surprising even himself.

'Miss Howard,' he said, 'you are a jewel.'

It seemed to Terrence that her face fell apart and came together again, so rapidly that it must have been an illusion.

'I'm happy to do it,' she said.

Miss Howard's willingness to have them stay after the baby came was a relief to Terrence, but it was only a partial solution. Sylvia did not want to stay. She was tired of living in another woman's house. She was sick of Miss Howard, and though she was not rude to her, she no longer put herself out to be agreeable. She had thought they would surely move out when she had the baby. It was only after Terrence took her downtown and showed her the kind of place of their own they could afford that she subsided.

'Remember it's only temporary,' he told her. 'You'll have your own house, your mansion. You'll have everything you want.'

'Yes, but when?'

'Sooner than you think.'

That seemed to comfort her a little, though it meant nothing at all. She might have thought he had some mysterious plan up his sleeve, but of course he did not. He was confident he would someday be a successful man and keep all his promises to her. He believed, as Aggie had and Miss Howard did, that he could do anything he set out to do. But he did not expect to manage it tomorrow. He had no idea when or how it would happen.

Meanwhile, he had to provide for the birth of their child and for his needs after he was born. Aggie had slaved and scrounged to keep him healthy and clean, but Sylvia had a husband to make motherhood a joy for her instead of a bondage. Their baby had a father, a da, to give him a real childhood.

'You're always talking about Terrence McNally the Second,' Sylvia said. 'Suppose it's a girl?'

'That would be fine. Especially if she looks like you. We can have boys later.'

'A girl is nice for a mother. I could dress her in such pretty little clothes, and we could go shopping and calling together as she got older.'

Terrence had to think of something to increase his income. The only thing that occurred to him at first was to take on some sort of extra job. He even considered going back to the Hoffman House and working as a waiter at night again. But he realized he could not do that. He was the editor of a national magazine. He associated with important people, well-known authors. He had even met one or two of them at the Hoffman House and sat at a table as a customer. It was one thing to affirm, as he had, that he had once waited on those same tables. That, in the light of his subsequent rise, was to his credit. But if he went back to it now, he would be seen as a failure, and the doors he had worked so hard to open would close in his face.

He was reading the Boston *Globe* on his way to Newburyport to see Harriet Prescott Spofford when the idea came to him. The by-line on one of the articles was familiar: Wallace Lane. Lane was the man who had not had enough money to tip Terrence after his free lunch at

175

the Hoffman House, the man who had later become a reporter for *The New York Times* and to whom Terrence had given the story of President Webb's dismissal of Jake for publishing in *Pharos* the article on the elective system that contradicted Webb's views.

Terrence, wondering idly why Lane had left the *Times* for the *Globe*, turned the page. Further on in the paper he saw a story by the popular author he was about to visit. Hamilton had allowed him up to $250 to persuade Harriet Spofford to write a story for the *Cyclist*. Probably the newspaper paid her no less. Suppose she would agree to write another story, in addition to the one for the *Cyclist*, sell it to him, and allow him to place it not only in the *Globe* but in newspapers all over the country. He could sell the story to a paper for, say, $25, which was $225 less than the paper would have to pay to the author directly – and if twenty papers agreed to buy it, he could double his investment.

The idea excited him so that he went up on deck and stood at the bow, mentally urging the Fall River Line boat to hurry to its Boston port. He would go to the *Globe* first and ask Wallace Lane, who owed him a favor, to help him get a quick interview with the right person on the paper. Then he would see Miss Spofford and point out the obvious advantages of appearing in newspapers in a dozen or more different cities. If both these interviews were successful, he would write to the newspapers and say that other newspapers, 'such as the Boston *Globe*,' were using his syndicate service and that he could supply stories by popular authors, 'such as Harriet Prescott Spofford.' To authors he would write that he could place their stories in prestigious newspapers, 'such as the Boston *Globe*,' as he had placed the stories of other well-known authors, 'such as Harriet Prescott Spofford.'

Though Terrence was not then aware of it, several syndicates were in operation in England and France, and in addition to the few, on a small scale, in the United States, Samuel McClure was developing the idea of a syndicate that would involve top-ranking authors and big metropolitan newspapers. But Terrence was sure that he had hit on something new that had tremendous possibilities. All he had to do was find the first $250 to pay Harriet Spofford.

Two weeks later he was ready to write the letters. He had Miss Spofford's promise of a story. He had an agreement from the Boston *Globe* and an introduction to the managing editor of the Philadelphia *Press*, who was related to Wallace Lane's wife. All he needed was the $250.

After thinking up and discarding a number of impractical schemes, Terrence had decided he would have to borrow the money. He had never borrowed money in his life, but he saw no other way to get it. He went to Mr Stern, assured him it was strictly a business proposition and he would get his money back with interest. Mr Stern refused.

'Business propositions betveen friends and family I don't believe in,' he said. 'Always it vorks out dot in the end somebody is mad at somebody. I'll give you the money if you vant, Terrence. A present.'

Terrence would not take it as a present. A grown man did not accept presents to start a business venture. He could tell by the way Mr Stern had clasped his hand and wished him luck that if he had accepted it, he would have been diminished in the older man's eyes.

Sylvia, to whom he had said only that he needed the money to make a profit on an investment, suggested that he ask Miss Howard.

'She thinks you make the sun come up. She'll give you anything you want.'

He said that was a silly way to talk and that he could not possibly ask a woman to lend him money.

'She probably doesn't have it anyhow,' he said.

'Of course she has it. How much does she spend money on?'

'It might be a good thing for her at that. I'd pay her

interest, of course,' he said, not to explain to Sylvia but to convince himself. 'She'd make a profit on it.'

'Are you sure *you'll* make a profit on it?' Sylvia asked him, and when he said he was sure, she put her arms around him and kissed him and did not ask him anything more.

He saw no reason why she should. Such matters were not a woman's province. But she was right about Miss Howard. 'Of course,' Miss Howard said. 'I'm glad you asked me. And please don't trouble about the interest.'

He told her he appreciated her magnanimity, but it was a business loan and there was no question of not paying her interest. She said a peculiar thing to that. 'You'll only be paying it to yourself.'

That night in bed, holding Sylvia's naked body in his arms, he told her he thought he must be the happiest man in the world.

When he awoke, the remnant of his dream lingered with him. Sylvia was in the water somewhere, drowning, screaming to him to save her. He had gone in after her, but he could not swim. Coming awake, he could still feel the terrible helplessness. He could still feel the wetness around his legs and hear Sylvia screaming.

'Oh, Terrence, I'm dying!' she screamed. 'Oh, God, Terrence, I'm dying!'

Daylight had just broken. It disclosed the wildness of her eyes in a face no less white than the pillow she tossed on. The wetness was real, too. When he threw back the covers, he saw the blood spreading on the sheet.

He leaped out of bed, covered her up again, and brushed the sweat-soaked hair back from her forehead. He had no consciousness of what he was doing.

'It will be all right, Sylvia darling,' he gibbered. 'I'll get the doctor. Everything will be all right.'

He could not find the armholes of his bathrobe. The simplest motion seemed to take him an endless time, as if he were still in the dream. Sylvia was screaming so steadily, the same words over and over, that he did not hear the knocking on the door. When he opened it, Miss Howard was standing there in a high-necked flannel nightgown, her hair falling in gray-brown straggles to her shoulders. She pushed past him without a word, bent over the bed, and then straightened.

'I'll call my doctor. Get her legs higher than her head. Put the pillow under them.'

When Terrence had done that, he followed Miss Howard out into the hall. He wanted to ask her what was the matter with Sylvia and whether she was going to be all right. But Miss Howard had already gone downstairs to the telephone.

'Of course, it's a disappointment,' the doctor said. 'Nobody knows why these accidents happen, but there's nothing to worry about. She was only three months or so gone, so she'll be fine in a few days. She's a young, healthy woman, and there's no reason she can't carry to term next time.'

Terrence nodded. He saw the doctor down to the door. On the stairs his knees felt as though they might give way. He had gone through Sylvia's death a dozen times before he knew she was going to live.

'She couldn't have been pregnant even as long as three months,' he said to the doctor.

He was going to add that he knew she couldn't have been because they had only been married a little over two months, but the doctor was shaking his head and saying they must have figured wrong.

'If anything,' the doctor said, 'it was more than three. But as I say, there's no cause to worry.'

The sewing room had not yet been turned into a nursery. Terrence went in there and closed the door. He sat down on the floor and put his hands over his ears. As if he thought that would keep him from hearing the world break to pieces.

PART TWO

Terrence McNally the Second

1890–1907

1

'Don't keep saying you remember. You couldn't possibly remember,' she said. 'You were only thirteen months old.'

'I do! I do! Listen, Grandpa, there were lots of people, and Father held me over his head so I could see the big cables, the steel cables that held the bridge up. The Brooklyn Bridge. And there were loud fireworks, all colors, whooshing up into the sky, like on the Fourth of July. I know when it was, too. It was in 1883.'

'He's making it up from hearing about it,' she said. 'He's always making things up.'

'Maybe he really does remember,' his grandfather said. 'It's not impossible.'

'I'm sure he remembers,' his father said, and smiled at him.

Terry felt better. The only one who didn't believe him was his mother. She didn't love him so much anyhow. The one she loved was Charles. The baby, she always called him, though he was three years old. She had him on her lap now, winding his hair around her finger to make curls and kissing his neck.

'I'll take the baby up for his nap,' she said. 'You come along, too, Terry.'

'Let him stay here,' his father said. 'He's old enough to spend some time around men. He's with women all week.'

'Yes, maybe he can give you some valuable advice on your latest world-shaking scheme,' she said. 'I don't doubt an eight-year-old boy can do as well as whoever advised you in your precious syndicate.'

'My precious syndicate, as you call it, has paid for all your . . .' his father began to say, but she had gone out with Charles and slammed the door.

The two men started talking. Terry very quietly took a footstool into a shadowy corner of the room and sat down on it. He had found that if he moved out of view a little and stayed still, grown-ups often forgot he was there. A great many things he knew about he had learned that way.

'I'm sorry, Charles. We usually keep our arguments private,' Terrence said. 'She hasn't had much sleep lately. Little Charles is just getting over a cold. He's been coughing at night and getting her up. It makes her irritable.'

'You don't have to apologize for Sylvia to me,' Charles Littlefield said. 'She's been difficult from the day she was born.'

He took two cigars from his vest pocket and offered one to Terrence. Both men rolled the cigars between their fingers before lighting them. Terry loved to watch the smoke. After a while it would hang in the air. You would think you could take hold of it, but if you tried, you could not feel anything. He loved the smell of it, too. His mother hated it.

'Was that just a dig, Terrence,' Littlefield asked, 'or is your syndicate in trouble?'

'It's not profitable anymore. It hasn't been for some time.' Terrence sat back and blew smoke at the ceiling. 'I've always had to compete with McClure's syndicate, you know, but I managed. Now all the top-ranking authors demand outrageous prices, and the newspapers want no others. McClure recently paid Mark Twain a thousand dollars apiece for some of his letters from Europe. I can't pay prices like that and make any money.'

'Your magazine's all right, though, surely? With cycling more popular than ever? I know nearly everyone in my chapter of the Wheelmen of America reads it.'

'The magazine is doing well enough. It keeps us comfortable, though Sylvia doesn't care for the house, and she'd like to have a nurse for the children in addition to the cook-housemaid. But it isn't my magazine. I run it, but Woodrow Hamilton still owns it.'

'Are you thinking of buying it? Is that what Sylvia meant by your world-shaking scheme?'

'No. I wouldn't buy it if I could. I've had ten years of editing the *Cyclist*, and I've learned everything I'm going to learn from it. I never intended to devote my life to a magazine about bicycling.'

Terry watched his grandfather blowing smoke rings. His father couldn't do it. He said it was because his mustache was so bushy that it broke up the rings before they got into the air. His grandfather had a beard that divided in the middle, under his chin, but no mustache.

He was quite a new grandfather. Before Charles was born, Terry had not had him. He had had only Papa and Mama Stern, who acted like grandparents but weren't really. He loved them anyway, but his mother didn't. He supposed she must love his real grandfather, though, because he was her own father. He had come right after Charles was born. Terry had heard the bell ring and run down from his room to see who it was, the way he always did. His father had opened the door, and there stood the grandfather, though at the time he only looked like a strange man.

'I've been a coward, Terrence,' he said, 'but that's behind me. If you can overlook my sins of omission, I'd like to see my daughter and my grandsons.'

'Come in. Do you know the new one is named after you, Mr Littlefield?'

'So I heard. That's what made me hope I might not be unwelcome.'

He sat down in the parlor and talked to Terry, holding him between his knees. Then Sylvia brought Charles down for him to look at.

'It was good of you to give him my name, Sylvia,' he said. 'I wouldn't have expected you to forgive me.'

'I've had enough of Irish names,' she said. 'Charles Littlefield once meant something in cultivated circles. He can always drop the McNally later if he chooses.'

His father never roared at Terry or Charles, but he sometimes roared at their mother. Terry had heard him doing it that night after he was in bed and the new grandfather had left.

'Don't ever let me hear you repeat – to Charles or to anyone else – what you said to your father about dropping the McNally. If you ever again slur my name or my Irish heritage in any way, so help me, I'll put you out of this house.'

Terry could not hear what his mother answered, but his father kept on roaring.

'No? Well, I'll say something now that I haven't said before and won't again unless you drive me to it. I was young and confused nine years ago, and too obsessed with you, in spite of everything, to let you go. But now you're here on sufferance because of the children. So be careful.'

Terry often did not know what grown-ups were talking about, but he liked to listen. Sometimes it was just voices going on around him while he played or read or thought about something else. Sometimes he remembered things later and understood them because he was older.

He moved his footstool to the window, so he could watch the people go by in their carriages for a Sunday afternoon drive. His father sometimes hired a carriage to take them around Central Park, but they did not own one, though his mother said they should.

'What is your scheme then?' Charles Littlefield asked Terrence. 'Or is it something I'm not to know?'

'It's no secret. In fact, one reason I asked you here today was to discuss it with you.' Terrence tapped his cigar ash into a jade ashtray. 'I want to start a new magazine. I've always planned on doing that someday, and I feel that this is the time. I believe the future of the magazine in this country has never been so bright, and I want to be in on it at the beginning. You may not know I inherited a little money a few years ago. I've never touched it.' He smiled briefly. 'Much to Sylvia's annoyance. She can't understand why money should be set aside. In her opinion, it's for immediate spending, and nothing else.'

'I know. Her mother's the same.' Littlefield shook his head. 'Women!'

'Yes. It was too bad she had to know anything about the inheritance, but since she was named in the will, too, she had to hear it read. At any rate, I've kept the money in the bank, gathering interest, until I was ready to start. I'm ready now.' He looked directly into his father-in-law's mild blue eyes. 'I have almost enough, but if I'm to launch this publication the way I think it should be done, I need a little more. I know you're not, by your standards, a wealthy man, but if you have a thousand dollars to invest in my magazine, I believe I can promise you a handsome return on your money in a few years.'

Littlefield set his cigar down next to the trumpeting elephant. He got up and walked to the window, saw Terry sitting there on his stool, patted his head absently, and returned to his chair.

'Terrence,' he said. 'I lost a fortune twenty years ago, and my gumption with it, and I've never recovered more than a fraction of either one. I won't say it doesn't frighten me to risk one thousand dollars. It frightens me very much. But I have as much confidence in you as I could have in anyone, and besides, I owe you something for allowing you to be reviled in my house. You'll have the money by the end of the week.'

'Thank you, sir. You won't regret it.'

Littlefield sighed. 'I believed in myself once, too. Financial failure shrinks a man, Terrence, strips him of the respect he had from his family and friends, leaves him less than he was. I hope—'

'I won't fail, Mr Littlefield. If I did, I'd start again another way.'

'Yes, well, perhaps you would.' Littlefield frowned at the end of his dead cigar and relit it. 'What kind of magazine are you proposing? I know nothing about the business, but if I'm investing in it, I should have some idea of your plans.'

'Of course you should. I'm touched that you agreed to invest on faith and ask questions afterward.' Terrence leaned forward in his chair. His cigar burned down, forgotten, in the ashtray. 'First of all, I intend to publish the world's foremost authors writing in English – men like Robert Louis Stevenson, Rudyard Kipling, and Thomas Hardy. In addition to fiction, my magazine will be concerned with social issues, politics, science, and I'll get contributions from outstanding writers in those fields. Illustrations will be done by the finest artists. I'm going to use the new photoengraving process for halftones instead of woodcuts, which will save thousands of dollars, so I'll be able to put out a superior magazine and sell it for as little as ten cents a copy. This means that everybody—'

'Pardon me for interrupting, Terrence.' Littlefield had been vainly opening and shutting his mouth for several moments, trying to slip a word into a pause that never came. 'As I say, I know nothing about the magazine business, but you mentioned before that your syndicate was no longer profitable because you had to pay so much to top-ranking authors. Then how can the magazine be profitable if you publish those same authors? You surely can't pay them out of the revenue from sales at ten cents a copy.'

'I don't expect to make my profits on the sale of the magazine. In fact, I plan to distribute several thousand free copies. I've already lined up a dozen men to take them around the city and out on the road. Once I've built up circulation, I'll have no trouble attracting advertisers. That's where the big profits will come from. Do you know what the annual flow of goods is worth now in this country? Something like twelve billion dollars. The only way to sell it all is through advertising, and the best medium isn't the local newspaper but the national magazine. Before long, in my opinion, magazines will be selling millions of dollars' worth of advertising a year, and *McNally's Monthly* is going to be in on it from the start.'

'Millions of dollars? Do you really think so?' Littlefield's cigar had gone out, too. His hands were clasped over the small paunch that interrupted the otherwise flat spareness of his body. '*McNally's Monthly*. It has a nice ring.'

'A nice Irish ring.'

Littlefield gave a crooked smile. 'I'd like to see you rub their noses in it.' He appeared to be watching this outcome on the ceiling, savoring the scene. 'Am I the only investor, Terrence?'

'My friend Jacob Stern has put a little money into it. Also, Woodrow Hamilton . . . Oh, yes, he knows I intend to leave him and start my own magazine. It won't, of course, be any competition for the *Cyclist*, which he has lost interest in anyway, and he thinks I'll make a success of my own magazine. After all, I made a success of his.'

'Yes.' Littlefield looked more and more content. 'Yes. And you mentioned having certain moneys of your own to put into it? An inheritance? I understood you had no family.'

'No – well, yes, I do have some family, as a matter of fact. Uncles and three brothers who live in Boston. But I wasn't brought up with my brothers, and I haven't seen them in years. The inheritance came from the woman who owned this house. I boarded with her after my mother died, and we've lived here since our marriage. She was a Miss Jessica Howard. She left me the house and several thousand dollars she had accumulated during years of teaching school. She left Sylvia her clothes. I don't know what was in her mind. She must have known Sylvia wouldn't wear anybody's used clothing, even if it wasn't an old spinster's frumpery. She must have meant it as a joke. If so, it was her first. In all the more than twenty years I knew her, I never saw a trace of humor in her.' Terrence gave a snort of amusement. 'Sylvia was outraged. She threw everything into the trash. And I rescued it and took it all down to my old neighbourhood. Maybe Miss Howard knew it would happen that way. Anyway, I think it would have pleased her. She taught the children of women like the ones who got her clothes. To them, they were finery.'

Terry had slipped off his stool and was lying on the rug, half asleep. He imagined it was beginning to snow, but when he roused himself to get up on his knees and look out, he saw the sun was shining. Besides, it was only the beginning of October, too early for snow. He lay down again. He thought he remembered his father saying something about Miss Howard. Aunt Jessica. That was why he had imagined snow. Aunt Jessica and snow went together in his mind.

His teacher in first grade had said they must all remember the date because nothing like it had ever happened before and might never again. March 12, 1888. The teacher said the city had not been prepared at all. Some of the men went out with wagons and shovels, but so much snow fell they might as well have used toys. The whole city was paralyzed. None of the horsecars or elevated trains moved. The street signs were covered with snow. No mail was delivered. The teacher said to remember it, the Blizzard of '88, so they could tell their grandchildren. Some of the boys giggled at the idea of having grandchildren. Terry raised his hand.

'I know something else to tell my grandchildren,' he said. 'I know something terrible that happened.'

The teacher had asked him if he wanted to tell it to the class. He had wanted to. He had had pictures in his head that frightened him at night, and he needed to talk about them. But not to his father, who had acted funny, as if he had pictures in his head, too, and not to his mother because she never really listened to him.

Aunt Jessica had waited in school, thinking the snow would stop and be cleared away and it would be easier to get home. But the snow got worse. By the time she decided to leave she couldn't walk through it. She could have spent the night in the school, but a man came along in a cutter he had hired with a horse and driver, and he said he would take her home. The only place for her to sit was on his lap, but that was all right because of its being a blizzard and the only way she could get home. The road was so uneven from the snow that the cutter kept tilting and almost falling over. Most women would have screamed, but Aunt Jessica never made a sound. The main trouble was that the driver could hardly see where he was going, and neither could the horse. They were driving along Third Avenue, and they drove straight into one of the pillars of the elevated. Aunt Jessica was thrown out of the man's lap. It would have been all right if she had just fallen into the snow, but first her head hit the pillar.

The man brought her home in the cutter. Terry had heard everything the man had to tell before his father remembered him and made him go upstairs to his room. He had seen the way Aunt Jessica looked. His father had pretended afterward that it was only as if she were asleep, but it wasn't. People didn't have blood on them when they were only asleep. Their faces were not like Aunt Jessica's face. Terry had kept picturing her flying out of the cutter and hitting her head on the pillar, though he had not seen it, and he kept picturing her face, which he had seen.

'She wasn't really your aunt or mine, you know,' his mother had told him. 'She was just an old lady who used to be your father's teacher.'

'She loved me, though.'

'Oh, all this talk about love. Your father gets it from those Jews, and you get it from him.' She meant Papa and Mama Stern. She never said their names. 'I'm sure Miss Howard *liked* you. That's enough.'

Terry closed his eyes again, and this time he fell fast asleep on the rug. He did not hear his mother come into the room or his grandfather leave. He woke when his mother and father were talking, but he kept his eyes closed and pretended to be still asleep.

'You talked him into it, of course,' Sylvia said. 'You always could talk the leaves off the trees.' She was lying on the sofa to rest after putting Charles down for his nap.

She plucked a lace handkerchief from the long sleeve of her white dress and patted her forehead with it. 'Not that Father is ever difficult to persuade. He's a weakling. The slightest poke, and he caves in.'

'He's a good man, but his big failure took the heart out of him, and he still pities himself for it, all these years later. His trouble is he never had to fight for what he wanted, and when the time came, he didn't know how.' Terrence got up from his chair and stood looking at the unlit logs in the fireplace. 'I wish he hadn't mentioned our agreement. It isn't your concern. But whether you believe it or not, he has made an excellent investment.'

'Why isn't it my concern? Do you think because I'm a woman I'm too stupid to understand it?'

'I never thought you were stupid, Sylvia. But business isn't a woman's province. And don't pretend you have any real interest in any part of it except how much money it will make for you to spend.'

'That's the purpose of business, isn't it? To make money?'

'Not its sole purpose. Not for me. Not for most men. I've waited a long time to start my own magazine. *McNally's Monthly.* Your father thought it had a nice ring. I want to make it heard in every household in the country.' He turned and looked at her. 'Now it's not just for myself anymore. I want it for my sons.'

Sylvia sat up. She felt with both hands to test the condition of the Psyche knot she wore in imitation of Lillie Langtry. 'I wouldn't count on Charles if I were you,' she said. 'That is, if your precious magazine is actually in existence when he's grown. Charles is cut out for something exceptional. He has the Littlefield breeding. Perhaps an ambassador.'

Terrence laughed. 'For God's sake, Sylvia, now you do sound stupid! How can you tell what Charles is cut out for? The child is three years old.'

Terry stood up from his place at the window, startling them both. 'I'm going to go to the magazine with Father,'

192

he anounced. 'Charles can be an am – what you said. I'm going with Father.'

His mother went over to him and took him by the arm. 'What are you doing here, Terry, hiding and listening like a little sneak? Go up to your room and stay there until I tell you to come out.'

'I wasn't hiding. I fell asleep.' He began to sniffle. 'Father told me to stay here. You know he did. I sat over there, and then I got tired and I fell asleep.'

'Don't cry. You're too big to cry,' his father said. 'Let him go, Sylvia. He didn't do anything wrong.'

She stopped holding his arm, but she said, 'He's always listening. You don't notice it. All you notice is how bright he is. I've seen him, though, sneaking off into corners to listen and then playing innocent when I find him. He hears more than is good for him.'

His father crouched down so as not to be much taller than he was. 'Is that right, Terry? Do you hide and listen?'

'I don't hide. You and Grandpa knew I was there.' He went closer to his father so he could get more of his cigar-and-shaving-soap smell. 'Sometimes I listen a little, but not much.'

His father hugged him. 'All right, son. Go on to your room and play.'

Terry started to run out and then stopped. 'Is Mother still angry?'

'She isn't angry,' his father said. 'She just misunderstood.'

'Don't wake the baby when you go upstairs,' his mother said.

2

They called him Terry at home to avoid confusion with his father. In school he was called Terrence. When he was in fourth grade, he began putting 'Terrence McNally the

Second' at the top of his papers, the way his father put 'Terrence McNally the First' on things he signed. One teacher tried to explain to him that the reason he was the Second was that his father was Junior. She would not believe him when he said his father was not Junior but the First. She said nobody would be Terrence McNally the First unless he was a king.

'She's wrong,' his father said, 'but leave it alone. You'll find as you go along that some people will accept it and some won't, and there's no use trying to argue the won'ts into it.'

'Roger Blake said I was stuck-up for writing my name like that.'

'It's no more stuck-up than when he writes Roger Blake. That's his whole name, and Terrence McNally the Second is yours. It's a family thing, and we're proud of it, so you mustn't mind what anyone says. If you do mind, you're letting Roger Blake, or somebody else, hold your reins, instead of holding them yourself.'

About once a month Terry and his father and, when he was older, Charles, had Sunday dinner at the Sterns'. His mother did not go. Nobody ever said anything about it, but Terry thought the Sterns knew his mother did not like them. He did not think they liked her either. His father said everybody was disliked by somebody, and there was not much you could do about it.

Terry loved it at the Sterns'. Even if only Uncle Jake was there, they all talked at once and laughed a lot and had so much to eat that even Terry, who, his mother said, had an appetite like a hod carrier, could not finish it all. ('Be thankful he can satisfy his appetite,' his father said. 'My father was a hod carrier who couldn't.') But usually Aunt Bertha or one of the other aunts was there, too, with her husband and children, even though the whole family had had dinner together two nights before, as they did every Friday night. Aunt Bertha had a boy, Sam, a few months older than Terry, and almost as smart.

'He's the image of you, Terrence,' Uncle Jake said, and

ruffled Terry's hair, which his mother said was the color of carrots and Mama Stern said was auburn. He liked that word. Auburn. 'The very spit,' Uncle Jake said, 'only not as ugly.'

'Ugly? Nobody here is ugly,' Papa Stern said. 'Dot's a handsome boy, dot Terry.'

Charles loved it at the Sterns', too, though he always pretended to their mother that he didn't feel one way or the other about it. Charles, their father said, was a born diplomat. Terry had not liked him much when he was little, but Charles improved as he got older. He had what Mama Stern called a sweet nature. He hardly ever got angry or said anything mean about anybody, and if you wanted anything he had, he would almost always give it to you; that usually made you feel like giving it back. He followed Terry around and tried to copy everything he did, even when he was much too little to do whatever it was.

Later Charles grew almost as tall as Terry, though not as heavy. Terry was built like his father – like a bull, his mother said – but Charles was slim and quick-moving. He had his mother's fair skin and hair, but his eyes were neither brown like hers nor blue like his father's and Terry's, but a clear sea green. He was so fast on his feet and so clever with his hands that much bigger boys did not dare bully him. Before that, when he was too little to do it for himself, Terry fought the bullies off. If Terry came home scratched up or with a black eye, he was punished by his mother. Charles always told her why it happened, but she thought he was just trying to protect Terry. She hugged him for being such a good brother and went on punishing Terry.

In the beginning Terry told his father when his mother was unfair to him, but he stopped doing that. It almost always started an argument between his father and mother. First the argument would be about Terry and Charles, but it would spread to other things. At night, in the room they shared, the boys could hear their father, who probably did not know how his voice got louder and louder. They could not hear their mother, but they could usually figure out what she said by what their father answered. Terry hated their arguments, but they did not upset him the way they upset Charles. Until Charles was eight or nine, whenever they argued, he crawled into bed with Terry, and the whole bed shook from his trembling.

When Terry was twelve, Papa Stern had a stroke. Jake called Terrence from the hospital, and he left the magazine office right away and went up there. He could not tell whether Papa Stern knew him or not.

'He can't speak. He can't move anything but his eyes,' Terrence told them that night at the dinner table. 'Jake thinks he can see awareness in his eyes, but to me they looked blank. I can't believe it. A few days ago he was a vital, alert man. Now he's a block of wood.'

Sylvia looked at Charles. 'I don't think this is anything to discuss in front of the children.'

'It won't hurt them to know that life isn't always gentle.'

'A seven-year-old boy doesn't have to know that. He has plenty of time.'

'Is Papa Stern going to die?' Charles asked.

Charles asked a lot of questions about dying. Once on their way to school he and Terry had seen a dead cat lying in the gutter. Charles had gone over and bent down close to look at it, his eyes getting bigger and bigger and his face going white, the way it had done now. Then he had kept talking about it, asking Terry why the cat was stiff and whether it knew it was dead and whether an animal or a person who had died ever came back to life.

'I don't know, Charles,' his father said to the question about Papa Stern. 'The doctor says he can't tell yet.'

'What's a stroke?' Terry asked.

'A sickness that happens to the brain, so that it can't make the rest of the body work the way it should.'

'Can a little boy seven years old get a stroke?' Charles asked.

'See what you've done?' Sylvia said. 'Look at his face!' She pulled Charles out of his chair and urged him onto her lap. 'Of course, a little boy can't get it, baby. It's something only old people get.' She rocked him in her arms. 'Don't think about it anymore. Just don't think about it. How would you like a nice big dish of ice cream? Your favorite flavor?'

Charles sat up, his long legs dangling down from his knee pants. With his curly blond hair and the pink that had returned to his cheeks, he looked like an oversized doll.

'Is it peach?'

'Yes, indeed, it's peach, and if you're very good, I wouldn't be surprised if Mary would let you lick the dasher besides.'

Terrence was staring at them, his mouth a straight line. Terry knew that expression. He knew his father was furious at the way his mother treated Charles but would not say so in front of him and Charles. They would probably hear him later, upstairs.

'Can Terry lick the dasher, too?' Charles asked.

Sylvia hugged him, told him what a good brother he was, and let him slide off her lap and return to his chair. Terry said nothing. He did not even want the ice cream in his dish, though normally he could not get enough, no matter what the flavor.

'You sick, boy?' Mary said when she came in to clear the table. 'You don't eat ice cream, I think you sick.'

Her name was not really Mary, but Mary was as close to it as anything pronounceable. She was a short, dark, heavy woman of indeterminate age, who came from Austria-Hungary and claimed her family were aristocrats. Sylvia said that was ridiculous, that she had the coarse features and big hands and feet of a typical peasant. She did not say it in front of Mary, though. Servants were plentiful, but one who was not only clean but a good cook was hard to find. They had had a girl who took off her shoes in the kitchen and walked around in bare feet with

197

long, filthy toenails and did not know enough to shut the door when she went to the toilet. She had claimed to be from a farming village in England, but Sylvia was sure she was Irish and told her so when she discharged her, adding 'dirty' as a modifier. The girl had answered by spitting into the soup on the stove.

'I'm not sick,' Terry said to Mary. 'I'm just not very hungry tonight.'

Terrence leaned across the table and squeezed his shoulder. 'He may get over it, son. The doctor says some people recover completely from a stroke and are the same as they ever were.'

But Papa Stern did not get over it. He died four days later, unable to give any sign of recognition to anyone.

Charles wanted to go to the funeral. He told Terry he wanted to see if Papa Stern really looked like a block of wood. But Sylvia said he was far too young to go, and Terrence did not insist. Terry went with his father. They had to wear hats and sit in a separate part of the synagogue from the women. Most of the service was in Hebrew and sounded like a kind of singing. Terry wondered whether they thought Papa Stern could hear it or if it was for themselves.

'He was an old man, you know, Terrence,' Mama Stern said afterward. 'Much older than I am, over seventy. You couldn't tell that, could you? Because he never looked very different. He never looked young and he never looked old.' Her daughters stood around her weeping noisily, but her eyes were dry. 'I'll miss him. We had nearly forty years together. I'll miss him every day, but I can't say it wasn't time for him to die. Only now – now that it's too late – I think of how he worked all those years. He didn't know anything else, Terrence. His family, the people he loved, and the fur business. That's what grieves me most. That the world is so beautiful, so – so varied, and he never knew it.'

'He was happy, Mama Stern,' Terrence said. 'He was immensely proud of you and his children and of building

198

up a business that kept you all in such luxurious comfort. That was all he wanted.'

'Ah, but Terrence, don't you see? He never had time to notice how much else there was to want.'

The editorial offices of *McNally's Monthly* were at 750 Broadway, almost directly opposite the building that housed *Scribner's Magazine*, the *Magazine of American History*, and the new magazine published by McClure, Terrence's former syndicate competitor. In this golden age of magazine publishing new periodicals were launched constantly, some to flicker out in a few months, but many to go on for years. There was always room for another attractive one, in whatever category – general, business, science, women, farmers, literary, children, church. More than three thousand American periodicals spilled from the presses, some weekly, some monthly.

In 1894, the year Mr Stern died, Terrence had begun taking Terry to the office on Saturdays. Once he had been shown around and introduced to the staff, the boy was left to himself and, in the constant hectic rush of getting out the next issue of the magazine, was often forgotten.

'I want you to get the feel of it,' Terrence had told him the first day. 'When you're a little older, I'll have work for you to do when you're off from school, but right now I just want you to watch, see what happens here, what it's like to get out a magazine. Don't get in anybody's way, but look around quietly. If you have questions, write them down and ask me when we leave.'

Terry was the only boy his age he knew of who could say he worked in his father's office on Saturdays and have it no more than an exaggeration of the truth. He did work after a fashion, though not at anyone's behest but his own. He delighted the office boy by keeping all the desks supplied with fresh paper and sharpened pencils and emptying the ashtrays and wastebaskets. When he could think of nothing else that required his attention, he turned to a story he had decided to write for the magazine, describing his father's rise from poverty. He intended to present it as fiction and only at the end reveal that it was a true story whose hero was none other than Terrence McNally the First, editor and publisher of *McNally's Monthly*.

At the office, where he was tolerated because he was polite and agreeable – and the boss's son – one of the men gave him the use of a decrepit typewriter. After he had taught himself the rudiments of typing on it, he started his father's story. He called it 'Rise to Fame' and set down three or four sentences, stopping frequently to admire the appearance of his own words in a close equivalent to print.

He was in the midst of this task the day Jake Stern appeared at the magazine office in the middle of the afternoon. Terrence was out, seeing an advertiser who owed him money, but Terry had heard him say he would be back soon.

'What are you writing?' Jake asked Terry.

'Oh, nothing.' Terry rolled the sheet of paper back until all his typing was hidden. Then, realizing this was rude, he said, 'It's a kind of secret, Uncle Jake. You'll know about it when it's finished. Nobody has seen it yet, not even Father.'

'Do you want to be a writer, Terry?'

'Maybe. I thought I did. I'm not sure, though. It's awfully hard.' He looked up at Jake, who was sitting on the edge of an empty desk. 'You look different. Did you get a new haircut or something?'

Jake shook his head. 'Not a new haircut.' He smiled and ran his fingers through his thick curls, the black already heavily flecked with gray, though he was still in his thirties. 'But something is different. See if you can tell what.'

Terry got up and walked around him. Jake had on his usual black lawyer's suit with the hard stand-up collar and black tie. He wore the same steel-framed thick-lensed spectacles. He was not growing a beard or a mustache.

'I know!' Terry said suddenly, but before he could go on, Terrence came striding into the office, his face, which was red with November chill, brightening when he saw Jake.

'Jake!' he shouted. 'What are you doing here? Have you been waiting long? Why aren't you wearing your yarmulke?'

Jake winked at Terry. 'Didn't you realize I only wore it for Papa's sake, Terrence? At first Mama thought maybe I shouldn't take it off, but she came around. Mama's a sensible woman. She doesn't really believe Papa still knows what I'm doing or not doing.'

'You look strange without it,' Terrence said.

'When you see me without it every day, you'll get used to it.'

'What do you mean, every day? I don't see you every day. Not that it wouldn't be—'

'You're going to,' Jake broke in. 'At least I hope so. That's what I came to talk to you about. I think I've waited a decent interval since Papa's death. I kept him happy while he was alive, and he died happy, and now it can't matter to him anymore.'

Terry, fastened to his seat by curiosity, watched Terrence's face. Usually the most incomprehensible things people said were clear to his father. But he could see this was not.

'If you need reassurance that you were a good son, Jake, I'll be the first to give it to you, but—'

Jake interrupted him again. 'What I need is reassurance about a job on *McNally's Monthly* because I've just handed in my resignation from the firm of Silverstein and Bernbach, and if you turn me down, I'll be among the two or three million unemployed.'

Terrence stared at him without speaking. 'You must be crazy,' he said finally. 'Do you mean you've actually given up your position in a prosperous law firm in times like these? When they were going to make you a full partner and you'd be set for life? How could you do such a crazy

201

thing?'

Jake shrugged. 'It was easy – one of the easiest things I've ever done.' He leaned back, balancing himself with his hands behind him on the desk. 'My distaste for the practice of the law has lasted, undiminished, for more than fifteen years. I feel as if I've shaken off a ton of iron that's been sitting on my shoulders all that time.' He smiled at Terrence. 'Now I can do what I've wanted to do since the days we sat in Room Three-twelve, and in Mama's sewing room, and worked on *Pharos* together.'

'Jake,' Terrence said. 'Jake. You should have waited. You should have talked to me first. There isn't anybody I'd rather have with me. Of course, you know that. But this isn't the time.' He lowered his voice. 'I'm barely hanging on, Jake. Everybody owes me money, and nobody pays. I even go out to see them personally – I was just out now talking to an advertiser who owes me more than five hundred dollars – but it does no good. Nobody has any money. I'm in debt myself. I've cut my own salary to the bone. Soon I'll have to cut my staff.' He took a deep breath, looking as if it hurt his chest. 'This depression can't last indefinitely, of course. I'll ride it out. If you had only waited instead of throwing everything over now. Now, of all times.'

'There couldn't be a better—' Jake looked around at the men working at their desks. 'Is there someplace we can talk more privately?'

Terrence looked at Terry, who pretended to be absorbed in typing. 'Yes, of course,' he said, a note of surprise in his voice, as though he had not noticed anyone else was there. 'Come into my office. Learning to type, Terry? That's fine, son. Very useful.'

Terry knew about the depression. It had been explained to him in school, and he had heard his father trying to explain it to his mother. Sylvia had wanted to hire a second maid to help Mary, and blamed the diminished income that made it impossible on Terrence's mismanagement. She seemed not to believe that the whole country was in trouble.

'I'm not really surprised,' she said. 'You botched the syndicate. Now you're botching your precious magazine.'

'It isn't Father's fault,' Terry said. 'It started a long time ago, when this English bank made some bad investments in Argentina. It would have gone bankrupt, only the English government guaranteed to pay its debts. What happened was—'

'Terry, I don't need instruction from you,' Sylvia said. 'You may be a very bright child, but a child is all you are. Nobody is talking about England in any case. England has nothing to do with us.'

'The boy is right, Sylvia,' Terrence said. 'When the British banking house of Baring failed, British investors in American securities began to sell, and gold began to move out of the country. Our railways were affected, too. They overexpanded with British capital, and when that was withdrawn, the railroad boom collapsed. That was the beginning that led to the Panic last year.'

'*The boy is right*' was evidently all Sylvia heard. 'No matter what I say, you always uphold him. It's no wonder he's full of himself and has no respect for me.'

Terrence sighed. 'I was foolish to discuss it. As I often remark, such things are not a woman's province. On the other hand, there must be women who have noticed the disaster. There must be a few who are aware that thousands of businesses have failed and millions of men are jobless. That the country is torn by strikes and mob violence and that anyone who has work or is able to maintain any kind of commercial enterprise and provide his family with a home and three meals a day is lucky.'

'What a talker you are,' Sylvia said. 'If you could only go into the talking business and be paid by the word, we'd be rich.'

On the way home from the office, the day Jake had come, Terry noticed a difference in his father. He looked pleased. It was a long time since Terry had seen him look that way.

203

'Is Uncle Jake going to be on the magazine?' he asked.

'Yes,' Terrence said. 'Yes, he is. Not only that, but he's going to put quite a bit of money into it. Enough, I think, to tide us over this bad time.'

'Is Uncle Jake rich?'

'Rich means different things to different people, Terry. When I was a waiter at the Hoffman House bar, any night I made five dollars in tips, I felt rich. If Mr Vanderbilt had to get along on Uncle Jake's money, he would consider himself poor. Papa Stern left Uncle Jake what by our standards is a considerable sum.' Terrence looked down at Terry. 'Does that answer your question?'

'Not exactly.'

Terrence nodded. 'That's right. I can't answer it exactly or inexactly. The question is unanswerable. Now, if you ask me whether Uncle Jake has enough money to do whatever he wants to do, that I can answer. He has. Do you know what he said to me, Terry? He said, "Even when I resented Papa, I loved him. Can you imagine how much I love him now that he's given me my dream?" He meant the magazine. All these years he's envied me. When I edited the *Cyclist*, he envied me. When I started *McNally's Monthly*, he would have given anything in the world to be in on it, but he thought it would break his father's heart if he gave up the law. I wish I could have had him on the magazine without the money, but it would have been impossible. I couldn't have paid him anything. And he's happier like this. He has a share in the magazine. Our names will be together on the masthead, the way they were on *Pharos*. "*Editors: Terrence McNally the First, Jacob Stern*".'

Terry loved it when his father talked to him. He didn't always understand it all, but that didn't matter. As long as he talked, Terry felt warm and important. He was with his father a good deal. In addition to the Saturdays, he often went along to visit authors or to see printers. His studies came so easily that his marks did not suffer if he missed a day or two of school. But sometimes his father hardly talked to him at all, seemed almost to forget about him, even when they were right next to each other. If Terry spoke to him, he always listened carefully and gave one of his long answers, but it was not like this, not as if he enjoyed it, but as if he had been dragged back from somewhere else to do it.

'I want you to discuss with me anything that's on your mind,' Terrence had said to him once. 'As you know, I never had a father to talk to. My mother was an exceptional woman, but she was a woman, and without education, so that there were many things I couldn't discuss with her. A boy needs somebody he can talk to about whatever may be bothering him. You know you can do that with me, don't you?'

Terry said yes, but it wasn't altogether true. He had to pick his topics to hold his father's interest. Anything related to the magazine or to people Terrence knew, any factual information Terry had or needed, these were unfailing. He had learned very quickly to recognize the look, the tone of voice, the hard surface against which some things he had to say no more than touched his father and slid off.

He had no real friends. He was too bright for his peers, too disinterested in most of the pastimes that engaged them. He was not well enough coordinated to be good at sports. Charles, at seven, threw a ball with more natural grace and skill than Terry ever mastered. Nor did he enter into the communal salaciousness—the dirty talk, the comparison of penises and the speed with which they could eject semen. He knew as many obscene words as any boy his age, and masturbated as steadily, but he had no interest in competition and preferred to relish these pleasures privately. He was fond of his brother and enjoyed being his mentor and the object of his adoration, but Charles was still too young to furnish companionship. As for his mother, it was Terry's secret hope that she would one day look at him in astonishment and wonder why she had not recognized his unique abilities all along.

Terry knew he was his father's favorite. Terrence, who could talk to anyone at staggering length, seemed to have little to say to Charles. They were so different. Terry looked like his father and tried to be more like him than he naturally was. Even at Charles's age he had known what to say to him, what questions to ask. Most of the time Terrence liked having him around. Terry liked being with him more than with anybody in the world, especially when he was in a good mood, the way he was now.

'Would the magazine have failed without Uncle Jake's money?' he asked.

'I don't think so. I think we'd have managed,' Terrence said. 'But it's possible, the state the country's in.'

'What would we have done?

'I'd have started another magazine,' Terrence said. 'I don't know how or when, but I'd have done it. Of course, I'd have had to call it something else, and I wouldn't have liked that. *McNally's Monthly* is the magazine I want to build up for you. Someday you'll be the McNally it belongs to.'

They were riding home in a parlour car on the Third Avenue el. Other cars were jammed with people, most of them standing, hanging onto the straps to keep their balance, ripe for the dips who profited by all the easily accessible pockets. But there were no standees in the parlour cars, which were wide and comfortable, with upholstered seats, armrests, rugs on the floor, and curtains at the windows.

'Why isn't Uncle Jake married?' Terry asked suddenly.

Terrence looked at him with curiosity. 'What makes you ask that?'

'I just wondered. Most grown people are married, aren't they?'

'It seems so. Man's natural state, I suppose. Woman's, at any rate.' He said nothing else for so long that Terry thought he had forgotten the original question. But then he went on. 'Jake was once in love with a girl who fell in love with somebody else. It was a long while before he got over that. When he did, he met and fell in love with a girl who wasn't Jewish. He couldn't even tell Papa Stern that he was going out with her, much less that he wanted to marry her. For some people the worst thing a person can do is marry outside his religion. That was the way Papa Stern felt. So that girl married somebody else, too. I guess Jake gave up after that. I guess he decided two heartbreaks were enough.'

'We're outside his religion, but Papa Stern loved us. He said we were like his own family. So why did he care if Uncle Jake—?'

'Marriage is different. It's complicated, Terry. Part of it is because the Jews are a comparatively small group of people, and they're afraid the children of a mixed marriage won't carry on Judaism. They also distrust Christians because so many have hated and persecuted Jews and still do. I'm not sure Papa Stern would have wanted me in his house if he had had a chance to object, but before he knew it, Uncle Jake had brought me home and Mama Stern had welcomed me and he was too kind a man to throw me out. After a while he took me for granted, and then slowly he began to feel affection for me and later for you and Charles. "My Irish son," he used to call me at one time.' For a moment Terrence looked sad. 'But you see, Terry, we were the only Christians he knew, and he thought we must be different from the others, all of whom he still distrusted, sight unseen.'

'But if Uncle Jake had brought her home, that girl he loved who wasn't Jewish, if he had brought her home the way he did you, maybe Papa Stern would have got used to her, too, and loved her the way he did us.'

'Uncle Jake must not have thought there was any chance of that because he never tried it.'

Terry thought about this for a while. Then he said, 'I didn't think a grown-up man still had to obey his father.'

Terrence looked at him. There was something in his face that Terry, who knew most of his expressions, could not read. 'It wasn't a question of obedience,' he said, much more softly than he usually spoke. 'He just couldn't bear to cause his father such heartbreak.'

3

Jake's money had saved *McNally's Monthly* from possible bankruptcy, but to keep it going and make it the magazine Terrence wanted it to be – the foremost general monthly in the country – required more money still, and more than money. On Jake's advice the magazine was incorporated and investors were invited to buy stock. Terrence talked Woodrow Hamilton into buying fifty shares at a hundred dollars a share. His father-in-law, Charles Littlefield, bought ten. Neither of these gentlemen knew how close he had come to losing his original investment. To them and to the others who bought the stock, *McNally's Monthly* appeared to be a thriving enterprise. No official audits existed to keep a publication from inflating its actual circulation figures.

Advertisers, however, knowing how inaccurate any magazine's figures were likely to be, were not easily taken in. Jake insisted that a first-rate advertising manager could overcome such obstacles and that the man Terrence had was obviously not right for the job.

'Look what happened when you went out to get advertising for *Pharos*,' he said. 'You were forceful and innovative. You went to people who had never before thought of advertising in a college journal and persuaded them it would be profitable. That's the kind of personality and approach we need, not—'

'Jake, this is not *Pharos*. This is not a college journal with a built-in supply of readers. This is a national magazine, competing with thousands of other national magazines for millions of readers of unknown persuasions, unknown tastes. If we can attract a large enough share of those readers, we won't have to sell the advertisers; they'll come clamoring for space. Our first, most important job is to build circulation.'

Terrence and Jake did not always agree on how to accomplish this. For the first time in all the years they had known each other, their arguments, on occasion, were acrimonious. Terrence told Jake he had a lawyer's mind, not an editor's. Jake countered that Terrence always thought that he knew better about everything than anyone else and that his stubborn arrogance might have been as responsible as the state of the national economy for the near failure of the magazine.

Terry, who often overheard these exchanges, was more upset by them than by the arguments between his parents. He was used to acrimony at home, but he had never before heard his father and Jake talk to each other with any trace of unfriendliness. He thought that they were becoming enemies and that someday his father would put Jake off the magazine and they would never see him again. Terry did not have so many people to love who loved him in return that he could afford to lose one of them.

Other things changed, too. Charles grew out of even Sylvia's concept of babyhood, too big for her lap or for curls or crooning. When she became less obsessed with him, he escaped to a life of his own, in which his obliging nature and his skill at games gave him instant popularity. He still admired Terry, but he needed him less. In the afternoon he was usually playing somewhere with his friends. Sylvia, no longer expecting him, was rarely home. Only Mary was there to greet Terry after school. She comforted him with milk and gingerbread, sometimes a dark, rich, molassesy kind; sometimes another kind, much lighter and paler but spicy with extra ginger and dusted on top with powdered sugar.

'You make the best gingerbread in the world,' he told her.

'*Ja*. For best boy.'

'What about Charles?'

'Charles is best boy, too, but you Mary's.'

He was nearly fifteen, in his second year of high school, before he was certain that his father was not going to fire Jake. By that time *McNally's Monthly* had almost doubled its circulation, and although its two top editors still argued, they no longer pummeled each other with bitter accusations. Terry understood for the first time that someone could be unpleasant to someone else not because of dislike, but out of some worry or fear or frustration that had nothing at all to do with the other person.

'You've been around the magazine for several years now,' Terrence said to him one day during the Christmas holidays. 'Tell me why you think we're doing so much better than when you first came.'

Terrence often tested him this way, asking him why he thought a story had been bought or rejected, a man added to the staff or released from it, a decision made on subscription or advertising rates. Once he had told him about an encounter with a well-known midwestern author during the last years of the syndicate. Terrence had gone to see the man at a New York hotel, where he was staying while negotiating with his publisher, and suggested that he write a series of essays for which Terrence would pay him $150 apiece.

'He told me he regretted very much that I hadn't come to him just a few days sooner,' Terrence said, 'because only a day or so before he had been visited by Sam McClure and had agreed to write a monthly essay for him for two hundred dollars each. We talked awhile longer on other subjects. He was a man of great charm, and I was much taken with him. As I was about to leave, he said that if I could top McClure's price, he would try to get out of their agreement, that he would much rather do business with me because although he liked McClure, he found him irritating. Now, Terry, what would you have done? Even one hundred and fifty dollars was a stiff price for me to pay, but here was an author in great demand, pursued not only by McClure but by *Scribner's Magazine* and others.

What would you have said to him?'

Terry had known part of the answer. He had known that the first thing to say was that he would think it over. His father had taught him that unless absolutely necessary, it was never advisable to make an immediate decision even if at the moment the right decision seemed obvious.

'Good. You'd have told him you would think it over. That's exactly what I did,' Terrence had said. 'Then what?'

'Well, then if I didn't have the money, I'd have got hold of it somehow. Borrowed it if I had to. Since he was in such demand, it shouldn't have been too hard to get an advance from some of the newspapers you were going to sell his essays to.'

Before he finished speaking, Terry had seen from his father's face that he had not passed this test.

'I didn't try to find the money, Terry. I wouldn't have done business with him at any price. If he was ready to repudiate his agreement with McClure, what assurance did I have that he would honor an agreement with me? As a matter of fact, McClure kept on trusting him, and the author repeatedly promised him material that he either did not deliver at all or delivered to a higher bidder. Never, son, no matter how attractive it may seem, no matter how high the stakes, *never* do business with an unscrupulous man. In the end you will lose out.'

But this test – to account for the magazine's rise – was easy. Terry had listened and watched, overheard and seen. He had been saturated with ideas and arguments and projects and with the reasons why some had worked and some had not. He knew that his father's refusal to consider Jake's proposal that they raise the newsstand price of the magazine to fifteen cents had paid off in readers who were rejecting higher-priced magazines. He knew that one factor in the magazine's success was Jake's talent for thinking up colorful popular subjects to publish and that another was Terrence's decision to employ a regular staff of writers competent to deal with the subjects, rather than depend wholly on uncertain free-lance submissions. He had heard Jake warn his father against the large sums he spent to entice the best novelists and artists in the country, and he was aware that his father had not listened and that the resulting profits from soaring circulation and increased advertising had far outstripped the expenditures.

Terry recited all this to Terrence and glowed in his father's approval. 'Yes,' Terrence said. 'Yes, you've learned well. When the time comes, you'll fill my shoes in a way to make me proud.'

Terry did not repeat what he had once heard Fanny Clayborn say to Jake, who had commented that Terrence was a genius. She had said, 'No. He's a brilliant magazine man. *McNally's* is one of the best periodicals in the country. One day it may well be the best. But a genius orginates. He has ideas no one has ever thought of before. McNally simply imitates and improves on the original.'

Terry wondered whether he would, when he was grown up, have ideas no one had ever had before.

Fanny Clayborn was one of Jake's ideas. He had read a piece she had written for *St Nicholas,* a magazine for children, explaining the operation of the telephone in such simple terms that an eight-year-old would understand it. He suggested to Terrence that they ask her to come in for an interview, with the prospect of employing her as a staff writer of a monthly feature to be called 'How It Works'. Thousands of people, he said, must be as ignorant as he was and would like to understand such inventions as, for instance, the incandescent lamp or the wireless telegraph.

'She could even go to see some of the living inventors and liven up the articles with colorful interviews,' Jake said. 'That is, if she's capable.'

Terrence was reluctant. He did not think inventions were a woman's field. Besides, they had never had a woman on the staff. She would be out of her element among nobody but men. The men would feel constrained.

'That's all nonsense,' Jake said. 'Your notions about women are antiquated. At least have her here and talk to her. If you're not impressed, nothing will be lost.'

Terrence was so impressed that he seemed to forget it had been Jake's idea to interview her and began trying to convince him that Fanny Clayborn would make a fine staff writer.

She enchanted Terry. His contact with females was limited to his mother, Mrs Stern and her daughters, his teachers, and Mary. There were no girls in his school, and he was not part of the band of boys who knew how to find them elsewhere. Terrence, at fourteen, had been sexually experienced, but Terry had no access to any comfort other than his own hand. Fanny Clayborn dazzled him like chain lightning.

She was in her mid-twenties, a tall, big-breasted woman with pink cheeks, large, brilliant brown eyes, and masses of dark hair that kept escaping its pinned arrangement and falling down her neck and high forehead. Everything about her was quick – her movements, her mind, her tongue. She could digest quantities of research material in a short time and translate it into clear, simple prose almost as fast as her flying fingers could type the words. The moment she arrived at the magazine office for her first day's work, she was totally at home, calling everybody by name before the day ended, laughing and joking as if they had all been her friends for years.

'Are you called Mr McNally?' she asked Terry when she met him. 'Or is your first name better, so as not to get you muddled with your father?'

No one had ever before dreamed of calling him Mr McNally. 'I suppose Terry would be less confusing,' he said, with no notion that he sounded more pompous than adult.

He made excuses to stop at her desk, hoping she would have time to say a few words to him. Even when she did not, she always glanced up and gave him her bright, pleased smile, as though the sight of him delighted her.

One day he met her on Broadway, a few blocks from the office, as she was returning from an interview with a man who had invented a two-cycle engine for running a horseless carriage. Terry, rapturous at the opportunity to be with her alone for several minutes, walked back with her, the errand he had been sent on wiped clean from his mind.

'I'm going to ask you a question,' she said. 'If you think it's too impertinent, don't answer it, but it's something I've been wondering about you.'

Terry nodded, unable to speak. He was not just a boy she saw around the office and then forgot. She thought about him, wondered about him.

'Are you really all wrapped up in the magazine?' she asked him. 'Or are you in the office so much because your father insists on it?'

'Oh, no, he doesn't insist on it. He wouldn't do that. You see, he saw Uncle Jake's father make him become a lawyer and how unhappy Uncle Jake was until he could be an editor. Father would never do anything like that to me.'

'I'm glad to hear it,' Fanny said. 'Fathers can be tyrants, but I didn't think yours was that kind. He's certainly fair and reasonable to his staff.'

She was silent for a moment. Terry tried to think how he could shift the conservation from his father back to himself, but she was so close to him that her arm brushed his, and everything else slid out of his mind.

'He has a lot of confidence in you, hasn't he? Especially considering how young you are,' she said. 'You surely can't be more than seventeen.'

He could almost feel himself growing, bursting out of his clothing. But his father or Jake might tell her he was a long way from seventeen. All he could risk was to add on a few months and say he was fifteen. He had to be content with her astonishment.

'I'd never have believed it,' she said. 'You seem so mature. I think it's because you're so serious.' She turned

214

to glance at him as they walked along. Her eyes were about on a level with his. He had to look away from their brilliant brownness. 'What do you do for amusement, Terry? Are you good at games?'

'No, but Charles is. He can learn any game in no time and be better at it than older boys who have been playing for a long while.' Why was he talking about Charles? She didn't even know who Charles was. But he went on. 'Charles is my brother. My mother says that the way he was put together, he must have been meant as a model for some kind of new, special race of people.'

'He sounds very unusual,' Fanny said in an odd, stiff voice. 'Games have their place, of course, but things you do are tremendously interesting, aren't they? Meeting and talking to famous authors. How many boys ever have a chance to do that or would know how to conduct themselves if they did?' She laid her hand on Terry's sleeve. 'You're a remarkable person, Terry. I don't know your little brother, but I'm sure that in many important ways he can't hold a candle to you.'

Terry was not sure what she was talking about. When he thought back on their conversation later, he wondered if he had missed something, some phrase or sentence that would have given it a central point. But he did not dwell on this. She liked him. She had called him a remarkable person. Everyone agreed he was smart, but nobody else had ever told him he was remarkable. She had also said he was mature, meaning she did not think of him as a child, years younger than she was.

Where she had touched his sleeve he fancied he felt something that lingered on the arm beneath – a warmth, a pulsing. He had dreams, in daylight awareness as well in the sleeping night, of her breasts crushed against his chest, of a nakedness he knew only from pictures, a penetration he could only hazily imagine. When he came to himself, he was ashamed, embarrassed, appalled that she should have been the victim of such riotous imaginings. All he consciously wanted of her was to idolize her and to have

215

her recognize his secret self, so different from the one that others saw: so much finer, wiser, quicker, and more winning.

He was too big, now, and too restless to melt into corners and stay listening for whatever might be said, but he was still an inveterate eavesdropper. It did not occur to him that there was anything underhanded in being alert to learn in this way what he would not otherwise know. He had long forgotten that Sylvia had once called him a little sneak for doing it. His way of dealing with his mother was to retain her rare expressions of approval and bury the rest.

It took a little time for Fanny Clayborn to establish herself as just another member of the *McNally's Monthly* staff. Terry heard one of the men in the advertising department say that he did not think she was quite a lady. If the man had not been so old, almost as old as Terrence, and his father's employee, Terry thought he would have punched him in the nose.

'She's so free in her manner,' the man said. 'That hearty laugh and the way she looks straight into a person's eyes, with no semblance of modesty. I wonder if there's anything there – if you know what I mean.'

He was talking to a younger man. Terry, clipping articles from rival magazines in an adjoining office, laid his scissors down soundlessly. What the older man meant was clear to Terry from the tone, if not the words. Terry's balled fists ached.

The other man laughed. 'There isn't, believe me. Not for you or me anyhow.'

'Ah! For somebody else then? Who?'

'I don't know. No one. I'm just talking. What I mean to say is, you've got her wrong. She's one of the new women, that's all. These days ladies don't all sit quietly at home with downcast eyes.'

'Well, I think it was better when they did. At least that way a man could distinguish them from the others.'

Terry found a roundabout method of discussing this

216

with his father on the way home. They owned a carriage now that took Terrence to the office every morning and called for him at night. It was drawn by two horses and driven by a coachman who also served as houseman and butler. That evening Terrence drove home himself, as he often did, sending Thomas, the coachman, to sit on the box in the rear.

'Do you think women should have the vote?' Terry asked him.

'I'm not certain. At one time I'd have said that politics is not a woman's province, but I'm beginning to see capabilities in women that I didn't realize they had. I don't know why it's taken me so long. My mother, your grandmother, could have done anything, I think, if she'd had a little education. I remember asking her once, when I was a child, why she couldn't be a ward leader.' He flicked the whip over the rumps of the horses barely touching them, doing it for the grace and dash of the movement. 'Of course, it depends on the woman,' he went on. 'Some have no interest in politics, no knowledge of anything outside their families and their own private concerns.'

'Like Mother. She probably wouldn't care whether she could vote or not.'

'You must not criticize your mother, Terry.'

'I'm not criticizing her,' Terry said, and added a disclaimer that he knew would be, to his father, beyond argument, 'I'm just stating a fact.'

'Yes, well, you must remember that she was brought up, like most girls of her class, to think of nothing except preparing herself for a good marriage and presiding over a household and moving in society. She's an intelligent woman, but she often quotes her mother as saying that she was sent to Normal School not to develop her mind but to get over the four awkward years between adolescence and eligibility for marriage.'

Sylvia was not the subject Terry had meant to introduce, but now that they were on it, he was intrigued. They had never discussed his mother like this.

217

'Couldn't you teach her about other things? If she understood politics, maybe she would want the vote. Maybe she'd be interested in that, or in something else, and not be bored all the time, like she says she is.'

'I'm afraid it's too late, son. People don't learn easily once they're grown. They don't learn at any age if they're reluctant.' Terrence looked around at him and smiled. 'Would you really want a mother who stood on a stump, haranguing a crowd to give her the vote, or who ran for the presidency of the United States, like Victoria Woodhull?'

Since Victoria Woodhull had been not only an advocate of women's rights twenty-five years earlier but also an actress and a part-time prostitute, Terry considered this a flattering man-to-man reference. He laughed.

'I wouldn't want a woman like Miss Woodhull for my mother, or for President either,' he said, and, knowing that the subject of Sylvia was closed, deftly shifted gears. 'I think somebody like Miss Clayborn deserves the vote, though, don't you?'

'Yes, I do,' Terrence answered with no hesitation. 'But of course, she's an unusual person. A real woman, yet with a mind as quick and searching as a man's.'

'Is she a lady?'

Terrence frowned, 'That's a peculiar question. Why should you have any doubt?'

'I happened to hear somebody at the office say he wondered if she was.'

'Who? No, never mind. I don't want you to tattle. Of course she's a lady, Terry. Her father is a distinguished professor, head of his department at Columbia University. Miss Clayborn lives with her parents.' Terrence paused. 'That's nonsense. That's not what makes her a lady. What does is that she's kind and considerate and never says unpleasant things about other people behind their backs.'

Terry glowed. He could have no stronger validation of his enchantment with Fanny Clayborn than his father's obvious enthusiasm for her.

The coachman took charge of the carriage as soon as they got home. They had moved, finally, the year before, sold Miss Howard's house, which Sylvia had always hated, and built one of red brick and gray stone on Fifth Avenue and Fifty-fourth Street. It was smaller than most of the other houses in that area, not, Terry had heard his mother say several times, the mansion Terrence had promised her.

Nothing they had was as big or as much as Sylvia wanted. She had claimed they needed an eight-bedroom house and had to make do with six bedrooms. She had demanded a four-in-hand coach, with a coachman front and rear, in which to ride along Fifth Avenue and in Central Park in their finest clothes and be seen and recognized. To her mind, a carriage with two horses and one coachman did not at all serve the purpose.

'You were going to be successful,' she said to Terrence. 'You were going to give me anything in the world I wanted. Talk, talk. That's what you are, all talk.'

'I've been very successful, Sylvia, as even you must know, and I will be more so, but I'll never squander my money for your foolish extravagances. It happens to be to my advantage, in a business way, to appear prosperous – perhaps more prosperous than I am. Otherwise, I'd have been perfectly satisfied to stay in the old house and rent a carriage when necessary.'

'Oh, of course, *you'd* have been satisfied. You've never known anything better. What about me? What about your promises to me?'

'You'd be well advised to consider those canceled, Sylvia, and be grateful for what you get.'

Terry wished they had stayed in the old house. He did not like the new one. The rooms were crowded with furniture, and he was always in danger of stumbling into one of the innumerable little tables and bringing the bric-a-brac with which it was laden crashing to the floor. He had once, with an awkward sweep of his arm, dislodged a

219

large garlanded bisque cupid from one of the marble mantelpieces. Only a deft catch by Charles had saved it. But his mother's comment on his clumsiness was offset by a private whisper from his father: 'I wish the ridiculous thing had broken into smithereens.'

Terrence's den was the only room in the house that had escaped the elaborate ornamentation and clutter that Sylvia had copied from the fashionable homes of the immensely wealthy. Once the furniture was installed, Terrence had forbidden her to add any decoration without his express approval. Layers of curtains, obscuring the light, had been hung before this edict. He had ordered all but one layer taken down.

'I've given you a free hand in the rest of the house,' he had said, 'but here in my private domain I don't intend to live in the dark like a mole or to be smothered by *things*.'

Sylvia had told him he had no eye for beauty. If that was so, Terry had none either. He thought the heavily draped rooms were gloomy. He did not see the sense of displaying on special shelves such silly objects as a vase in the shape of a hand, a porcelain shoe with spats, or two ceramic children sitting in a ceramic basket. He had his own room now, instead of sharing a room with Charles, but he did not feel at home in it. The fringed pink seat cover on the straight chair, the pale blue upholstery on the rocker, the lace-edged bedcover and curtains, and the elaborately carved bed and bureau – all seemed to him more suitable for a girl than for a nearly fifteen-year-old boy.

Charles's room was even fussier, but he was too young to care. What Charles minded was his separation from Terry. He came into Terry's room on any pretext and often, claiming to be frightened by one thing or another, crawled into his brother's bed at night.

'You're getting too big to be scared,' Terry told him. 'A big athlete like you.'

'I'm not so big. I'm only ten years old. Anyway, I get lonesome in there. I like it here with you.'

Terry considered it suitable to pretend displeasure, but he was glad when Charles came. He was used to his company, even though their conversation was limited by the difference in their ages. Besides, he enjoyed the role of protector and comforter. No one else ever came to him for help.

'Why do they fight so much?' Charles asked, a question that recurred at intervals. 'Don't they love each other anymore?'

'Of course they do. Married people always argue, no matter how much they love each other,' Terry answered, though he did not know whether or not this was so. 'There's nothing to worry about.'

'What if he hurts her?'

'Father wouldn't hurt anybody. He just makes a lot of noise, that's all. Did he ever hurt you?'

'No,' Charles lay on half of Terry's pillow with his hands under his head. 'He doesn't notice me so much.'

'That's because you're young. When you're older, he will. Anyway, he has to pay more attention to me because I'm going to be on the magazine.'

'Why can't I be on the magazine?'

'You know why. What are you asking me for? You know you're musical. What good would that be on the magazine?'

Charles turned around and patted Terry's cheek. 'Don't be angry, Terry. I won't be on the magazine. I'll tell you a secret if you stop being angry.' He lowered his voice to a whisper. 'Madame Violet says I'm not musical. She says I'll never be a good violin player. She wants me to tell Mother because she's afraid to, but *I'm* afraid, to, too. But don't worry, I won't go on the magazine.' He turned onto his back again. 'I might be an actor. I was in a play at school today called *A Midsummer Night's Dream*. I was a merry elf named Puck, and Miss Gordon said I was as good as a real actor.'

'I don't think Mother will let you be an actor,' Terry said.

'Yes, she will,' Charles said. 'If I'm a very good one, she will.'

'All right. You'd better go back to your own room now,' Terry suggested a moment later. But Charles, in that moment, had fallen asleep, or pretended he had. Terry, with some half-formed notion of making amends for not wanting to share the magazine with him, let him stay. Allowing him more than half of the bed besides, Terry moved as far over as he could, closed his eyes, and thought about Fanny Clayborn.

The following Saturday he heard her mention his name to Jake. She was in Jake's office with the door closed, but the transom was slightly open. Terry stopped and listened. If anyone came by, he would knock on the door as if he had just arrived there. Over the years he had perfected a number of such strategies. He had even, on some trumped-up errand, gone into a room where he suspected something interesting was being said behind closed doors and left the door slightly open on his way out, so he could hear. He never used anything he learned this way except to enlarge his own knowledge. It did not cross his mind that it could serve any other purpose.

'What kind of woman is she to make a remark like that in Terry's hearing?' Fanny was saying. 'Making it plain she thinks the little brother's some special being and he's just ordinary! How could any mother be so insensitive? It's a wonder Terry doesn't hate the boy.'

'Charles is a hard boy to hate. Anyhow, Terry's all right, Miss Clayborn. He's Terrence's favourite, and he knows it.'

'If you think he's all right, Mr Stern, I beg your pardon, but you're not very sensitive either. He's not all right. He doesn't play or have any fun. He has no life of his own. He's a boy pretending to have a man's interests because that way he can feel closer to his father. He's so hungry for affection that a smile sends him into transports. He's—'

'Well, if it's your smile, Miss Clayborn, I don't think it

222

requires any special hunger to be transported.'

'Please. I'm serious. Terry's a fine boy, and I'm very fond of him. It worries me that nobody else seems to see what's happening to him.'

'It's wonderful of you to be so concerned about him. You're a very tenderhearted woman, aren't you? But I think you may be exaggerating Terry's difficulties. The fact is, he's surrounded with affection. Aside from his father, his little brother worships him; he's like another grandson and nephew in my family; even the McNallys' cook adores him. It may be true that he doesn't spend enough time just having fun. That's something I haven't thought about, but I can't believe it's as critical as you seem to believe.'

'His father should have thought about it. He's the one who uses all of Terry's free time for the magazine.'

'Miss Clayborn, you have to understand that Terry's father doesn't know anything about free time. He never had any from the time he was ten years old. The kind of fun and play you're talking about is something he never experienced. His first real fun was editing a college magazine. His fun now is editing *McNally's Monthly*. Why wouldn't he think this was the best kind of fun he could give his son?'

'I see. Yes. That would explain it. Mr McNally seems such a considerate man in other ways that I did wonder how he could—' Fanny broke off. There was a silence before she went on again. 'If you pointed it out to him, then, in some tactful way, he'd surely be glad to know.'

'I wouldn't have any idea how to go about being tactful with Terrence. We've known each other too long. You'd better talk to him yourself, Miss Clayborn.'

'I? Pry into my employer's personal affairs? How could I? He'd tell me it was none of my business, and he'd certainly be right.'

Jake chuckled. 'But you are prying into his personal affairs. With the kindest of motives, I know, but you're doing it. So you might as well go ahead with it. You'll be

223

much better than I at finding a tactful way to approach the subject.'

'No. I won't be. I'm not tactful. I just plow ahead and say what I think. He'll probably throw me out before I'm halfway through.'

Terry left. He was not sure whether he had heard someone coming or pretended to himself that he had. In any case, he did not want to listen anymore. He felt too unsettled. Enraptured by Fanny Clayborn's interest in him, but apprehensive, threatened by something he could not name, and dizzy from the whirl of words in his ears. When later that day he saw Fanny go into Terrence's office, he made no attempt to eavesdrop.

4

Nothing happened as a result of what Terry had overheard between Fanny Clayborn and Jake. He did not know what he had expected to happen, but was relieved when everything went on the same as before, except that Fanny Clayborn went into his father's office much more often than usual and stayed there much longer. Terry thought it might be because of him. If she had told his father what she had told Jake about him, maybe his father hadn't believed it. Maybe she kept going in there to try to persuade him. Terry could have listened, but he didn't. In a way he wanted to know, but in more of a way he didn't.

It was a few weeks later that something finally did happen, and by then Terry had almost forgotten about it.

He and his father and Charles went to the Sterns' for Sunday dinner for the first time in more than a month. Terrence asked Sylvia to go along, as he always did, and as usual, she refused. Sometimes she complained about being left alone while they all went off to see 'those Jews'. When Terrence reminded her that she was free to come with them, she said he knew how she felt about the matter

224

and that by going without her, he was encouraging her children to disregard her feelings.

That day, though, Sylvia was in a fine, gay humor, smiling and hugging Terry as well as Charles, kissing Terrence good-bye, and telling them all to have a good time. Whenever this happened, Terry thought maybe everything had changed, and she would go on in the same agreeable way. But the mood never lasted. As a small boy he had been afraid it was his fault when she relapsed into captiousness and discontent. He knew now that it was not, yet he often felt guilty just the same.

Mrs Stern kissed Terrence and did her best to hug both boys at once. Her plumpness had expanded and softened with the years. To be in her arms, against her breast, was like sinking into mounds of pillows. The fullness of her still almost unlined face diminished the size of her nose, so that she was prettier now than she had been when she was young.

'You shoot up from month to month. Terry, you're almost as tall as your father. Come in, come in,' she said, sweeping them along with an arm around each of them. 'Only Aunt Bertha will be here today, with Sam and Emily. And Uncle Jake, of course. The others are all busy somewhere else. It seems to me everyone is busier now than they used to be. Do you feel that, Terrence? That the pace of life is speeding up? Or is it just my age?'

At this point they had arrived in the drawing room, where Jake rose from the overstuffed chair that had been his father's.

'That's no question to ask Terrence, Mama,' he said. 'His pace is twice as fast as anyone else's to begin with. If it were speeded up, he'd fly off the face of the earth.'

'Pay no attention to him, Mama Stern. He likes to make me out a freak,' Terrence said. 'I *do* feel what you're talking about. I think there is a heightening of activity, of excitement, a promise of amazing things to come.' He walked to the window and looked out, as if expecting to see the amazing things lined up outside the house, and

225

then came back and took Mrs Stern's hands. 'Soon we'll be in a new century. That's a stirring fact in itself. Think of all the wonders this century has produced. Now we have a whole new one ahead of us. Who knows what unguessed-at marvels the twentieth century has in store!'

Mrs Stern laughed. 'I was deploring the change. You, typically, think it will be better. Everything, always, better and better. Terrence, I love you.'

'And I you, madam,' Terrence said with a low bow. 'And I you.'

Terry was delighted when his father was like this, so alive and full of humor. The Sterns made him happy. They made Terry happy, too. He could count on things here. When Papa Stern died, Terry had been not only sad but afraid his death would mean changes. But except for Papa Stern's absence, nothing was very different. Mama Stern and Uncle Jake still lived together in the same house, with the same furniture. Sunday dinner was still a family occasion, even if not everyone in the family was there every time. Mama Stern still cooked the meal herself, and the menu never varied, except that the vegetable that went with the roast chicken and mashed potatoes changed with the season and that the pie was apple in the fall, lemon in the winter, rhubarb in the spring, and blueberry in the summer.

After dinner Charles went off to play with Emily, not minding that she was a year younger than he was and a girl. Sam usually disappeared as soon as the meal was over, whether into another room or out of the house, Terry had no idea. They were the same age, but they had never found any meeting ground. It was so usual for Terry to have nothing in common with other boys that he scarcely thought about it. He was content to sit with the adults and listen to their conversation or, if he did not understand what they were saying or lost interest in it, read a book or daydream. Only here was he free from the nagging restlessness.

This Sunday, though, Sam did not leave when everyone

got up from the table but followed the others into the drawing room. He did not sit down but stood leaning against the wall with his hands in his pockets, observing Terry. Whenever Terry caught him at it, his gaze moved lazily to his uncle and Terrence, who were continuing a lively argument about the new President, William McKinley.

He was a short, dark boy, with black hair that grew low on his forehead and thick black eyebrows that would, in manhood, be shaggy. In repose, his expression was somber, but when he spoke or smiled, his near scowl smoothed out, and he looked more his age, lively and even roguish. His father, Saul Bernbach, who had been close to forty when Bertha married him, was now in his middle fifties, and Sam had the unyouthful manner of the child of an older parent.

Terry pretended to read the book he had brought with him, *The Master of Ballantrae*, by Robert Louis Stevenson. The fact that his father had met the author added a fillip of pleasure to the novel. But he was too conscious of Sam's stare to concentrate on what he was reading. Something was in the air. Soon his peripheral vision picked up Bertha's raised-eyebrow glance at her son and Sam's shrug, and he knew, before Sam spoke to him, exactly what it was.

'Do you want to go out someplace, Terry?'

Terry could shrug as well as the next one. 'I don't know. Not especially.'

'Go on, son. Go along with Sam.' Terrence said in a fake-hearty voice. 'It's a nice day. No sense in you boys hanging around inside with us all afternoon.'

Terry did not want to go. Sam certainly did not want him. He did not think his father would really care if he stayed. The only one he knew would be pleased if he went was Fanny Clayborn, who thought he was a fine boy who did not have any fun. She would think going out with Sam would be fun.

'Where are we going?' he asked Sam when they were in

the street.

'No place in particular, unless you have some ideas.' Terry shook his head. 'Well, let's walk to Broadway.'

They walked in silence. Terry saw no reason to search for topics of conversation. He would put in the time, go where he was led, and let his father know afterward that it had not been fun. Somehow let Fanny Clayborn know, too. That he had tried it, but that it really was the magazine he enjoyed most.

Sam had a funny way of walking, with his head hunched up between his shoulders. It made him look older than he was. He looked older anyway, older than Terry, though he was a head shorter. He had a dark stubble on his face, and when he took off his jacket in the warm late May sun and rolled up his shirt sleeves, a mat of thick black hair showed on his arms.

'Why don't you take yours off, too?' he said. 'Go on. Nobody we know is going to see us.'

Terry was perspiring under the heavy woolen jacket, but he hesitated. He thought of Sylvia. She would say only a Jew or an Irishman would appear in public without his jacket, not a gentleman.

'Go on,' Sam said. 'Don't be a ninny.'

Why should he care about being a gentleman anyway? 'That's better,' he said, and hung the jacket on one shoulder so he could roll up the sleeves of his shirt as Sam had done. He regretted that the hair on his arms were barely visible, a red-gold down that glinted in the sun, but there was nothing to be done about that. 'It's too hot for a jacket.'

Sam patted him on the shoulder as if he had passed a test. 'Listen, whatever we see or do or talk about this afternoon is between you and me, all right? As far as anybody else is concerned, we took a walk and looked in shopwindows and – I don't know – raced each other around the block, anything. All right?'

'Yes, all right.' Without warning, Sam's nervous secretiveness made Terry giggle. 'What are we going to

228

do, though? Murder somebody?'

Sam grinned and patted him on the back again. 'Not this afternoon. Maybe some other time.' He swung his jacket with one hand, almost wiping the street with it, and then folded it carefully across his arm. 'Have you ever had a girl?'

Terry felt that he had somehow made himself acceptable to Sam, that Sam was beginning to like him, and that the wrong answer to this question could set everything back again.

'It depends,' he said, 'on what you mean.'

Sam curled the fingers of his left hand against his palm to form a hollow cylinder. With a little smile and a sidewise glance at Terry, he thrust his right forefinger into the hollow.

They had turned onto Broadway now. They could have been on the moon for all Terry knew. The prickling of his skin and the moisture that sprang out on his face had nothing to do with the weather, but he made a great show of feeling the heat, running a finger under his stiff collar and mopping himself with his handkerchief. Sam, going along in his hunched-up way, did not seem to be watching him, but Terry felt that he was, nonetheless. Watching and waiting.

Terry gave a final 'Whew!' and stuffed the handkerchief back in his pocket. 'Well, no, I haven't had a girl yet,' he said, having decided against claiming an experience for which he might have to give details beyond his ability to improvise. 'But there's somebody I've been seeing. She likes me. So it's going to happen soon. I just have to convince her. You know how it is.'

'Sure. I know.' Sam looked up at him and winked. One man of the world to another. 'What's she like? Is she in your school or what?'

Terry, carried away by this unaccustomed camaraderie, said, 'Oh, no, she's an older woman. I met her at the – in the – well, you know I work on the magazine, and sometimes when I go with Father when he interviews

229

authors and everything, I meet a lot of people.'

'An older woman. You can learn a lot from an older woman.' Terry was enthralled by the awe Sam could not altogether conceal. 'Is she an author?'

'Well, I wouldn't call her exactly an author. I mean, she isn't anybody you'd know about from reading her novels or stories or anything, but she is a writer.' Terry cleared his throat. 'I guess I'd better not tell you any more about her. I mean, I have to protect her reputation.'

'Yes, sure. Of course.' Sam began swinging his jacket again, scowling down the street. It did not seem possible that he could see where he was going, but abruptly he stopped. 'Here,' he said. 'Have you seen this?'

Terry looked around him. They had arrived at Herald Square on Thirty-fourth Street. Ahead of them was the marble arcaded New York Herald Building, the clock on its façade reading twenty past three. Farther on, lettering on the side of the Hotel Normandie assured the public that the hotel was 'Absolutely Fireproof'. On the left a sign as high as the four-story building to which it was affixed spelled out 'JIM CORBETTS,' in huge letters outlined with light bulbs. The cobbled streets were quiet, except for the trolley cars on Broadway and the trains on the Sixth Avenue el, which crossed Broadway at the square. One empty delivery cart was drawn up at the curb, the horse standing patiently between the shafts. Few people passed by. It was not a section for fashionable strolling, and the shops were all closed.

'Have I seen what?' Terry asked.

'Right in front of you.'

Terrence had been to Herald Square before. He had been inside the Herald Building with his father, met the editor, Mr Bennett, whom his father knew from the syndicate days, and seen the printing presses with which the building was crowded. But he had not noticed this building or the posters that adorned it, and his father had not called them to his attention.

The place was called Koster and Bial's Music Hall.

Among the attractions featured on the posters were three buxom, bejeweled girls in tights, with gaily colored plumes in their hair and purple, green, or red stockings, which were fastened above the knee with bright silk garters. An expanse of well-rounded flesh showed between the stockings and the tights. The bosoms of all three beauties were so ample that they seemed about to burst out of their inadequate confinement.

'Golly!' Terry said, instantly restoring Sam's good humor and approval.

Sam poked Terry in the ribs. 'You wouldn't have to protect *their* reputations.'

'I guess not. Of course, we wouldn't have a chance with them. Those are the girls rich whatdyecallems – ne'er-do-wells – go after, and they buy them whatever they want to get their – uh – favors.'

'Of course,' Sam agreed, to Terry's relief. 'We can see them, though, if you want. We can see them in the flesh. And not just them. There's dancers and gymnasts and a lot of other things. Look at that.'

He was pointing to another poster. 'THE VITASCOPE,' it said in large black letters. 'Thomas A. Edison's latest marvel. Presenting selections from the following: "Burlesque," "Boxing," "Umbrella Dancer," "The Bar Room," "Kaiser Wilhelm Reviewing his Troops," "Butterfly Dance," "Venice, Showing Gondolas," *and more.*'

Terry had never been to any kind of public entertainment. Once in a while, to mark some occasion, his parents went to the theatre or to a restaurant for dinner. It had never occurred to them to take Terry, nor had he had any thought that they should. Since he was sure his father did not care for such things and went only to please his mother, he took it for granted that he would not care for them either. Yet now, with all these advertised delicacies spread before him, he was overcome with longing to experience in actuality what he saw in print and picture.

'We can't,' he said despairingly. 'It's closed today.'

'I didn't mean today, you ninny. We'll come tomorrow

night. Listen—' Sam gripped his arm. 'Have you got any money?'

'I've got a little. Most of it's in the bank.'

'Well, you can get it out, can't you?'

Terry had never thought of getting it out. His father paid him for working at the magazine, instead of giving him an allowance, and every week Terry put half his pay into the savings bank. He did this not so much to accumulate the money as to indicate to his father that he was not a spender like his mother or like Charles, who spent most of his small allowance on the sweets he loved and the rest on treats for his friends and Terry. Once the money was in the bank, Terry did not think about it. With the half he kept out of the salary Terrence gave him weekly, he paid his minor personal expenses, such as fares or an occasional ice cream soda or sarsaparilla. The excess he put away in a coin bank to use for Christmas and birthday presents for his parents and Charles and the servants. This bank held ten dollars and supposedly could not be opened until it was filled, but since Terry spent much less than ten dollars on the individual presents, he had figured out how to get it open when each occasion arrived. He had never opened it otherwise.

'I don't know,' he said now, cautiously. 'I might be able to get some out. Why?'

Sam still had hold of his arm. He moved so close that Terry could feel his breath. He lowered his voice, though no one was anywhere near them.

'We could see this show. When it's over, we could go to Sixth Avenue and get some girls – women. Did you ever hear of the French Madam's? Some of the fellows at school go there for women. We'd say we were older. Even if they don't believe us, they won't care, as long as we have money—'

'What is it? Is it a' – in spite of himself, the word emerged in a dubious hush – 'a brothel?'

But Sam was too wrought up to notice. 'Well, sure. That's the safest. If you get one in the street, she might have a disease or rob you of your money.'

Terry glanced at the fleshy beauties on the poster, and away again. He wanted to forget the whole thing, get out of it, go home and pretend he had never seen the posters, never heard what Sam had proposed. At the same time he burned to see more, to know more. He did not believe he could go through with it – the show, maybe, but certainly not the rest – yet he wished he could. His whole ordinary self seemed on the verge of shedding itself from him, like dead skin.

'I don't know,' he said again. 'How much money would we need?'

'We'd better take plenty. We don't want to get to the French Madam's and find out we don't have enough. We'd better take twenty-five dollars. You've got that much, haven't you?'

Terry, who had been looking everywhere but at Sam, looked at him now. 'What about you? If we did it – and I'm not saying we will – what about your share?'

'My share?' Sam pushed away from him, scowling. 'Listen, it's all my idea, isn't it? You wouldn't have thought of any of it.' He shrugged. 'So I'll put in five dollars, that's fair enough.'

'No, it isn't fair. It doesn't matter whose idea it was. That has nothing to do with it. You have to pay half.' Terry stood with his hands in his pockets, comfortably aware that control had passed from Sam to himself. 'If you don't, I'm not going.'

Sam shifted his feet. His scowl deepened. 'I don't think I can get it. All my father gives me is a dollar a week. He thinks if I have more I'll get in trouble. Sometimes he'll give me a little extra if I ask for it, but I have to tell him what I want it for, and he has to approve.' Sam looked up at Terry and gave a brief grin. 'You can bet he wouldn't approve this. He probably doesn't even know there *are* places like the French Madam's.'

'Well, then, I guess we'll have to give it up,' Terry said with both relief and disappointment. 'I don't know, anyway, how I could get even half the money. The bank would be closed by the time I get out of school. I have about eight dollars besides, but I don't think I'd want to use that. I put it away for something else.'

'No listen, Terry, let's not give it up.' Sam grabbed his arm again. 'I'll get my half some way. You can get it, too. You can leave school before the bank closes, say you're sick. We'll do it Tuesday, not tomorrow, to give us more time. I'll meet you here Tuesday night at eight o'clock.'

'I don't know. I'll have to see,' Terry said. 'If I'm not here by ten after eight, you'll know I'm not coming.'

5

Terry was never sure afterward whether, if it had not been for the telephone call, he would have gone anyway. That Sunday night, when he had left Sam and was home alone in his room, he had certainly not intended to go. The idea that he had even contemplated invading his savings account and breaking open his coin bank for the purpose filled him with guilt. Of course, if he had had the money in hand, he would have liked to see the show, especially the Vitascope moving pictures, but he must have been out of his head even to think of going to that place later. He would not know how to act, what to do. They would laugh at him, a boy his age trying to fool around with grown women. He thought of what he had told Sam about an older woman, suggesting that he was on the point of an affair with one, not mentioning Fanny Clayborn, but with her in mind. How could he have demeaned her that way, even in make-believe? How could he have considered soiling what he felt for her by having anything to do with some low woman at the French Madam's?

Yet when he finally fell asleep, his dreams enthusiastically embraced everything that, awake, he had repudiated. In the morning his sheet was damp and sticky, and he felt unrefreshed. By evening he had begun to wonder whether he might not be better off trying to find out what all of it was really like, instead of dreaming it.

The telephone call came while he was in his room, doing his homework. Automatically he slipped out into the hall, closing his door behind him. He heard Thomas, the houseman, answer in the hall below and then go into the library. A moment later his father came to the telephone. Terry moved out of sight to listen.

'Hello, Miss Clayborn,' his father said in his loudest voice. 'Yes, I understand . . . yes, you were right to call me at home in this case—' He stepped back a little from the wall where the telephone hung, looked up into the darkness where Terry stood hidden, and then spoke again, much more softly, so that Terry had to strain to hear. 'I'm disappointed, too, of course . . . Yes, tomorrow night then, but . . . it's hard to wait . . . Goodnight to you, Fanny. Get a good rest—'

There was another word at the end, a whispered word that Terry could barely hear. He was not absolutely sure he did hear it, but he did not have to be absolutely sure. He heard his father's tone, the lowered voice that could have reached no one in the house except Terry.

He went back into his room and lay down on the bed. He began to shake and could not stop. He stayed there without finishing his homework or getting undressed. When he fell asleep, or how long he slept, he had no idea. He did not know that he had cried until he felt the moisture on his pillow and on his cheeks. If he had been asked what the tears were for, he could not have said.

He was still lying there, dressed, in the morning, when Charles came in. 'What's the matter?' Charles came over to the bed and stared down at him. 'Are you sick?'

'How many times have I told you to knock before you come busting in here? Get out!'

The viciousness in his voice surprised himself. Charles's eyes grew large and his chin quivered. He turned and started to run out of the room, but Terry caught hold of

235

his jacket.

'I didn't mean to yell at you, Charley. I've got a headache, that's all, and it makes me cranky.'

Charles came back to the bed. 'Are you going to school?'

'No, I don't think so,' Terry said, though he had not thought of it until that moment.

'Should I bring you a cold compress, like Mother gets for a headache?'

'No. Just go on down to breakfast. Tell them—' He turned over on his side, his back to Charles. 'Tell them I'm going to sleep and not to bother me.'

Terry waited. When he heard his mother coming upstairs, he closed his eyes and breathed deeply. She tiptoed into the room, felt his forehead with the back of her hand, and tiptoed out again. As soon as he heard his father leave, he got up and took the coin bank out of the bottom drawer of his bureau. He opened it by inserting the point of a letter opener under one edge of the metal piece that enclosed the bottom and prying it loose. Without counting the money, he spilled it all out and stuffed the coins in his pockets.

He had planned to tell his mother that he felt a little better and thought the air would do him good, but by the time he got downstairs she had gone out. He told Mary instead. He said he didn't know when he would be back; he might even go to school later if his headache went away.

At the bank he changed his coins into bills. Then he went to another teller, choosing one who did not know him, and drew out all the money from his savings account. When he counted everything together, it came to $19.50.

Sam arrived at the theatre a moment after Terry. He came running along, not hunched up at all, waving and grinning.

'I got the money! Eleven dollars!' he said breathlessly. 'What about you?'

236

'You're supposed to have twelve fifty,' Terry said.

'Oh, don't be a ninny! This is all I could get. If it isn't enough, you can lend me some of yours, can't you?'

'I don't know. How would you pay me back?'

'I'll get it the way I got this. From Grandma. I told her it was for a present for Mama.' He snickered. 'It was easy. I don't know why I never thought of it before.'

'What are you going to say when she asks you where the present is?'

'Oh, I don't know. I'll say I was robbed before I could buy it, or something.' He put his arm around Terry's shoulders, stretching up to reach them. 'Come on. What are we standing here talking for? The show's going to start in a few minutes.'

The price of the seats was twenty-five cents – hardly a dent in Terry's money. He had a fortune in his pockets, and he did not know how he was going to do it, but he intended to spend it all. In some obscure way he felt this to be an appropriate vengeance. This, and the entire evening ahead of him.

He strode in grimly with Sam, scarcely thinking of where he was, scarcely thinking at all. His whole body seemed sore, exposed, as though a layer of skin were missing, but there were no words in his mind for what he felt or why.

'What do you think of this?' Sam said, making a grand gesture with his arm, as if he had produced the hall they had entered and everything in it. 'Isn't it dandy?'

They were seated at a table on one side of the hall. The better seats, occupied by well-dressed ladies and gentlemen, were at tables in the center, near the stage. Below the stage a violinist and a pianist were tuning up. They struck a chord, and a young woman glided out and began to sing against a backdrop representing a woodland glade. She was all in white: plumed hat, long dress, stockings, high-heeled buckled shoes. As she sang, she swept her full skirt aside with a flick of her hips, revealing an entire length of leg, and pointed one toe toward the audience. She was slender, almost fragile, but her voice filled the room.

'Isn't she fine?' Sam said. 'Now just wait till the ones we saw outside come on!'

Terry was not listening. He was trying to look everywhere at once, hear everything at once. The large, crowded room; the laughing, chattering people; the violinist's sweeping bow, the pianist's flashing fingers, and their music, much louder and clearer than any music he had ever heard on the talking machine; the painted scenery with its real-looking trees; and the singer, who sometimes turned her head and sang to him, smiled right at him.

Five acts followed: a Russian clown; a woman billed as an 'eccentric dancer', whose gyrations required righteous gasps from the ladies in the audience; the buxom tights-clad trio on the posters outside, in an act entitled 'Satanic Gambols', performed in suggestive pantomime; two gymnasts; a song and dance number by 'Mons and Mme Delarue, naughty French duettists'; and a comedy called 'London Life'.

Then the lights went out. Terry could see nothing but the blank whiteness of a twenty-square-foot screen above the stage. Suddenly flickering, life-sized figures appeared on the screen. A woman danced; two men burlesqued a boxing match; a blurry gondolier poled his exotic boat along a quivering canal . . .

When it was over, Terry followed Sam outside with no recollection of having risen from the table. People streamed around him, Sam prattled in his ear, but he was on a different planet, living another life.

'Listen, what's the matter with you? Are you walking in your sleep or what?' Sam grinned and punched Terry's arm. 'Come on.' He lowered his voice and spoke through barely opened lips. 'The women are waiting for us.'

Terry came jolting back to Thirty-fourth Street and Herald Square. No longer anesthetized, he glared, angry and wounded, at the world he had left when he entered the music hall. They crossed to Sixth Avenue, an area lined with sleazy hotels and lodging houses, gambling halls, dance halls, and houses of prostitution that catered to every class of clientele, and paid up to six thousand dollars a year for police protection.

'We've got to look for the lamps,' Sam said. 'The French Madam's has two electric lamps on the stoop.' All at once he sounded subdued. 'I think I see it.'

Terry saw it, too. It was not one house, but two adjoining houses, the lamps, one on the outer edge of each stoop, uniting them. The French Madam's. A brothel. A place with low women inside, prostitutes, waiting, expecting him to know exactly what to do.

If Sam had not been there, he would have turned and run.

'We may not have enough money,' Sam said. 'I mean, we've got to pretend we're about eighteen, and they'll think that's a joke unless we have plenty to pay them.'

'You sound as if you're getting cold feet.'

'Don't be a ninny! I'm just preparing you in case they won't let us in. Come on.'

The French Madam herself opened the door to them. She did not appear to be French. Her name was Mrs Hermann. Terry thought she looked like anybody else, like any older woman he might see on the trolley car, except she was more dressed up and her cheeks and lips were rouged. She smiled at them and called them dear and asked them if they each had five dollars.

That was all there was to it. The next thing Terry knew, he was alone in a small room with a girl not much older than he. Nothing was in the room but a straight chair, a washstand, and a brass bed. The girl sat on the bed. She had on a pink silk negligee, edged all around with white feathers. Her cheeks and lips were rouged more than Mrs Hermann's, and her bright yellow hair hung down to her shoulders. She smiled at Terry, showing large, crooked, but reasonably white teeth.

'Why don't you come over here?' she said in a low, timbreless voice.

Terry stood in the middle of the room, his hands clenched in his pockets. He looked in the direction of her ear and hoped he would seem to be looking at her. She was obviously naked under the negligee. He knew that should arouse him, but instead, he thought he could feel his penis shrinking, disappearing.

'I won't bite, you know. Unless you want me to.' She gave a shrill little giggle, patted the bed next to her. 'Sit down here, why don't you?'

He sat stiffly beside her. He cleared his throat. 'This is a nice room,' he said.

She giggled again. She leaned forward and looked up into his face. 'It's your first time, isn't it?'

'Of course, it isn't,' he said, and then blew out a chestful of breath and said, 'Yes, it is. I don't – I think I'd better just go.'

He started to get up, but she pulled him down. 'You don't have to go. You don't have to worry. I'll show you. Wait and see. You'll like it.' She took hold of his hand and placed it under the pink silk, between her legs. 'See? Isn't that nice? Now I'll do you.'

He felt warm skin and a cushion of thick, springy hair against his palm. Under his fingers it was warmer still, fleshier and moist. She unbuttoned his trousers and began softly stroking him, and he blossomed in her hand.

'My, you're big!' she whispered. 'You might even hurt me a little, big as you are.'

He did not know whether she undressed him or he did it himself, but he was naked, and she was naked under him, and she did not have to show him what to do or how to do it because his body found the way by itself. She was saying words in his ear, dirty words, like a chant, but he was intent on the wave that rose inside him, filling him, bursting out of him, finally, into her warm receptacle. He lay with his hot, wet face buried in her hair, gasping for breath, exultant.

'All right,' she said. 'Get off me now. I've got to wash.'

Sam was waiting for him out in the street, slouched

against a lamppost. When he saw Terry, he straightened up and went to meet him, staring up into his face.

'Well,' he said, 'how was it?'

Terry smacked his lips and rolled his eyes in a way he knew to be vulgar. 'How was it for you?'

'Oh, fine,' Sam said. 'Dandy.' He started walking, his head hunched between his shoulders. 'Jim-dandy.'

Terry went along beside him. Sam had little to say. If it had really been fine and dandy, Terry was sure Sam would have talked about it. Probably it had been no good at all. Probably, for all his man-of-the-world manner, Sam had not known how to do it.

Just before they separated, Terry gave him five dollars. 'Now you've got what you started with, so you won't have to make up any story for your grandma.' Sam protested a little, but Terry stuck the bill in his jacket pocket. 'I don't need it,' Terry said. 'I've got a lot more.'

'Well, thanks.' Sam grinned for the first time since they had left the French Madam's. 'You saved my life. I didn't ask for the money. I took it. Now I can put it right back, and she'll never know the difference.'

'You mean you *stole* the money? From your *grand-mother*?'

'Oh, don't be such a ninny! I didn't steal it. I borrowed it. I'd have put it back sooner or later,' he said airily, and then was silent for a minute. 'Listen, you know Sunday when I asked you if you wanted to come out for a walk? Mama made me. It wasn't my idea. I always thought you were a ninny. Well, you're not.' He patted Terry's shoulder. 'I'm glad Mama made me ask you.'

As Terry began trudging up Fifth Avenue toward home, his satisfaction with the evening and himself began to drain away. He had not been home since morning. He had telephoned and told Thomas he would not be there for supper, but he had given no reason. It was the first time he had ever stayed away alone and of his own accord. He did not want to go back now, but he was tired and hungry, and he seemed to have no other choice. In books

241

boys his age left home and made their own way, but he did not know of any in real life who had done it. Of course, his father, at his age – but he did not want to think about his father.

He let himself into the dark hall and tiptoed toward the kitchen stairs at the back of the house. No one would hear him in the kitchen. It was below street level, far from the family's bedrooms on the second floor, farther still from the servants' quarters under the roof. If Mary noticed anything missing from the icebox in the morning, she would not say anything. Terry and Charles both often sneaked downstairs for a sandwich or a slice of cake after everyone was in bed, and she never gave them away. She was pleased that they liked her cooking that much.

Once on the back stairs Terry no longer tried to be quiet. By the time he saw the streak of light under the closed kitchen door it was too late to escape. The door opened, and his father stood in the entrance.

'Ah, Terry!' he said. 'You're just in time to join me in a ham sandwich. Come along. I'll slice some more ham.'

Terry followed his father into the kitchen without thinking, because that was what he would have done at any other time. Once there, the sight and smell of the glazed pink meat held him riveted. He loved ham, and he had eaten nothing since breakfast but a bag of peanuts, which he had consumed while distractedly roaming the streets until time to meet Sam.

'Sit down,' his father said. 'I'm making tea. Do you want a cup?'

'No, thank you.'

Terry would have liked a cup of tea, but he was not going to accept everything. He could do without the tea. He sat down on a white chair at the white enameled-top table. His father finished slicing the ham and went to the stove for the teakettle. He was in his business clothes, but he had taken off his dark jacket and draped it over the back of a chair and had laid his hard collar and black tie carefully on the seat.

242

When they both were settled with their sandwiches, he said, 'I'm told you didn't come home for supper. Why was that?'

'I telephoned.'

'Yes, I know you did. I'm not finding fault. You're old enough to stay out for supper if you want to. I just wondered where you were, what you've been doing all this time.' His tone was mild. 'I've never known you to go out and not come in until this hour. I just wondered.'

'I was with Sam. We went to the show at Koster and Bial's Music Hall.'

His father nodded. 'They say that's a pretty good show.' He waited a moment. 'It must have been over at about eleven, isn't that so?' He was still wearing his vest, his gold watch stretched across it. He took the heavy gold watch from its pocket and snapped open the lid. 'It's not far from one A.M. now.'

Terry said nothing. He chewed on his sandwich, not tasting it. His father had a sliver of ham caught in his mustache, but when he took a sip of tea, it disappeared. He put down his cup and leaned a little toward Terry.

'Son, were you with a woman? A girl? If you were, you don't have to be afraid to tell me. It's natural enough.'

Terry stared into his plate. All at once he was so tired that he wanted to put his head down on the table and go to sleep right there. The heaviness inside him seemed to shift a little, its edges to soften. He could have misunderstood that telephone call. It might not have meant what he thought it did. Maybe an employer would sound that way, talking to somebody who worked in his office and was sick or something. He might even call her Fanny, thinking it would be more sympathetic than Miss Clayborn. That other word – that whisper. He was not at all sure he had heard that. He could have imagined it . . .

'Did you go to a house, son?'

Terry still stared at his plate. 'The French Madam's.'

'Yes. I've heard of it.' His father cleared his throat. 'There's nothing to be ashamed of. It's perfectly natural.

We males have urges that must be satisfied. I'd be worried about you if you lacked them at your age. But are there no girls? When I was a boy and a young bachelor, there were always willing girls. I never had to go to a house.'

'I don't know any girls.'

'Well.' His father cleared his throat again. 'Is there anything you'd like to ask me? About all this, I mean. Anything you're not sure of? You know, I've always told you I want you to feel you can talk to me about whatever is on your mind. Anything at all.' Terry shook his head. 'Well, then we'd better get to bed. You have school tomorrow, and I have an early appointment at the magazine.'

Something filtered into Terry's consciousness. He looked up from his plate. 'Why are you up so late?' he asked.

'I had to see someone.' His father rose and put the ham back in the icebox. 'You know how authors can talk sometimes. I didn't get home until a few minutes before you did.'

I'm disappointed, too, of course . . . Yes, tomorrow night then, but it's hard to wait . . . Good night to you, Fanny. Get a good rest – darling.

Darling . . . Yes. Oh, yes. That was the word he had heard all right.

By the time his father had turned back from the icebox Terry was out of his chair. The doorknob was so slippery under his hands that he could not turn it. He took out his handkerchief and rubbed it between his palms, watching as carefully as if he were manipulating a knife.

'I want to tell you something,' he said in a voice unlike his own. 'I'm not going to the magazine anymore.'

'Terry! Why! What's happened? Has somebody—'

'I'm just not going, that's all. I'm never going. I'm not going to be on the magazine, ever.' He felt as though he had been running. It was hard to catch his breath. 'I hate the magazine!' he gasped. 'I hate it!'

He tried to leave but his father crossed the room and

took him by the arm. 'Look at me, son. Tell me what's happened. If anyone has said anything to you, I'll take care of it. You know I'd never let anyone hurt you. Or if it's something else – whatever it is – I'll straighten it out. We'll straighten it out together. Don't be afraid to tell me. You know you can trust me.'

Terry stood rigid, choked, until his father sighed and dropped his arm.

'All right, Terry. I can't force you to talk to me. I can't force you to stay with the magazine either, and I wouldn't want to. But I hope you'll change your mind. I'd miss you, son. Everybody on the magazine would miss you. Uncle Jake, Miss Clayborn—'

Terry's voice went out of control. 'Miss Clayborn can go to hell!' he shrilled. 'You can go to hell, too!'

6

'Talk to your father,' Mama Stern said. 'Whatever it is, tell him. You owe him that.'

'Why?'

'Because he's your father. Because he loves you. Because if he has done anything to hurt you, he doesn't know what it is. How can he set it straight unless he knows?'

It was a little more than two weeks after the night Terry had gone out with Sam. Terry had scarcely spoken to his father since, answering him with a word or two when he had to, avoiding him when he could. He had stayed in his room on the two Saturdays until he heard Terrence leave for the magazine without him.

'Why are you angry at Father?' Charles had asked him.

'None of your business,' Terry had told him. 'Don't bother me.'

His mother had come up to his room the second Saturday, after his father had gone. She rarely came to his

245

room. He was embarrassed about the way it looked, as if she was a visitor. The lace-edged bedcover was on the floor at the foot of the bed. A pile of his dirty clothes was on the floor, too. He had covered the pink chair with an old torn towel and instructed the servants not to remove it. The overflow of school books and papers on his desk was scattered everywhere. He had to remove a pile of books from the blue rocker so his mother could sit down. He sat in the other chair, hoping to conceal the towel that covered the fringed pinkness he detested.

If Sylvia noticed any of this, she said nothing. Often she had her breakfast in bed and stayed there until almost noon. This morning she had breakfasted in the dining room with the others. She had on a negligee that reminded Terry uncomfortably of the girl at the French Madam's, though his mother's was made of heavy satin in a deep rose and without a marabou edging. She was still slender, fragile-looking, her tiny waist only slightly thickened by child-birth. Her hair, down her back in a braid for the night, was still fair. Except for the few faint lines around her dark eyes and the beginnings of a downward droop at the corners of her mouth, she might have been in her middle twenties instead of ten years beyond them. Terry thought she was beautiful.

'What's the matter,' she began without any sort of preliminary, 'between you and your father?'

'Nothing,' he answered.

'Oh, come now, Terry. Don't tell me there's nothing. You've followed him around like a puppy since the day you could walk and hung on every word he spoke. All of a sudden you hardly look at him. This is the second time you haven't gone to the magazine with him on Saturday. You might as well tell me what's wrong. I'll find out sooner or later, you know.'

He shook his head. 'There's nothing to tell.'

'Nonsense. You're behaving like a stupid, stubborn child, instead of a great big fifteen-year-old who's supposed to be so bright.' Her tone was half exasperated –

the tone she most often used when she spoke to him – and half wheedling. 'I have a right to a truthful answer. After all, I'm your mother.' She smiled at him. He had never noticed that she did not show her teeth, like other people, when she smiled. 'It will be just between the two of us, I won't mention it to your father.'

Terry wondered how many things she and Charles had just between the two of them. Terry, in all his life, had not shared a secret with her. If he could have thought of something now, made something up, he would have done it, but his mind felt blocked, frozen. He shook his head again without speaking.

Her mouth tightened. 'Well, I can't drag it out of you. Anyway, it's probably a good thing it happened, whatever it is. You've always thought he was some kind of god. Now I suppose he's been unfair to you or something, and you realize I'm not the only one who has faults, no matter what he says.'

'He never—' Terry began, and stopped. He had almost defended his father, almost told her he had never talked to Terry about her faults.

'He never what?' she prompted.

'Nothing,' Terry said.

She got up so abruptly that she set the blue chair rocking violently on its own. 'Oh, you're impossible, Terry.' Now she looked slowly around her. 'Have you any idea how much trouble I took to make this room beautiful for you? I should have known you'd turn it into something out of an Irish slum,' she said, and slammed the door behind her as she left.

Mama Stern had called him up on the telephone a few days later and asked him to come see her on Thursday after school. He had known she wanted to question him, too, but he could not refuse Mama Stern.

'Because he's your father,' Mama Stern said. 'Because he loves you . . . How can he set it straight unless he knows?'

They were alone in the Sterns' house. The big, soft-cushioned, wide-armed chair he was sitting in was as familiar to him as his own skin. He had once snuggled into it with his legs sticking straight out. Now he filled it, and his feet reached the floor, but it still comforted his body; it still smelled the same.

'Nobody can set it straight,' he said, and then, because he could feel a weakness starting in his throat, he hardened his voice. 'Did he tell you to get me up here and ask me questions?'

She was sitting on the sofa, her fat little body taking up enough room for two women of average size. Because of her weight, she moved like a woman of seventy-five, but her smooth, plumped-out face gave her the look of someone in her early fifties. Terry did not think of her as old or young, homely or not. She was Mama Stern.

'I haven't spoken to your father at all,' she said. 'He told Jake about it. That's natural, isn't it? Jake is his closest friend. Even a grown man needs somebody to talk to when something as troubling as this happens to him.'

'Why did Jake tell you?' It was the first time Terry had omitted the 'Uncle'.

'He told me with your father's permission. Because Jake has never had a son, and I have. We both love you, but I've had more experience with boys. They thought I might be better at getting you to talk.' She smiled at him. Her teeth were so small and even that they looked false, but they were all her own. 'Is there anything else you'd like to know?'

He shook his head. She watched him in silence for a moment and then said, 'What about the practical considerations? I understand you've quit the magazine. What will you do for spending money? I'm sure you don't expect your father to give it to you under these circumstances.'

'No,' Terry said, although he had not thought about this at all. He still had a good part of the money he had drawn from his savings account and taken from his coin bank. It had been his intention from the beginning to spend it all. He had not considered what he would do when it was gone. 'I don't need his money,' he said.

She pushed herself forward with difficulty, leaned over, and put her hand on Terry's. 'Listen to me, please,' she said. 'Don't do this. Don't set yourself on this road out of stubbornness. If you go too far along it, there may be no turning back.' She searched his face. 'Do you understand what I'm saying, Terry? An estrangement between you two would be a tragedy for both of you.'

Terry looked away from her. He kept his eye fixed on the painting of an old bridge over a wild stream, a canvas by Turner that had always hung there.

'I can't help that,' he said.

She sighed. 'Try to change your mind,' she said, patting his hand. 'Please try.'

'I can't.' He withdrew his hand and stood up. He wanted to leave before the steadiness of his voice crumbled, but he had to ask her something first. 'Can I come here sometimes anyway?'

'Oh, Terry, what do you think?' She levered herself up from the sofa and put her arms around him. 'Of course, you can come, darling! Of course! I love you. Jake and I both love you. Nothing you say or do can change that, now or ever. Come whenever you like.'

He felt he would have to cry as soon as he got outside, but he turned his mind to the thing only he knew, and the feeling went away. If Mama Stern had known, she would not have tried to get him to change his mind. Nobody would. They would blame his father, not him.

At the edge of his awareness was the wish that he did not know either. That he had not overheard the telephone call. He did not put this wish to himself with any explicitness. But he knew he would never again listen in surreptitiously to other people's conversations.

It was a few days after his visit to Mama Stern that his father exploded. There was no warning. He had seemed as calm that evening at dinner, as accepting of Terry's withdrawal, as he had all along. From time to time he had

249

directed some casual remark to Terry and seemed undisturbed at the minimal response. Then Charles asked him about the new horseless carriage that was being demonstrated by the Duryea firm in a store on Broadway.

'Does it really go, Father, without even electricity?' Charles asked. 'Is it really safe?'

'I don't know, Charles, I haven't seen it yet. Have you, Terry?'

Terry said, 'Yes.'

He had gone to see the demonstration model the week before, gazed at it in wonder, admiring its handsome lines, its look of an elegant carriage. He had pictured himself at the wheel of this marvel, propelled in some miraculous way by gasoline, traveling at incredible speeds.

'What did you think of it?' his father asked.

Terry shrugged.

He did not know at first what had happened. He had not been looking at his father, had not, in fact, looked at him directly since the night they had met in the kitchen. He heard a sound as if something had fallen, a great rattling of dishes and glassware, and a small frightened squeal from Charles.

His father had risen from his chair and was pounding on the table. His face was red, and his voice filled the room. Terry had never seen him like this. He had never heard this voice except muffled by the walls between his parents' bedroom and his own.

'This is intolerable!' Terrence roared. 'I've had enough of it. I won't be dealt with this way, shrugged off by my own son in my own house. Either change your behavior, Terry, or get out!'

Sylvia said something, but Terry's eyes were filled with his father's roaring, and he could not make out her words. He left the table and went up to his room, opened his drawers, and began throwing his clothes into a valise. When the pile began to spill over the sides, he took everything out again and tried to fold it, but his hands were awkward at best, and now they shook so that he had

250

to give it up. He left out half the clothes and was trying to close down the lid of the valise on the rest when Charles came bursting in. He was crying, the tears pouring down his pink cheeks like rain.

'Don't go, Terry!' he wailed. 'Please don't go!' He threw his arms around Terry's waist and buried his face in his stomach. 'Father didn't mean it. You don't have to go.'

'Yes, I have to. He meant it all right.' Terry unwound his brother's arms and pushed him away. 'Get back downstairs or to your room or someplace. I don't want anybody in here.'

Charles looked at him mournfully. 'If you did what Father said, you could stay., If you changed your—'

'Shut up, will you? You don't know anything about it. Just shut up!'

'I don't see why you have to yell at me.' Charles's chin trembled. 'I don't like it when everybody yells.'

'All right, I'm sorry I yelled at you,' Terry said, still yelling. 'Now go away and leave me alone.'

Charles did not move. 'Can't I come with you, Terry? I won't be a pest or anything.'

'No, you can't!' Terry said, and then, more gently: 'You're too young, Charley. You have to stay with Mother and go to school.'

'Why couldn't . . .' Charles began, but he saw Terry's face and stopped. 'Where are you going?'

'I don't know.'

'Will you ever come back?'

'I don't know. Please go away now, Charley. I'll come and say goodbye to you before I leave.'

When Terry was alone again, he returned to the task of closing the valise. If he had taken out one more article of clothing, he could have shut it more easily, but he kept trying to force the lid down over the whole bulge. He was angry because it would not work, yet he did not really want it to. The anger felt better than the fear. Finally he got so furious that he threw the valise on the floor. It landed upside down, so that he had to pack it all over again. While he was doing that, someone knocked on the door. He thought it was Charles again and did not answer.

'Terry, can I come in?' his mother said, and was in the room before he could speak.

He went on with what he was doing until she laughed. Then he looked up. 'Are you laughing at me?' he said in a tone he had never used to her before. 'Do you think I'm funny?'

'My, you're touchy tonight.' She sat in the blue rocker and began gently rocking. Her dress was the same color as the chair, tucked from neck to ankle, the sleeves buttoned tight at the wrist. She wore her hair piled high on her head and full around her face, in the style of the girls by Charles Dana Gibson. 'I was laughing at that jumble of clothes in your valise, not at you.'

He gave the valise a kick and turned to face her. 'Well, what do you want?'

'Don't snap at me, Terry,' she said. 'I'm not the one who told you to get out.'

Terry had no answer to that. It was true. She had nothing to do with any of it. He did not know why he was angry with her too. Yet he was.

'Of course, he doesn't really want you to leave,' she said. 'Where would you go? You're only fifteen years old.' She was no longer laughing, but she still sounded as if she were. 'I don't think you're ready just yet to make your own way in the world.'

'I'll get along. I look older than I am. I'll get a job. He was earning a living at my age. I'm just as smart. I'll get a job. Anyway, I'm not going to stay here and—'

'Stop prowling around the room, Terry. You're making me dizzy. You may be as smart,' she said, 'but you've had a different life. You've been brought up like a gentleman, not in the streets. Your father was a man at your age. You aren't any more equipped to take care of yourself than a baby.' She rose from the chair and smiled up at him. 'So

252

put your clothes back where they belong and do your homework and go to bed.'

He did not know whether he was infuriated by her smile or the way she looked or what she said or by something else altogether, but all at once he was shouting at her. His voice lacked the volume of his father's, and it shook, but his mother backed away from him as if she thought he might strike her.

'What do you care what I do or where I go? You'd be glad to get rid of me. You'd be glad if you never saw me again in your life.'

She stood still and stared up at him. When she spoke, her voice was so soft that in contrast with his, it sounded like a different instrument.

'How can you say such a thing, Terry? I'm your mother.'

'Yes, but you wish you weren't.' He was not shouting now, but gasping, his throat too clogged for the breath he needed. 'If I weren't here, you wouldn't have to bother about me. You'd just have Charles. That's what you want. Just Charles.'

'Oh, I see. You're jealous of Charles,' she said flatly. 'You know you're being ridiculous, don't you? Naturally I've spent more time with him. He's much younger than you are, and he's a sensitive boy. He needs me more than you do. Your father doesn't understand him. But that doesn't mean I wish I had only him and not you. You're my son the same as he is.'

He turned away from her and looked down at the valise on the floor. He saw himself shutting it, picking it up and starting toward the door, and his mother coming after him, throwing her arms around him to keep him from leaving. But he felt that the valise would be too heavy, that he would not have the strength to lift it. His anger was gone. It was as if everything had dropped out of him, leaving him hollow.

'Do you want me to stay?' he mumbled.

'Of course I want you to stay.' He heard the rustle of

253

her dress behind him as she moved. 'Now let's forget all this nonsense.' She went past him to the door. 'Speak to Charles when you have a chance, will you, Terry?' she said. 'He's terribly upset.'

She did not come to breakfast the next morning. When Terry saw she was not at the table, he started to back out of the dining room, but his father stopped him.

'Come and sit down, Terry,' he said mildly. 'Mary has made hot cakes this morning. No, Charles, stay here, please. I want you to hear what I have to say too.' He pushed away his plate of half-eaten pancakes, wiped his mouth and his mustache with his napkin, and looked at Terry. 'I apologize for losing my temper last night and saying something I didn't mean. I'm still responsible for you, Terry. I couldn't put you out of the house even if I wanted to. And I don't want to.' He spoke with his usual rapid fluency, never pausing for a word. 'In spite of your peculiar behavior, which I don't understand and you won't explain, you're my son and I love you, and I hope that in time we can talk together and clear things up. In the meanwhile, I will, of course, continue to provide for you, pay for your clothes, schoolbooks, all your necessities. Your pocket money you will have to earn – either on the magazine as formerly or in some other way. The choice is yours.'

Terry had discovered that if he stared steadily at his father's face, he could blur it into near invisibility. When Terrence stopped speaking, it took Terry a moment to realize he was waiting for an answer.

'I'll get a job,' Terry said.

His father never again questioned him or referred in any way to what had happened between them. For a week or so Terry managed to go on answering him in monosyllables when it was impossible to avoid him, but he could not keep it up. He began to forget, to be caught off guard. Before long they were talking to each other normally. No outsider would have noticed anything. But it was as if his father were in one room, and he in the next,

254

and they were speaking through a closed door.

Terry found a job before his savings ran out. He worked after school and on Saturdays as a clerk in a grocery store, earning less than his father had paid him for Saturday alone. But he had saved half of everything he had made on the magazine. He never saved another penny.

When the grocery job palled, he got the idea of tutoring failing students for pay. Since he was proficient in nearly any subject and knew from years of helping Charles with his studies how to go about it, he soon had as many pupils as he wanted. He also spent one evening a week reading to a blind man, who left the choice of books to him and paid him well. He continued with the tutoring and the reading all through college. He did not make much money, but it was enough for his needs. Whatever he earned went for the pleasures that had first come to his attention that night with Sam.

Charles was thirteen, a year older than Terry had been, when his father began taking him to the magazine on Saturdays. His mother did not want him to go. She knew by now that he was no musician, but she still thought he was meant for something finer or rarer than magazine work.

A few years earlier his parents would have fought over it. The boys would have heard Terrence roaring in the bedroom, still unaware that he could be heard all over the house. But they seldom fought anymore. Much of the time Terrence shrugged and let Sylvia have her way.

Besides, they were together far less than they had been. Terrence was often out of the house in the evenings, claiming he had an author to see or other magazine business to transact. Sylvia did not sit at home waiting for him but went out, too, going off in one of the elegant carriages sent to pick her up. Now that they lived in the 'right neighborhood', she had a coterie of friends with whom she went to tea or shopping in the afternoons – all 'silly women', Terrence had once observed, 'who never think of doing anything useful, such as helping the poor, only of gossiping and adorning themselves in the latest fashion'. When Sylvia had answered that her friends came from a class he knew nothing whatever about, he had let it drop. Their arguments were never long sustained now.

Charles did not understand the change, but he did not puzzle over it. He was simply relieved not to hear that terrible voice that he had always feared, in spite of Terry's reassurances, might preface some monstrous episode. But Terry was aware that his father, a naturally temperate man, was no longer so involved with his mother that she could goad him to distraction. His mother might have thought it was *McNally's Monthly* that absorbed his father, but Terry had been around the magazine enough to know that its business was not conducted in the evening and that authors rarely had to be seen at night.

'I'm not forcing Charles to come to the magazine,' Terrence said when Sylvia objected. 'If he has another career in mind, he has only to say so.'

Charles said he hadn't. 'Mother, it isn't as if I was really good at something else. Of course, I could be a professional baseball player if you think that's better.'

For a moment Sylvia looked horrified. No one was used to humor from Charles. 'Well, don't be afraid to say so if you find you don't like it on the magazine,' she told him. 'There are many other things you could do. You can't possibly know, at thirteen, what you may be capable of later on.'

'That's understood, isn't it, Charles?' his father said. 'We can only tell whether or not the magazine is the place for you by trying it out.'

Charles came to Terry's room later. He sat on the floor with his back against a chair, his long legs arranging themselves with none of the ungainliness that had plagued Terry at thirteen.

'Do you mind me going to the magazine, Terry?'

'Mind?' Terry sprawled on the bed. He had deliberately torn a hole in the lace-edged spread the year before and now had one in maroon damask, still not to his taste but at least more suitable. 'Why should I mind?'

'Well, you always liked going, didn't you? I thought you might think I was sort of taking your place.'

'That's silly. You know I gave it up of my own accord. I found I just didn't care about it anymore.'

'I hope I will.'

'Sure you will. Of course, it's not much like being an actor.'

'An actor? Oh.' Charles laughed. 'I forgot about that. It didn't last long. I didn't like memorizing lines.' He paused. 'What if I'm not good at it? The magazine, I mean?'

Terry snorted. 'Don't be an ass. What do you think you're going to be doing? Writing editorials? Most of the time you'll just hang around, watching the way it all works. Once in a while Father may take you along when he has to see an author or somebody. In a couple of years, maybe, you'll get a chance to cut clippings out of other magazines or make sure the pages of a manuscript are in the right order. A fool could do it.' He lay back on the bed and looked up at the ceiling. 'If you expected it to be exciting, you're in for a big disappointment.'

'I didn't know what to expect,' Charles said. 'Father just told me to wait and see what it was like when I got there. Anyhow, one good thing is I'll have a chance to be with Father more.'

That Saturday, when Charles and Terrence went off together Terry had such a pain in his stomach that he spent the morning lying on a hot-water bottle. He thought he must have eaten something that disagreed with him, though nothing ever had. It might have been all the beer he had drunk the night before, but he didn't think so. He had been drinking for only a few months, since he had entered college, yet he seemed able to consume a great deal without feeling sick or losing control of his legs or tongue.

When, in an hour or so, the pain went away, the

257

pillowcase under his cheek was wet. Terry was disgusted with himself. An eighteen-year-old boy, crying over a stomachache.

7

The January 1900 issue of *McNally's Monthly* featured an article headed 'The Twentieth Century in a Crystal Ball.' Among the predictions offered by various prominent men was one by a young writer named H. G. Wells, who at only thirty-four years of age had acquired a reputation as a seer. According to Wells, the new century would see the development of automobiles (also tentatively known as motorcycles, petrocars, viamotes, and mocles) capable of traveling three hundred miles or more in a day. Roads would be built not for iron horsehoes and the filth of horse traffic but for soft-tired conveyances. They would be made of asphalt or of some new substance not yet developed, and their traffic would be strictly separated. The 8,000 automobiles then in existence in America would proliferate to perhaps as many as 100,000.

A fellow in Terry's fraternity at Columbus wrote some verses on the subject, which were taken up and chanted by the brothers at one of the fraternity's famous drinking parties. They concerned 'that pipe-dreaming writer HG, who would just as soon soothsay as pee', and derided *McNally's Monthly* as a 'too credulous periodical to fall for such stuff idiotical' as 'this Wellsian joke, or delusion, about carts of such speed and profusion'.

Terry chanted as gleefully as the others, although he did not consider Mr Wells's prediction so laughable or his fraternity brother's doggerel so hilariously clever. He might have said what he thought about automobiles except that it could have seemed a defense of his father's magazine, rather than of Mr Wells.

Terry was too newly pledged, and too unsure of his

acceptance in the fraternity, to express himself freely. He did not know why they had pledged him. He was not, like many of the others, from one of New York's first families. He was not an athlete. He had not distinguished himself in any way except by devoting his time outside classes to frequenting places of entertainment and chasing women, yet managing to maintain a C average, and by his ability to drink a great deal without showing any effects. But before long he understood that these very pursuits and abilities were what had commended him to the fraternity and overcome the liability of his plebeian background. Whatever more lofty purposes may have been expressed, the objectives that welded the brothers together were to have fun, to experience numberless sexual triumphs, to drink vastly and imperturbably, and yet to get by in their classes so they could stay in college and continue enjoying these pleasures together.

In the fall of his junior year Terry asked Charles to a football game and to a fraternity party afterward. Columbia was swamped by Pennsylvania, but that in no way put a damper on the party. Instead of drinking to celebrate, the boys drank to blur the pain of defeat. A few of the more daring girls were persuaded to take a sip, too, but they all professed to find the taste too harsh for their delicate palates.

Terry's girl was not one he would ordinarily have invited. He had met her at another party and knew how little to expect. If he was attentive and charming to her all evening, she might go out into the dark hall with him and let him rub himself against her and fondle her breasts through her layers of clothes. But she had a younger sister, suitable for Charles, whom she was willing to bring along.

Terry thought it was time to introduce his brother to the possibilities of female society. Charles still had numerous friends, school athletes like himself, but he seemed totally unaware of girls. They were not unaware of him. He was a striking boy, his hair and skin as fair as in

259

childhood, his eyes the same clear green, and his slim, nimble body grown, at fifteen, to nearly six feet in height.

But if Charles recognized the effect he had on women, Terry saw no sign of it. He had been innocent himself, but not as innocent as Charles, who, as far as Terry knew, did not even have fantasies about girls. And he thought he would have known. Charles had the same trust in Terry, the same openness, as when he was ten years old. He still came to him with questions and to talk out his fears and worries. None of them ever concerned girls.

Terry drank less than usual at the party. He wanted to keep an eye on Charles and make sure he remembered Terry's warning that he was too young to drink. Nothing that went on with the girl would show, but if Terry brought him home drunk, he, not Charles, would be blamed.

He need not have troubled. Charles went nowhere near the liquor. Normally as graceful and easy-moving as a cat, he sat stiffly in a chair too low for him, his knees bent at an awkward angle, his hands clutching the arms of the chair. The girl Terry had arranged for him was pretty and just his age, but whenever she tried to talk to him, he turned scarlet and stammered some monosyllabic response. As soon as she gave up on him and went to find livelier company, he relaxed and began chattering animatedly to one of the new pledges who had come without a girl.

'I'm sorry,' he said on the way home. 'She was nice. I liked her. But girls – I don't know – they scare me. They're so – well, not like us. I don't know how to talk to them. I think of things to say, but they're always things I'd say to another fellow – like what a great coach Hurry-up Yost is – and that wouldn't interest a girl. I don't know what interests girls.' He put his hand on Terry's sleeve. 'I'm really sorry, Terry. You went to all that trouble, and I acted like a fool.'

From the time they had left the party until they had

deposited the two girls at their home, Terry had been simmering with frustration. Charles had spoiled his evening. If it had not been for him, Terry would have had a rollicking time. He would probably, at that moment, have had a willing girl with him. Instead, he had had no real fun at all, a few quick feels that had barely raised his peter and not enough whiskey in him to compensate. And it had all been for nothing. Charles had behaved like a little idiot, and Terry could hardly wait to tell him so.

But now Charles had beaten him to it. There was nothing left to say. Terry tried to hold on to his resentment, but it melted away.

'Don't worry about it, Charley,' he said. 'I just thought it might be fun for you, but I guess you're not ready yet. No harm done.'

They were walking home from Morningside Heights, cutting through Central Park to Fifth Avenue, a distance of about four miles. They always walked when they were together. It was the only form of exercise Terry liked and could share with his athletic brother. At that hour, well past midnight, Central Park was empty except for an occasional derelict sleeping peacefully on a bench. Terry and Charles might have been alone in an abandoned world.

'I don't know if I'll ever be ready,' Charles said slowly. 'I don't mean just about girls, but the whole thing. I can't – it doesn't seem like fun to me. Having a party to get drunk and stagger around and get sick—'

'I never get sick.'

'I don't mean you, but when I went to pee, there was a fellow in there puking all over the floor, and I can't see what fun that is. And I can't—' He glanced at Terry and then away again. 'The thing with girls. When you were fifteen, were you the same as now? I mean, wanting to do it more than anything else? With any girl you could get?'

'Charley, that was five years ago. I don't remember how I felt then,' Terry said. 'Anyway, everybody's different. You love baseball. You once said you thought a game was like a concert. When I watch it, I just get bored.' He linked arms with Charles, matching his long stride. 'By the time you get to Columbia you may have different ideas. Anyway, you'll have lots of choices. Maybe you'll meet a beautiful Barnard girl and marry her right after graduation.'

'I may not even get in Columbia. I'm not as smart as you.'

'Your grades are all right. You haven't failed anything. Sure you'll get in.'

'Sam didn't.'

'Don't you know why? It's because Sam's a Jew. Columbia only takes a certain number of Jews a year.'

'That's crazy.'

Terry had said the same thing to Sam, and Sam had shrugged.

'It's the way it is,' he had said, and he had gone all the way across the country to some college called Azusa Pacific that nobody had ever heard of, pretending he didn't mind.

For a time Terry had thought of going somewhere else himself. He had even written a letter refusing his admission to Columbia, carefully numbering his reasons.

3. When Dr Barnard wanted to admit women, one of the arguments against it was that it was mostly Jewish girls who wanted to go to college and they would turn Columbia into, and I quote, a Hebrew seminary . . .

But he had not sent the letter. He wanted to be in New York and go to Columbia, where he could have the kind of life he enjoyed. He did not want to miss out on things the way Papa Stern had done. What good would it do Sam if Terry went someplace else?

'I might never get married,' Charles was saying. 'I don't see what's so wonderful about it. You're supposed to love each other, but look at Mother and Father. If they do, they don't act much like it.'

They had come through the park and were walking down Fifth Avenue, their shoes on the pavement making the only sound in the deserted streets. Terry withdrew his arm from Charles's and put his hands in his pockets.

'You've been worrying about that as long as I can remember. You used to think something terrible was going to happen because they fought all the time. Now they hardly ever fight, and you're still worrying. It's—'

'I'm not *worrying*, Terry. I didn't say I was worrying.'

'Well, whatever you're doing, cut it out. Talk about something cheerful for a change, will you? All you've done since we left the party is moan.'

There was a pause. Then Charles laughed. 'Well, you have to admit I'm not just like everybody else. A party is supposed to make people cheerful, and I get gloomy instead.'

They walked several blocks in silence. 'I didn't mean to snap at you, Charley,' Terry said finally. 'Everybody feels gloomy once in a while. If you can't tell me the way you feel, who can you tell? I guess I'm just tired.'

But it was a long time before Terry fell asleep. He kept thinking of things he did not want to have in his mind, and for this he began blaming Charles again. It was easy to be angry with Charles when he was not there. Terry had often been angry with him, often hated him, but he could only sustain these emotions in Charles's absence.

8

Terry was twenty-one when he was graduated from Columbia in 1903. America was prosperous, with a surplus of close to fifty million dollars in income over expenditures. Prices were low – a turkey dinner could be bought for twenty cents. More and more ordinary people were able to afford the new appurtenances that made life easier and pleasanter: the sewing machine, the telephone, the self-binding harvester, even the automobile. It was an age of optimism. A minister in Brooklyn said, 'Laws are becoming more just, rulers more humane; music is becoming sweeter and books wiser.' A businessman was quoted as saying that anyone who could not make money in America was a hopeless case.

Terry, however, had no profession, no trade. At the beginning of his senior year in college, his father asked him whether he had any plans for the future. The future, for Terry, was no farther off than the next party, the next show, the next girl, but he told his father he had something definite in mind that he was not yet ready to discuss. He was sure something would turn up. It always had.

Toward the end of the year reality began to trickle in, but it was only at the farewell party of his fraternity that it hit with full force. The entire focus of the evening – whether in sobriety or drunkenness, jest or seriousness – was on the approaching horrors of going to work. Three of the wealthier boys were making the Grand Tour first. Two were entering medical school. Most of the others were starting with their fathers' businesses or law offices. Terry was sure they had taken their college years no more solemnly than he had, yet they all had mapped out their life's work.

They took it for granted that Terry was going to the magazine. He had never denied it. Everyone knew *McNally's Monthly*. To be associated with it gave him added prestige in the fraternity He had not thought of what he would say when they found out he was not there.

Charles wanted him there, but of course Charles had nothing to do with it.

'I don't think it's what I'd like to do for the rest of my life, Terry,' Charles had said about a year before. 'I get bored. I make a lot of mistakes and annoy Father. I'm a rotten speller. I'm no good at writing, and I'm not even crazy about reading.' He had given a little laugh. 'What am I doing on a magazine?'

'Have you said anything to Father?' Terry had asked him. 'It was only supposed to be a trial. If it isn't working out, you ought to discuss it with him.'

'I can't. Not unless you change your mind and take my place. He talks all the time about handing the magazine down and hoping a McNally will always carry it on. I know I'm an awful disappointment to him, but at least I'm a McNally. If you'd come—'

'No, Charley. I'm sorry. I have other plans. Why don't you try it a little longer and then, if you still feel the same way, make up your mind to tell him? He'll get over it.'

Charles had heaved a heavy sigh. 'I wish you'd change your mind. He'd much rather have you. He keeps calling me Terry by mistake.'

For one fanciful moment Terry had thought it might be possible. But of course it was not. Whatever Charles said, Terry did not know how his father felt. He could not cross the distance between them and ask to be taken back on the magazine. He could not risk a refusal. Mama Stern had been right when she had talked to him six years ago about the road he was taking. There was no turning back.

He could not recapture the sense of himself as he had been then, a boy of fifteen, concealed in a dark hall, listening to his father speak lovingly to a woman who was not his wife, arrange a meeting with her, call her darling. He could not remember exactly what he had felt, or why. Had he been outraged because of his mother? Disillusioned by the misbehavior, the deception of the man he had admired above anyone on earth? Jealous because he was himself in love with Fanny Clayborn? He no longer knew. He was not sure he had ever known.

None of it seemed valid to him now. A young boy's crush. A young boy's idealized image of his father. A young son's fantasy about his mother, scarcely disturbed by the knowledge that she cared nothing for him, that he was too much like his father for her taste. He had been beyond all that when he got a little approval from her, after he had been accepted into a fraternity that included some of the sons of socially prominent families. He knew she would wear this as an ornament to flash at her friends, as she flashed Charles's startling good looks. Terry was no longer sure she loved even Charles, except as a showy extension of herself. The word itself was alien to her. *All this talk about love . . .* He did not blame his father anymore. But he had gone too far along the road. There was no turning back.

The first week after graduation Terry got up early every morning, saying he had appointments relating to positions he had been offered. He did not, he said, want to talk about them at all until he had made a final decision. Every morning he went to Central Park and sat on a bench in the summer sun, watching the ladies who had been up before breakfast riding along the bridle paths. Ordinarily he would have flirted with one or two of them, if only as an exercise, but he had no heart for it. When he got tired of sitting, he walked up to the Metropolitan Museum of Art and looked at the paintings. He had learned a little about paintings from Mama Stern and a little more in a course of art appreciation he had taken at Columbia because it was a snap course, but these mornings he did not know what he was looking at. After he left the museum, he got on the Fifth Avenue bus and rode all the way downtown and all the way uptown and then downtown again to Fifty-fourth Street. By that time he could have completed his fictitious business, so he went home.

Terry followed this same routine the entire week. Eventually, he knew, he would have to do something about finding work, but he could not do it yet. He could not even think about it. He felt he should have had the summer, like some of his fraternity brothers, to make the transition from college boy to workingman. He should have had a chance to go to Europe, like Charles.

Charles had been invited by a friend to go with him and his family, who had reserved a suite of staterooms on the

Campania. Since he would be company for their son, and the second berth in their son's stateroom would be unoccupied unless Charles came, they proposed to pay his passage.

At first neither of his parents wanted Charles to go. His mother said he was too young, and she knew nothing about the people, though she had met the son. He was a handsome, dark-complexioned boy whose name was Sidney Keller, which Sylvia thought sounded Jewish. To Terry's delight, Charles pretended to think he was half Jewish and half Indian, a bit of knowing mockery of which Terry would not have thought Charles capable. If Sylvia wondered about it after Mrs Keller had spoken to her on the telephone, she did not mention it. The Kellers were immensely wealthy and distantly related to the Schermerhorns, one of the foremost families in New York society. How Mrs Keller managed to convey this information over the telephone, Sylvia did not say but after the call she decided that Charles might, after all, benefit from a summer abroad.

Terrence was outraged at the Kellers' offer to pay his passage.

'What do they think we are? Poor Irish trash that can't pay our own way?'

'No, Father, of course they don't think that. It's just that money doesn't mean anything to them. It's as if they were treating me to a soda,' Charles told him. 'They know all about you, and they're very impressed. Just the other day Mr Keller was saying you must be quite a man. "I look forward to meeting Mr Terrence McNally the First," he said.'

It was the first time Terry had ever heard Charles try to change his father's mind. Whatever Terrence told him to do or not to do, Charles had accepted, not always happily, but at least with resignation. Terry had often suggested that he argue for something he wanted, but Charles was too much in awe of his father, too eager to please him. Now, without any practice, he seemed to know exactly how to soften him up.

'I'd learn a lot in Europe, Father,' he said. 'I'd be more use to the magazine after seeing something of the world.'

Terrence finally agreed. 'But they're not going to pay your passage,' he said. 'I don't care how rich they are, if you're going, it will be on my money, not theirs.'

When Sylvia heard this, she said, 'I could go to Europe with friends myself. You know I've been wanting to go for years, but you've always said you couldn't afford it. Now that you evidently can afford it, there's no reason why I shouldn't go too.'

'It will have to be either you or Charles. I can't sent you both.'

'Then let the Kellers pay for Charles. The money isn't important to them. They're glad to have—'

'No, I will not let the Kellers pay for Charles. Nobody has ever paid for me or mine, and as long as I have anything to say about it, nobody ever will.'

His roar might be worse than his sting, but they all knew this quiet, hard voice and that nothing it said was negotiable.

'You and your ridiculous pride!' Sylvia said. 'Terrence McNally the First, king of the Five Corners!'

Even Sylvia could not bring herself to say she should be the one to go instead of Charles, but Terry thought she would have let Charles persuade her. He was relieved that Charles did not try. It was the kind of thing his brother was likely to do, but this time what Terry considered Charles's abnormal selflessness was overcome by his eagerness to go.

'It's the most wonderful opportunity,' he told Terry. 'We're going everywhere. If Sid and I want to see some place his parents don't, they've said we can go off on our own, even if it's for two or three days. Sid and I already have some ideas.'

Sid and I. They had been close friends for months, constantly in and out of each other's houses, doing everything together. Charles was friendly to everybody, but he had always had one or two special friends. Terry, an outsider in grade school and high school, had made friends in college, but they had been group friends. He saw them at the fraternity house, caroused with them, but had never asked one of them to his home or been asked to any of theirs. Sam Bernbach was the nearest to a personal friend he had ever had, but their relationship had been based more on convenience and the pursuit of pleasure than an affection or shared interests. He had had no word from Sam since he had gone to college in California and only knew from Mama Stern that he would not be back, that he was engaged to a Californian girl and was going into her father's business instead of into his father's law office.

'We might even visit Ireland,' Charles said. 'I'd really like to go there and see what I can find out.'

Terry knew that what he wanted to find out about was their great-grandfather, the first Terrence McNally, the man whose existence had been negated when their father was named Terrence McNally the First. The story had always fascinated Charles.

'What did he do?' Charles had asked as a child. 'Was he a werewolf?'

'Werewolves aren't real,' Terry had answered, 'so he couldn't have been one. I don't know what he did. Father doesn't know. Nobody knows.'

But Charles had never believed that. He was sure someone knew.

'I don't see how you can expect to find anything out,' Terry said now. 'He's been dead about ninety years. Nobody who knew him could be alive anymore.'

'Somebody who's alive may have heard about him. Where he lived is a very small place. Sid and I could go around talking to people.'

Sid and I.

'I wish I could go with you,' Terry said before he could stop himself.

Charles looked at him and then came and put his arms

269

around his shoulders. 'I wish you could, too, Terry. I'll miss you. I've never been away from you before.'

They were in Charles's room, which was decorated exactly as it had always been, too fussily draped and ruffled and dainty for a boy of ten; absurd for a sixteen-year-old six-footer. But Charles endured the room in silence. He did not tear holes in the dotted Swiss bedspread or cover with a towel the old rose velvet armchair in which he now sat down. He did not want to hurt his mother's feelings.

'I guess I really shouldn't be going,' he said. 'I'm not sure Father can afford to send me. The magazine isn't doing as well as it was.' He sat with his hands between his spread knees, looking down at the floor. 'I'm not supposed to tell that to anybody, but I guess it's all right to tell you.'

Terrence never mentioned the magazine to Terry or discussed it in front of him. Terry knew nothing about what was happening on the inside except for the little Charles told him voluntarily. Terry never asked. He did not want to ask now, like an ignorant, curious outsider, but he had to know.

'Why isn't it going well? What's happened?'

'I don't know exactly. Father and Uncle Jake argue about it a lot. Uncle Jake says *McNally's Monthly* isn't keeping up with what the public wants. He says the magazine ought to be more like that one they edited in college – what was its name?'

'*Pharos.*'

'Yes. Well, Father says *McNally's Monthly* isn't a college journal, and he's just going to go on publishing the same solid magazine because it will outlast any faddist changes. But I think he's worried.'

'What faddist changes is he talking about?'

'I don't know, Terry. I'm just repeating things I hear. I don't really understand it or feel part of it. I don't think I ever will.' He sighed, still staring at the floor. 'I guess I picked a terrible time for a trip to Europe. I should have

270

thought more. Maybe I still ought to cancel it.'

All the excitement had drained out of him. He looked listless, quenched. He had been this way at intervals since before Christmas, changing almost overnight into a moody stranger who could be his usual self one minute or one day and the next sit brooding in his room, looking as he did now. Terry, to whom he had always told everything, could get nothing from him except that he was feeling a little glum and that nobody should be expected to feel cheerful all the time – this said in a gentle, reasonable voice, as if everything were now explained.

Although he insisted he was not sick, Sylvia sent for the doctor, who prounounced him a perfect physical specimen and suggested that he was probably suffering from what the doctor called spiritual growing pains. This seemed to Terry a more plausible diagnosis than his father's conjecture that Charles was in despair over some girl – 'a not uncommon ailment of young fellows' – and should be let alone to recover in his own way. Terry thought Charles would have told him about a girl.

Whatever the trouble was, it had lasted most of the winter. Then Charles had become friendly with Sid Keller, and his periods of melancholy had vanished as suddenly as they had begun.

'Sid and I feel the same way about everything – baseball and everything else,' he had told Terry. 'Any crazy thought I've ever had, he's had it, too.' He had stopped then, looked into Terry's face, and laid one hand on his sleeve. 'Sid hasn't any brother or anybody he can talk to. For me, it's just that it's somebody my own age.'

No matter how many friends Charles had had, it had always been Terry to whom he had come when he was troubled. Terry knew it never would be again. He felt mean and small-minded for resenting this, for resenting Sid, but he couldn't help it. So many things would never be the same again. But he had been relieved when Charles was once more the old Charles, and he was alarmed to see signs of a relapse.

271

'Listen, Charley, don't be an ass,' he said. 'You know Father doesn't throw money around. He wouldn't let you go if he couldn't afford it. Magazines have their ups and downs like any other business. By the time you come back *McNally's* will probably be going better than ever.'

Terry knew nothing about the ups and downs of magazines or the future of *McNally's Monthly*, but since he was saying what Charles wanted to hear, his brother was easily persuaded. The color came back to his cheeks, and he began to burble again about all the places they were going and the strange, wonderful foreign things they would see. *Sid and I.*

The final day of Terry's park-museum-bus routine he went with his parents to the Cunard pier on the North River to see Charles off. They went aboard the *Campania* to look around this new ship that its owners called a floating palace. Terry had never seen a palace, but he thought there could not be one more magnificent. In the lavishly decorated drawing room, on a Persian carpet, stood not only a Collar grand piano but an American organ besides. The reading room was lit by electric lamps of beaten copper, in the shape of rosettes. In the dining saloon long rows of tables seemed to stretch to infinity. The 430 seats were revolving armchairs, with the Cunard lion rampant on their backs. Illumination was furnished by a crystal dome in a light well that extended down through three decks. A special saloon was set aside for the ladies, with wide lounges, soft cushions, and vases of fresh flowers. The men's smoking room had a fire burning in an open grate, the hearth made of Persian tiles, with an Oriental rug in front of it.

'Isn't it stupendous?' Charles said. 'I can't believe I'm on a ship. I can't believe I'll be living in such luxury for over a week.'

'This is the way I expected to be living all the time,' Sylvia said, 'but your father—'

'Mother, please don't,' Charles pleaded. 'This is the most exciting day of my life. Please don't let anything

272

spoil it.' He went over to Terrence who was peering out a porthole at the crowd on the pier. 'Father, I've got to thank you again for sending me. I know it must have cost you an awful lot.'

Terrence patted Charles's shoulder without turning all the way around. Terry had never seen his father embarrassed by anyone but Charles. 'That's all right. The cost doesn't matter,' Terrence said. 'Just make the most of the chance.'

They went to see the staterooms. Mr and Mrs Keller had a parlor and bedroom, furnished in satinwood and mahogany, with tables and chairs, a brass bed, and wardrobe. The two staterooms for the boys were simpler, but large and airy, the old-fashioned wooden berths replaced by what were called triptic beds, the upper one of which folded up against the bulkhead.

Charles pulled it down to see how it worked. 'You could get in there, Terry. I'd fold it up again, and nobody would find you until after the ship sailed.' Without waiting for a comment he loped across to the porthole, tried opening it, gave that up, and went to peer out the door. 'I wonder where Sid is,' he said. 'Oh! Here come Mama Stern and Uncle Jake.' He ran out to greet them.

'Did you ask them to come?' Sylvia hissed to Terrence.

He went close to her and took her by the shoulders. Terry's practised ears heard him whisper, 'Be courteous to them. I'm warning you.'

Terry shivered. Terrence was not an alarming man. Even Charles, who had once trembled at his distant roar and was still in awe of him, did not actually fear him. But several times since his childhood Terry had heard his father speak to Sylvia in this obscurely threatening way, and each time, though he did not expect his father to do her physical harm, it frightened him. It was something like the fear he had felt as a little boy, going alone into a dark room where some nameless thing might jump out at him.

But Sylvia shrugged Terrence off, turned away from him indifferently, and whispered back, 'Of course, I'll be

273

courteous. I'm a lady. But I wonder what the Kellers will think.'

Charles came in with his arm around Mama Stern's enormous waist. Jake followed them. Terry and his father kissed Mama Stern, each taking a fleshy, no longer resilient cheek. Jake hugged Terry and then pushed him away.

'What am I doing?' Jake said. 'I don't even know who you are.' He made a show of peering closely at Terry through his thick glasses. 'The face is familiar, like a face I used to know a long time ago or maybe in a dream.'

'Don't tease him,' Mama Stern said. 'He's a busy young man, graduating from college, getting ready to make his way in the world. He can't run to see us now the way he used to.' She reached up to pat Terry's cheek. 'Never mind him, Terry. We don't have to see you all the time to love you.'

Sylvia, who had withdrawn to a corner of the state-room, made an ambiguous sound. Mama Stern turned.

'Mrs McNally,' she said. 'I didn't see you with all these huge males in front of me. How are you?'

Sylvia did not move except to incline her head in a minimal bow. 'How do you do, Mrs Stern,' she said distantly.

She wore a dress of primrose faille, tightly nipped in at her small waist, with white satin collar and cuffs, black satin revers, a lace-edged jabot, a full floor-length skirt, and an overskirt that flowed to a graceful point in the front and at both sides. Her hat was a toque with a silk crown and bow to match her dress and a black velvet brim against which her hair appeared almost as palely blond as in her youth. Mama Stern, her bulk encased in a steel-boned corset over which her long dark gray dress fell shapelessly, lumbered across the cabin like some disabled, mothballed battleship.

'What a long time it is since I've seen you! I think you're even lovelier now.' Mama Stern plucked Sylvia's limp hand from her side and held it between both of her

274

own. 'I've always wanted to tell you how much credit your two wonderful boys do you, Mrs McNally. I'm glad to have this chance. They've given me so much pleasure through the years. I couldn't love them more if they were my own grandsons.'

Sylvia stepped back a pace, withdrawing her hand. 'You're very kind,' she said.

Only Terry saw and heard all this. Terrence and Jake were examining the triptic bed, and Charles was watching out the door for Sid. When Sylvia started to turn away, Terry came and swung her back, with one arm around her and the other around Mama Stern.

'Isn't it nice that Mama Stern and Jake are here to see Charles off, Mother?' he said. 'It makes it a real family occasion.'

Mr and Mrs Keller and Sid came in at that moment, led by Charles, who introduced them to the Sterns. At once Sylvia's demeanor changed. She talked with charming animation to Mrs Keller, a plain woman who had the serene air of a person born with impeccable credentials. She smiled enchantingly, just short of flirtatiously, at gray-haired, austere-faced Mr Keller, inducing him to smile with obvious pleasure in return. Terry saw his father watching her and could not read his face. He wondered if this was the way his mother had been when his father first knew her and if he was remembering that.

Then Sylvia positioned herself so that Mama Stern and Jake were behind her. She gave the impression that they were people she did not know, who had wandered into the cabin by mistake.

'You must know Susan Van Rensselaer,' she said to Mrs Keller. 'She gives the most exquisite luncheon parties. You must have been at some of them.'

'I don't attend many luncheon parties,' Mrs Keller said. 'But I do know Mrs Van Rensselaer. We work together at the Henry Street Settlement.' She spoke over Sylvia's shoulder to Mama Stern. 'Haven't I seen you there, Mrs Stern? Your face is so familiar to me. I've been trying to think—'

'Yes, I used to work there very regularly,' Mama Stern said. 'Now I can't move around well enough.' She maneuvered herself with difficulty from behind Sylvia to the other side of Mrs Keller. 'I've told them at the Settlement that I'm too old, because that's something I can't help. What would they think of me if they knew I was too fat?' She smiled and shook her head. 'A fine thing! Too fat for charity!'

'She talks as if she's some kind of renegade, Mrs Keller. Don't listen to her,' Jake said. 'I had to get two doctors to help me convince her she's done her share. Even now I come home every Tuesday and Thursday and sit on her to keep her from going down to Henry Street.'

'My son,' Mama Stern said, 'is a teller of tall stories. If I made up my mind to go, he could no more hold me down than if a fly sat on me.'

Mrs Keller chuckled, a rich, unexpected sound from her pale mouth. 'I believe you, Mrs Stern,' she said. 'I remember all about you now. You're the woman I once heard the great Lillian Wald herself call a ball of fire.'

A powerful gong chimed somewhere on the ship and chimed again before the first reverberations had died. This was followed from place to place by a voice shouting through a megaphone.

'ALL ASHORE THAT'S GOING ASHORE! ALL ASHORE THAT'S GOING ASHORE!'

Charles grabbed Sid's hand. 'They really say that, Sid. Listen to them. They really say it.'

'Of course they really say it.' Sid, who was half a head shorter than Charles, smiled up at him. His teeth were so white against his dark skin that Terry thought they looked painted. 'We're ready to sail.'

'Listen, everybody, we're ready to sail,' Charles yelled. 'You've got to say good-bye to us now.'

He was so excited that Terry thought he scarcely knew which one of them he was hugging. Terry, when it was his turn, said nothing, only squeezed Charles's shoulder and

276

ruffled his hair. He was afraid to try speaking.

On the pier it no longer mattered, though it was absurd. A twenty-one-year-old man crying because his younger brother was going away for two months. But the others were too busy locating their passengers at the rail to notice, and the passengers were too far away to see.

Even so close to the water it was hot with the midday June sun burning down on the pier. The ladies in their high-necked, long-sleeved and long-skirted dresses held parasols over their heads and pretended not to notice their unladylike perspiration. Periodically the gentlemen mopped at their necks under the hard collars and removed their gray or black silk hats to dry off dripping foreheads. As the *Campania* began to move, smoke pluming from its tall funnels, handkerchiefs waved from both the ship and the pier below, some on the pier attached like flags to the end of canes. People shouted good-byes to each other across the widening strip of water and were heard only by those for whom the shouts were not meant.

Sylvia was unusually subdued. 'I hope he'll be all right,' she said. 'He's so young, and it's so far away.'

'He's sixteen years old, nearly seventeen. When I was his age . . .' Terrence let that sentence dangle. 'Anyway, he's not going alone.'

Sylvia looked out the carriage window. 'I didn't care much for that Mrs Keller. If I'd met her, instead of just talked to her on the telephone, I'm not sure I'd have let Charles go.'

'That's nonsense. She's a perfectly nice woman. They both impressed me as being fine people.' He looked at Terry. 'What was your impression?'

'I didn't see anything wrong with them,' Terry said.

Sylvia kept looking out the window. Terry wondered whether there could be tears in her eyes, as there had been in his. He had never seen her cry. He thought of putting his hand over hers, but what she said next shriveled the impulse. 'I don't think she realized they were Jewish.'

Terrence, whose attention had wandered, said, 'Who?

What are you talking about?'

'Mrs Keller. A woman in her position wouldn't know any Jews. She wouldn't dream she might meet Jews in our son's stateroom, seeing him off to Europe. She probably thought they were – I don't know. I don't know what she thought.' Sylvia sounded more despairing than angry. 'That dreadful Mrs Stern! How can a woman let herself get so disgustingly fat?'

Conscious of Thomas, the coachman, on his box above them, they all had been speaking in low voices. Now, without warning, Terry felt a surge of rage that was not altogether of this moment, and heard the pitch of his voice get away from him.

'Don't you dare talk about Mama Stern like that! She's the most—'

'*Dare*?' Sylvia turned from the window with a small, incredulous smile. Her eyes were dry. '*Dare*?' she said again, and leaned across Terry to look at Terrence, lifting her hands, palms up, to underline her amazement. 'Did you hear your son telling his mother what she *dare* not do? Screaming it at me?'

'No one in the vicinity could have avoided hearing,' Terrence said, gesturing with his chin and raised eyebrows at Thomas's back. 'I disapprove of your talking to your mother in that manner, Terry.' He took his cane between his feet, clasped his hands over the silver head, and rested his chin on his intertwined fingers. He looked at neither Terry nor Sylvia. 'However, I applaud the sentiment. Mama Stern is, as you were about to say, the most – whatever splendid adjective comes to mind, including beautiful. If you see her otherwise, Sylvia, please don't offend us with your distorted vision.'

'You never take my part. You never . . .' Sylvia began, but Terrence had not finished.

'As for Mrs Keller, whose ideas seem to weigh with you even though you don't like her, I can assure you,' he went on, 'she certainly has known Jews – at the Henry Street Settlement, if nowhere else. You heard her speak of the

278

founder as the great Lillian Wald, who called Mama Stern a ball of fire. The great Lillian Wald is a Jewess. Mrs Keller certainly knows that Mama Stern, the ball of fire, is also a Jewess, and Mrs Keller was obviously pleased to meet her again. I feel sure all your fears that you would be found socially unacceptable because the Sterns were there to see Charles off are totally unfounded. On the contrary, as far as Mrs Keller is concerned, it's probably a feather in your cap.'

Sylvia leaned back and closed her eyes. 'You're exhausting me with talk. You always have. Talk, talk, talk. I'm sick of all those people,' she said. 'I wish I'd never have to hear any of their names again.'

9

Terry got a job as a salesman for Tommy Togs, a line of boys' clothing that was sold to retail stores, primarily in the East. His territory ran from Maine, in the north, to as far as western Pennsylvania in the west and as far south as southern Maryland. Each week he called on approximately sixty customers and potential customers in small and medium-sized towns, leaving New York City (a separate plum of a territory that was not his) at six on Monday morning and returning the following Saturday night, or the Saturday after that, depending on business, any time from six to midnight.

In order to get this job, he had agreed to work on straight commission. He was not a good salesman. In fact, he made little effort to push a sale, but simply showed his line and let the customer make up his mind. He acquainted himself only sketchily with such matters as fabric, color, and style, and often could not answer pertinent questions.

But he was liked. He was considered a good fellow, much as he had been in college. He always had a good story to tell – an incident or racy joke he had heard in another town, or some real or imagined exploit of his own. He was always ready to go out for a drink or to find a woman, or both, and he knew how to hold his liquor and his tongue. What he sold was goodwill, enough of it to produce modest sales of Tommy Togs as well. He put in as much time as any laborer, fifty-nine hours a week, though it was not all work. The average laborer earned $9.42 a week. Terry's average weekly earnings were about $12.

He had not expected the job of selling to interest him, but he had thought the life would be attractive. He would travel all over the country, see everything, have all the freedom he wanted, all the pleasures that dozens of different places had to offer.

It was that way for a while. It served his restlessness to be constantly on the move, rarely going to bed at night in the same place where he had awakened in the morning. He liked the unfamiliarity of the different towns. He enjoyed his ready acceptance by men with whom he had neither age, education, experience, nor interests in common – nothing but tweed knickers or a sailor suit – and who expected nothing of him except a funny story and a little agreeable, discreet debauchery.

He was glad, too, to be seldom home. Sylvia was usually away, visiting friends in their summer house at Newport, or Bar Harbor, or Saratoga Springs. Alone with his father, Terry was more conscious than ever of the strain between them. And he missed Charles. On the road he seldom thought of his brother, but when he was home, he could not get over listening for his voice, looking for him in his empty room. Sometimes he thought he could sense in his father's face or manner the judgment that he should move out and rent a room of his own somewhere. It would have been better to do that, but he couldn't afford it. Terrence did not know how small his income was. Terry talked little to him about his job, and most of that little was a lie. In the beginning, when he left for the train on a Monday morning, lugging his heavy sample cases, it was with relief and anticipation.

The anticipation did not last. He got tired of the hot, smelly trains with their continual starting and stopping – every forty or fifty miles – to water the thirsty locomotives. The difference between one town and another seemed much slighter than at first. They all had narrow main streets crowded with narrow stores, their windows jammed full of as many attractions as they would hold. There was always a bank on the main street and a saloon that offered raw whiskey, usually a meal in an adjoining dining room, and often roulette. The food all began to taste the same. The hotels he stayed in were all alike in their sleaziness: the cramped, dimly lit rooms indifferently cleaned. The lumpy mattresses were redolent of stale sweat and semen. So were the women.

Finally he could endure it only by telling himself that it was temporary, that something else was bound to turn up very soon, and by drinking more heavily. If he drank enough, he could consider himself a vagabond, an adventurer, leading a gay, free life and caring nothing for the future, nothing for material comforts. Sober, he was often on the verge of quitting, even with no other prospects, but he kept on. He could not have said whether this was because he was stubborn or because of what he imagined his father would think.

When Charles came home from Europe at the end of August, Terry had just set off on a two-week selling trip. He was in a rudimentary town in northern Maine, drinking with Mr Purdy, the owner of what was more a trading post than a store, except that it sold, rather than bartered, everything but food. It was a dismal town without a hotel. Mr Purdy let Terry sleep on sacks of grain behind a counter, with a horse blanket to cover him.

When he told Charles about it later, Terry turned it into a tale of comedy and high adventure in the hinterlands of the north. He did not say that in that part of Maine late August nights were already bitterly cold, and that after the whiskey had worn off and the fire Mr Purdy had kindly left burning in the Franklin stove had died down, he thought he might freeze to death. He did not say that Mr Purdy had ordered two boys' shirts and four pairs of boys' woolen hose – because he thought Terry was 'a nice young feller' and it would be too bad if he came such a 'fur piece' for nothing – and that Terry's commission on this sale came to sixteen cents.

This glorified recounting took place before the end of the two weeks. Terry was in Pennsylvania, nine days after he left Maine, when he got word that Charles Littlefield, who had been failing for several years, was dead. He had had such a small part in Terry's life for so long that Terry could mourn him only by remembering the grandfather of his childhood – the slim, fair man who had appeared out of nowhere to see his baby namesake, who had made perfect smoke rings for Terry's pleasure, and talked to Terrence in his soft, apologetic voice while Terry sat quietly out of range and listened.

No one else in the half-empty church seemed to mourn him at all. His wife, Terry's grandmother, whom neither he nor Charles had ever seen before, sat motionless in the front pew with her son, Peter, looking perfectly composed and contented, as if she were at a concert or a play. Terry, glancing at her from the pew across the aisle, had the feeling that she had been placed there, an old lady chiseled out of stone for her husband's funeral with the wrong expression on her face. Her son simply looked bored.

Terry could not imagine being related to these people, nor had they acknowledged the relationship, sitting alone in one pew while Charles Littlefield's daughter, son-in-law, and grandsons sat in another. Terry felt an unaccustomed sympathy for his mother. What kind of woman would refuse, at such a time, to look at or speak to her daughter or any member of her daughter's family because their name was McNally? Sylvia, though she had inherited her mother's prejudices, would surely not disown a child for what she considered his distasteful Irishness. Sylvia

282

had a distaste for Jews, too, but at least she acknowledged their existence. With such a mother, worse might have been expected of her.

Charles agreed with all this. He laughed at the story about Mr Purdy's store in Maine. But his mind seemed to be on something else. Throughout dinner, after the funeral, he had talked to Terry about his trip, repeating anecdotes his parents had obviously heard before, not pausing for questions, as though in a hurry to get it all told. Now that he and Terry were alone, walking on Fifth Avenue in the autumn twilight, he seemed to have nothing more to say. He walked with his hands in his pockets and his head down, not in dejection but as though he were searching for something he had dropped.

'You're pretty quiet all of a sudden, Charley,' Terry said. 'Is anything the matter?'

'No.' Charles looked up and smiled. 'No, I just have so much to remember – so much happened – I keep trying to sort it all out.'

'Well, don't do it now. You're wasting my time.' Terry gave him a playful punch in the arm. 'We've got two months to catch up on and not much time to do it in. I have to leave in the morning.'

'Do you *have* to?'

'Of course I have to. I'm a working man, not a high school boy like you.'

'Don't remind me. School starts Monday.' Charles sighed. 'I've got to start going down to the magazine again, too. I've got to start this Saturday. I guess I'll never get out of it now that you have your own career.'

Terry did not want to pursue this subject. He did not want to discuss his 'career'.

'Say, listen, Charley,' he said, 'you haven't told me anything about Ireland. You haven't even mentioned it. Didn't you go there?'

'Sure we went there. Sid and I did. I must have mentioned it.' Charles began speaking in a rush again, the way he had done at dinner. He began walking faster. 'We

283

loved Dublin. We loved listening to the people talk. Do you know they speak the purest English of anybody? That's what we were told. And they're so nice. Wherever we went they were nice, not loud or fighting or – what Mother always says about them. Crude. They're gentle and polite and not crude at all. Especially when I said my name was McNally. They didn't believe it at first because of the way I look. I started wishing I looked more Irish, like you—'

'Whoa!' Terry said, reaching out for Charles's arm. 'Slow down, Charley. I can't keep up with your gallop. I'm not an athlete. Did you go to—?'

'We went by jaunting car in some places. That's a cart with two wheels and you sit in back-to-back seats.' Charles slowed the place of his walk but not of his tongue. It was unlike his father's easy, rapid flow. Charles stumbled over words. He sounded, Terry thought, almost feverish. 'The countryside is so green. It rains a lot, and especially after it rains, the grass and everything is the greenest you ever saw. That's why green is the national—'

'Charley, wait a minute. You're wound up like a top.' Terry took his arm again. 'Let's sit down and catch our breath.'

He urged Charles towards a bench that stood outside the stone wall that separated the avenue from Central Park. They both sat with their legs stretched out, black socks showing below the black stovepipe trousers of the suits they had worn for the funeral. They were exactly the same height, but there was no other resemblance. Terry was much broader and heavier. The slight softness above his belt, the slight looseness around his eyes – early marks of the heavy drinker – were perceptible only in contrast with Charles's perfect tautness. Away from Charles, Terry was attractive, strong-featured. Beside his brother, he looked coarse, his dark red hair and bright blue eyes flamboyant, his body thick and clumsy.

'Look, there's a Great Arrow,' Charles said. 'The Kellers have one like that.'

They watched the automobile roll past the carriages and the lesser motorcars, its six gold-plated lamps – two in the front of the hood, two in front of the windshield, two at each side of the driver's seat – glowing importantly along the avenue. A chauffeur sat stiffly at the wheel. No passengers were visible behind him.

'I wish we had an automobile,' Charles said. 'Mr Keller thinks it won't be long before nobody will be driving carriages anymore, only automobiles.'

'He must think everybody's as rich as he is,' Terry said. 'The Bernbachs have a Haynes touring car that they keep at their country house. Sam once told me it cost three thousand dollars, and three thousand dollars a year to run it. A Great Arrow must cost even more.' He looked curiously at Charles's hands, which were clenched so hard together that Terry could see the whiteness of the knuckles in the light from a nearby street lamp. 'Anyway, to get back to Ireland—'

'Oh, I guess I've told you everything that's interesting. We spent much more time in England. Mr Keller even hired horses for us in London, and Sid and I went riding in Regent's Park. We had—'

'Charley, why are you so nervous? All you've told me about Ireland is that you liked Dublin and the grass is green. What about your reason for going there? Did something happen? Did you get to Lisdoornoo?'

Now Charles was sitting straight up on the bench, his knees bent, his toes on the ground, as if getting set to sprint.

'Nothing happened. What could have happened? It was just like you said it would be. Nobody in Lisdoornoo ever even heard of Terrence McNally. That's why I didn't tell you about it. There wasn't anything to tell.'

Terry did not look at him. He looked across Fifth Avenue at the French Renaissance houses that faced the park.

'You're no better at lying than you ever were, Charley.

Why don't you want to tell me what you found out? You never used to have secrets from me.' He couldn't help adding, childishly, 'I'm sure Sid knows all about it.'

'Sid was with me,' Charley said softly, and said nothing more for several moments. Then he unclasped his fingers and put a cold, moist hand on top of Terry's. 'I'm sorry I lied. I thought it was easier than—' He broke off, shook his head a little, and began again. 'I don't want to keep it secret from you. I'll tell it to you. I always meant to. But not right now, Terry. I can't right now. I have to – sort it out.'

Terry took his hand away. 'Where did you get that "sort it out"? What is it, some kind of English expression?'

'I don't know. What's the difference?' Charles asked with uncharacteristic asperity. 'I'm sorry if you're annoyed, but I can't help it. I just don't want to talk about it until later on.'

'I'm not annoyed, Charley,' Terry said, trying to sound as if he weren't. 'If you don't want to say anything at all, even about how you found whatever it is, that's up to you. I can wait.'

After another long pause Charles said, 'I guess I don't mind telling you that. There was an old man they said would know if anybody did. He didn't want to tell me. He said it was nothing for a boy to know. But I gave him a dollar. It was like a fortune to him. He mumbled a lot of prayers over me, thanking God, or blessing me, or something, and then he told me.'

'How did he know? He couldn't have been old enough to—'

'He heard his father telling another man. He was only a boy, but it was – something you'd remember.'

'He could have been making it up to earn the dollar. You have no way of knowing if it was true or not.'

'It was true.' Charles got to his feet. 'Let's go, Terry. I'm not going to talk about it anymore.'

They walked home almost in silence. Terry, who had

once been as curious about the first Terrence McNally as he was about everything, had long ago put him out of his mind. He still could not believe that Charles had simply gone to Ireland and found an old man who knew all about him. He did not trust this old man. He could picture him, a wrinkled, humpbacked faker, clutching Charles's dollar bill, mumbling blessings, while he concocted his story. But what could he have said that had upset Charles so much that he could not talk about it? How had he so totally convinced Charles, who was childish and naive, but no fool, that it was true? In fantasy Terry knocked Charles down, sat on him, and began slowly choking him until he told. He had often had such fantasies and despised himself for them. No decent human being could want to hurt Charles, even in imagination.

'One other thing I'd like to know, Charley, if you don't mind telling me,' he said as they approached the house. 'Is what this old man said our great-grandfather did so terrible that – well, say he did it today, here in this country – would we feel the same way about it?'

Charles spoke as if his lips were stiff. 'What way?'

'Well, a family couldn't really erase a man like that now. Not in New York City in the twentieth century. That was pretty primitive. So it occurred to me that their idea of something bad enough to deserve that treatment might be primitive, too.' He was saying too much, talking against a look on Charles's face that he could not interpret. 'Like burning women who were supposed to be witches,' he finished.

'If he did it today,' Charles said, 'his family would erase him, too.'

Ordinarily Terry did not drink when he was home. He always had whiskey with him, carrying it in a cigar-shaped flask that he kept in his breast pocket, but he saved it for the train, taking his last swig before he arrived at the station and leaving the rest untouched until he was in his seat, on his way out of New York. He thought it was all right for his father, who did not drink at all, to know that he took a nip now and then, but Terry did not want him to smell it on him constantly. That night, though, he drank almost half the whiskey in the flask so he could get to sleep and stop thinking about the first Terrence McNally, and the way Charles had looked and sounded when he talked about him.

The next day Terry returned to Pennsylvania, to finish up there, and then went to see his customers in New Jersey. One morning he woke up in his hotel bed with the beginning of a sore throat and his legs full of bites, bloody where he had scratched them in his sleep. It was not the first time he had been attacked by bedbugs, but he had never seen such a swarm as this, crawling over the mattress and the adjacent headboard. He decided he could not go on through New Jersey and then to Delaware and Maryland without a night or two in a clean bed and a few good, tasty meals to fortify him.

He considered joining his mother and father and Charles in nearby Atlantic City. For the past three years they had been spending five days there every September before school started. It was his father's only vacation, the only time the family all went somewhere to have fun together. Terry liked the beach and the ocean and walking on the boardwalk, smelling the salt air, watching the peep shows and bazaars, and having his fortune told by a brooding-eyed woman with a bandanna around her head and gold-colored hoops in her ears. This was the first year he had not gone along. It would be a good place to soothe a sore throat.

But he did not go. His mother would say, as she always did, that no fashionable people went to Atlantic City, and only someone with cheap tastes could enjoy its crude amusements. She would dip herself gingerly in the waves at the water's edge, barely wetting her black stockings and the skirt of her knee-length black and white suit, and wonder why Terry churned the waves so furiously with his hands and feet while Charles glided

288

through them like a ship in sail. His father, after the first day, would go off somewhere by himself, returning only for meals. Charles – Terry did not really want to see Charles now. He could not deal with all that mystery and strangeness so soon again. Especially when he was not feeling very well.

Instead, he went home. It was the perfect solution. Nobody would be there – not even Mary or Thomas, who always got time off when the family went to Atlantic City. He would have the house to himself. Unless he felt like going out, he could stay there the whole time, sleep all day if he chose, drink as much as he wanted to. There would be food in the icebox. Mary always cooked too much of every dish she made.

He arrived home late the following night. By that time, since he had been drinking steadily for medicinal purposes, he was quite drunk. He did not miss the keyhole of the front door, but he had to direct his hand slowly and with great concentration. He did not stagger, but his walk was stiff and careful, and when he climbed the stairs, he held firmly to the banister. When he reached his room, he turned on one small, heavily shaded lamp, so as not to assault his eyes with too much light, and started to undress.

The first sound he heard was so indistinct that it could have been nothing more than one of the various noises all houses knew how to make. Terry paid no attention until he heard something else. He did not know exactly what the new sound was either, but he knew a person had made it. He knew that with absolute certainty. Someone else was in the house.

He had a cane in his wardrobe, his mother's gift for his twenty-first birthday, a gentleman's heavy-headed ebony cane that he had never used. It would make a good weapon. Whether or not he could actually hit a burglar over the head with it, Terry had no idea. He had never been called on to exhibit physical courage and did not know whether or not he had any. As he tiptoed along the dark hall with the cane in his hand, he felt only moderately frightened. He thought if he had been sober, he might have been terrified, but he had no way of confirming that now.

After he had gone a few steps, he could hear whispering. There were at least two of them, and they were in Charles's room. Terry did not stop to think how he would manage more than one burglar. He opened the door, held the cane at the ready in one hand, and turned on the light with the other. Then he stood like that, frozen, as if he would never move again. Finally his arm came down slowly. He did not know he had let go of the cane. He did not hear it clatter to the floor.

'God!' he said. 'You filth!'

Terry spent the night in Central Park, sleeping on a bench with his head on his sample case. He did not remember going there. When a shabby, reeking old man woke him in the morning, he did not know where he was.

'You'd better get up, young man,' the old man said in a hoarse, cultivated voice. 'The cops will be around soon. They have a nasty habit of rapping on the soles of shoes.' He looked with red-veined wet eyes at the ankle-high button shoes that Terry wore on the road. 'Your soles are thick, of course.'

'Thank you.' Terry sat up and rubbed his face. He felt terrible, as if he had a fever. 'I just sat down to rest for a few minutes. I must have fallen—'

The old derelict was not interested in Terry's excuses. 'Some of the men who sleep here every night are dishonest. Bums,' he said. 'They'd as soon rob you as look at you. I deplore that. A sleeping man is helpless. When I see one like you, who no doubt has money in his pocket, I watch over him.'

Terry looked up at him vaguely. It took him a few seconds to understand why the fellow, having delivered himself of this message, did not go away and leave him alone.

'Oh. Yes.' Terry felt for the pocket that held his money. It did not occur to him until much later that the old man may have been not so much virtuous as thwarted by the fact that Terry had been lying on that pocket, with the money under him. 'Here you are. Thank you very much.'

'Not necessary. Not necessary at all. But if you insist.' The tramp folded the dollar bill into his dirty palm with one-handed deftness. 'Thank *you*, sir. God bless you.'

He was gone. Terry shuddered. He felt chilly. His throat ached. He began to think he had imagined the old man, taking a dollar from him in return for a favor; a wrinkled, humpbacked man, clutching a dollar bill and mumbling blessings . . .

He got up abruptly, stumbled into the bushes, and vomited until nothing was left to come up but a watery sourness. How he made his way to the Sterns' he could not afterward remember.

Mama Stern came to the door herself. She wore a dark blue silk robe that minimized her size and trailed the floor like a train. Her two nighttime braids, pinned up now to encircle her head, resembled a silver crown.

'Terry! Come in.' She reached for him and held him against her with one arm. 'Come and have breakfast with us. We're just sitting down.' When he shook his head, she looked into his face and then felt his forehead with the back of her hand. 'Go on into Bertha's old room. The bed is made.'

'Can I stay a few days, Mama Stern?'

'Of course, darling. As long as you'd like.'

Over the new few days, whenever he drifted into awareness, she was there, laying a cool compress on his forehead, turning his pillows, sitting quietly beside the bed. One of the maids brought the trays, but she fed him, spooning broth into his mouth, holding a glass of fruit juice to his lips.

'Mother,' he said once.

Mama Stern leaned close to him. 'Do you want me to call her, Terry? I don't know if they're back home yet, but I can try.'

'No. I thought you were her.' Terry closed his eyes, sinking into sleep again. 'I thought I was a little boy.'

He got out of bed the third day, a little shaky but otherwise recovered. His suit had been pressed, his shirt and collar laundered and starched, his shoes polished. He could not find his sample case. Mama Stern said he had not had it with him when he arrived.

'Do you know where you could have left it?'

'In Central Park,' he said.

They were in the dining room. In place of the invariable white damask cloth of the Sunday chicken dinners, the table was covered with a yellow linen breakfast cloth, bordered with hand-embroidered daisies. Terry, his appetite restored, was finishing off a plateful of scrambled eggs and a stack of toast with sweet butter and homemade strawberry jam. Mama Stern, who had eaten breakfast earlier with Jake before he left for work, was having a second cup of coffee to keep Terry company. She did not ask him what he had been doing in Central Park. She did not ask him anything except whether the loss of the sample case was disastrous.

'I'll have to replace it, that's all,' he said, as if it were not disastrous. Replacing the sample clothes in the case, and the case itself, would cost almost as much as his average commissions for two weeks. The only money he had was what was in his pocket, seven dollars. No, six. Like a fool – or like someone in a dream – he had given a dollar to that tramp, who, for all he knew, might have gone off with the sample case.

Terry did not want to think about the tramp. He did not want to think about anything that had happened. He did not know what he was going to do, how he was going to pay for the lost samples, how he was going to live, how he could ever go home again. He was sorry he was well. He would have liked to go back to bed in

Bertha's old room and stay there.

'You don't have to leave here unless you want to,' Mama Stern said, watching his face. 'I love having you. You're like my own grandson, Terry, you know that, don't you?'

'I know. I love being here, too.' He contrived a smile. 'The accommodations are first class, and the service is excellent. But I guess I can't loll around here anymore. I've got a living to make.'

She nodded. 'Yes. Of course. You're a man now. It's hard for me to realize that. Sometimes I even think of Jake as a boy, and he's forty-six years old.' She still had her eyes on his face, but so softly that he had no urge to look away. 'It isn't always an easy thing to be, is it, Terry? So much is expected of a man. No matter what happens, he's supposed to know what to do. He's supposed to take charge and never show any weakness or softness. I'm not sure that's right. I don't think men are as different from woman as they're made out to be. They shouldn't have to act like lords of the universe all the time.' She reached for his hand, held it in one of hers, and stroked it with the other. 'Whatever it is you're going through, don't try to live it all in advance. Just do the best you can with it day by day.'

'Thank you, Mama Stern.'

It was the only thing he could think of to say. He felt a little better, but he could not be sure her words were what had done it. He was not sure he had heard everything she had said or altogether understood it. But some of his panic had subsided. He could go downtown and face his boss, tell him he had lost the sample case and had no money to replace it. That was the first thing. After that, if he kept his job or got a new one, he would see about living somewhere else, maybe moving to another town where he could rent a cheap room. All it had to be was clean. He was on the road most of the time anyway.

Nothing will ever be the same again, he said to himself.

'Have another cup of coffee before you go.' Mama Stern was a great believer in coffee. 'There's nothing like it to invigorate you, especially when you've been sick.'

The coffee, which Mama Stern made herself, was thick and powerful. Terry, lacing it with abundant sugar and heavy cream to make it potable, had just begun to drink it when Jake walked in.

Mama Stern started to say something to him and stopped. Terry put down his cup. Jake stood with his thighs pressed against the table, his hands coming together and flying part. His face, normally pale, was so white that the skin did not look alive. His mother and Terry stared at him, waiting.

'It's—' He had to clear his throat and begin again. 'Something terrible has happened.' He looked at Terry with his hugely magnified, swimming eyes. Terry looked away, watched Jake's throat, which moved up and down, up and down. 'It's Charles.' Terry knew what he was going to say. It seemed to him that he had known the moment he saw Jake's face. 'He's dead, Terry. He killed himself.'

They had found him when they got home from Atlantic City. They had found his note first, stuck into the foyer mirror where they could not miss it; where it would prepare them for what lay upstairs.

Dear Family [the note said],
    Please forgive me for this, but it's the best way. I've found out I have an incurable disease. It will be easier for me and for you if I don't try to live with it. You'll find me in the bathroom. Don't let Mother see me until you fix me up a little.
    Thank you for giving me such a happy life. I love you all.

Charles

'He cut his wrists,' Terrence said. 'He was lying in the

bathtub with the water running to wash the blood away. Even then he was thinking of us, trying to make it less horrible for us.'

As soon as Terry had walked into the house, he had smelled his father's cigar and followed it into the den. Terrence had been sitting in his Turkish leather rocker. The curtains had been drawn. Except for the glowing tip of the cigar, the room had been dark.

Terry had said, 'Father,' and then his throat had closed and he had stumbled across the room, dropped to the floor, and put his head on his father's knees. He had not done such a thing since he was a small boy. Almost instantly it had embarrassed him. But he had felt his father's heavy hand stroke his hair, then rest on his head, and he could not move right away.

Finally he had asked, 'How—?' and got up and sat in a chair. 'I didn't wait for Jake to tell me.'

Terrence had told him. They were the first words he had spoken. He knew the note by heart.

'Where – is he?' Terry asked.

'In his room upstairs. Your mother's with him. She wouldn't let him be taken away yet. Why don't you go to her?'

'She won't want me, Father. She'll want to be alone with Charles.'

Terrence did not answer this. 'I don't think I should be smoking. It feels wrong to do the ordinary things,' he said. 'But it comforts me.'

'Of course it's not wrong.' Terry could not remember ever before reassuring his father. 'Do you mind if I turn on a lamp, Father? It's awfully dark in here.'

'Yes, it is dark, isn't it? I hadn't noticed. Turn on the lamps.'

In the light Terry could see that his father had been crying. His eyes were red, and his face looked curiously streaked, not wet, but as if the tears had worn furrows in his cheeks. Terry had not cried. His torment was beyond simple sorrow.

'An incurable disease,' his father said. 'Only months ago the doctor pronounced him physically perfect. What could he have had? What doctor told him?' Terrence squeezed his eyes shut and opened them again. 'Among the things that have been torturing me while I've sat here is the possibility that it was a mistake, and he didn't have this disease at all, that he listened to someone who didn't know.'

'He wouldn't have listened to one man, Father. He loved life so much. He'd have made sure.' For a moment Terry's throat was again too clogged for speech. 'I think he must have suspected it for some time,' he went on slowly, choosing his words. 'Do you remember how strange he was last winter? I think he was worried then but finally convinced himself it was nothing. The night of Grandpa's funeral, when we went for a walk, he was strange again, talking as if he were delirious. I think he either knew that night or was pretty sure and found out definitely afterward. But anyway, you don't have to worry that it was a mistake. He'd never have done it if there was any doubt at all.'

'You must be right. You knew him better than I did.' Terrence touched his cigar to the edge of an ashtray, easing off a long gray ash. 'That's another thing. I never knew him well enough. I never seemed to know how to talk to him. But probably if I'd tried harder, spent more time – I suppose I'll regret that the rest of my life.'

Mary came in from the kitchen, trying to tiptoe but unable, with her big, splayed feet, to do other than clump. Her ageless face was swollen, the black eyes almost shut.

'Excuse, please, Mr McNally, is no good you don't eat.' The intricacies of English construction were still, after so many years, beyond her. 'I fix you nice sandwich now, yes? You, too, Terry. Nice ham sandwich, the best you like, and chicken to take Mrs McNally.'

Terry began to say he didn't want anything, but Terrence spoke quickly, telling her sandwiches would be wonderful, with tea for him, please, and coffee for Terry.

'Soon ten years I work here. You think I no know tea and coffee for which?'

'That's her comfort, like my cigar,' Terrence said when she had gone. 'It would have been unkind not to let her feed us, even if we throw it all out when she isn't looking.'

'I didn't think of it that way.'

'One day – maybe I was a little younger than you are now, but not much – I was unkind to somebody without realizing it, and Mama Stern told me to erase unkindness quickly before I learned it too well. After that I tried. I haven't always succeeded.' He sighed. 'Charles didn't have to try. He had nothing to erase. He was kind by nature.' Terrence's voice broke. 'Oh, Terry, I should have loved him more!'

Terry said, 'You – you—' and then doubled up with pain.

'Cry,' his father said. 'There's no shame in it at a time like this. Cry, son. You'll feel better.'

Terry shook his head. 'I'll never feel better. The last thing I said to him— We – had a fight. And the last thing I said to him was – something rotten.'

'Ah, Terry, he knew you didn't mean it. Didn't he say in the note he loved us all?'

Mary brought the sandwiches and beverages, and in a little while they both ate most of the food and drank all the tea and coffee.

'I know how you felt about the cigar,' Terry said. 'It doesn't seem right to be having all this – letting everything just go on, as if it didn't matter that Charles – that he'll never—'

'But what Mary said makes sense,' his father broke in. 'Is not good we don't eat.' He smiled at Terry. 'Is no helping nobody.'

Terry smiled back. If his father could do it, he could. 'Even with a Hungarian accent, you sound Irish.'

Outside the house the day went on. Inside, it could

have been any hour. Terry never looked at his watch or heard the chime of a clock. He did not know what time it was when Charles's body was removed from the house. Terrence went upstairs with the men. Terry could hear him talking to Sylvia, but not what he said. He heard his mother give one short, sharp scream. Then he heard the men start downstairs, moving carefully, and he went across the room where he could not see.

'She won't come down.' Terrence said when he returned. 'She's just sitting there in his room, next to the bed. I'm thankful you're here.' He came to the fireplace where Terry was standing and took him by the shoulder. 'It's been a long time since we've been together like this.'

'Yes,' Terry said.

They both sat down again. His father said, 'Will you tell me something, Terry? Are you really happy in your job?'

'Father,' Terry said, and stopped, and plunged on. 'Father, is there still a place for me on the magazine? If there isn't, it's all right. I'll—'

Terrence began to shout, and then remembered, and went on quietly. 'Is there a place for you on the magazine? Terry, it's MCNALLY'S *Monthly*. Not *Terrence McNally the First's Monthly. McNally's.* Yours and mine. Someday yours. That's how it was meant to be from the day you were born.' He had leaned forward in his chair, moved to the edge of it, as he had done long ago in Woodrow Hamilton's office – an excited boy about to become the editor of a bicycling magazine. Now he sat back again. 'Suddenly you turned against me and the magazine. I've never known why.'

'It doesn't matter why, Father. It was a boy's reason. I've wanted for a long time to go back to the way things were – the magazine, everything, but I – couldn't.'

'I should have talked to you again. I should have tried. All these years I've waited for you to come to me. Watched you growing further and further away and never thought something could happen to you and it would be too late.' Terrence wiped his eyes with the back of his hand, then smiled and shook his head. 'We're a couple of proud, stubborn Irishmen, Terry, and often that's useful for getting on in the world. But not between father and son.'

Now Terry began to cry. He sat hunched over in his chair with his chin thrust into his chest and his arms crossed around his body, as if holding himself together. He tried to cry silently, but he could not stop the hoarse sounds that came tearing out of him. His grief was vast and formless, encompassing the death of Charles and its reason, merging with guilt and revulsion, and embracing sorrow for the wasted years of isolation that it had taken a tragedy to end.

Terrence did not speak until the weeping was over. 'Try a cigar,' he said then. 'I think you'll find it soothes the spirit a little.' He opened the humidor on his desk, took out a fresh Havana for himself and one for Terry, and clipped both ends with a cutter shaped like a guillotine. 'It's a companionable thing as well, two men smoking their cigars together.'

When the cigars were lit, they sat in silence for a while, puffing small gray-white clouds that floated across the room.

'I remember watching you and Grandpa smoking,' Terry said. 'I used to wonder what held the smoke up in the air.'

After another silence Terrence said, 'The magazine never meant very much to Charles, you know. I was doing to him what Papa Stern did to Jake, except Papa Stern thought Jake cared about the law, and I knew Charles's heart wasn't in magazine work. I told myself it would grow on him, but I knew better.' He paused. 'Don't let me do it to you, Terry. Don't come to the magazine to make me happy. I might not see it at first, but I would in the end, and it would be far worse for me than not having another McNally on the staff. One such wrong is enough to live with.'

Terry looked down at the cigar in his fingers. 'I don't think I'd come to the magazine just to make you happy, Father. Not just for that. I'm not as dutiful as Charles or Jake. I'm doing it because I hate my job and I'm a rotten salesman and I don't know of any other job I could get that I'd like or be good at. Also, I've run out of money, and I wasn't sure how I was going to get along until I could earn some more.' He looked up at his father, whose face had gone still. 'But I'd do it anyhow. I never thought of doing anything else, or wanted to, until – the thing that happened. It's as if I went away somewhere after that – a kind of exile, where I had to live and work like – well, a foreigner. And now I can come home.'

'What sort of creatures are you?' Sylvia said. She was standing in the doorway, her face so white above her black dress that it seemed to float without a body. 'Sitting here chatting happily and smoking your foul cigars, before my son is even in his grave!'

10

Terry started at the editorial desk. His job was to handle any editorial correspondence that did not require the special attention of a more exalted member of the staff; to see aspiring authors who brought story ideas to the office in person, and to get rid of most of them, but to learn to recognize the few with possibilities; and to keep a schedule of all material planned for future issues, so that his father and Jake could see the format of any issue at a glance and locate the placement of any article or piece of fiction that they might later decide, for some reason, to include in a different issue, or not use at all.

It was not a glamorous or prestigious job, and the need to sit still at a desk for long hours was a trial to him, but he was so grateful to be there that he would have spent his days scrubbing the floors rather than ever go anywhere else again. As a boy he had taken the magazine for granted. He had belonged to it as he belonged to his family and the house he lived in, absorbing it without particular consciousness. Now he was sharply aware of everything – the vitality of the office, the fierce scribbling of the staff writers, the excitement of a new idea or the discovery of a talented new author, the frenzy to meet the deadline of the current issue, even the smell of the magazine when it came fresh from the printer.

He tried to concentrate so totally on his work that he could not think of anything else. His habitual evening diversions sickened him now. He could not drink without tasting the whiskey that had sent him down that dark hall with a cane in his hand. He could not enjoy a woman without seeing, as if in terrifying mockery, what he had seen when he opened that door. Occasionally he went to a show or with his father to the Lotus Club, the members of which were journalists, authors, actors, musicians, and artists, and which afforded informal entertainment on Saturday nights and gave banquets to honor distinguished visitors like Mark Twain or Sir William Gilbert. More often he stayed home. If Terrence was out, he sat in the den, reading or rereading one of the books in his father's glass-enclosed bookshelves, losing himself in other worlds, in the visions of other men. One day he would have to confront the death of Charles and its cause. But not yet. He could not do it yet.

It was some time before he knew the magazine was in trouble. He had known it once – Charles had told him – but with all that had happened since, it had gone out of his mind.

His father did not speak of it to him. In the office he treated Terry like any other member of the staff, his manner pleasant but businesslike and often rushed and abstracted. As they went back and forth in the carriage, their conversation was limited by Thomas's broad back looming above them. It was limited at home by Sylvia, who sat rigidly at the table, either in tragic silence or in cold disapproval of something Terry or his father said. When she went to her room or, as time went on, frequently left for the evening, Terry did not want to discuss the magazine. He wanted to recover the closeness of the day he and his father had grieved and regretted and smoked together.

'Why do you put up with it, Father?' he asked one evening after his mother had gone out, escorted from the front door by some friend's chauffeur.

His father didn't pretend not to know what he meant. He puffed for a moment on his after-dinner cigar – they were still at the table – and said, 'What do you suggest I do? Order her to stay home or go out with me? There's no pleasure in someone's unwilling company. If others can distract her from her grief, that's fine. I have my own distractions. My work, my club.' He smiled at Terry. 'You.'

And Fanny Clayborn, Terry thought. He said, 'I wonder why you stay with her.'

His father stiffened, and Terry wished the words unsaid. He had overstepped some invisible boundary, perhaps endangered the intimacy he meant to foster. He took up his own cigar, which he had not yet started – he cared little for tobacco and smoked only in his father's company – and occupied his eyes with the ritual of clipping and lighting until Terrence spoke.

'Yes, well, I suppose you have a right to question that. You're not a child anymore,' he said. 'It's obvious ours is not a marriage made in heaven. But it's a marriage. We've had a home together, a closed circle in which children were born and raised. Your mother gave you birth, watched over you, took care of you when you were sick. While she did that, I provided for all of you and protected you. Together we made a family. That's a valuable thing, Terry, to a man who never had one. Whatever else happened between your mother and me,

302

she helped give me a family. I can't turn my back on her.'

A few days after this Terrence called Terry into his office. Fanny Clayborn and Jake were there, too, Jake sitting directly in front of Terrence's desk, with Fanny at his right and an empty chair for Terry on his left.

The first time Terry had seen Fanny again after returning to the magazine, memory and knowledge had made him as self-conscious as if he were again a boy of fifteen. But it was not possible to stay ill at ease for long with Fanny Clayborn. She was too thoroughly at ease herself, too warm and open. She did not seem to Terry at all changed. Her cheeks were still as pink as a girl's, her brown eyes as brilliant, her dark hair still too thick and abundant to be contained by pins.

She could have been Jake's daughter, Terry thought. Ordinarily he was too used to Jake to see him. Now it struck him that Jake was only a year older than his father, yet it was impossible to imagine him as Fanny's lover. His pale face was thin and lined, with pouches under his eyes that drooped below his glasses. His hair was completely gray; his shoulders were stooped. In contrast, Terrence's vigor seemed almost excessive. He had recently shaved off his mustache and looked younger without it, his large, freckled face luminous with health, the red of his hair somewhat muted, but untouched by gray.

He said, 'Sit down, Terry. This is an informal conference. No one is here in any official capacity. I've asked Miss Clayborn in as an idea person, rather than a staff writer. I wanted you because I think it should be part of your experience to understand some of our problems. Jake and I have already conferred at length with the managing editor and the production manager and others.' He put his elbows on his desk, tented his fingers, and looked at the wall above their three heads. 'The magazine is not, at the moment, doing well. Our circulation is slipping. We've lost several of our writers to other magazines. Some of us think that the situation is temporary and that we can ride it out with no essential change of policy. Jake disagrees. He thinks— Well, why don't I let him tell you himself. Jake?'

'Yes.' Jake shifted his chair around to the side of the desk, so that he could look at Fanny and Terry as well as Terrence. The moment he began to talk, in a voice that had lost none of its depth or timbre, he was transformed from a pallid, unimpressive, aging man into someone vital and authoritative. 'I believe we have only to look at what's happening around us to see we have to change. Terrible things are going on in this country. Terrible corruption. Terrible abuses of power and privilege. Who wants to read a sweet little romance or an article about an obscure scientific discovery when they can get the inside story on some of these scandals? That's what interests people in these times. That's what we have to give them if we expect our circulation to grow. But there's another angle. These things ought to be exposed. We have the power to expose them. It's our duty to do it.' He glanced quickly at Terrence and then looked from Fanny to Terry. 'When we were young, in college, we cared a great deal about duty and the uses of power.'

'You're an idealist,' Fanny said, but not with disapproval.

Jake smiled. 'I'm a practical man. When what is right and what is profitable comes in one package, I buy it.'

Terrence said, 'I'm as appalled by what's going on as Jake is and as eager to see it exposed. If we were the only ones who could do it, I'd agree that we should. But since we're not, I don't believe it's necessary or advisable to change the character of our magazine and turn it into some sort of scandal sheet. That's not what people who read and love *McNally's Monthly* expect or want. I think we'd lose more of them than could possibly be made up by the new readers we might attract, so that I can't agree with Jake that the change would be profitable. People open the pages of *McNally's Monthly* not to be assaulted by all the evils of our society but to forget them – to be entertained.'

'If that's so,' Jake said, 'why have we lost readers while magazines that publish these tirades, as you call them, have attracted more and more? Terry, you may not know this, but three such tirades appeared in the January *McClure's. Three*, in one issue. One was on government corruption in Minneapolis, one on the illegal maneuverings of the Standard Oil Company, one on the lawlessness of some members of the United Mine Workers.' He looked at Fanny. 'Instead of losing readers by this triple assault, *McClure's* circulation has soared.'

Terrence barely gave him time to finish. 'I thought that too, but it isn't true,' he said. 'Their circulation has not by any means soared. The figures they claim are greatly inflated. According to Ayer's *Directory*, which you've apparently been too trusting to check, Jake, they gained fewer than seven thousand new readers soon after the articles appeared, and now that figure is declining and may even fall below last year's average. This supports my conviction that articles such as you've cited may stir up reader excitement, but sustaining it is something else. In my experience, public indignation can very quickly turn to boredom.'

Jake settled back in his chair. 'Ah, well, you may be right, Terrence. You usually are. Or you manage to make me believe you are. Still,' he said softly, 'I wish *we* had published those three articles.'

For a while no one spoke. Terry had questions, but he was not sure this was the moment to ask them. It was not the first time he had been aware of tension between his father and Jake. Now, as on other occasions, he sensed something deeper than their disagreement on a particular issue. If he had not known how close they were, he would have called it antagonism. He tried to think of some bland comment that would show interest without opinion, but Fanny was quicker and, as always, perfectly direct.

'Are you gentlemen waiting for us to take sides?' she inquired. 'I can't speak for Terry, of course, but I'm not going to do it. In the first place, I don't know enough. In the second – no, what's the difference? The first place says it all.'

Terrence did not look at her. It struck Terry that he seldom did, and that it must be for fear of giving himself away. The idea was disconcerting. He could not imagine his father with an expression on his face, in his eyes, so intimate, so burning, that it would instantly proclaim what his public voice and manner concealed.

'It's ideas I want, Miss Clayborn, not votes,' Terrence said. 'As I pointed out in the beginning, we've lost circulation and we've lost writers. I don't deny for a minute that it's because *McClure's* and others have come out with some sensational material and everybody is jumping on the bandwagon. But I am convinced it's a temporary trend, and what I'm looking for are ways to combat it without doing such violence to our magazine that it will be unrecognizable as *McNally's Monthly*.'

'All right. I have an idea or two. Or questions. As long as you accept that they're not votes.' Fanny poked uselessly at her tumbling hair, the ever-present pencil in her hand only disarranging it further. 'Would it compromise the magazine forever if we *occasionally* published an exposé? Not three in one issue, of course, maybe not one in every issue or every other issue. But occasionally, while the trend lasts. Would that make *McNally's* unrecognizable and turn away our regular readers? If we got hold of the best writers available?'

Terrence took a cigar from his vest pocket, ran it under his nose, clipped it, and, after a silent gesture to Fanny for permission, lit it. He did not offer one to Terry, who did not know whether this was an oversight or whether it was not considered fitting for an editor-in-chief to smoke with a desk editor.

'I'd like to hear your other idea. Or question,' Terrence said.

Fanny had no difficulty looking at him in a quite ordinary way. She smiled. 'Before you comment on the first one? All right,' she said again. 'If you're reluctant to print any of these sensational *facts*, would it be possible to handle some of them *fictionally*? Get a writer like, say, Will Irwin to write a story that would contain all the elements of some actual case of corruption, or whatever, but use a fictional situation and fictional characters.'

'Yes,' Terrence said.

Fanny raised her eyebrows. 'Yes, what?'

'Yes, those are interesting suggestions.' Terrence smiled at Fanny's ear. 'We'll consider them.' He turned to Terry. 'Have you anything to say or ask, Terry? Anything at all that comes to your mind? You have an advantage over the rest of us. You don't yet know all the complexities of the magazine business, and you haven't had a chance to harden into a point of view. If you have thoughts on any of this, they're likely to have the value of freshness.'

Terry hesitated. His father, no doubt meaning to reassure him, had on the contrary given too much importance to his response. The only idea he had that might conceivably be fresh might also be preposterous. But they were all looking at him, waiting, and he was not willing to say that nothing whatever had come into his mind.

'I was wondering – it's a wild notion, I suppose,' he said, 'but would it be possible for us to publish a new magazine? In addition to *McNally's Monthly*, I mean. And give that one a different character, make it more – sensational, if that's the word, so we could use it for the kind of material you've been talking about – exposés – and leave the old one just as it is? Would that be at all . . . ?'

He trailed off because Fanny had opened her mouth to speak. It was Fanny he had chosen to look at while he was talking, whose barely perceptible nod at the beginning had encouraged him to go on firmly.

'You're right,' she said to Terrence. 'He is smart.'

'He always was,' Jake said. 'My papa used to say he must have Jewish blood.'

'He has McNally blood,' Terrence said. Terry looked at his father now and saw he was smiling. 'It isn't a wild notion, Terry. It's a good, sound idea. But not for us. I don't rule it out as a possibility for the future – we've talked about such a possibility – but it would be impractical now. *McNally's Monthly* takes all our time and attention. All our money, I might add.' He waved his cigar at Terry. 'But you're thinking shrewdly. Like a magazine man.'

'Your father knows I don't agree with him,' Jake said. 'I think we could carry another magazine now. To our profit.'

'Yes. Well.' Terrence again addressed the wall above their heads. 'Jake can afford to gamble. I can't. *McNally's Monthly* is my son's inheritance.' He sat up abruptly and mashed the remains of his cigar in an ashtray. 'That's all, Miss Clayborn, Terry. Thank you for your suggestions.'

When they got outside and were walking back to their own desks, Fanny said, 'Your father's awfully proud of you, Terry. Without you I don't see how he could have stood your brother's death.'

Terry winced. 'Father's a lion. I don't think there's anything he couldn't stand.' He changed the subject quickly. 'What do you suppose will happen? Will he pay any attention to what you proposed?'

Fanny laughed a little. 'Oh, yes, he'll pay attention. He'll adopt both proposals.'

They had reached her desk, which stood in a cubicle at one end of the room. All the staff writers and minor editors worked in cubicles that varied in size and position, according to the importance of the individual. Typists and clerks occupied the center of the room, sitting at rows of desks. All the cubicles were known as offices, but only Terrence, Jake, the advertising manager,

308

the production manager, the managing editor, and the editors who headed departments enjoyed the privacy of real offices with doors. The largest of these were Terrence's and Jake's. They were of equal size, but Terrence's rug was Turkish while Jake's was domestic. Fanny's was one of the larger cubicles and had one wall that was not shared with another.

'You see,' she said, 'I only proposed a way of doing what he has wanted to do all along. Can you really imagine your father staying completely out of something like this? A chance to use the power of the magazine to bring down some of these high muckamucks?'

'But then why hasn't he just gone ahead with it?'

Fanny went in and sat down. Her desk was wildly disordered, but except for her hair, she herself was neat and immaculate in a crisp black and white striped blouse and floor-length black skirt with a wide leather belt. Terry thought that this businesslike outfit only underlined her lush femininity. He stood in the open entrance of her office, watching her arrange herself in her chair before she spoke, smoothing her skirt and then giving it a tomboyish little kick to settle the hem around her ankles.

'He couldn't just go ahead with it,' she said. 'Not when Sam McClure thought of it first and he'd just be following along. Not when Jake told him he thought this was a crusade *McNally's* ought to join.'

'Do you mean he'd oppose it, or pretend to oppose it, because Jake's in favor of it? I don't understand.'

'He isn't pretending, Terry. He doesn't pretend. His opposition is perfectly genuine. He's very reluctant to pattern *McNally's* after any other magazine or change its character. And the thing with Mr Stern—' She shook her head. 'He can't let Jacob Stern tell him what kind of magazine *McNally's* ought to be. Advise, suggest, the way I did, yes, but not tell him what his duty is.'

'But they're coeditors.'

'That's what it says on the masthead. It doesn't work

that way. Your father loves Jacob Stern. He wants him standing with him, next to him. But not on the same spot. You know that college journal they edited together? Your father told me Jacob Stern started it – the whole thing was his idea – but that's not how it ended. Your father always comes in first.'

'You make him sound ruthless.'

'No. He's a kind man. He honestly doesn't know how it happened that Jacob Stern lost control of the journal. If he crowds other people out, it's because of some force in him that they can't resist and that I don't think he even realizes he has. Something I suppose he had to have, or develop, to get where he is from where he once was. As long as Jacob Stern has known him, and as close as they are, he doesn't understand this about him. Mr Stern keeps trying to push against that force and failing.'

'You, though, seem to understand my father very well,' Terry said, and did not know what had impelled him to say it. 'I suppose it's woman's intuition.'

She looked at him for so long without speaking that he had all he could do not to drop his eyes.

'You know, don't you?' she asked him then.

'Know what?'

But she would not let him retreat. 'Don't play games with me, Terry.' she said impatiently. 'Maybe I talk too much. I know I talk too much. But I'm honest with people, and I expect them to be honest with me. How long have you known?'

'A long time.' He was inside the cubicle now. They had both lowered their voices. 'Since the beginning.'

She nodded. 'That's what came between you and your father, wasn't it? I always suspected it might be, but he said there was no way you could have known.'

'I heard him talking to you on the telephone,' Terry said, and paused. 'I stayed and listened.'

'Of course you did. Who wouldn't?' She smiled and then stopped smiling. 'And you were terribly shocked and angry. I'm sorry, Terry. Not about anything between your father and me. I've never been sorry for one minute of that. But I do regret what it did to you and the way it tore you and your father apart.'

'It wasn't your fault. I was young,' he said inadequately. 'Anyway, everything's all right now.'

'It's not – it never was – just a casual affair, you know. We love each other very deeply. I believe we always will.'

Terry looked away, as if the sun were in his eyes. 'Please don't tell my father I know about it,' he said.

'How could you think I would? That's something for you to tell him yourself, if you want to, or for him to bring up when he feels it's the right time. Now,' she said briskly, 'I think we'd better both get back to work.'

He started out and then stopped. 'I'm not sorry you know I know,' he said. 'I hope it doesn't bother or embarrass you.'

'No, Terry, it doesn't. I'm not exactly a shy, blushing damsel.' She laughed gaily. 'I haven't been embarrassed since I was eight years old and my petticoat fell down in the grocery store.'

As Fanny had predicted, Terrence adopted her proposals. In one issue of *McNally's* he published the first chapter of a fiction serial about the thinly disguised tinplate trust and its watered-stock activities. He had Fanny investigate a reported case of bribery of a Chicago alderman and, when it turned out to be an attempt by criminals to run the city, printed the story in the next issue. After the serial had run out, he wrote an editorial in which he said that the lawlessness and the abuse of power invading every segment of American society had grown to such proportions that no responsible publication could ignore it.

McNally's Monthly is, and shall always be, a family magazine [he wrote]. Its purpose from its inception has been, first and foremost, the entertainment and edification of discerning readers, and this will not change. We shall go on publishing great fiction by the finest of contemporary authors and outstanding articles by recognized experts in the fields of art and science. But in these parlous times, when the very foundations of our free nation are threatened by callousness, greed, and the misuse of influence, we must do more. It is our duty, as we see it, to inform our readers of this widespread debasement of values by which all Americans of principle wish to live. Thus we have begun, and will continue in future issues, fearlessly to cite instances and name names, until, through the mighty power of the pen, we have cut this malignant growth out of the body of our society.

From then on, at careful intervals, *McNally's Monthly* attacked such individuals as a senator who represented a corrupt political machine; a lumberman in Wisconsin who had acquired great tracts of forest land and a huge fortune by the use of illegal political pressure; a political boss in Oregon who used his power to direct the route and stopping places of a railroad; a manufacturer of cash registers who fixed prices by showing any new manufacturer reluctant to comply a warehouse filled with the registers of those he had put out of business.

Terrence never acknowledged that Fanny Clayborn had suggested the approach he used. When he wrote the editorial to explain it to his readers, he wrote as if *McNally's* alone were fighting the good fight, although *McClure's* had started it, and *Collier's*, *Leslie's*, *The Cosmopolitan*, *Everybody's*, and *Ladies' Home Journal* all had begun to engage in what President Theodore Roosevelt was later to call muckraking.

'I see what you meant,' Terry said to Fanny, meeting her on the way out to lunch one day. 'Father comes in first even when he doesn't.'

'He does, though, Terry. You'll see,' she answered. 'By now not only does he believe the whole thing was his idea, but he's making it his. No other editor is handling it the way he is, featuring an individual instead of an entire industry. No one else has treated it as a temporary departure, a duty. Some of the others have changed

312

direction entirely, even given their magazines new names, but he assures readers that *McNally's* will stay the same. And look at the piece in last month's issue on the greatness of Mayor Seth Low – do you understand how brilliant that was?'

'It was a good article. After all, Lincoln Steffens wrote it. But brilliant?'

'I don't mean the writing. Having it written was brilliant. I didn't realize it myself until your father showed me a letter from a reader that arrived the day the Seth Low piece was published. "Haven't you anything good to say about the country?" this reader wanted to know. And if he's asking that question, so are other readers. They're getting tired of reading about all the rottenness. Your father knew they would. That's why he published an article about good government in New York under an honest mayor – *before* he got that letter. Look at your schedule. How many exposés are planned for future issues? *McNally's* will be back to normal long before the magazines that changed their names and their entire policies know their day is over.'

Terry grinned at her. He was more at ease now with her than with any woman he had ever known. He had never been comfortable with his mother. With Mama Stern, whom he loved like a grandmother, he felt the need to appear better than he was. He had no friends among women his own age, no intimacy that was not sexual. Fanny treated him like a trusted younger brother, and he enjoyed the role. She was so forthright about her relationship with his father that he had come to take it for granted.

'My, you're impassioned! Your cheeks are so red you look feverish,' he said. 'I wish you'd champion me like that.'

'When you become a great magazine man like your father, perhaps I will.' She tossed her head, spraying hairpins all over Broadway. 'Anyway, if my cheeks are red, it isn't passion; it's this miserable March wind.'

313

They were approaching Twenty-third Street. Terry was going to a bookstore to buy Theodore Roosevelt's *Oliver Cromwell* for his father, who had an appointment with the President the following month and wanted to read the book first so he could say something knowledgeable about it. Fanny was taking the crosstown streetcar to have lunch with Alice Paul, a suffragette with militant ideas on whom she wanted to write a feature article.

'I wish you could have lunch with me,' Terry said. 'On the other hand, maybe it's as well you can't. I've just read in *The Cosmopolitan* that too much female company is mentally enervating for a man.'

He ducked, laughing, as she swung her handbag at him, and watched her board a streetcar, trying vainly to keep her skirts down in the whirlwind produced at that corner by the peculiar structure of the Flatiron Building.

11

When he got back to the office after lunch, a tall, thin middle-aged man with a tired face that might have once been handsome was sitting in his cubicle. He had on a cheap but neat gray suit under a worn brown overcoat that he had opened but not removed. He started to rise when he saw Terry but then evidently thought better of it and settled back again.

'They told me to wait in here,' he said. 'You're young Terrence McNally, are you?'

He had an accent that Terry could not place – not precisely foreign but unfamiliar. An out-of-town writer down on his luck, Terry guessed, though he had no manuscript with him. Still, Terry smiled and held out his hand, which the man took in a surprising iron grip.

'Yes, I'm Terrence McNally the Second. What can I do for you?'

'I don't know as you can do anything for me. It's your

314

father I wanted to see, but they tell me I must see you first.'

'That's right.' Terry sat down at his desk. 'My father, as you can imagine, is a very busy man. I try to see as many people for him as I can so that he's able to work without interruption. Is it a story or an article you wanted to discuss with him?'

'No, no, nothing like that.' The man folded his hands over his flat stomach and looked at Terry as though deciding whether or not to say anything more. Then he cleared his throat and said, 'My name is Sean McNally. I'm your father's brother. Your uncle, that makes me.'

Terry's first thought was that the man was a fake. He almost said so. He almost told him his father had no brother, before he realized that of course he did. Three brothers. He could not recall when his father had last mentioned them. Once, years before, Terry had asked him why they never saw each other.

'We've led different lives,' his father had said. 'It would only be awkward to try pretending we're brothers when, except in the strictest sense, we're complete strangers with nothing in common.'

This, like many of Terrence's pronouncements, had been over Terry's head at the time, but he remembered the gist of it now.

'I'm glad to meet you, Uncle Sean.' He thought this was the least he could say, whether it was true or not. 'What brings you here after all these years?'

'Well, I thought I'd tell your father that.'

Unlike Terry, he was perfectly self-possessed. Terry did not know how to deal with him. He was accustomed to hopeful, nervous writers who might wish to see his father or Jake but would not dream of insisting. This was altogether différent. This was his father's brother, yet his father might want to be protected from him, too.

'I'll have to find out. If he's in the midst of something – talking to somebody—'. Terry stood up. 'You might have to wait quite a while.'

315

'That's all right. I don't mind waiting.'

Terry went to his father's office and knocked on the door. Terrence answered, 'Yes?' in a testy voice, but when he saw who it was, his tone softened a little. 'Yes, Terry? Is it important? I'm struggling with an editorial.'

'I don't know if it's important or not,' Terry said. 'Your brother Sean is here.'

Terrence whirled around in his chair. 'Sean?' He said the name as if it made no sense to him. 'Here? Where?'

'In my office. He wouldn't tell me anything. He wants to see you. I told him you might be busy for a long time, but he said he'd wait.'

Terrence stood up, and then sat down again. 'I can't imagine—' He shook his head. 'There's not much sense in speculating, is there? Go and get him. Wait,' he said as Terry started out. 'Are you sure it's Sean? Sean McNally?'

'How can I be sure, Father? I've never seen him. He doesn't look like you.'

'No. None of them ever looked like me. I'm the homely one. All right, Terry, bring him in. Then stay with us. I want you to hear whatever he has to say.'

When Terry came back with his charge, his father was standing at the window. He turned around, looked at the man in the cheap gray suit and worn brown overcoat, and then said, 'Sean.'

'Did you think it would be an impostor, Terrence?'

'It's possible. Peculiar things happen to men whose names are always in print. But I recognize you. I wasn't sure I would. How often have I seen you, after all? The last time was when my mother died. Twenty-seven years ago. You were – what? Nineteen? Still, I do recognize you.'

'Our mother.'

'Well, yes, she bore you too.' They had been standing a few paces apart, facing each other, but now Terrence moved to his desk and waved his brother to a chair. 'All right, sit down, Sean, and tell me why you're here.'

316

Terry moved a chair into the far corner of the room. As he sat down, he felt as if he were again a child, creeping into the shadows, making himself unnoticeable so as to hear and learn the secret things that grown-ups knew – except that this time his father had told him to listen.

Sean sat at the side of the desk opposite Terrence. He still did not remove his overcoat. He looked to Terry like some of the old-time salesmen he had met on the road, the has-beens who did not know how to sell modern merchandise to modern buyers and did not know how to do anything else. His clothes were like theirs, and the grayness of his face, the way he sat in his overcoat with his hat held between his knees. But unlike them, he had neither an air of defeat nor a mask of bravado.

'I wanted to come many times before,' he said. 'Maybe you'll remember I tried to say so on the day of the funeral. To see her, our mother, in the early days. Later to see you. I got the idea, watching you the one day, that I'd get along better with you than I did with Paddy or Mike. They were great pals and still are. I was always the outsider.'

Terry could not make out the oddities of his speech. The flat vowels were clearly Bostonian, but there was a cadence, an occasional turn of phrase, that puzzled him. It was, in any case, the speech of an intelligent but not highly educated man.

'If you wanted to come,' Terrence said, 'why didn't you?'

'For mean, vain, and foolish reasons.' Sean's tone was so quiet and unstressed that the words did not sound theatrical. 'When I was young, and you lived in that dismal place we came to after the funeral, I couldn't stomach it. I surely hoped you'd come back to Boston with us, but I was proud of you when you wouldn't. Then you went to college, and I was ashamed to come with my ignorance.'

'How did you know I went to college?'

'That lady – the teacher – she wrote to tell us. She thought we should know, since the uncles offered help, that you were fine on your own. Then I married, you see, and had the six children, and I couldn't leave Boston at all. Later I couldn't bring myself to come, with my little country Irish wife and my Boston Irish ways, and you, married into high society and living in a mansion. Not commendable, Terrence, any of it, but there it is.'

Irish, Terry thought. That was the cadence, the turn of phrase. If his father had stayed in an Irish ghetto, he would talk the same way, his American English laced with that charming, lilting speech. How Sylvia would have hated it!

'You've come for no other reason than to see me?' Terrence asked. 'No other reason at all?'

Sean smiled for the first time, and it was possible to see how attractive he must have been as a young man, dark-haired and blue-eyed and with fine high cheekbones. 'Ah, now I didn't say that, did I? I've been speaking the truth about wanting to see you all these years, and I'll speak it still.' Now he set his hat down on the desk in front of him and straightened in his chair. 'I've come as well because there's nothing left for me in Boston. The uncles are dead. My wife died in the summer – the same month as your boy, Terrence. I read about that in the paper—'

He was saying how sorry he was, but Terry shut that part out. He could only bear to think of Charles alive and innocently happy.

'My children are married and moved away, either from Boston or from me. I was always working, you see, and it was their mother they were close to. And the business – I think I told you that day I didn't care for the shoe business, but I stuck it out. With the uncles it was bearable. But now Paddy's the boss, and Mike's next, and I've nobody to look out for but myself, so I quit.'

'Come, Sean, get to the point,' Terrence said, but Terry could hear a shade more warmth in his voice.

318

'What do you want from me? Money?'

'Ah, no, Terrence, after all these years I'm not here for a handout. I never in my life took money and gave nothing in return. I'm a worker. I've always been a worker. But when a man is well past forty, it isn't easy to find a new employer.' Sean held up his hand as though to stop Terrence from speaking, though he had not opened his mouth. 'Now I know you'll say I should have thought of that before I quit my old one. I did think of it. I thought of it, and I said to myself, *I'll go to see Terrence, who I've been wanting to see anyway all these years, and if he has no work for me I'll stay in New York in any case and get acquainted with my brother, and surely in that big city I'll find it possible to earn enough for my simple needs. A man willing to work will surely never go hungry*, I said to myself.'

Terry put his fist to his mouth to keep from laughing. The man was like a phonograph record, the sound increasing and accelerating as the handle was cranked. He had thought his father was a great, glib talker, but in comparison to Sean, Terrence was an inarticulate man.

Terrence thought so, too. He made no attempt to check his laughter. 'If I'd doubted you were my brother before, I wouldn't now,' he said. 'You're even wordier than I am, and that, let me tell you, is a feat.' He turned serious again. His voice was naturally much louder than Sean's, much harder. 'How is it you have no money, Sean? You must have made plenty of it, all those years in a successful business. What happened to it?'

'A good bit of it went for the raising of six children and putting them all through college. A good bit of it.' He looked down at his hat and back at Terrence. 'The rest of it – well, you see, Terrence, after my Margaret died, it was like the sunshine went out of my life, and so I took to the drink, and I played cards in a state where I hardly knew a spade from a club, and so I lost the rest of it. I tell you, Terrence, there's something in the Irish blood, I think, that makes it so a man can't drink in the ordinary way, take it or leave it. At least in my case the only one harmed by it was myself. I've always thought it must have been the drink that took that grandfather of ours, the first Terrence McNally, and caused him to do some fearful thing that couldn't be spoken of, though nobody will ever know.'

If Terry had been warned in time, he would have covered his ears against these words of Sean's and against his own silent answer: *But somebody does know.* Instead, he focused with desperate attention on his father's response. 'Let's not get off on tangents, Sean. Just tell me this – in one very short sentence, if that's possible for you: How much are you drinking now?'

'Oh, I've given it up entirely. It's not a thing I can do a little of, you see. All or nothing is the only way, and I chose nothing.'

'Well, that's three sentences, but all right. Another question: Do you know anything whatever about the magazine business?'

'Not about any part of it that isn't like the shoe business, no, but—'

'Then what qualifications do you imagine you have,' Terrence broke in, 'that would fit you for any sort of work on *McNally's Monthly*?'

Terry did not think his father need be this caustic. The man was, after all, his brother. But Sean seemed altogether unruffled.

'No special qualifications, but a few general ones,' he said. 'I'm a fast learner and, as I've told you, a hard and willing worker. I have, as you've noticed yourself, a way with words, which is a useful thing in any business, but surely a large advantage in one that's mostly words.' He smiled. 'Also,' he added (was the shrewdness accidental? Terry wondered, or had he so rapidly sized up his brother?), 'don't forget I'm a McNally and so, you'll surely agree, no ordinary man.'

Terrence relaxed in his chair. He smiled, too. 'Sean, either I take to a man right away or I don't. I've always

320

been like that, and I've always gone along with it, and so far I've not once had reason to change my mind. Have you a place to stay?'

'I found a room in a lodging house.' He extracted a slip of paper from his vest pocket and read it. 'On Forty-sixth Street near Ninth Avenue. I was told I'd find something there within my means, and so I did.'

'You can't stay there. If it's not a brothel, it's the next thing to it, in that neighborhood. When we've finished here, you must go and get your luggage out of the place. For the time being, you'll stay in my house. We have plenty of room.' He stood up. 'Now come and meet Jacob Stern, my coeditor. I think—' He looked at Terry, who thought his father had forgotten he was there. 'Starting tomorrow morning, Terry, your uncle will spend his time with you in your office, learning to do your job. I think that's the place for him to begin. When he's ready to take it over, I'll see about getting you out of the office.' Terrence turned back to Sean before he could have seen the pleasure in Terry's face. 'Terry doesn't belong at a desk. You probably do. Anyway, we'll try it.'

Sean followed Terrence out of the room. 'I note you're a man who makes up his mind and then acts, no dilly-dallying,' Terry heard him say. 'A man after my own heart, and that's the truth.'

Later in the day Terry saw his father alone for a moment – long enough to say, 'Mother isn't going to like it. Uncle Sean staying with us, I mean. She'll make him feel uncomfortable. Wouldn't it be better to send him to a hotel, pay for his—'

'He wouldn't let me do that, son. He'll stay in our house because that's the natural thing for a brother, but he wouldn't go to a hotel at my expense. Don't worry. He won't be uncomfortable.' Terrence spoke as if he and Sean had grown up together and never lived apart. 'I doubt that anyone has ever made him uncomfortable or ever could.'

Sylvia reserved for Terrence her open outrage at having this uncouth, too-Irish brother-in-law suddenly foisted on her. She treated Sean with the cold courtesy she used to keep Jews, tradespeople, and other inferiors in their place. But Sean, as Terrence had predicted, was not in the least affronted. In fact, he seemed not to notice. He went on in his amusing, long-winded way, behaving like an old-time member of the family, the amiable uncle who charmed everybody and was always welcome. Sylvia's name for him was a frigid 'Mr McNally,' to which he invariably replied with a genial 'Sylvia,' often accompanied by a pat on the cheek or hand, apparently oblivious of her distaste.

She avoided him as much as possible, never coming down from her room until he had left with Terrence and Terry in the morning, and going out even more often than before for dinner and the evening. Though he made no apparent connection with Sylvia's attitude, Sean spoke once or twice of looking for a place of his own. Terrence discouraged this.

'There's no hurry,' he said. 'Give yourself a chance to accumulate some savings first.'

'I don't want to start smelling like they say fish and guests do if they're around too long.'

'You're not a guest, Sean. You're my brother.'

This acquisition of a brother in his middle age gave Terrence evident pleasure. He had told Terry that his brothers were strangers to him and that if they had met, they would have nothing in common, but now, with Sean, it did not seem to be so. The two men talked endlessly, sometimes interrupting each other, sometimes both going at it at once, Terrence's loud voice rising above Sean's soft one, yet never quite drowning it out. When Terry joined them, they both tried to draw him in, but before long they were back to a duet.

One evening they were discussing President Roosevelt, who was Sean's idol. 'Such a joyful man, such a fighter,'

Sean was saying. 'I'm surprised he's not a man after your own heart as he is after mine.'

'He is and he isn't,' Terrence said. 'I like the joy and the fighting spirit all right, but he's too wild and inconsistent for a President, and he's too much of a politician for my taste, too much of an opportunist, making deals with a senator like Aldrich, cuddling up to J. P. Morgan, and—'

'A President *must* be a politician; you won't deny that, surely, and if Teddy deals and cuddles, it's in a good cause. Look at all his reforms – busting the big trusts and all. I'm a lifelong Democrat, but Teddy—'

'*We've* instigated his reforms, Sean. We've clamored for them in issue after issue. But does he recognize this? On the contrary, he called me down to Washington to tell me we've done nothing really effective to combat the evils, that we're just lurid sensationalists, building up a dangerous revolutionary feeling in this country. Luckily, as you know, Terry, I foresaw the growing unpopularity of our clamor and have let it die away.'

'What do you think of Teddy yourself, Terry?' Sean asked. 'We haven't heard your opinion.'

'I think he's basically an honest man, but he's superficial. I don't believe he really understands the difference between the common good and the special interests. When he compromises—'

'That's right!' Terrence broke in. 'Why do you think he amended his bill to regulate and control the railroads, Sean? The President of the Pennsylvania Railroad persuaded him that—'

'In the end, though, Terrence, his deals and his compromises and all do lead to the common good, so what does it—?'

Terry slipped out of the smoke-thick den, leaving his cigar to burn itself down in an ashtray. He did not think the other two had noticed his departure, but his father followed him into the hall.

'If you're provoked, Terry, I don't blame you,' he said.

323

'I know it sometimes seems we're shutting you out. It's only that Sean and I have so much to catch up on, so much we don't know about each other – ideas, opinions, all that.' Terrence put his hand on Terry's shoulder. 'He won't be staying here forever, son.'

'I'm not provoked, Father,' Terry said, though it was not altogether true. He said, 'I like to listen to the two of you,' which was true. 'I left because I have tickets for *The Belle of New York*.'

This was also true. Terry had loved the theater since the night he and Sam had seen the show at Koster & Bial's Music Hall. It was the only entertainment he had resumed after his long period of near monasticism since Charles's death. Often he went alone. Tonight, as a favor to Fanny, he was escorting her niece, a gawky, frightened girl from Vermont who had never been to New York before, never seen a show, never, Fanny guessed, been out alone with a man.

'Give her a memory, Terry. How often can you do that for anybody so painlessly?'

He did it for Fanny, not the girl. She was a dead weight, so shy she could scarcely talk. But he was unexpectedly moved by her rapture in the theater. She sat motionless, openmouthed, as the Salvation Army lassie sang her way to fame, singing, 'They never proceed to follow that light, but they always follow me.' She was utterly bedazzled, and Terry had made it possible.

In the theater he decided to take her to Rector's for a bite afterward, but once out in the street, with her gulping and stammering beside him again, he changed his mind. Fanny would not expect it of him. It would make it too late a night anyway. He had to be up early to go to work with his father and Sean.

Sean had quickly become a favorite among his co-workers. He was an artist at balancing between deference and camaraderie with his superiors; between authority and friendliness with typists and clerks. He mastered the routine aspects of Terry's job in two weeks and was by nature better than Terry at easing out hopelessly untalented authors and other unwanted visitors without destroying their dignity. It took him longer to learn discrimination. His knowledge of literature was limited, and he often recommended as distinguished an author's offering that was no better than pedestrian. But he had, as he had told Terrence, a way with words himself and recognized a happy turn of phrase, or a clumsy one when he saw it. The works he approved were never totally worthless, and he never overlooked real competence. In six months or so he acquired enough judgment so that he no longer needed to be monitored. Terry, because of his personal urgency to get away from the desk job, scrupulously did not hurry the day. It was Sean himself who decided the time had come.

'There's no way to measure, anyhow, what's good and what's better. I've found that much out, Terry,' he said. 'I've heard enough tales of some piece of writing called hopeless by some editor and allowed to slip away, only to be snatched up by another editor and become a great success. Or the other way around. If I make mistakes, likely as not I won't make them any oftener, and they won't be any worse than anybody else would do.'

Long before this happened, and Terry was set free from his desk, something more cataclysmic took place. Sean was still living in the house at the time. His presence may have precipitated the event, but even Sylvia made it clear that he was not in any sense its cause. It astonished Terry that she bothered to do this. In fact, her behavior was altogether so uncharacteristic that at the moment it almost obscured from Terry the enormity of what she was saying.

She had not dined with them that evening, but she was still in the house. Terry heard her come down into the hall while he and his father and Sean were having dessert and coffee. She said something to a chauffeur who had arrived at the front door a moment earlier. Now he went upstairs and she came into the dining room.

For a time, after Charles's death, she had appeared to fade and age, but it seemed to Terry now, watching her enter and stop just inside the doorway, that the process had been reversed. She looked beautiful. She could have been mistaken for a young woman. Her hair, under a two-toned velvet and chiffon picture hat trimmed with ostrich feathers, was as fair as it had ever been. She wore an evening gown of peach satin, the puffed sleeves, the bodice, and the long skirt lavished with lace and velvet ribbon, a row of bows marching from the neck to the girlishly small waistline. Her skin bloomed with youthful color, and her dark eyes glowed.

'I'm leaving,' she said.

Terrence nodded. 'Have a pleasant evening.'

'I don't mean I'm leaving for the evening.' For an instant she fingered a ruby necklace that Terry had never seen before. 'I'm not coming back,' she said.

Terry wanted to look away from her, but he was unable to shift his eyes. He heard Sean's chair scrape.

'You needn't go, Mr McNally. This isn't a secret.' Sylvia glanced at him. 'It has nothing to do with you. In case you think it has, I assure you that I'd have left whether you were here or not. It isn't your doing either, Terrence.' She gave her husband a little nod, the shadow of an inappropriate smile. 'I realize that by your standards you've become a successful, important man, but your standards have never been mine. You know that. I haven't pretended they were. In spite of that, I've stayed with you a long time, longer than I'd have thought possible when I married you. But now that Charles is dead, there's nothing here for me anymore.' She looked at Terry, the remains of the smile still on her lips. 'I did my best for you, Terry. Nobody can do any more than that. I wasn't cut out to be a mother. Well—' The smile changed, became the fixed social expression of a departing guest. 'I wanted to make all this clear before I left. I'll go now.'

She had already started to turn away when Terrence

326

said, 'One moment.'

Terry, finally detaching his gaze from his mother, saw that all the color had gone out of his father's face. The freckles that had faded with age into near invisibility stood out like fresh stigmata against the pallor.

Sylvia spoke without facing him again. 'There's no use saying anything more, Terrence. You can't stop me.'

'I don't intend to try. There are, however, certain practical considerations that make it necessary for me to know how to communicate with you.'

'I can't imagine what they could be. I'm getting out of your life entirely and going to another one that has nothing to do with anyone here. I'll even be living in another country. France, you might as well know. Paris,' she said on a note of triumph. 'So there won't be any reason at all for any communication.'

'You seem to forget,' Terrence said, 'the little matter of divorce.'

Sean pushed his chair away from the table again and stood up. 'I shouldn't be listening to this. It's not proper,' he murmured, and fled the room. Terry supposed he should leave as well, but he made no attempt to go. As so often in the past, he felt that no one remembered he was there.

'Oh, well, you needn't worry about that,' his mother said. 'I won't let you divorce me. Not without an ugly scandal that I'm sure you'd want to avoid – if not for yourself, certainly for – someone else. If I should ever decide to divorce you, you'll be informed.'

She went out. They heard her talking to the chauffeur in the hall. 'You'd better not put this small package with the others, Jean-Paul. I think it will be safer on the seat between Monsieur and me.'

For several moments after the front door closed, neither Terry nor his father spoke. Then Terrence sighed, offered Terry a cigar from the humidor on the table, took one himself, and held it in his fingers without lighting it. The color had come back into his face.

'That seems to be that,' he said. 'I'm sorry you had to hear it all.'

'You needn't be, Father. It's a long time since I've had any illusions about her.' Terry paused. 'Or do you mean you're sorry I heard what she said about a divorce?'

Terrence gave him a quick glance and then examined his cigar. 'If you had to hear it, I'd have preferred—'

'Father, I've known since I was fifteen. Fanny knows I know. You can ask her what I said. She's worth ten of my mother. I don't blame you.'

His father smiled. 'I'm very glad. I don't blame myself. For many things I do, but not for that. Fanny has given me everything your mother did not. *Could* not, Terry. We should remember that about her. The capacity to care for another human being was left out of her nature.'

'Charles?'

'She has always cared about owning lovely things. Charles was her most beautiful possession.'

Terrence sold the Fifth Avenue house at a large profit and rented an apartment in the Dakota. The apartment was so named when it was built in 1884 because its location on Seventy-second Street and Central Park West was so far uptown from any fashionable district that it was considered an outpost. The apartment was luxurious, with a huge mahogany- and oak-paneled drawing room, two marble bathrooms, and four bedrooms, but it was still an economy move. The house was much larger and much more expensive to maintain. For one thing, in the apartment they needed only one full-time servant and someone to come in twice a week to do the heavy cleaning.

Mary came with them, but Terrence gave Thomas a modest settlement and let him go. When public transportation was inconvenient, he hired a hansom cab, as he had once, to Sylvia's annoyance, hired a carriage instead of owning one. He never owned an automobile. By the time he might have considered it, he found it less trouble to travel by taxicab or hired limousine with chauffeur.

'This is a reasonable way to live,' he said to Terry. 'Maybe now I can stay out of debt.'

He was standing in the doorway of Terry's room, watching him arrange his books. The room's furniture was sparse, plain and heavy, with dark red rough-textured draperies and a bedspread of the same fabric.

'I didn't know you were in debt,' Terry said.

'I'm not now, since the increase in the magazine's advertising revenue, but I was for years. Between the money I poured into *McNally's Monthly* and Sylvia's extravagances—'

'Couldn't you have put a stop to her extravagances, Father?'

'If I had, I believe she'd have left long before she did. I wasn't willing to risk that while you and Charles were young. Charles still needed her. At least I thought so. He still seemed to me, even at seventeen, very much a child.' Terrence came into the room and briefly touched Terry's averted cheek. 'You're not over his death, are you, Terry?'

'How can anybody get over a thing like that?'

'Yes. How can anybody?'

They had tried to persuade Sean to come and share the apartment with them, but he refused. He had his bearings now and a little nest egg, and he wanted to be on his own.

'It was fine of you, letting me live with you for a time. I was happy doing it, fitting in as best I could, and all. But I have my own ways, and at my age I'm set in them, so it's best I have a place where I can do as I like, when I like, and no bother to a soul.'

He took a room in a comfortable boarding house on Seventy-eighth Street between West End Avenue and Riverside Drive. The proprietor was a jolly German woman, Mrs Schiller, who cooked plain but nourishing meals for her six gentlemen boarders. She kept the house

329

immaculate with the help of a husky niece and a young colored man whose outfit changed with his functions – a striped canvas apron for cleaning, a white coat for answering the doorbell or serving in the dining room.

Mama Stern died in her sleep one snowy night in January 1906, at the age of seventy. The doctor said it was a wonder she had lived that long, with the weight she had carried. She was buried the next day, according to Jewish custom, and that night, after all the other mourners had left, Terrence, Terry, and Sean stayed with Jake.

'Please, you stay, too,' Jake said when Sean started to leave. 'Terrence is my brother, so you're my long-lost brother as well as his. I've felt that from the first. Mama did, too.' His face dripped with tears, but he smiled at Sean. 'I'm a sentimental man. Jews are sentimental people. Humor me, please.'

'*Humor* you?' Sean pulled a chair over to Jake, who was huddled in a corner of the sofa, and sat in front of his knees. '*Humor* you, man? I'm proud to stay. I'm honored. How long is it I've known you? Not two years or so, surely. It feels like all my life. And the same for her, your wonderful mama. Our wonderful mama, Jake, for she was truly like one to me, especially since I hardly knew my own, so I'm proud and honored when you call me your brother and want me to stay.'

Terry had moved across the room, away from the wash of words. He liked Sean. Everybody liked Sean. But sometimes his talk was too extravagant for Terry's taste.

A silver-framed snapshot of Mama Stern stood on top of the piano. Terry had seen it often before, but now he leaned closer to examine it again because he felt that her face had already begun to fade from his memory. Jake had taken the snapshot six years earlier with Kodak's new Brownie camera, one of four the company had presented the magazine when the issue came out that advertised the camera: 'You press the button, we do the rest.' What Kodak could not do was hold the camera still for the button presser. Jake had moved it, rendering Mama Stern's features indefinite, fuzzy, as though they might be disappearing. Terry had an urge to snatch up the picture and hide it while the face was still visible. But all he did was walk to the window and stand with his back to the room until he was sure he was not going to cry.

When he joined the others, Jake was asking Sean about Mrs Schiller's boardinghouse.

'It might be the place for me,' he said. 'What do I want with this house now, one man alone?'

'Come and live with us, Jake,' Terrence said. 'You'd certainly find Mary's cooking much more to your liking than Mrs Schiller's.'

'Thank you, Terrence, but you know it would be a disaster. We'd bring our business and our wrangling home with us, no matter how we tried not to, and there wouldn't be any peace for either of us.'

'I don't think you'd like it at the boardinghouse, though,' Sean said. 'It's not what you're used to.'

Jake caught something in Sean's tone that Terry missed. 'No Jews allowed, is that it? . . . Yes, of course. Mrs Schiller. I should have—'

'I don't think it's her so much. I can't see her refusing to take you, a nice woman like her. But some of the others. I've heard remarks. For all I know, they make them about the Irish as well when I'm not there.'

'Then it won't be Mrs Schiller's boardinghouse.' Jake sighed. 'Mama warned me, of course, years ago. "I've had my life," she said. "Go out and live yours. If you stay here with me, you'll end up a dried-up old man with nobody and nothing." Ha!' he said suddenly, sitting up and taking off his glasses to wipe his eyes. 'Listen to me, mourning for myself! I'm not the one who died.'

'If you'll excuse me for asking, as long as you brought it up,' Sean said, 'why didn't you go and live your own life? It isn't as if you were her only child or she was destitute or anything.'

Jake put his glasses back on. He shrugged. 'Maybe Mama gave me an excuse not to try it.' He slid along the sofa, past Sean's knees, and stood up. 'What I think Terry and I need now is a little of that good scotch my brother-in-law Saul brought. Sean, would you like a glass of this new beverage, Coca-Cola, that everyone's talking about? You, Terrence?'

'Fine,' Terrence said.

'I think I'll have a little of the scotch. Just a very little,' Sean said. 'Just this one time. I think the sad occasion calls for it.'

Terry and his father took Sean back to Mrs Schiller's boardinghouse shortly after ten o'clock. The house had a number of stone steps, leading up to a high front stoop. They had trouble getting him up the steps. Even with one of them on each side of him, holding him up, he kept sliding back. They made so much noise that the door opened before they reached the top. The colored man in his white coat peered down at them and then came quickly and took Sean from them, holding him expertly under his arms.

'That's all right. I'll take care of him now, Mr McNally, sir,' he said to Terrence.

'Can you manage him alone?'

'Oh, yes, sir, I'm used to it. I always take care of him. He'll be fine in the morning. You just leave him to me, Mr McNally, sir.'

12

Terry sailed for Europe in February of the following year. He was to interview several American writers who were living in France and persuade them to submit stories involving the country and its people, from the

American point of view.

'No one else is doing this,' his father said. 'Everything in the magazines is about Americans in America. That was all right once, but I believe readers are less provincial now, more curious about other countries and other ways of life. It's an interesting assignment for you, Terry. See what you can develop.'

An exchange of letters would have accomplished the purpose well enough. It was, Terry thought, his father's way of appeasing him and, at the same time, getting rid of him for a while.

He was delighted to go. His normal restlessness was exacerbated by frustration on the magazine. Once relieved of the desk editor's job, he had anticipated rapid progress, but his father persisted in holding him back. The authors he was permitted to deal with were minor ones. He had a natural understanding of popular taste – Fanny and Jake both said so – but everything he read had to go through two other readers before it reached his father, who made the final decision on every piece that appeared in the magazine. He was full of ideas, too. Some of them were wild, he knew, but some were not. He was certain, for example, that they should be publishing more than one magazine, but his father continued to reject this, as he rejected most of Terry's suggestions.

'A magazine for women, Father. At least that. It would be tremendously popular. Look at the *Ladies' Home Journal*.'

'Not yet, Terry. The timing is wrong for us. You haven't been in the business long enough to sense such things.'

It was always the same. He did not know enough; he had not had enough experience; he was too young; he was too impatient. Once Terry lost his temper and said something he regretted as soon as it was out of his mouth.

'You have to know better, don't you, Father? You

333

have to come in first. Even if it means keeping your own son back. Or your closest friend.'

They were not in the office at the time but in the apartment, where they had agreed never to discuss magazine business, yet often did. Terrence got up out of his chair abruptly, walked to the windows, and stood staring at Central Park.

Terry spoke to his back. 'I shouldn't have said that. I'm sorry.'

'No, you shouldn't have said it, Terry. It's nothing a son should say to his father. However, there may be some truth in it.' He did not turn around. 'You'll have my place on the magazine one day, when you can do the job better than I can. It may be that I'm restraining you because I'm afraid otherwise your cleverness will bring the day on sooner than I'd like. I don't think that's so. I think what I want to curb is your contentment with superficial skill, your tendency to chafe at anything you can't master overnight and then go on to something else. I think what I'm afraid of is that unless I do this, you won't be the superb magazine man I've hoped you'll become. But I could be deluding myself.' He was silent a moment. 'As for Jake—'

'Please, Father. I was angry. I just said the first thing that came into my mind. You don't have to explain to me.'

'I know I don't, but I'd prefer to have things clear between us. We had enough misunderstanding in the past.' Terrence came away from the window now and sat down again. His manner eased. 'Jake has made himself, Terry. *Un*made himself, I suppose, would be more accurate. He has always put himself under somebody's thumb. Out of goodness or weakness or something else, I don't know, but he's done it. Mine, on *Pharos*. His father's. Mine again, after his father died. His mother's. If he had married, he'd have been under his wife's thumb. It's the strong women who attract him. Like Fanny—' He stopped and went on quickly again.

334

'You've seen how he argues with me, how he comes alive then. But it's only the argument itself he enjoys. Winning makes him uncomfortable.' Terrence grinned suddenly. 'On the other hand, there's nothing you like better, is there?'

Terry grinned back at his father and said, 'I'd like it if I could do it. How can anyone win an argument with you, Father? By the time you've finished talking it's impossible to remember what the argument was about, all those words ago.'

Temporarily Terry was always pacified. His father could explain away anything. Sooner or later, though, Terry's resentment revived. It was not altogether because of their differences over his role on the magazine. They were two strong-willed men, working in the same office, living in the same apartment with no one else there as a buffer between them. Terry, though he had not resumed his immoderate drinking and whoring, went out often, and Terrence visited Fanny several times a week. Still, they were together too much.

'Why don't you let Fanny come here and live with you, and I'll get my own place?' Terry had asked his father.

But Terrence had been shocked. 'I don't know how you can suggest such a thing. If I were willing to see her reputation in shreds, I'd have divorced your mother, let her spread whatever ugliness she wished, and married Fanny.'

Terry had hesitated to say that he thought he should move out anyway. He did not like leaving his father to rattle around in that cavernous apartment, but he did not intend to live his life with a parent. He was twenty-five years old, and it was time to be on his own. This trip to Europe gave him an easy way to make the break. By the time he came back his father would be accustomed to his absence, and he would immediately find another place to live.

He went first to Paris and stayed at the small hotel on

the Left Bank near the Seine where Oscar Wilde had died seven years before. Andrew Pruitt, the writer he was to see, was a young man not much older than Terry. He had written one very successful novel and promptly gone to Paris to write another in a more inspirational atmosphere than that of the small American town in which he had written the first. His muse, however, had apparently remained at home. Since he had made five starts on a new novel in the eight months he had been in Paris and torn them all up, Terry easily persuaded him to abandon it, at least temporarily, and write something for *McNally's*.

Once that was out of the way, Terry, with Pruitt as a knowledgeable guide, devoted himself to savoring the delights of the city.

Pruitt was a stocky man with a cadaverous, bearded face that did not seem to belong to his husky body. He affected the clothes and mannerisms of a French artist and spoke a competent French with a midwestern twang that gave the entire performance a comic quality. At home Terry would not have chosen him as a companion, but here he was part of the enchantment of Paris. He lived on the rue du Bac in a seventeenth-century building, its doorways decorated with the elaborate stonework of the Art Nouveau architect Jules Lavirotte. He rented his apartment from the impoverished French widow of an Italian count. Her portrait, a distorted, brilliantly colored fauvist painting by André Derain, hung on one red damask wall, beside one of a churchman ancestor of her late husband's by the fifteenth-century painter Antonello da Messina.

'Think of it! This building, this room, all these things!' Terry made an enveloping gesture. 'Most of them were here, part of people's daily lives, centuries before our country was even an idea. Think of knowing who your fifteenth-century ancestor was, much less owning his portrait!'

Pruitt smiled indulgently. 'One gets used to it,' he said.

'I suppose so. You might use something like it, though, in your piece for the magazine. An American's first impressions of Paris.'

'I might.' Pruitt took a notebook and a pencil stub from the pocket of his long, loose blue jacket and began scribbling. His smile did little to relieve the pale melancholy of his face. 'You don't mind my stealing your idea?'

'You're not stealing it. I gave it to you. That's one of the things an editor is for.'

Pruitt assumed an air of amused boredom with Terry's awestruck response to the city, his eagerness to see everything and go everywhere. He also hinted that he was running out of money. But he knew all the likeliest places, and once he realized that Terry would foot the bill for those that had a price, he took him around willingly.

He took him to the great, soaring, coal-soiled twelfth-century Cathedral of Notre-Dame, its masses of carved stone figures representing the religious, legendary, and day-to-day life of Paris, and to Sacre-Coeur, the huge, white Byzantine-Romanesque basilica dominating the city from the top of Montmartre, begun in 1875 and not yet completed. They went to the Eiffel Tower, which some Parisians considered 'arrogant ironmongery' and in which some, like the writer Blaise Cendrars, saw the poetry of iron and bolts, of 'tangled girders' and of mass and height, carrying the viewer's gaze up toward the sun . . .

They walked through the snow-dusted Tuileries Gardens across from the Louvre and looked through Napoleon's little Arc de Triomphe du Carrousel to his great Arc de Triomphe, the largest triumphal arch in the world, at the end of the Champs-Élysées. They walked through the crowded market on the ancient, winding rue Mouffetard, popularly known as La Mouffe, once part of a Roman *via* that led to Lyons. They walked along the Seine, where barges floated so slowly that they barely seemed to move and where, even in February, fishermen lazily dangled their lines and lovers sat entwined on the stone banks in the winter sunshine . . .

'The light is so marvelous,' Terry said. 'What makes it like this? So that you can look across there to Napoleon's Tomb, for instance, and see it one way, and then the next minute the light shifts and it's something new?'

Pruitt didn't know.

They went to hear *Manon* in the vast opera house and to see Molière's *Tartuffe* performed by the Comédie Française, though Terry did not understand French at all and he could tell Pruitt only pretended to follow the flashing dialogue. They saw the show at the Moulin Rouge, the best-known music hall in the city, and then drank a great deal of wine in a café. Afterward Pruitt introduced Terry to a *pissoir*, one of the city's numerous street urinals, enclosed so that only the legs of the men inside, and sometimes their heads, were visible to passersby.

They spent hours strolling through the Latin Quarter, where twelfth-century students from all over Europe once sat on bales of straw to hear Abélard and other teachers lecture on logic and theology, and made Latin their common tongue. Terry was fascinated by the belligerence of the modern students, who were constantly shouting and shaking their fists, protesting against some law, Pruitt said, or against conditions at the University of Paris, or arguing with each other about politics.

'They've always been like this,' Pruitt said. 'Way back in 1200 they demanded that the current king exempt them from civil jurisdiction, and he did it, too, made them answerable only to the church. They'd been in some kind of brawl with an innkeeper, and the populace and the sheriff went after them. The students did battle with all of them, and five boys were killed. The only difference now is that nobody dies. At least nobody has so far.'

'What a docile bunch American students are by comparison!' Terry said. 'I thought we were pretty freewheeling at Columbia, but we'd never have considered making any kind of demands or battling the authorities. It couldn't happen there.' He listened to a boy screaming at a group of hecklers who had gathered around him, apparently to shout down his political views. 'Political views?' he said to Pruitt. 'I can't imagine any American student having any, much less fighting over them. Why do you suppose it's so different here?'

'I don't know about the politics,' Pruitt said. 'I think they fight because that's their disposition. What the French call *mauvais caractère*. Parisians in general, not only the students, tend to be rude and unpleasant, especially to each other.'

'Don't put that in your story.'

'Why not? Even if it's only partly true, it's amusing.' Pruitt yawned, bored now that he had finished displaying his knowledge. 'Let's leave them to it. I know where we can find some women if you're interested.'

Terry surprised himself by rejecting the suggestion. He felt a casual one-night encounter to be inappropriate to the grandeur of the city. He knew this was absurd. Paris had its bawdy, squalid side, and he was not, surely, a romantic. But he told Pruitt he was serious about a girl at home and had no eyes for other women.

Later that night he stood alone on the Pont Royal, looking down the river at the twin towers of Notre-Dame, and thought suddenly of Charles, who had been to Paris and said nothing about it that would prepare anyone for its magic. Probably he had not noticed the magic. If he had been there on the bridge beside him, Terry would have showed him how eerily the jagged river reflected the ancient buildings along its banks, and the marvel of the distant cathedral, standing for eight centuries in rain and snow, darkness and sunlight, and now under a cold winter moon. Charles would have listened and learned. He always had. If Terry could have shown him how not to die—

He twitched his shoulder, as if shaking off a hand, and went back to his hotel. The next day, after telling Andrew Pruitt he would return to Paris and pick up his story in about two weeks, he took the train to Nice.

Terry stayed in the south of France for nearly two months. In a letter to his father he said that he was writing his own impressions of the country and its people, that he thought they were decidedly publishable, and that he wanted to stay on the ground until he had finished them. He was also negotiating with two writers in the area and with an excellent artist whom he was trying to persuade to come back to New York and do illustrations for *McNally's*, instead of painting Mediterranean landscapes that he hardly ever sold.

All this was true, but none of it was his primary reason for staying so long.

> I'm delighted with your decision to do some writing of your own [his father wrote]. An editor who doesn't write seems to me an anomaly, but I've never noticed any definite tendency in that direction on your part, other than an abortive piece that I found in an old typewriter at the office when you were a young boy – something that I believe set out to be the story of my life.

His father was as prolix on letter paper, Terry thought as he read, as he was in person.

> I certainly don't want to discourage you now, though you know, of course, that we won't publish your work unless it is up to the high professional standards we demand of any author. In any case, it's excellent practice – a writer learns only by writing – and I trust it will make you more valuable to the magazine to stay in France and complete it than to

return now, though it was certainly not my intention to have you spend more than a few weeks there. As for the two authors with whom you are negotiating, I think I would not be too vigorous about that if I were you. We will have Pruitt's piece, and possibly yours, and we don't want to overdo it. I would by all means drop your efforts with the artist. We are leaning more and more toward photographs for our illustrations now, and when we do want to use original paintings, we have enough fine, proven illustrators like Gibson and Flagg to draw on ...

Terry could not abruptly drop his efforts with the artist, but he tapered them off. It was only a game anyway – a spurious reason for staying on with Frank, who knew the real one, and an excuse for not going home that he thought his father might accept.

Frank Gabriel was a landscape artist, not an illustrator. He had no wish to become an illustrator. He had no wish to leave France. Money did not interest him. He had a small inheritance from a lonely man he had once befriended, and he needed no more.

He was a natural befriender, an entirely generous and trusting man. The first time they met, Terry had told him it would be difficult to keep going back and forth from Nice to transact his business and asked him if he knew anyone there in St-Paul-de-Vence who would rent him a room.

'Oh, you must stay here,' Frank had said. 'I have a room that's gone begging since the artist I share the place with went home to Italy. He won't be back till late spring, so you can stay as long as you like ... No, no rent, I won't hear of it; the room is empty and it costs me nothing. We'll go halves on the food, and you can help me with the every-now-and-then cleaning up.'

It was Margaret Gabriel, his niece, who took Terry to meet him. Meg. She worked in a little shop in the walled town, selling wooden figures and bowls and other objects carved by local artisans. Terry first saw her the day he came to St Paul to talk to the two American writers who lived there. He had finished his preliminary discussion with one of them, and had stopped in the shop before going back to Nice, idly looking for gifts to take home with him.

She had come from somewhere in the rear of the shop, begun 'Qu'est-ce . . . ' and then stopped and smiled. 'You're American, aren't you? Can I help you?'

He turned around. The shop was so dim that he could not see her distinctly. His impression was of a tall woman, young, with a cloud of tousled hair that reminded him of Fanny. Over her proper high-necked blouse she wore a cotton coat of the type worn by workmen in Paris. Beneath it her skirt was so short that it showed her ankles and a few inches of skin. Terry had never seen a woman so eccentrically dressed.

'Why does everyone know I'm an American,' he asked her, 'Before I even open my mouth?'

'It's a matter of the clothes Americans wear, the way they move, the cast of their features, a lot of little things all together.'

'They? I haven't your expertise – I can go only by the way you speak – but you're certainly an American, too, aren't you? Why do you say "they" as if you weren't?'

'Oh, I've been in France so long I almost forget I'm not French.' She turned away with an air of businesslike briskness and picked up a figure from the table Terry had been browsing through. 'Is this what interested you? It's a very fine replica of the statue of St Paul that stands in the courtyard of St Paul's Without the Walls in Rome. Look at the way the folds in the cloth are carved, and the beard, and the fine detail in the features. Come to the light so you can get a better look at it.' She went ahead of him to the doorway, where she put the figure in his hands. 'Isn't the wood beautiful? It's olive, from trees in this region. Feel the smoothness of it.'

Terry tried to examine the figure with convincing intentness and at the same time look at the woman in the

342

light. She was younger than he had judged from her manner, no more than twenty or so, with tan-flecked green eyes, a thin nose, and a large mouth. Her skin had a golden cast, as from a light suntan, and was so taut that it seemed barely to cover the prominent bones of her face. Terry's taste in women ran to obvious prettiness, but this girl, who was not pretty at all, intrigued him.

'Are you this enthusiastic about everything you sell?' he asked her.

'No, I'm really not. Some of the things I don't like a bit, and I'm afraid I'm not very good at concealing it. This, though – of course, I hope you'll buy it, but I'll be sorry to have it go out of the shop, where I'll never see it again. It's a very special piece of work.'

'Either you're sincere or you're a clever saleswoman,' he said, meaning to provoke her out of her impersonal role. 'How can I know which it is?'

'Unless you're a judge of character, you can't. You'll have to rely on your own taste.'

The quickness of her response delighted him. He laughed. 'I'll take the figure.' He followed her back into the dimness of the shop. 'I'd also like to take you out to dinner. I realize you have no idea who I am, but I can refer you to the author Elliott Britt, who'll confirm that I've just been persuading him to write something for my father's magazine, *McNally's Monthly*.' He stopped for breath, thinking he must sound as wordy as his father. 'I'm Terrence McNally the Second.'

'The Second,' she repeated, but then made no comment on it. 'I admire Elliot Britt's work.' She wrapped the figure in newspaper. 'I don't know him, though, except to say *bonjour* to, and I've never heard of *McNally's Monthly*. We don't see American magazines here. But I'll have dinner with you anyway. I'm not very conventional. It will be a change.' She said all this while busily arranging the table where the figure of St Paul had left a gap. 'It's beautiful here, and I love it, but it does get a little monotonous sometimes.'

He was absurdly excited. 'Where shall we go? I don't know my way around here at all. You'll have to recommend a restaurant. Tell me where you live, and I'll call for you at whatever time you say. In the meantime, I'll—'

'You needn't call for me. We'll go now.' She began unbuttoning her workman's coat. 'There aren't any restaurants. We'll buy some food, and I'll cook it at my uncle's.'

'Your *uncle's*? Will he be there?'

'Yes, of course. I'm not that unconventional.'

The sharpness of his disappointment was as absurd as his excitement. He had wanted to be alone with her, to – what? Persuade her into bed? It was what he always wanted of women. The rest was all preliminary, more or less tiresome, depending on the artfulness of the woman. For this girl he had met a few minutes ago, he did not have to endure anything as tiresome as an uncle. There must be prettier women in Nice.

'Are you sure your uncle won't mind?' he said. 'Isn't it a little presumptuous of a perfect stranger to drop in on him for dinner?'

'He'll enjoy it. He loves company.' She led the way out of the shop, leaving the door wide open. 'We're very informal here. No one bothers about the things that are considered proper or improper in ordinary society, as long as we don't annoy or offend anybody.'

'Still, you wouldn't have dinner with me in your uncle's apartment unless he was there.'

She glanced at him, raising her eyebrows. They were perfect crescents, with a silky look. Everything about her was neat, spare, except for the soft tumble of brown hair, which Terry found welcome, like a bump in the nose of an otherwise faultless face.

'It would be unkind,' she said. 'It might tempt you to annoy or offend me.'

He gave such a whoop of laughter that a man carrying a canvas along the cobbled street looked up sharply and then smiled and waved.

'*Bonjour, Mademoiselle Gabriel. Comment allez-vous?*'

'*Très bien, Monsieur Matisse, et vous?* He's a painter from Collioure, here on a visit,' she explained to Terry after the man had passed. 'He's making a name for himself. You may have heard of him. Henri Matisse?'

'I'm afraid I'm not that much abreast of art. But I'm indebted to Mr Matisse. At least now I know your name, Miss Gabriel.'

'Oh, I'm sorry. Didn't I tell it to you? Margaret Gabriel. When you know me well, you may call me Meg.'

'Am I going to know you well?'

She frowned and changed the subject. 'If it's your first time in St-Paul, there are things you must see. We'll buy what we need for dinner afterward.'

She did not ask him if this suited him. He did not understand why it did. Women who took the initiative with men, whether in lovemaking or anything else, were not to his liking. Or never had been before.

She led him outside the walls first, down a curving road to a spot where they could see the fortified town in the best light of the day. It rose high above the olive and cypress trees in the glow of the late afternoon sun, the bell tower of its thirteenth-century church the highest point, with a glimpse of the brilliant blue Mediterranean beyond. Terry almost forgot the girl beside him.

'It's like something out of a fairy tale. A golden city,' he said finally. 'I thought I couldn't possibly be as moved again as I was in Paris, but this—'

'Yes.' After a few minutes she touched his arm. 'Come. It's like this every sunny day at this time. Let me show you around the town before it gets dark.'

They went back, walked up the hill and through the entrance arch, guarded by a cannon that in the sixteenth century had turned back an attack by a neighboring town with, in the absence of other ammunition, a volley of cherry pits. The narrow streets wound under other arches, between high stone walls and through a small square with a fountain shaped like an urn. There they took a flight of stone steps to another level of streets, visited the church, and went up on the ramparts for a broad view of the sea and the snowcapped mountains.

'We'd better get inside,' the girl said. 'It's cooler here in the hills than it is near the sea, especially toward evening, and you haven't brought an overcoat.'

'It was as mild as spring when I left Nice.' Terry followed her down, watching the way she moved, with a free, swinging stride like a boy's, yet not boyish. 'But I wasn't shivering from the cold,' he said. 'I think I'm bewitched.'

'St-Paul's a bewitching place. That's why I've stayed so long.'

'It isn't all St-Paul.'

She did not answer this. Other women evaded with lies or foolishness the comments or questions they did not care to deal with, but she simply said nothing. He knew that about her now. He knew also – she had told him as they walked – that she had lived in France since she was fourteen, first at a school near Nantes, then in Paris while she attended the university, and here in St-Paul for the past eight months.

'Haven't you been home in all that time?'

'Home? That's wherever I happen to be. It certainly isn't back there.'

'Don't your parents—?'

'My parents are not like other people's. They were so besotted with each other – are still, I suppose – that they wanted no one else. I was a mistake, an intrusion. I don't blame them. They did the best they could, looked after me and were kind to me for fourteen years, and then saw to it that I was well educated and had everything I needed. My father is still generous to me. I work in the shop only for fun.'

'But how could they leave you on your own like that? A young girl?'

346

'I wasn't on my own. The school was very strict and watchful. By the time I went to the Sorbonne I was a woman.'

'That may be, but most women aren't—'

'I'm not most women.'

She had come to St-Paul to visit her uncle, whom she had not seen since childhood, but who had from time to time written her charming letters, urging her to make the trip when she could. She had a tiny room over the bakery, rented from the baker, adequate for the week or two she had meant to stay. She had not bothered moving when the time stretched out.

'It sounds uncomfortable.'

'That kind of comfort isn't important to me. I don't notice it very much.'

Terry thought she must have a lover or at least some man who attracted her enough to keep her here. He fastened with sharp dislike on that artist they had passed earlier but then discarded him as only a visitor, and too old besides, probably near forty.

'Still, I don't understand why you stay on and on.'

'St-Paul betwitches people. You said so yourself. And there's my uncle. You'll see when you meet him.

They were at the uncle's iron door before it struck him that he had been alone with her for more than an hour, often with no one else in sight, and that he had been simply talking to her, listening to her, watching her. He had not touched her. She might not have let him. But he had not tried.

The iron door, set in the stone wall, looked as though it might lead into an ancient dungeon. Instead, it opened into a garden overlooking the snowy Alps, and from there to a spacious studio with the artist's accoutrements at one north-lighted end and a living area at the other.

Frank Gabriel was just cleaning his brushes after the day's work. He still had on a paint-daubed smock, and a navy blue beret that had paint on it, too.

'I used to get paint in my hair,' he explained later,

'until I decided to wear my beret indoors, even if it does make me look like somebody's "Portrait of the Artist."'

He was a short man, almost as wide as he was tall, with merry little brown eyes in a broad face webbed with lines and topped by thick, crisp gray hair. His niece had not finished the introductions before he came bounding across the room, hands outstretched, beaming with a show of large, yellowish teeth. He took both Terry's hands.

'Oh, this is nice! You're *very* welcome! I enjoy company, as Meg has probably told you, and don't get enough of it. Especially not American company. Come and sit down.'

He indicated a piece of furniture resembling a sofa, except that it had no back or arms and was covered with a ribbed brown throw and with a number of cushions that rested against the wall. This, Gabriel explained, turned into a bed at night and was where he slept. Terry had never known anyone who slept in his sitting room.

'I like to be near my paintings. I'm something of an insomniac,' he said. 'When I can't sleep, I get up and look at what I'm working on. Often I see something I didn't notice during the day. There's a regular bedroom inside, but I chose this.'

Meg had disappeared into the kitchen with the food. Except for the discourtesy it would have been to the uncle, Terry would have followed her. He did not want her out of his sight. He was afraid that the next time he came to St-Paul, unless he pressed his advantage, she might not care to see him again, might wish she had told him less about herself.

That was why, later in the evening, he asked Gabriel whether he knew of a room he could rent in St-Paul. If he were there all the time, he would see her every day and she could not – get away from him, was the way he thought of it. When Gabriel offered him the bedroom in his own apartment, he had to put on a show of reluctance, but he was elated. She could not very well avoid him while he was living with her uncle.

They ate at a table of fruitwood, with beautifully carved legs. Gabriel had made it all by hand. He had been a cabinetmaker in Virginia and had painted only as a hobby. But his wife had died three years before, and he had 'run away', as he put it, from everything familiar, everything that reminded him of her. They had had no children.

'Except Meg,' he said, smiling at her. 'I like to think of her as mine. My rediscovered daughter.'

'Yes.' Her own smile was rare, but she had an appealing little trick of narrowing her eyes in a way that affirmed affection and approval. 'Incidentally, Uncle Frank,' she said, 'Mr McNally has bought your carving of St Paul.'

'Ah! Did she bring undue pressure on you, Mr McNally? Meg's a formidable young lady when she has a goal in mind.'

'No one would have to be coerced into buying such a beautiful piece of work,' Terry said.

'I did coerce him a little, but you make me sound like a battleship. Formidable!' She turned to Terry and asked, somewhat flirtatiously, 'Did you find me formidable, Mr McNally?'

'Yes,' he said. 'But not in the way your uncle means.'

'Let's all be quiet now and savor the food,' Gabriel said. 'Meg's cooking deserves reverence.'

He was right. She had created what seemed to Terry a kind of miracle out of the few simple ingredients they had bought. It was a simple, substantial meal. The main course was a thick soup, brimming with vegetables, delicately flavoured with garlic and basil. With this they had slices of bread, cut from the long, crusty loaf called a *baguette*, and a red wine followed by cold sliced celeriac in a piquant mustard sauce that Terry's palate was too untrained to appreciate. For dessert she served fresh pears with a sharp cheese.

'The way to eat it is a bite of pear, then a bite of

cheese,' she told Terry. 'You don't mind my telling you, do you? It's the best way to enjoy it.'

'Of course not,' he said, though he might have minded if some other woman had instructed him. 'The meal was delicious. I don't know how you did it all with such ease and so quickly.'

'She does everything that way,' Gabriel said.

Terry brought his valises from Nice the next morning and settled into the bedroom of Gabriel's apartment. The artist worked at his canvases all day and talked as he worked, but Terry discovered that it was not necessary to answer him. He talked as someone else might have hummed or whistled. His landscapes were strange, with wild streaks and blobs of color, and did not sell very well, but he painted happily on.

Terry thought he was the happiest man he had ever known. He did not expect to persuade him that he would be happier illustrating magazine stories in New York, but he made a show of trying. He had finished his business with writers. He worked a little every day on his piece about France for the magazine, but he did not have to do it in Gabriel's apartment. He could have written anywhere, gathered other impressions in some other part of the country.

'I'm going to stay here until you say yes,' he told Gabriel.

'That's no threat, my boy. I'd be delighted if you never had to leave. I have an idea Meg would be, too.'

Of course he knew. Meg and Terry were together constantly. Sometimes he took her to Nice, to restaurants for dinner and twice to the opera. She obviously enjoyed these excursions, but she seemed just as content to prepare a meal in Gabriel's apartment and to take walks through the cobbled streets or outside the walls. She let Terry kiss her and hold her, but nothing more. She would not let him come to her room.

'Are you afraid of me?' he asked her.

'Yes, and of myself.'

'Have you ever been with a man?'

He thought she was not going to answer. They had stopped outside the entrance to the town. She leaned against the stone wall and looked beyond his head and then up into his face.

'Yes, I have been. Once,' she said. 'I thought I was in love with him. It isn't a mistake I intend to make again.'

'Then you aren't in love with me?'

He heard the words as though someone else had spoken them. He had never said them to himself, never thought *love*. She was a girl he was enormously, perhaps obsessively attracted to, a girl he was after and meant in time to have. But the bleakness out of which he had spoken was not because he was afraid she could not be seduced. *Then you aren't in love with me?*

'I've known you only a few weeks,' she said. 'That's what happened the other time. I was too young to understand that it takes longer. What I felt, what I feel now, isn't enough. Some day I'll love a man for everything he is, and what he isn't won't be a surprise I get too late and can't accept.'

'Some day.' He put his hands against the wall on either side of her, as though he intended to imprison her there until she gave him an answer he had not known he wanted. 'Does that mean I can't be the man?'

'I don't know. It's too soon to tell. But it can't matter anyhow because for me it will have to be a lasting thing and you have to go away.' She paused. 'It might be better if you went soon.'

'Is that what you want?'

'No,' she said.

So he stayed. He opened himself to her so that she would know everything he was and everything he wasn't. One night in early April, a week before he was to leave for home, they sat on a hill outside the town and he told her about Charles. She knew Charles was dead, but now he told her the rest of it. He told her what Charles had heard from the old man in Ireland, and he told her about finally going to see Sid Keller, forcing himself to go, because there were things he had to know. He had thought he would never be able to talk about any of this to anyone as long as he lived, but he told her all of it.

When he had finished, she leaned toward him and took his face between her hands. She said, 'It doesn't matter, Terry. I wish I could make you see that it doesn't. I wish I could stop it from haunting you.'

'Come with me then,' he said. 'Please, Meg. Come home with me.'

PART THREE

Megan's Voice

1919–1958

1958

We are alone again now. He sent the others away, saying
he wanted to sleep, but he told me to stay. I don't think
he's sleeping, though his eyes are closed. Maybe he does
doze off now and then. I can't tell. Nothing changes; not
the pallor of his face, nor his stillness, nor the way his
fingers accept my hand, neither holding it nor letting it
go. Only when he talks can I be sure he's awake.

He still talks. I am told he may slip into a coma before
the end, but I don't believe it. I believe he will talk until
his final breath. His voice is no longer strong, but he
makes himself heard. If his mind wanders, he gives no
sign of it. I can imagine him testing himself behind his
closed eyelids, making sure he is thinking in proper
order, in the right time span. He would do that, if there
was need for it.

'Megan,' he says now, 'I made it.'

I fancy he smiled a little, but the change is so small, so
quickly gone that I can't be certain it was there at all.

'You sure did,' I tell him.

'Who got them to send the telegram? Terry?'

'Yes.'

'I thought so. You wouldn't.'

'Why wouldn't I?'

'Silly nonsense. As if I'd believe it came personally
from the President. As if I didn't know they've got clerks
that send them out routinely, all the same, just fill in the
name.' This time there is no question about the smile.

'The name might have stopped them, though. "Here's a really dotty one. Terrence McNally the First. Wonder what he thinks he's king of."'

He hasn't said that much at a time since yesterday. It seems too trivial to use up breath on. But that's not for me to judge. I believe he knows as clearly as he ever did what he needs to say.

'Come on, now, Grandpa, who do you think you're kidding?' I tell him. 'You loved the telegram. To Terrence McNally the First, from Dwight D. Eisenhower. Silly nonsense or not, it proves you made it.'

'Whom,' he says.

'What?'

'*Whom* do you think you're kidding. I should have been born in 1852. Six years earlier, and I'd have got Truman's signature on the telegram. That would have suited me better. He might even have signed it himself.'

He says nothing more for a while, dozing or not. I can hear the sounds of the others. A man's voice, a woman's, several voices at once. The clatter of a glass or a cup on the table. Sounds, but no words. This is a well-built, well-carpeted house, designed for privacy and quiet, though not for deathly silence. We could always hear the children laughing.

Someone laughs now and quickly muffles it. For whom? He can't hear anything that far away, though his ears still serve him well enough. Even if he heard, he wouldn't mind. One reason he wanted them out of the room was their gloominess.

'They're rushing things,' he said to me after they'd left. 'Acting as if I'm dead while I'm still alive. Silly nonsense, anyway. Nobody can honestly grieve for a man a hundred years old.'

'Why not? I can't imagine a world without Terrence McNally the First in it. That's reason enough for grief.'

'When FDR died, Mac told me – no, it wasn't Mac; it was Sheila. She was crying because she couldn't imagine a world without him in it. She was thirteen years old, and he was the only President she'd ever had. But that's not real grief.'

Well, she was eleven. Mac was thirteen. My father, at seventy-six, wouldn't come anywhere near that close. Even on their birthdays. I always had to tell him how old my children were.

'I know what you're after, Grandpa,' I said. 'You want me to tell you we all love you so much that we don't see how we can go on without you.'

He didn't answer that. I'm not sure he heard it. I thought he looked a little happier, but I don't know what made me think so. With his eyes closed, he doesn't look happy or unhappy. So many wrinkles scrawl across his face that any particular expression is scratched out. It's hard to find his mouth unless he opens it. Only his nose is changeless, bold and unshrunken, but there is no expression in a nose.

'Are they all staying in the house again tonight?' he asks me now, waking suddenly. Or awake all along.

I tell him they are. He knows they were to leave today. They always leave the day after his birthday. But this year they are staying. I wait for him to comment on it, and of course, he does.

'I suppose they won't go until I'm dead,' he says. 'It's hard on you. I'll have to be quick about it, but I doubt if I have much authority.'

'Don't be an ass. You know I like having them here, and so do you. You were always big on family. Or was that just something you thought a nice little girl ought to be told?'

'You were never a nice little girl.'

I haven't wept yet, but that makes me want to. That gets to me. The love and pride still contained inside that ancient, withered shell. Sheila admires him; even, I think, cares about him, in her way, but he repels her. She says he looks and smells like a mummy. I wonder why it matters. Terrence McNally the First is in there, at least for a little while longer. And it's true I can't imagine a

357

world without him in it. Poor world.

'You're brooding, Megan. Stop it. I like you cheerful and sassy.'

His eyes are open now. I think if they could sparkle, they would. They can't, of course. They have that filmy, rheumy look that very old eyes have, that stiff way of moving, as if actuated by a puppeteer. Their color is so faded there is no way of telling what it was. But I think I can sense the sparkle and the blueness. I think they are only hidden.

'I'm not brooding. I'm hungry,' I say to him. 'Why don't I go down and get us something to eat?'

I am not hungry, but I want to try once more, even though I know it isn't any use. He isn't going to eat again. His birthday dinner, what little he had of it, was his last meal. He made it. He was determined to make it. Now he's ready to let go.

'Get something for yourself. I'm not hungry,' he says, and closes his eyes. 'Go on. I'll take a little nap. Go on, Megan. Don't worry,' he says, though I have given no indication that I'm afraid to leave him. 'I'll wait for you.'

'Is there anyone else you want to see when I come back?'

It takes him awhile to answer this. 'Terry,' he says then. 'Fanny . . .' His voice trails off, then resumes. 'Don't worry,' he tells me again. 'I know she's not here. I was wishing, that's all.'

I get as far as the door when he speaks again. 'Megan, is the magazine all right?'

'Flourishing, Grandpa.'

'Good. Terry would tell me it was if it were on its last legs, but I know you wouldn't lie to me.'

I would, of course. I have. I do. When he says 'the magazine,' *McNally's Monthly* is the one he means. *McNally's Monthly* is not flourishing. *Woman's World* is keeping *McNally's Monthly* alive. He wouldn't want to hear this. He's proud of me. He boasts about me. But

McNally's Monthly is his magazine, his special baby, and he is Terrence McNally the First.

'Megan? Are you still there?'

I was almost out the door, but I come back to the bed, alarmed at the weakening of his voice. Then I realize it hasn't weakened. He is whispering, meaning to whisper.

'No secrets between us,' he says.

I'm not sure what he means, and I tell him so. I tell him there is no need to whisper. They all are downstairs.

'I know,' he says, 'but how can you mention secrets without whispering?'

It isn't brilliant humor, but it's humor. From a man one hundred years old and dying.

'I don't want to end with any secrets between us,' he goes on, still whispering.

'All right,' I say. What secrets can he have, worth hearing, that I haven't already heard? The secrets I know that he doesn't aren't mine to tell, and if they were, I'd keep them from him. But I say, 'I'll see what I can dig up,' whispering, too.

When I get downstairs, I feel as if I've walked in on a scene from the wrong play. Except for the cast, it could be any ordinary social evening in Westchester. Everybody has a glass in hand or nearby. Everybody is munching the cashew nuts that someone has found and put around in dishes. Everybody is talking in intimate groups of two or three. My indignation is probably unjust. Do I expect them to sit on the edges of their seats, silent, hungry, and thirsty, until he dies?

They all stop what they're doing or saying and look at me. I thought Pa would be the one to ask, but Sheila gets in ahead of him. That's a trait of Sheila's.

'How is he?'

'The same. Talking. Joking.' I tell this to all of them, calmly, and then unexpectedly I have tears in my eyes, and I say, without advance planning, 'Oh, God, what a man!'

My father looks as if he might start toward me, but I manage to make my voice brisk enough to stop him.

'He wants to see you later, Pa. He's napping now, but he said I should bring you up in a little while.'

'Doesn't he want to see any of the rest of us?' Sheila is tactless enough to ask, so that I have to say of course he does, later, not knowing whether he does or not.

Sheila, I know, makes him a little uncomfortable. He says she strongly resembles Pa's mother, that awful woman, Sylvia. Only in looks, of course, but still, it must be disturbing. Yet I think it's exactly this resemblance that enchants my father. In spite of the way Sylvia treated him, he seems always to have felt some kind of attachment to her. He used to try to find her whenever he went to Paris, and even today he will talk about how beautiful she was.

Apparently Sheila is, if anything, more beautiful. 'A little more character in her face,' Grandpa says. 'McNally character.' But I think he imagines that. I see no McNally in her at all. She has her father's long chin and the pronounced cheekbones that I inherit from my mother. Sometimes, though, I see nothing familiar when I look at her. Who is this self-possessed-to-the-point-of-brashness young woman? It is absurd that she is not my contemporary, or older, but my twenty-four-year-old daughter. I have to look in the mirror to be convinced this is possible.

'You don't really mean he's joking,' she says. 'How can he joke?'

Maman answers. 'He can. Of course he can. God, what a man, as Megan says.'

I smile at her. I think it was brave of her to come. But no circumstance can make her ill at ease, and no one can feel ill at ease around her. I used to watch the way children and peasants and laborers ran away in panic when tourists asked them for directions, but they never ran from my mother. She is sitting next to Angela now, right next to her on the love seat, and there is no hint of strain between them. Of course, they are old, and it was all a long time ago, but I don't think that's more than a fraction of it. Passions may cool a little with age, but they don't burn out, not at all.

'This is awfully hard on you, Megan. These last few days when he won't let you out of his sight,' Pa says. 'I wish he'd let me take your place for a while.'

I say I don't mind. But it isn't a question of minding or not minding. I've had a birthday dinner for him every year since he retired. I'm the only one with a house big enough to accommodate all of them overnight. Mind? It's as if, when I was pregnant, I'd said that I didn't mind having a baby.

'Megan has the stamina for it,' Angela says.

Whatever Angela means by stamina, it's something admirable. She knows all about everybody's faults, but she is never critical. Grandpa once told her that blanket approval was not the way to express love. She said it was the only way she knew.

She often comes across saintlike and sappy – profoundly irritating to people like Maman. She is, on the contrary, clever, stubborn, and manipulative, but her gentleness conceals it. She stills looks wonderful, slim and elegant, though she is deep into her sixties, but sitting there next to Maman, she seems just a thin, neat old lady with a surprising tumble of smoky hair.

'Stamina, yes,' Maman says in response to Angela's comment. 'But there's more than that to it. It's an act of love.'

Angela says, 'Yes, of course. I know how special they are to each other.'

She says it in that uncertain way of hers, but she means she knows better than my mother does. They are rivals still. I am the child between them, discussed as if I weren't here. I always feel a little like a child, anyway, on these occasions, though I manage them and the house is mine. After all, how many women of forty-nine have parents and a grandfather alive to remind them of their childishness?

My father and Sam have gone over to the bar to freshen their drinks. They seem to be on intimate terms, though they have seen each other only once since they were boys. Sam has never been in this house before. He happened to be in New York on a client's business and – on impulse, I imagine, since he hasn't done it in all this time – called Pa at the office. They gave him this number.

'I told him to come,' my father said. 'I thought it was fitting. It's all right with you, isn't it, Megan?'

I said it was, but it wasn't. Since he had been asked, however, and could not very well be unasked, the question was academic. But uselessness never bars Sheila from saying what she wants to say.

'I think it's ridiculous,' she told my father. 'We never saw him before the funeral, and we haven't seen him since. You might as well have asked a stranger to come. That's all he is, a stranger.'

My father said, 'It will mean a great deal to Father to have Jake's nephew here. Not personally, maybe, but as a symbol.' He patted Sheila's cheek. To her credit, she didn't flinch, though she hates being touched. Even as a small child she squirmed away when anyone tried to hug her. 'I don't expect you to understand,' Pa said.

He and Sam come back and sit down now with their refills. They talk in low voices, but not the voices of mourners. My father once told me about going to a music hall with Sam and seeing his first movie. They look as though they could be talking about that as they sip their drinks. Sam nudges my father with his elbow, and they both grin and then look around guiltily like boys with forbidden smokes. Boys not far from eighty. Instead of retiring or dying, they both go to their offices every day and enjoy a drink and a good meal and, probably, their wives at night. One of them even has a living father. A dying father.

'I think you're disgusting.' It is Sheila who says this, coming out of the kitchen, where she has been making coffee. Saying what I am too rational to say and know it is unwarranted to feel. 'He's upstairs dying, and you act as if you're at a cocktail party.'

'Oh, Sheila, that's nonsense,' I say quickly, making light of it before anyone can make it heavier. 'Do you think he'd want us to sit around weeping? His family? The McNallys? That isn't what the Irish do, even after one of theirs dies. And he isn't dead yet.'

She turns around and goes back to the kitchen without a word. Angela apologizes for her, saying people react oddly when they're upset. Nobody else says anything. Sheila is undoubtedly crying in there, but she would be furious if I went in and saw her at it or tried to comfort her.

I call to her from the kitchen door, without looking in. I tell her if anybody gets hungry before I come downstairs again, there are cold cuts on a platter and a bowl of coleslaw.

'In the *frigo*,' I say, forgetting how the word annoys her.

Sheila can't believe that sometimes a French word comes naturally to my mind. I tried to teach both children French and had Mac chattering away in it before he started school, but Sheila is totally incapable of grasping a foreign language. She considers my occasional reversions an affectation.

'If you mean the referigerator,' she calls back, predictably, too irritated to care that her voice is thick with tears, 'why don't you say so?'

I go upstairs again, my father clumping along beside me. He has always been a clumsy man. I don't know why I find that endearing. Maybe because he once told me how he envied Charles's agility.

'Fanny?' my grandfather says as I open the door, and then, almost immediately: 'What's the matter with me? I must be getting senile. You were gone a long time,

363

Megan. Come around here where I can see you. Is Terry with you?'

I think his voice is weaker but still perfectly clear. When the nurse was here, she tried to get him to take his teeth out.

'We want to be comfortable, don't we, dear?'

'We do, dear, but we're used to our teeth, darling, and we don't want to sound like a mumbling idiot, honey.'

She laughed, so he was willing to have her come back tonight.

'I'm here, Father,' Pa says. He draws up a chair next to mine at the bed and takes Grandpa's hand. 'How do you feel?'

Grandpa's eyes are open. 'You used to ask intelligent questions, son,' he says, and actually winks at me. 'I've been waiting for my whole life to pass before my eyes, but it hasn't . . . Another piece of misinformation. There's more of that on earth than is dreamed of in anybody's philosophy.'

He has to pause for breath. My father leans forward, as if to tell him to stop talking, but I nudge him with my knee, and he sits back. What better way for Terrence McNally the First to die than talking?

'Let's see if we can get it started passing before my eyes,' he says. 'Let's prime the reel.'

'Pumps get primed, not reels,' my father says. Good. That's what Grandpa wants.

He answers back with pleased asperity, or as close to asperity as he has the strength to come. 'Whatever reels need to get them going, then. I'm not a mechanic.'

He closes his eyes, waits a minute, opens them again. 'Ma,' he says. 'Aggie.' I'm sure he's wandering this time, but no, he ties it up. 'You're like her, Megan. What she would have been, with your advantages.' His eyes shift jerkily to my father. 'The opening of the Brooklyn Bridge. The fireworks. We took you, Terry. Do you remember?'

'Yes, of course I do. And I remember insisting I

364

remembered, and nobody believing I possibly could, except you, Father.'

'You were so bright. You delighted me,' he says. 'You've often delighted me.' I know without looking that this brings tears to my father's eyes. Then he adds, his voice cracking in what I think is a kind of chuckle, 'How could anyone with your brains do so many damn fool things?' He doesn't wait for an answer. 'But you gave me Megan. You saved her for me. At least you were wise enough for that.'

I don't think it was wisdom. I'm not even sure it was willingness. Not at first. A well-grown, ready-made daughter on his doorstep? No, I think it was simply circumstance. And, of course, Angela.

1

Until I was eleven, I lived with my parents in a brownstone house on Seventy-fourth Street near Central Park West. My grandfather lived two blocks away, in the Dakota. Every morning my father and I called for him, and we all walked together to Broadway. I left them there and walked up to my school, PS 9, at Eighty-second Street and West End Avenue, and they took a taxi to the magazine offices.

On bad days we all took a taxi, but I got out at Broadway no matter what the weather was. I did not want any of the poor girls from Amsterdam or Columbus Avenue to see me arriving at school in a taxi. One of my friends, Helena Sutton, came every day in her father's Peerless, driven by a uniformed chauffeur. Helena seemed untroubled by this ostentation, and I never heard anyone else object to it either, but I didn't think it was nice.

On the other hand, I did not play with the girls from Amsterdam Avenue or Columbus. They were mostly

Italian or Porto Rican. Three of them were colored. The Italian and Porto Rican girls did not play with the colored girls. I considered this to be the natural order of things and gave it no thought.

One day Helena Sutton told me she could not play with me anymore.

'I'm not allowed to play with Irish girls,' she said.

'I'm not Irish. I'm American.'

'My mother says if your name's McNally, you're Irish.'

I did not know, and it was doubtful that Helena knew, what was behind this. It had begun with the anti-German sentiment that generated such inventions as 'liberty measles', 'liberty cabbage' for sauerkraut and 'liberty pups' for dachshunds. Former President Teddy Roosevelt thought it was not patriotic enough simply to hate the Germans. He started a campaign to turn all 'hyphenated Americans' into '100 percent Americans' who would forget their origins and drop any trace of the customs or languages of their forebears. He did not insist that foreign names be changed – after all, his own was Dutch – but a name as blatant as McNally was suspect.

I did not have to know any of this to decide what to do. I punched Helena in the stomach. This was not a good idea, however, because Helena had just had breakfast, and I got as much of it on me as Helena did. After we were cleaned up, I was sent to the principal, who told me little ladies did not punch people. Since I had no interest in being a little lady, I was not impressed. Nor did it bother me to take a note home to my parents. The poor girls were beaten when they brought notes from school, or so everyone said. But my mother only talked to me or, if the offense was serious, kept me from going out to play. She must have known I was perfectly happy to stay in and read, yet this apparently did not concern her. Could she help it if I did not feel punished? As for my father, he was rarely involved in such matters at all.

'She said I'm not American,' I explained to my

mother. 'She said she's not allowed to play with me because I'm Irish. She said if my name's McNally, I'm Irish. So I punched her.'

'I can see your point,' my mother said. She could always see my point. 'I'd want to punch someone, too, who didn't think I was good enough to play with. I wouldn't do it, though. It's no use. Punching her didn't change her mind, did it?'

'It made her cry and throw up, and I don't care.'

'Still, if you hadn't punched her, she might be sorry she couldn't play with you. Now she probably won't be.'

'I don't care. She said I'm not America. She said I'm Irish. That's a lie, isn't it?'

My mother explained what it meant to have Irish forebears.

'Megan's a British name, you now,' she said. 'We called you that partly because of my nickname, Meg, but mostly because of pride in the McNallys. We might have called you Marguerite or Margharetta because you have French and Italian ancestors on my side, but Megan sounds much better with McNally.'

'Italian?' I was aghast. 'Like those Ottavianos who live on Columbus Avenue and smell?'

My mother seemed interested in this. 'What do they smell of?' she asked. I didn't know. 'You see how it is,' my mother said. 'Maybe there's an Irish child or two who isn't fit to play with, but that doesn't apply to Megan McNally. For all I know, the Ottavianos do smell, but so do some Americans.'

'They're poor. They live in a tenement.'

'The Ottavianos? Your grandfather was poorer. Columbus Avenue is the Garden of Eden, compared to where he lived.'

My parents sent me to public school in order to have me mix with girls from all kinds of backgrounds and to have me learn to be 'democratic'. But hardly anybody mixed. Hardly anybody learned. Even after my mother's explanation I didn't play with any of the girls who lived on Amsterdam Avenue or Columbus Avenue. The lines were strictly drawn. From Riverside Drive to, but not including, Amsterdam Avenue, and from, but not including, Columbus to Central Park. I could not have crossed these borders without being considered eccentric by everyone involved. The worth of eccentricity is likely to escape ten-year-olds. It was awhile before I recognized it in my mother, longer before I valued it.

At this period of my life the days followed each other in smooth, orderly, predictable, satisfying progression. After school I played in Central Park or, in bad weather, at home or at a friend's. Wednesdays at five Miss Holmes came to give me my piano lesson. Saturday mornings I went to dancing school. Once a month, Miss Letty, the seamstress, spent half a day to a day in the sewing room. I regularly got dizzy from the endless standing and turning while Miss Letty pinned my hems, and had to lie down. Grandpa came for dinner on Thursdays and played casino with me afterward until my bedtime, chortling when he won, which was usually. When my parents had guests for dinner, I ate in the kitchen with Christine and Sig, our Swedish couple. Some of my friends had to recite for their parents' guests, but I only had to shake hands and curtsy.

If America was, as writers of the time suggested, in a period of ferment and unrest, bewildered, disenchanted, questioning all the old social traditions, I was unaware and unaffected. True, the War to Make the World Safe for Democracy, later to be known as World War I, had provided a little extraordinary activity. I had sold two Liberty Bonds, one to my father and one to my grandfather, knitted a scarf for one of our brave boys in the trenches, and saved enough silver foil to make a ball four inches in diameter – for what purpose I never knew.

The day I turned nine I was allowed to go all by myself for the first time to see my grandfather. I had been waiting for the elevator to take me back down when the whistles started blowing and people came bursting out of their apartments in the staid Dakota, laughing and crying, screaming that the war was over. I screamed along with them, but since I knew no one who had been in it, and had not suffered much on wheatless Mondays or meatless Tuesdays, mine was more the excitement of contagion than of joy or relief.

But that had happened last year, and now everything seemed to be the same as always. Nothing outside of my personal concerns really disturbed me. Cocooned in the egoism of a sheltered childhood, I was serene – as serene as my temperament allowed – in the midst of such turbulence and change in both the country and my immediate world that neither would ever be the same again.

My fifth-grade teacher, Miss Burns, was a fervent advocate of rights for women, a spare-time suffragist, who practiced on our class. Ordinarily we believed in our teachers, convinced they knew everything. Miss Burns, however, had a nervous disorder that caused her head to shake at irrelevant intervals. This nullified her omniscience and made her fair game for baiting. One of the girls, whose mother was opposed to women's suffrage and thought Miss Burns should be dismissed for filling our heads with such dangerous nonsense, kept bringing in published anti-suffragette statements to pass around the room. Miss Burns invariably confiscated them and invariably, to the delight of the class, became so infuriated when she read them that her head appeared in danger of shaking itself off her neck.

May Irwin, a popular actress, said she was sick of hearing about women's rights and thought it was doing more harm than good. 'I have more rights than I can properly attend to,' she said. *The Woman Patriot*, a magazine devoted to defeating the suffragette movement, stated that the suffragists were 'bringing America to the culmination of a decadence which has been steadily indicated by race suicide, divorce, break-up of the home, and federalism, all of which conditions are found chiefly

369

in primitive society.'

I would have liked to bring in copies of *McNally's Monthly,* which was eloquently on Miss Burns's side. Not because I believed in women's rights myself – I neither believed nor disbelieved – but to show off my father's magazine and the name McNally, my name, in print. I couldn't do it, though. I could not appear to support Miss Burns while all the others derided her.

But when Miss Burns's moment came, most of us were not moved to ridicule. Perhaps in some evolving segment of our savage beings we recognized that it was our moment, too.

'Remember the day,' she told us. 'June fourth, 1919, the day Congress passed the Nineteenth Amendment to the Constitution. Finally, girls, we've won a right denied until now only to criminals, lunatics, idiots, and women. The right to vote.' If her head shook, as it must have, I did not notice. I noticed the tears in her eyes, which in themselves were awesome. Children cried, and actresses in the movies, but not teachers. 'Finally, girls! Finally!' she said. 'It means that when you grow up, you'll have a chance to help shape the world!'

I had no interest in shaping the world. I was satisfied with it the way it was. What interested me was the outcome of D'Artagnan's duel with the Three Musketeers and my father's return that evening from one of his trips abroad. He always brought presents.

This time he brought me a dress from Switzerland which was much too small for me. I did not regard clothes as presents anyway.

'I'm sorry, kitten,' my father said 'You grow so fast I can't keep up with you. Here.' He fished out a couple of dollar bills and pressed them into my hand. 'Buy yourself a nice doll instead.'

A doll. I hadn't played with dolls since I was four years old, and not much then. My father knew very little about me, but I thought that was natural. Fathers knew about boys. He would have known what my brother wanted, but my brother had died of scarlet fever, which he had caught from me when I was four and he was two. Terrence McNally the Third. The last McNally, I had once heard my father say. I thought I would buy myself a Mysto Magic set. How could I expect my father to know I liked boys' toys?

As additional consolation for the dress that didn't fit, I was allowed to bring *The Three Musketeers* to dinner with me. This was a special treat, so rarely permitted that it did not contravene the rule that it was rude to read at the table. The rule did not seem to apply at all to my father, who read the newspaper at the breakfast table every morning.

Ordinarily, when I was reading, I heard nothing that was going on around me. I paid little attention at any time to adult conversation. Yet that evening maybe I was not wholly absorbed in the book. Maybe the topic caught my ear. Maybe I sensed some tonal dissonance. In any case, I listened, without looking up.

'The states haven't ratified it yet, of course, but there's no doubt they will,' my father was saying.

'I think Terrence believes it was really *McNally's Monthly* that brought it about.' My mother always called my grandfather Terrence. 'He gives credit to the suffragists, but I think he doubts they would have accomplished it without the strong backing of the magazine.'

'Father tends to magnify McNally power. He probably knows better.'

'Anyhow, he's genuinely pleased at the outcome. Are you?'

'That's a funny question. You know I am.'

'I don't know it. I'm not sure you're convinced women have the capacity to vote intelligently.'

'What do you mean, Meg? Haven't I always come out for women's suffrage? I don't understand your—'

'Oh, I know you've been for it publicly.'

'Not only publicly. I can remember asking Father

371

when I was just a young boy whether he didn't think Fanny should be allowed to vote.'

'But Fanny, surely, is in a class by herself.'

There was a pause. In case they were watching me, I put a forkful of string beans in my mouth and turned a page.

'We're not really talking about women's suffrage, are we, Meg?' my father said.

My mother answered in a funny, very soft voice. 'I'm glad you're listening. So often you don't. No, Terry, that isn't what we're really talking about.'

'Meg—'

'Not now ... Megan, your food is getting cold. You'd better put your book away for a while and finish what's on your plate.'

I always kissed my father good night in the living room, but my mother still came after I was in bed to tuck me in and turn out the light. I was big for this now. I didn't need much tucking in, and she could have turned out the light later, but I was glad she didn't stop coming in. If I had things that were hard to say or ask in the daytime, this was when I could do it. In the dark, with my mother sitting on the edge of my bed.

'Are you angry at Daddy?' I asked that night.

I could see my mother fairly well in the light from the hall, but I knew my own face was in darkness. I liked looking at my mother's face. I wished mine resembled it more. I wished I did not have red hair and freckles. My mother said the freckles would fade when I got older, and I would be attractive, which was better than being just pretty. My mother never told lies, so I guessed I wasn't going to be ugly-looking. But I still wished that I had dark hair and that I had no freckles.

'No, I'm not angry,' my mother said now. 'I'm a little sad because Daddy's away so much, and when he's home, he's so busy with the magazines, or thinking about them, that he hardly has time for anything else.' She leaned down and kissed my cheek. 'It will be all right, though. Don't worry. We'll work it out.'

I asked my mother to tell me the story of how she and my father had met in France and come to America to get married and live happily ever after. It was like a story in a book. I had heard it so many times I knew it by heart, exactly the way my mother always told it, but I never got tired of it. That night I had a special need to hear it, though I could not have said why.

'. . . It wasn't sensible to go with him. We had known each other such a short time, less than two months. We had led such different lives. I was more French than American. I was living alone and free in a little French village. Now he was asking me to come to New York and be an American wife, act like other American wives, dress like everybody else—'

'But you loved him so much you couldn't let him go without you. If you did, you were afraid you would never see him again.' This was the part I liked best. Usually I let my mother tell it, but that night I wanted to tell it myself. 'So you came with him even though you had mis – misgivings, and you were married in Grandpa's apartment. Grandpa was there, and Aunt Fanny, and Uncle Jake and Uncle Sean. You never saw them before in your life until you landed at the pier with Daddy, but they made you feel like part of the family right away. Grandpa said he hadn't ever had a daughter, and you looked to him as if you were going to fill the bill. So then you were happy you came, and Daddy was happy, and after a while you started having me, and then you were even happier.'

After my mother had kissed me good night and shut the door, I took *The Three Musketeers* from the night table and the flashlight from under my pillow and read under the covers until I was too sleepy to read anymore. I did not think about the dinner-table conversation again.

In January, not long after my eleventh birthday, my grandfather and Aunt Fanny were married. This wedding also took place in the Dakota apartment. My mother was matron of honour, my father was best man and I was the bridesmaid. Uncle Jake was there, too, but not Uncle Sean. Uncle Sean had fallen down the subway stairs at Seventy-second Street and broken his neck. I had heard Christine say that he died a drunkard's death.

I had always known that my grandfather and Aunt Fanny were not married, but since I did not know what else they could be, I always thought of them as husband and wife. Except that they did not live in the same place, they were together all the time, just like any married couple. The wedding was therefore a surprise to me, and a little embarrassing. I had never heard of old people getting married.

'Why didn't they do it before?' I asked my mother, who was curling my hair around her fingers to see how it would look for the wedding.

'Because he had a wife,' my mother said. 'Daddy's mother. I told you that long ago.'

'I thought she was dead.' I had not thought about her at all. I had forgotten her existence.

'She isn't dead. Some rich old Frenchman with a title wanted to marry her, and I suppose she was ready to jump at the chance. She must be – what? Nearly sixty. Anyway, it finally suited her to divorce Terrence and let him marry Fanny after all these years.' My mother jerked her fingers out of my hair and said, '*Merde!* This isn't going to work. You look as silly in curls as I would. Why don't we go down to Best's and have it bobbed?'

At the hairdresser in Best's department store my mother sat in the next chair and had her hair bobbed, too. I had considered crying when mine was done, like girls in stories whose hair had to be cut off because of some terrible sickness, but when I saw the way it went into soft little tendrils, I loved it. I wished my mother had kept hers the way it was, but by the time we got home and she pulled off her hat, the clipped, tamed dark hair was all over her head again and did not look so strange.

'Anyway, it will be less bother for both of us,' she said.

My father did not notice it at all at first. When he finally did, he didn't like it.

'I've always loved your hair, Meg,' he said. 'It's all right for a little girl like Megan to have it cropped, but long hair is part of a woman's femininity. Why didn't you ask me first?'

'I didn't think I needed permission,' my mother said, and walked out of the room. A minute later she was back. 'It isn't fatal, Terry. If you really hate it, I'll let it grow back.'

I had never been to a wedding before. I didn't think it was very exciting. All I did was stand there in my blue organdy dress and patent leather shoes, holding a bouquet of flowers, while the judge asked my grandfather and Aunt Fanny questions, and they answered, 'I do.' Then the man said they were married. I had never seen them kiss each other before. I thought it was an embarrassing thing for old people to do. When Aunt Fanny started crying, it was even worse.

'My God, will you look at me?' Aunt Fanny said, sniffling and blowing her nose into a white handkerchief with lace around it. 'Did you ever see such a fool?'

'What's foolish about it?' Grandpa said in his loud voice. 'A woman who has finally caught me after trying for twenty-three years has a right to cry with relief.'

'It's not relief, you big boob. It's sorrow. All these years I've managed to elude you, and now you've trapped me at last.'

My grandfather beamed around at everybody. 'Come on, all you people, let's partake of the wedding breakfast so my bride and I can get started on our honeymoon.' He put his arm around Aunt Fanny. 'Come along, Mrs Terrence McNally the First.'

After eating, everybody stood around drinking more champagne, except Uncle Jake, who had ginger ale. I had ginger ale, too. I drank it in front of the bay window, looking out across the park. You could look all the way over and see the lights in the houses on Fifth Avenue. You could see the lake. When the white flag with the red ball in the middle was up, meaning the ice on the lake was safe, I often skated there. But in the dark it looked different, mysterious. I liked to imagine that fairies, invisible to humans, skated on it at night, though of course, I did not believe in fairies.

'It's beautiful, isn't it?' Grandpa had come up beside me. 'When I was born, it was just rocky hills and scrubby woods, far out of town, but some men had the vision to transform it into a garden spot for the public to enjoy. I find it heartening that though every prospect pleases, not all men are vile.'

He always talked to me as if I were grown up. Sometimes I didn't understand everything he said, but I liked it anyhow. My mother talked to me the same way.

'I wrote a poem about the park once.' I had never told this to anyone before, not even to my mother.

'*Did* you, Megan? I didn't know you wrote poetry.'

'Only that one.'

'Can you recite it to me?'

'I only remember a little of it. It's not very good. "At night when children go away, are you the same park where we play?" It's hard to think of the right words to rhyme.'

'I think it's very good indeed, Megan. A very profound thought. But poetry needn't rhyme, you know. When I come next Thursday, I'll bring you some that doesn't.' He stroked my hair. His hand was so big that almost my whole head fitted into it. 'I like your new haircut.'

'Daddy says long hair is part of a woman's femi – femi—'

'Femininity. Well, that's a matter of opinion and the times we live in. Our ideas about women, and almost everything else, have changed since the war. By the time you grow up I think it will be taken for granted that women are equal partners with men, not decorative

376

inferiors.'

I had once seen my mother smoking a cigarette. None of my friends' mothers smoked. None of them dressed the way my mother did, either, or said words like *merde*. I took what Grandpa said to mean these things were all right now and I did not have to feel embarrassed because my mother did them.

'That reminds me, Megan,' he said. 'I've been meaning to ask you. As you know, when your father was twelve years old, I began taking him down to the magazine offices on Saturdays. Now next year you'll be twelve years old, and I wondered if you'd like to come along on Saturdays and start learning the business.'

I was astounded. I was delighted. I felt as though I had grown up from one moment to the next.

'Oh, I can't,' I said, not meaning it. 'I have to go to dancing school on Saturdays.'

He grinned at me. 'You wouldn't consider giving it up?'

'Well, I don't really like it very much. The boys have sweaty hands.'

'Then that's all right. I'm sure if I talk to your parents, they'll let you quit. Anything else?'

'I don't think Daddy will want me to do it.'

'Why not?'

'Because I'm a girl.'

'We have lots of girls working for us. Aunt Fanny has one of the most important jobs in the company.'

'Mommy says Aunt Fanny is in a class by herself.'

'She's that, all right.' He looked over my head to where Aunt Fanny stood talking, waving her champagne glass, her cheeks pink as a girl's, her hair, wilder than my mother's, escaping the restraint of a flowered chaplet. 'But so are you in a class by yourself, Megan, and don't you forget it.' He put his arm around me and pulled me close against his cigar-scented morning coat. 'If you want to start next year, I'll see to it that you do. I'm the boss, you know.'

377

'I do want to, Grandpa.'

'Then the first Saturday after your twelfth birthday will be the day.'

But it did not work out that way. The first Saturday after my twelfth birthday I was in St-Paul-de-Vence, France.

It began one morning at breakfast just before school closed for the summer. Sig brought in the mail on a tray, the way he always did, and put it on the table in front of my mother. When she had finished sorting it, she always passed it to my father, who did not stop reading his newspaper to look at it unless my mother said one of the letters looked important.

That morning, when I reached for the sugar to put on my cornflakes, I saw my mother reading a pink letter. It was not the letter that surprised me, but the expression on my mother's face. Her mouth looked stretched, as if she were smiling, only she wasn't.

'I have a communication here, Terry, from Columbus, Ohio,' she said in a funny, tight voice, and threw the pink letter across the table to my father. 'You might be interested in reading it.'

When my father heard my mother say it, he dropped the newspaper right on the floor. He did not answer until he had picked it up and folded it and then looked at the letter. He was perspiring. I could see the drops on his forehead and under his nose.

'The little bitch,' he said.

I had never heard my father use a bad word before.

'I didn't make her any promises. You must believe that, Meg.' He looked at my mother for the first time. 'It was nothing. It meant nothing.'

'I don't suppose it did. I don't suppose any of them did.'

'Any of—'

'I'm not a fool, Terry. 'I've—' She looked at me and stopped, as if she had just noticed I was there. 'Go get

378

your books and things, Megan. It's almost time to go.'

I did not understand what they had been talking about, but it made me nervous. A week or so later, when my mother came to tuck me in and kiss me goodnight, she sat down on the bed, took my hand, and said, 'I have something to tell you, Megan. Something serious.'

By then I had stopped worrying about the morning at breakfast and the pink letter. I thought I must have done something I shouldn't and was going to get what my mother called a talking-to, though I could not remember doing anything.

'I know it will be hard for you to understand, but I'll explain it as well as I can,' my mother said, and took my other hand, too. 'Daddy and I are going to end our marriage. Daddy will stay here, and you and I will live somewhere else.'

I could feel something start to thump and shake inside me, as if my heart had come loose. All I could think of to say, or ask, was: 'Where?'

'In France. You'll love it there, Megan. It's beautiful.' She sighed. 'Listen to me now. Listen carefully. This is the most important part. Nobody is to blame. Will you remember that? Things go wrong in any marriage because people aren't perfect. Very often the wrong things can be straightened out, or accepted, if the husband and wife care enough and are able to change. But sometimes they can't, and then it's better to separate and try to make new, happier lives without each other.'

'Is it because Daddy's so busy and goes away a lot, like you said that time?'

'That's a little part of it, yes. But you see, Megan, many husbands work hard and aren't home much, and their wives make the best of it. If I'm not ready to make the best of some of the things I don't like, it's because I'm the wrong kind of person for this marriage.'

My fingers were tight and cold around my mother's. 'You didn't do anything wrong.' I said.

'It isn't what I did. It's what I am. Until I met Terry, I

lived in my own way, by my own standards, answerable to nobody.' I knew, by the way my mother said Terry instead of Daddy, that she had forgotten she was talking to me. 'I realized that I had to change in marriage, but not how much. Not how much freedom this life, in a brownstone house with two servants in New York City, was going to cost me. For a long time I thought it was worth it. Now, because of a number of things, I'm finding the price too high.'

'Couldn't we *all* move?' I asked, knowing it was a stupid question.

My mother did not answer this. She might not have heard it because I had spoken in a very soft voice.

'You'll love it in France,' she said again. 'You won't have to dress up. Of course, you'll go to school, but you won't have to take any lessons just because other children are taking them. You'll—'

'I wasn't going to take dancing lessons anymore anyway,' I interrupted despairingly. 'As soon as I was twelve, Grandpa was going to take me to the magazine on Saturdays. Now I'll be in France and I can't go.'

I pulled my hands away and rolled over onto my stomach so I could cry into the pillow. My mother sat quietly, stroking my head, and I did not stop crying. In a little while she got up and went out of the room. She left the door open. I heard her voice in the hall.

'I made a hash of it,' she said.

I stopped crying when I heard my father come into the room, but I did not turn around. He did not sit down on the bed, but was just standing there in the dark.

'Kitten,' he said. 'Kitten, don't make me talk to the back of your head.' He waited. 'All right. You're upset. Of course you are. I'm upset too, believe me. I don't want you to go. It isn't what I want at all. I'll be very lonely without you and Mommy, and I hope you'll come back here to me after a while, because I love you both very much.'

I said. 'You don't. You like boys, not girls. You wish I

380

was the one who died, instead of Terrence McNally the Third. That's why you and Mommy can't stay married and we have to go away.'

But I said this in a whisper, after my father had gone out and shut the door. I was not sure I believed it. I did not know what I believed. My mother said nobody was to blame, but I did not think that could be so. In my experience, when anything bad happened, somebody was always blamed for it. This was the worst thing that had ever happened in my life, so it had to be somebody's fault. If it wasn't my father's or my mother's, it had to be mine. At least I thought it did. I thought that for a long time.

2

My father wrote to me often, but he didn't know what to say. He could write brilliant magazine pieces, fine editorials, but letters to a daughter were beyond him. Though my own letters must have indicated some development, he wrote to me as if I were frozen in time – with the same kind of stilted cuteness when I was fifteen as when I was eleven. Soon he became unreal to me, a kind of obligatory pen pal whom I had never met and never would meet. I could no longer remember his face.

In one sense this helped heal me. In the first months of separation I missed him with an anguish that was curiously sharp, considering that he had never been deeply involved in my life. I was as enraged at him for not being there as someone bereaved is enraged at the loved person who has deserted in death. Sometimes I hated him for letting us go. Sometimes I hated my mother for leaving. More often I hated myself for not being the boy I was convinced he would have kept with him – the boy I would have preferred to be anyway when I was eleven. But in time his foolish letters dimmed my perception of him and diluted my confused wretchedness until it was washed away.

The letters from my grandfather were something else again. He wrote to me every week, talking to me as though I were there beside him, listening, changing, growing. He always included some mention of what he began calling 'our magazine empire'. Right from the beginning he cannily reported to me as though I were a member of the staff who was temporarily out of the country, perhaps on assignment.

Magazines are not having an easy time, what with the competition from radio and the movies [he wrote in one letter the second year we were away]. I think we need some young, fresh ideas. The editor-in-chief of our *Woman's World* is a good man, but he is a man, and not a young one. I believe this will be the ideal spot for you in the future. After all, who can understand the problems and interests of women as well as another woman? I know you will bring us a forward-looking approach on your return.

If it had not been for my grandfather's letters, I might have stayed in France the rest of my life. Not because I was happy there but because I would have had no visions of happiness anywhere else.

Actually I was miserable in France at first. I went to school in Vence, a little under three miles from St-Paul, and sat in sullen, helpless silence while a gush of meaningless syllables cascaded around me. The children all jabbered at me, sometimes raising their voices to penetrate what could only be my deafness, or speaking with exaggerated care as though to a moron, and finally, disdainfully, ignoring me.

My mother tried to teach me, but I wanted nothing to do with French at home. Not that I thought of it as home. We lived in four rented rooms that were part of a villa owned by a Madame Roche, whose husband had been killed in the war. By renting to us, she could afford to live in the remaining six rooms herself, with her two young children and a maid, who also cleaned for us and did our laundry.

I did not recognize it as a lovely place, only as an alien one. It was about half a mile outside the walled town where my mother had lived before she married my father. We had our own separate entrance and our own little garden, flanked by two lemon trees. The furniture, odd and ugly to my eyes, came from the French provinces and was spare and simple. The living room, where we also ate meals, had a fine view of the Maritime Alps, snowcapped in Winter. Off this room were my mother's bedroom, a rather primitive bathroom, and a small kitchen. My tiny room, obviously meant for a maid, was beyond the kitchen. My mother had suggested that I share her room, which was big enough for two beds, but that would have been an added strangeness. I had always had my own room. If I wanted to cry at night, as I did every night for the first couple of weeks in St-Paul, I could do it in private.

For want of other companionship I sometimes played after school with Madame Roche's older child, Paul, a boy of seven. He was, like most young French children, a solemn little boy, careful not to get himself dirty. But he could throw and catch a ball, and he treated our language barrier as though it did not exist, speaking French to me and not caring whether I answered in English or not at all. Inevitably, between Paul and my exposure, however reluctant, in school, I learned the language. Paul learned a little English, as well as one-a-cat, still-pond-no-more-moving, and how to climb trees. The first time he came home with dirty, scraped knees his mother spanked him, but I think my mother's example persuaded her to give it up.

Though they lived in the same house for so many years and were always courteous to each other and helpful in neighborly ways, Madame Roche and my mother never became friends. My mother had no talent for friendship.

She liked men – I'm sure now that she had lovers in St-Paul, and she was devoted to her aged uncle, Frank Gabriel, who lived inside the walled town – but was essentially a solitary. She talked to me constantly, but I have often thought since that she talked less as a mother to a child than as a person who is much alone talks to herself. That she loved me deeply, however, I never questioned, even when she let me go.

She forgot to tell me about sex. I believe she often lost sight of how young I was, how little I knew about many things that she neglected to tell me, how little I understood many things that she did tell me.

One winter day, when I was about twelve, I had to stay after school to do over some examples involving fractions and missed my usual autobus to St-Paul. This happened from time to time for various reasons. When I did not arrive home at the regular hour, my mother would borrow Madame Roche's Daimler, which she had, with great exuberance, learned to drive, and come to Vence to pick me up at a certain agreed-upon tree in the square.

That night, as I waited in the dark, a boy or a man I had not noticed and never did see, pulled me behind the tree, imprisoned me with his arms, muzzled me with his mouth, and began rubbing himself rhythmically against me. It lasted only a few seconds before he heard the car, or saw the headlights, and disappeared. I was as puzzled as I was frightened. Kissing and hugging between the sexes were not new to me – the books I read and the movies I had seen in New York (there were none in St-Paul or Vence) were full of romantically embracing couples – but I had never heard about rubbing. I did not understand why anyone wanted to do that, especially with a strange twelve-year-old girl. I did not understand, either, why it had given me such a funny feeling in such a funny place.

I did not mention the incident to my mother. At one time I had told her almost everything, but I was beginning to keep things to myself, to enjoy, I think, the power it gave me to have knowledge that she did not. In this instance, besides, I suspected I might be freakish and wanted no one else to know.

A few weeks later I ran screaming into her bedroom one morning, blood running down my legs, and gasped that I was dying.

'What do you mean, dying?' she said, looking at me in utter astonishment. 'Can't you see you're just menstruating? Get a serviette out of the bottom drawer. My belt is there, too. You can use it until I buy you one later. Go in the bathroom and put them on. Wash your legs off with warm water. Dying!' She smiled. 'What a silly girl!'

I found the things only because there was nothing else in the drawer that could have fitted the description. I had never seen a sanitary napkin or belt before. I stood blankly holding them. 'I don't know how to put them on,' I said. 'Is it a sickness, Maman? Do you have it, too?'

She had been lying in bed all this time, her short hair a mass of tangles around her face, the covers up to her chin. In New York she had worn silk nightgowns that my father brought home from European trips, but in St-Paul she slept naked, winter and summer. Now, when she sat up abruptly in the unheated room, she dragged the quilt up around her. Except for her tight-skinned, elegant face, she reminded me of the *clochardes* we had seen in Paris on our way to St-Paul – women who lived in the streets and wore all the clothes they owned at once, often with added rags or blankets pinned over them for warmth.

'My God!' she said. 'Do you mean to tell me you don't know what menstruation is? Haven't I ever discussed it with you? Go clean yourself up while I start breakfast, and we'll talk.'

She told me the whole thing that morning. By the time my own daughter was the right age for it, mothers commonly gave such information to their daughters. Articles and books explained how to go about it, how to

385

treat it so as not to disturb tender psyches or distort healthy but restrained sexuality. My mother had no articles, no books. She just told me, without embarrassment, drama or sentimentality, the way it was.

I immediately told Jacqueline. By then I had several good, though not intimate, friends, among whom I considered Jacqueline the best. She was a small, homely, blurry-featured girl who, presumably because she had three older brothers, could not make her own decisions about anything and so allowed me to dominate her. I decided she ought to have the knowledge I had acquired.

No doubt my mother's calm, lucid objectivity was lacking. Jacqueline screamed and turned white. I thought she was going to faint. Instead, she ran back into the school building that we had just left. When I followed a moment later, I saw her talking breathlessly to our teacher. That liar, Megan, she said, had told her a boy sticks his *machin* into a girl's *pipi* and lays an egg to make a baby, and she didn't think I should be allowed to say such dirty things and frighten people, and she knew her mother wouldn't like it.

The teacher turned red instead of white. She quieted Jacqueline by telling her that of course everyone knew it was God who made babies, but that Americans had different ideas about such matters. Then she took me aside and threatened to have me expelled from the school if she ever heard of my talking such filth again.

'It isn't filth. My mother told it to me, and she doesn't talk filth,' I said, though I knew this was not strictly true. She said *merde* all the time.

The teacher advised me not to answer back, '*Pas de répliques!*' and concluded that she would have to discuss the entire affair with my mother.

My mother drove to the school in the Daimler. She had on the outfit she wore in the shop where she worked half a day, decorating pottery for sale; a blue workman's smock over a tweed skirt that showed her calves, though short skirts were not yet in style. I waited outside the building, wishing she had dressed like other mothers. I hoped she would not smoke a cigarette.

When she finally emerged, she was smiling. 'Everything's all right,' she said. I asked her if she had told the teacher that what I had told Jacqueline was not filthy but true.

'Oh, she knows it's true. We didn't talk much about that,' my mother said. 'I congratulated her on being so sensible and open about things old-fashioned women thought shouldn't be mentioned, and I told her how pleased I was with the progress you've made in her class. I said she must be an excellent teacher and asked her if she was educated at the Sorbonne, which, of course, she wasn't.' By this time we were in the Daimler, and she lit a cigarette, puffing at it as we drove off. 'You don't have to worry with her anymore. If I were you, though, I'd let their mothers tell the other girls what I told you. They may want to do it in their own way in their own time.'

'Did you smoke in there?' I asked her.

She did not answer this for a moment. 'Megan, one reason I left your father was that I had lost myself and become what was expected of me,' she said then. 'Here I am myself again. Just now, in the school, as myself I would have smoked a cigarette if I felt like it, and I would not have flattered your teacher. For your sake, I put on another false face. But I'll never again live my life by other people's standards, and I hoped when I brought you away with me that you wouldn't either.'

I didn't know what to say. I understood that I had disappointed her, but I had a feeling 'I'm sorry' would not cover the situation.

'Do you think it's wrong to smoke?' she asked me in a gentler voice.

'It looks funny.'

'Does it look funny when men smoke?'

'No.'

'Then why does it look funny when a woman does it?'

'Well, because most women . . .' I began, and stopped.

387

'You see? I'm not most women. I'm me. And you're you, not what the world decides a girl should be.' She paused to negotiate the narrow, hilly road. 'As a matter of fact, Megan, women are smoking everywhere now, outside of small provincial towns. You're growing up in much freer times. Even so, unless you're careful, freedom can slip away from you. Love cost me mine.'

She seemed to be talking about something else now. Love. I was interested in love only in an academic way, as a fictional subject. I knew no boys but Paul Roche, for whom I had little use, now that I had girls my age as friends. I cried when Jo, in *Little Women*, refused Laurie and felt I would have married him, but such fantasies had no foundation on real feelings. I certainly made no connection whatever between them and my mother's enlightenment about the vagaries of male and female bodies.

She said nothing more until we reached the outskirts of St-Paul and stopped while a solid mass of sheep came jostling by, prodded by a boy with dull eyes and a loose, mumbling mouth.

'I still love him, you know. I suppose I always will.' She spoke without apparent emotion, meanwhile lighting another cigarette, sticking it in the corner of her mouth, and talking around it. 'I know he loved me. "I have been faithful to thee, Cynara! in my fashion." We loved each other in our fashion, too. It wasn't enough. He was too scarred by his mother's rejection and too full of guilt. I thought I might enjoy a buttress, after all the years with no one to lean on, but probably I couldn't have anymore. I don't know. What I got was an absolute governor.'

A week or so after that a copy of *Woman's World* arrived in the mail from my grandfather. The contents were about equally divided between romantic fiction, beautifully illustrated with handsome, strong-jawed men and sweetly pretty women, and kitchen lore, beautifully illustrated with pictures of food. A poem by a woman with three names anthropomorphized sunbeams. Dr Philip Burroughs, identified as a child specialist, told mothers what to expect of babies from birth to six months.

'What woman's world?' my mother said after leafing through it. 'Not mine.'

I felt vaguely outraged. Some day I was going to be the editor of *Woman's World*, though I was even vaguer about this prospect, with little notion of what it entailed or how I could get to New York to engage on it.

'Grandpa says millions of women read it,' I said, quoting one of his letters. I never showed her his letters or my father's, and she never asked to see them. 'He says when he started the magazine—'

'He didn't start it,' she broke in. 'Your father started it.'

We had brought chairs outside the house and were sitting in the mild October sun. It was the midweek school holiday (we had classes on Saturdays) and my mother had finished her half day in the shop.

'Grandpa doesn't tell lies,' I said.

'Of course not. I'm sure he believes by now that he started it. I'm sure he forgets how he fought against the idea of expanding. If it hadn't been for your father, he might never have gone beyond *McNally's Monthly*.'

She had no use for any of the magazines. They had absorbed my father's life. Whatever other reasons she had for leaving him, this was certainly one of them. But she was proud of his accomplishments. I think he may never have understood this. I think he may have believed it was only his shortcomings she saw with clarity.

'He began talking about launching another magazine when he started as a desk editor,' she said. 'Terrence kept saying it was a good idea, and some day they would do it, but it was always the wrong time.'

I was watching the antics of a *rouge-gorge*, a little French bird something like a robin, but smaller, with a red throat instead of a red breast. It kept hopping to within a foot of the bread crumbs I had thrown out earlier for the birds and then, nervous of our presence, hoping back again. I felt at first sad, and then annoyed, that it should fear its benefactor.

'What your father finally did,' my mother said, 'was go out and get backers for a new magazine, and then tell Terrence they were men who believed so strongly in Terrence's editorial genius that they envisioned an eventual magazine empire that would dominate the whole publishing world. This was, of course, your father's dream, not what the backers said.'

'What are backers?'

'People who invest in something like a new play or a new magazine. Put money into it, hoping to make a profit. These were presidents of railroads, bank directors, newspaper publishers. Some were men your father knew in college, fraternity brothers. Some were men he knew only by reputation. He convinced them all that the time was ripe for another women's magazine and that it was sure to be every bit as successful as the *Ladies' Home Journal*. He told me he was never any good at selling boys' clothing – you know he did that once, don't you? – but when it came to this, he discovered he had a silver tongue.'

My grandfather, according to my mother, believed in his editorial genius himself, and certainly wanted to think that others believed in it, too, but he still raised objections. He knew how powerful corporations could manipulate the press. He had seen it done in former times, when insurance companies, railroads, patent-medicine manufacturers paid press agents to sell to the newspapers material favorable to their interests, disguised as news, or used the threat of canceled advertising to kill unfavorable editorials or news items. Fifteen years earlier one of the great oil companies had controlled a leading periodical with an annual subsidy, and succeeded in so watering down its contents that the magazine did not survive to receive a second year's payment. It had been bad enough during the war, my grandfather said, when *McNally's Monthly* had to echo every government policy or have its mailing privileges canceled by the post office, but he was not going to put himself deliberately under the thumb of private interests.

'Your father said this was all ancient history,' my mother said, 'and the backers he had enlisted were men of the highest caliber, many of them personal friends, none of them interested in controlling the new magazine, or the company, but only in profiting from a successful enterprise.' She tossed her crushed cigarette into the grass across the path, frightening the *rouge-gorge* that I thought was just about to come close enough to eat the crumbs. 'Fanny and Jake both sided with your grandfather, but Fanny told your father later that this was just a tactic to—'

'What's a tactic?'

My mother looked at me in that way she often did, as if suddenly aware it was a child she was talking to.

'It means they really agreed with your father, but they pretended they didn't,' she said. 'They knew if they all opposed Terrence, it would only make him more stubborn. But if everybody seemed to be against your father, they were pretty sure Terrence would begin to defend him and to see some value in his idea. That's exactly what happened. But by the time *Woman's World* was published Terrence forgot it was your father's idea. He gave him credit for getting the backers. He boasted about your father's ability as an editor. But Terrence must always be the initiator and the chief.'

'You sound as if you don't like Grandpa much,' I said.

'Like him? I love him. And I haven't loved many people in my life. I'm not one of your warm, loving women with open arms, like Fanny. Terrence, though, I'd have chosen for my father if I'd had a choice.'

'But you said—'

'That he's flawed? Of course he is. You don't love a person for being flawless. Who is? Terrence is a giant of

391

a man.' She looked at me thoughtfully for a moment, then lit another cigarette and watched the smoke floating on the quiet air. 'You're one of the ones I love, of course,' she said.

It hadn't occurred to me that I might not be. Still, I said adopting her matter-of-fact tone, 'And Terrence McNally the Third.'

She sighed. 'Yes, well, he was such a baby, though, Megan. I hardly had time to get to know him.'

I was glad to hear it.

3

If I was freer in St-Paul-de-Vence than I had been in New York City, I was not conscious of the difference. What I knew were the little changeless days of school and homework and books and friends with whom I chattered in French.

Two or three times a week my mother and I visited Uncle Frank Gabriel, who could no longer hold a paintbrush in his crippled hands and needed an attendant to look after him, but was unfailingly cheerful and talkative. Once in a while my mother was able to borrow the Daimler on a Sunday and drive to Nice, where we walked along the oceanfront on the Promenades des Anglais and drank café cappuccino, sitting in the sun at a sidewalk café.

Every Christmas Eve I went to church with Madame Roche and Paul and little Jean (my mother never went) not because I was religious but because I loved the walk up to the ancient church to the tolling of the bell; the townspeople, all of whom I knew, crowding inside; the large wooden crèche that Uncle Frank had carved years before; the priest, transformed from a little man in a shabby soutane, carrying his groceries in a basket on his arm, into a resplendent white-clad figure invoking Jesus.

I could not really imagine that any of this would ever be different, or that it would go on and I no longer a part of it.

Uncle Frank died the winter I was fourteen. A few months later my mother got a letter from a lawyer in the United States, informing her that her parents had been killed in a train collision in Italy and inviting her to come to Charlottesville for the reading of the wills. She mourned Frank. She did not mourn her parents, whom she had not seen in years. She said that they had never needed anyone but each other and that it was good that they had died together.

'Italy's so close,' I said. 'Maybe they were on their way to see you.'

She doubted that. 'I had become a stranger to them,' she said. 'They wouldn't have cared about seeing me.'

'Like my father.'

She looked startled. 'What do you mean?'

'Like my father doesn't care about seeing me,' I said, just as an item of conversation, not because it distressed me anymore.

'What makes you think he doesn't?'

'He says he does, but he never comes here. I know he's in Europe sometimes because Grandpa says so, but he doesn't come to St-Paul.'

We were sitting in our living room. My mother had the letter from the lawyer in her lap. She began folding and unfolding it.

'He has wanted to come, Megan. I wouldn't let him,' she said. 'I suppose I should have told you.'

'Why wouldn't you let him?'

I could see she did not want to answer this. Sometimes she forgot to tell me things or meant to keep them from me, but she never lied to me.

'I was afraid,' she said finally. 'This is where we met, where we fell in love. I was afraid if I saw him here again, I might go back to him. He keeps asking me to. As long as he's three thousand miles away, it's easy to

393

refuse. If he came back here, I might forget all the reasons why I left. He says things would be different now, but I know they wouldn't be.'

'I should think he'd just come if he really wanted to. How could you stop him?'

'He wouldn't just come, Megan. He wouldn't feel he has the right to do that.'

She seemed suddenly soft and vulnerable, though I did not think of it in those words. I had never seen her this way before, and it made me uncomfortable. I needed her strong, impervious. 'I suppose I could arrange for you to meet him somewhere,' she said. 'You're old enough now to travel by yourself.'

'I don't want to meet him,' I said. 'I don't even remember what he looks like.'

'It shouldn't be that way. My father was a stranger to me, but I shouldn't have let it happen to you,' she said in a voice unlike the clear, crisp one I knew. 'You have a right to know your father.'

The following morning she looked as though she had not slept. The golden tan of her face was yellowish, like faded suntan, and her eyes were ringed with purplish shadows.

'I've decided to go to Virginia for the reading of the wills,' she said as she put our breakfast on the table. 'You'll come with me, of course. We'll take the first sailing we can get.'

The idea of going anywhere, even to Nice, excited me. I didn't know what the reading of wills entailed or why we were going all the way across the ocean to hear them read, but I was not concerned with such questions. If I had not been fourteen years old and conscious of my supposed maturity, I would have jumped up and down and clapped my hands. Instead, I asked judiciously, knowing the question would not change my mother's plans, 'What about school?'

'It won't hurt you to miss a few weeks of school,' she said. 'You're smart enough to catch up.'

My mother had grown up in Charlottesville, but she had no evident attachment to it. She pointed out the university, with its lovely old Colonial buildings, but we did not go inside the gates. After all, she had never been a student there. Nor did she look for the house she had lived in, though we later learned it now belonged to her.

Her parents had left her the house and everything else they owned, except for a few small bequests to servants. She told the lawyer to sell the house and give the servants their pick of the personal possessions.

'Surely you'll want to keep something,' the lawyer said. He was a spindly man who could have been any age from forty to sixty. 'Some memento of your mother perhaps.'

'All I want is the money,' she told him.

'Very well.' He could not keep the distaste out of his voice. 'You'll be quite a rich woman.'

'You should have told him the reason you only want the money,' I said when we had left the office.

'Why? I'm sure he believes they left it to me because they were fine, loving parents. What good would it have done to tell him it was their substitute for love?'

'Well, he thought you were awful. If he knew—'

'What difference can it possibly make? A man I'll never see again? My God, Megan,' she said, 'don't ever be concerned with what people who don't matter in your life may think of you. That's really enslavement.'

The lawyer told her she would be rich, but she said nothing about this to me, and I did not ask. Money had no importance to me. I knew that whatever we had, aside from the little my mother made in the shop, came in monthly checks from her father; that she had refused to take anything from my father. I had no idea and no interest in the amount of our income. Whatever I wanted, unless my mother thought it unsuitable or unsafe, I got. I could not imagine any way in which we might live better, or differently, now.

We took the train to Washington. My mother was

bored by buildings and monuments, but she went dutifully around with me to see everything she thought I should see. I was titillated by the White House, where I pictured President Harding cowering at his desk while the scandals in the Veteran's Bureau, and in the departments of the Interior and Justice, swirled around him. My history teacher at the lycée had used Harding's administration as an example of corruption in American government.

'As long as we're here, we might as well spend a few days in New York,' my mother said when we were again on the train. She looked out the window of our compartment, though it was night and there was nothing to see. 'Maybe I'll take you to visit your father tomorrow. It's a Sunday, so he's likely to be home.'

In many ways I was childish for my age. I knew no boys. I saw no movies. I heard little adult conversation other than my mother's. I had no responsibilities except setting the table, drying the dishes, and keeping my room in order. Yet I understood at once that my mother had not just now conceived the idea of visiting my father.

'That's really why we came over here, isn't it?' I said.

She sighed. 'You're right.'

'But I told you I didn't care about seeing him.'

'I know. That's wrong, though. It's my fault. Whatever happened between him and me has nothing to do—' She stopped and turned away from the window to look at me. 'Oh, who am I fooling, Megan? That's only part of it. I want to see him myself.'

'How do you know he's not away someplace?'

'I don't. I'm – I suppose what I'm doing is playing a game. A kind of superstitious game. If he isn't there, it isn't meant to be. If he is, and he asks me again—' She shook her head. I had never seen her cry, but she looked now as though she might. 'I'm probably out of my mind. It would only be the same old trap. But there isn't a day in the three years that I haven't missed him, and I can't—' She broke off again. Instead of crying, she gave

396

a little laugh and said, in a voice much more like her usual one, 'I don't suppose you have the faintest idea what I'm talking about.'

Before she was awake the next morning, I slipped out of my berth and went to examine myself in the mirror over the washbasin. I wanted to get an idea of how I would appear to a father who had not seen me since I was eleven. But I couldn't tell much. In the first place, I didn't remember how I had looked at eleven. Besides, the mirror was too small to show anything but my face and hair. My freckles were fading, as my mother had promised they would, and I thought he might notice that. I put no particular stock in the emergence of cheekbones, but I thought it was nice that my cheeks were losing their roundness, and I thought he might notice that, too. Now that I was actually going to see him I was anxious that he like me. My hands and feet were cold, the way they were before a test in school.

'Don't get your hopes up,' my mother said on the way uptown in the taxicab. 'He may not be there. You said that yourself.'

'Will we stay here?' The thought had that moment come hurtling into my mind. 'I mean, if he's here, and he wants us to stay, will we – just never go back home again?'

'Oh, we'd have to go back.' She spoke dreamily, not noticing my panic. 'We'd have to get our things and clean out the apartment. We'd have to pay Madame Roche.'

This city had once been my home. I could remember living here. But the years between eleven and fourteen are immeasurable. The child of my memory was as remote to me as one of the children I had sometimes played with in Central Park. I could not imagine that it had ever actually been home to me, or ever would be, this crowded, noisy place. I had never seen so many people or so many automobiles. It had evidently snowed sometime before, and shabby-looking men were shoveling what was left of it into soiled piles along the curbs. I had never seen snow in St-Paul except for the clean white caps on the distant mountains. It had hailed once, huge stones that clattered on the roof and bounded on the ground, white bullets that soon melted in the Mediterranean sun. Here it was cold – surely I could never have felt such cold before – and everything looked dirty.

My mother must finally have seen something in my face because she put her hand over mine and said, 'We'll see your grandfather, too, if we can. He lives only a few blocks away. You'll like that, won't you?'

I said I would, but I didn't know. I wasn't sure. I knew him in letters. I loved him in letters. Sometime – in that same vague, distant future that would somehow transport me to the staff of *Woman's World* – I would see him. I had not thought of seeing him now.

'Your hand is so cold,' my mother said. 'You're nervous, aren't you? I know, I know. I'm nervous, too.'

As soon as we turned into the street, I recognized the house, though it looked like all the other brownstones. We went up the steps to the high stoop, and I remembered standing there with my roller skates over my shoulder, waiting for Christine or Sig to let me in.

It was neither of them who answered the bell now. It was a maid in a black uniform with a starched white apron and a starched white frill pinned to her black hair. When she spoke, her teeth were a gleaming contrast to her dark brown skin. I never saw colored people in St-Paul. I had forgotten they existed.

'Mr McNally isn't home right now,' she said.

I didn't look at my mother, as much because I was afraid my relief would show as that I didn't want to see her disappointment.

'Do you know when he'll be back?'

'Just a minute, ma'am.' The maid started away from the door and then came back and opened it wider. 'Step inside, ma'am, young lady. It's too cold to wait out there. Who should I say is calling?'

'Mrs McNally and Megan,' my mother said.

The maid seemed pleased. 'Oh, yes, ma'am. Relatives. Just one minute,' she said again and scurried down the hall.

'To whom is she going to say who's calling, I wonder,' my mother said. 'Maybe Terrence is here. Wouldn't that be nice? Maybe your father has just gone out for a newspaper or something and will be right back. Do I look all right?'

I had never heard her ask such a question before. She did not seem to care how she looked, as long as she was clean and her clothes, however outlandish by fashionable standards, were neat. They were neat now and more conventional than usual. Her dark coat, warmer than she needed in St-Paul, was new and well below her calves, and she wore a new cloche hat that restrained her wild hair a little. I told her she looked fine.

A woman was approaching us from what I knew to be the direction of the living room. I thought she might be an aunt, or somebody, that I had forgotten, but I could tell from my mother's face that she had not seen her before. She was tall, taller than my mother, and as thin, but fragile-looking, which my mother certainly was not. When she came closer into the light, I saw that she was quite beautiful, in the pale, ethereal style of Lillian Gish, with long fair hair that she wore around her head in an unmodish braid.

'Oh, my, I'm sorry! Annabel shouldn't have left you standing here,' she said in a sweet, light voice. 'You're Margaret, aren't you? Meg. Meg and Megan.' She held out her hands to us. 'Please come in. I've asked Annabel to bring us coffee in the living room.'

She pressed our hands and then turned and led the way. Behind her back my mother smiled at me, raised her eyebrows, and shrugged, but she looked worried.

The living room seemed only faintly familiar, but then I had not spent much time in it, preferring my own room or the kitchen. The black-lacquered, ornately decorated cabinet, however, was clearly not from my time in the house. I knew it was not my mother's taste.

'Isn't this delightful? I'm so glad to meet you both at last,' the woman said when we had sat down. 'Terry will feel dreadful to have missed you. He's in Washington, interviewing some senators about the Teapot Dome thing. Will you be in New York long? Maybe he'll be back before you have to leave.'

He had been in Washington when we were there, I thought. We could have bumped into him in the street. I wondered if I would have recognized him, or he me.

The maid came in at that moment with the coffee and set the tray down on the table in front of the woman, who poured gracefully, without spilling anything into the saucer, as my mother usually did. When my mother said, 'No sugar,' and I said, 'Two lumps, please,' I realized these were the first words either of us had spoken since the woman had appeared.

My mother took a sip of her coffee and then put the cup down. She looked straight into the woman's face.

'If you don't mind my asking,' she said, 'who are you?'

The woman stared at her with large gray eyes gone huge. 'Why, I thought you'd realize. I'm so sorry,' she said. 'I'm Angela.'

'Angela,' my mother repeated. 'Angela who?'

'Oh, my!' the woman said. 'You must not have received Terry's letter. How stupid of me to take it for granted! He wrote you a month ago, but the transatlantic mails are so slow.' She looked at my mother, whose face was a wood carving. 'I'm Angela McNally. Angela Wentworth McNally. Terry and I were married on Christmas Day.'

I don't know how my mother did it. She smiled. She said how lovely it was, and she hoped they would be very happy. She said she had had business here and had suddenly had the impulse to come and bring Terry's daughter to see him, and it was too bad we had to leave for home before he came back, but it couldn't be helped.

Her voice never faltered.

'I wish we could wait, but we're expected home. I'm sure you understand,' she said, and even I, who knew better, pictured some anxious, well-rooted man, pacing our St-Paul floor, watching out the window for us.

We stayed a polite twenty minutes. At the door Angela took my hand. 'You look like your father. It's rare to see a girl with a strong face who is pretty at the same time. I'll try to describe you to him.' She kissed my cheek. 'I hope you'll come back someday, Megan. It would make Terry so happy, and I'd like so much to know you better.'

She had called a taxi for us. As soon as we were inside it, the door closed, my mother said, 'My God, what a sappy woman! I suppose that's what your father always wanted. She's probably exactly right for him, mooning and sighing and telling him how wonderful he is—'

'Where to, lady?' the cabby inquired.

'Where to? I don't know. Wait a minute.' She scrabbled in her handbag, found her cigarettes, and lit one unsteadily. 'The Waldorf-Astoria, that's where to,' she said then. 'Why not? I'll never be in this town again in my life. Why not do it up brown for once?' The driver had started off and had his back to us, so I assumed she was talking to me, not him. 'Let's celebrate. Let's—'

She was frightening me a little. I had never seen her like this before. 'Our valises,' I said, trying to switch her to some practical commonplace. 'How are we going to get them?' We had left them in the checkroom at the railroad station. 'Could we go for them now on our way to the hotel?'

'Absolutely not! We'll send someone for them. Some minion,' she said grandly, 'from the Waldorf-Astoria. And tonight we'll see a play. You've never been to the theater, have you, Megan?' She leaned forward and tapped the cabby on the shoulder. 'What's the best play in town?' she asked him.

'Well, there's *Abie's Irish Rose*. I ain't saying it's the

best, but it's been going a year, so plenty people must like it a lot.'

'*Abie's Irish Rose.* Well, it's apt. "Meg's Irish Fizzle."' She gave a hoot of unnatural laughter, and said it again. '"Meg's Irish Fizzle."'

While she was registering at the hotel desk, I watched the people going in and out. They all looked rich and in a hurry. I saw a girl about my age who seemed to be waiting for someone, tapping her foot and watching the door with an impatient, displeased expression. She wore a beaver coat, the skins arranged to form stripes of dark and light brown. Her mouth was red with lipstick that shaped it into a Cupid's bow.

My mother had planned to buy me a winter coat in Best's if we stayed in New York. The one I had on was a lightweight navy blue wool with brass buttons, with a sweater under it for added warmth. The best dress in my valise – the best dress I owned – was also navy blue, with detachable white piqué collar and cuffs. I had considered it very grown-up because it had a long skirt, my first, but looking at that girl I knew, though I could not see her dress under her coat, that she would not have been caught dead in it.

Upstairs in the large, hushed, perfumed gray satin room, my mother appeared calmer. She said, 'We didn't see your grandfather. I'm sorry, Megan.' She sat down on one of the satin bedspreads. 'I forgot all about it.'

'I don't mind.' I looked at my scrubbed, pale-lipped image in the dressing-table mirror with none of the approval I had given it on the train. 'It probably would have been embarrassing anyhow.'

She didn't seem to hear this. 'I've been saved from my own insanity, you know, Megan,' she said. 'It never would have worked out. A man of forty-one doesn't change. Or a woman of thirty-five, for that matter. I've made the kind of life for myself that I want and that I'm fitted for.' She looked around the room and shook her head. 'How could I have thought of coming back to this?'

We were going to have dinner in the hotel dining room before the theater. My mother had pointed out the corridor between the dining room and the grill room, where chairs were placed for people to watch the passersby. To watch them strut by, she said, loving to be watched. Peacock Alley, the corridor was called. I could not bear the thought of walking through there in my navy blue dress.

'I want to wear lipstick,' I said. 'I'm old enough.'

'In St-Paul you aren't, but I suppose you are here.' My mother shrugged. 'Go ahead if you feel like it.'

'I want to borrow one of your dresses, too.' We wore the same size. 'I can't wear mine.'

'Why not?'

'It's too childish. It's all wrong. I can't go down there in a dress like that.'

She frowned. 'I don't see why you care. I told you this in Virginia. You'll never see any of the people here again in your life. Why should it matter to you what they think of the way you're dressed?'

I seldom opposed her – not because I was docile, certainly, but because there were few things I wanted to do that she thought objectionable. Now, though, I made up my mind that nothing, nobody, was going to get me downstairs in that navy blue dress.

'I care how I look,' I said, which was, of course, not the answer to her question. 'I don't have to think the way you do about everything.'

'No,' she said. 'No, you certainly don't.' She got up and opened the door of the closet where she had hung her clothes when our valises arrived. 'Take your pick.'

I was sorry, then, that I had been so snippy, after what had happened to her in my father's house. She had brought only two dresses besides the one she had on. I chose the pale green because I knew green was supposed to go well with red hair. It had cap sleeves, a peplum, and a spray of darker green leaves embroidered across

403

the bosom. I had not yet grown as tall as my mother, so that I had to hold the skirt up with one hand to avoid tripping over it. I also had trouble making a Cupid's bow out of my full-lipped mouth. But I was satisfied. I thought I looked reasonably elegant and sophisticated and, above all, not like a little French schoolgirl.

My mother did not comment. 'Go on down awhile,' she said. 'I'll finish dressing and meet you in the lobby.'

I said I thought I might as well wait in the room. She raised her eyebrows. 'What's the matter? Do you think you're too young to go down alone?'

So, of course, I had to go. I sat down in Peacock Alley and assumed a bored expression. One or two people looked at me with what I was not sure was admiration, but hardly anybody looked at me at all. I was both glad of it and disappointed. After a while a young man in evening clothes came toward me, got close enough for a good view, and then veered away. I was both glad and disappointed about that, too, though mostly glad. I would have had no idea what to say to him.

I saw my mother before she saw me – long enough to prepare myself. By the time she came up to me I had put on what I felt was a natural bland smile.

She had scrubbed her face. Her nose was shiny, and she was not wearing lipstick. She was wearing my navy blue dress with the white piqué collar and cuffs.

'I thought you were never coming. I'm starved,' I said. 'Let's go in and eat.'

I was not, after all, my mother's daughter for nothing.

4

The letter from my father telling of his approaching marriage to Angela arrived about a week after we were back in St-Paul. My mother said it was short and almost

404

impersonal. She tore it up into tiny pieces.

He wrote to me after our visit. It was the first of his letters to recognize that I was not still eleven years old. Angela must have brought it to his attention.

'If only I had known you were coming. I could have arranged something,' he wrote. 'I could even have taken you along to Washington. If you're going to be on the staff some day, as Father assures me you will be, it would have been a good experience for you.'

Grandpa wrote that he did not understand why I had not come to see him when I was there, 'practically around the corner', but he was sure there must have been a good reason. In any case, when I finally came to stay, we would make up for lost time.

After that everything settled down again. My mother did not mention our trip or anything that had happened, except to tell me, as she had before, that *Abie's Irish Rose* was really a terrible play, and she was sure the only reason I had liked it was because it was the first play I had ever seen.

'It's like falling in love with the first boy you meet,' she said – a remark that turned out to be prophetic. 'You have nothing to compare it to.'

'If it's such a terrible play, why do so many people keep going to see it?'

'Because most people don't know any better. Taste has to be educated. Yours will be. Wait till you see the Comédie Française.'

This was to take place when I was living in Paris and attending the university, the Sorbonne, as my mother had. She often talked to me about it, but although it was now only a few years off, it was as hazy to me, as dreamlike, as my future on *Woman's World*, which was never mentioned between us.

Yet I knew that all my studies at the lycée were aimed at preparing me for the Sorbonne. In the first weeks after our return from America (no one in St-Paul called it the

United States) I did little else but study to make up for the work I had missed. It was not easy. School hours were long, and the work was piled on with little concern about overburdening the students. Those who could not keep up were weeded out by an examination, the *bachot*, taken at the end of secondary school, and were denied certain desirable positions for the rest of their lives. But much of the work was memorization, and I was blessed with a photographic memory. The rest I always managed to learn well enough to pass, even if I promptly forgot it afterward.

Before long our trip had become a dream to me, too. Someone has said that the past is another century. It was certainly that for me. The past and the future. Strange countries with strange customs that I had heard about but that had no clearly perceived connection with, for example, my daily after-school visits to the *patisserie* for pastry and coffee with a group of greedy, chattering girls.

Yet it was there, in the *patisserie*, shortly before my sixteenth birthday, that my slow, unrecognized journey to the country of the future was quickened, as if a sudden wind rose in the doldrums.

We talked of boys as we wolfed our *mille-feuilles* and our *croissants au sucre*, but few of us, except those with brothers, knew anything about them. I had once seen Paul Roche make *pipi* against a tree and caught a glimpse of his penis, but since he was four years younger than we were, this information seemed too trivial to share. Jeannine Albert, the only one with a brother the right age, was a closemouthed girl who would not discuss him and changed the subject when any of the brasher girls asked to be introduced to him. I thought there was probably something wrong with him, like the child with a huge, lolling head whom we sometimes saw wheeled along the street in a carriage and who, one of the girls said, was not a child at all but a twenty-five-year-old man.

The image of Jeannine's brother had lodged itself so securely in my imagination that it added considerably to my confusion when she took me aside one day and spoke to me about him.

'Let the others go ahead,' she whispered. 'I want to ask you something.'

She was a slight dark girl who still had an undeveloped body. I was fully matured by then, strongly built, with rather large hands and feet. Jeannine made me feel oversized and un-French.

'It's about François,' she said when we were alone at the table. It took me a moment to remember that François was her brother's name. Instantly I pictured the wobbly great head and vacant eyes. 'He's preparing for the *bachot*.' How could that poor creature possibly—? 'He's very smart in everything, but English gives him trouble. He could get somebody in school to help him, but of course they're all French, even the teachers. I told him you would know more than any of them, English being your native tongue.'

She was asking me to tutor her brother. I didn't know how to tutor anybody, certainly not a boy. I didn't even know how to talk to a boy. But the idea excited me. I was not so much afraid of newness, of change, as unable to believe in it until it happened.

The Alberts lived in Vence in a house built of stone, like most of the houses in this lumber-poor country. It was near the village, so that I could walk there after school. On cold days, Madame Albert and the four girls sat around the coal stove in the large kitchen, but François and I, in order to have privacy and quiet, worked in the damp, unheated, seldom used living room. Monsieur Albert was a butcher in the village. He considered his only son a genius and wanted him to go to the university instead of becoming a butcher, too. It would kill his father, François announced to me, if he failed the *bachot*.

407

He was dark, like his sister, with the same withdrawn look that bordered on sullenness, but he was tall and husky. I expected to be uncomfortable with him, and if he had treated me with normal courtesy, I'm sure I would have been. But he made me too angry. He resented taking instruction from a girl and evidently saw no reason to hide his feelings. After all, his family doted on him no matter what he did.

One day he snarled, '*Merde!*' I was used to hearing my mother say it, but it was not a fit word for a boy to say, much less snarl, to a girl. 'You talk too fast. If you weren't so stupid, you'd realize nobody can understand you when you talk like a railroad train.'

I stood up from the table. I grabbed the book we were using. 'Find somebody smarter, then, to tutor you. I've had enough of your rotten disposition,' I said, and threw the book at him. 'I quit, and I hope you flunk the *bachot!*'

An edge of the book hit him on the mouth, knocking his lip against his teeth and making it bleed. He stood stunned for a moment, dabbing at the lip with his handkerchief and looking incredulously at the blood. Then he went for me, moving so fast, in spite of his size, that he had me by the arms almost before I saw him coming.

'*Garce!*' This word meaning 'bitch', lent itself more to hissing than snarling. His fingers dug into my flesh. He began to shake me. 'I'll teach you to—'

'Take your hands off me or I'll yell.'

He loosened his fingers a little, but he did not let me go. 'All right, yell. I'll say you threw the book at me because I got a word wrong. Do you think they'll blame me for shaking you?'

'Let's find out,' I said.

I prepared to yell. I got as far as opening my mouth. The next thing I knew his tongue was in it, and his hands had shifted, one going around my waist and the other

408

cupping a breast. I tried to kick him, but he was holding me too hard against him. I considered biting his tongue, but the prospect seemed unappetizing. I remembered the time somebody had grabbed me from behind a tree and rubbed himself against me, and I had the wild idea that maybe it had been François. He was not rubbing himself against me now, but I could feel his hard bulge pressing my leg, and I knew, in spite of my innocence, that it meant he was enjoying himself. Maybe he had been secretly in love with me all this time. Maybe, since I was beginning to enjoy it, too, I was in love with him. I was just about to stop struggling when we heard someone coming. François let go of me, pushed me frantically down into my chair, and scrambled into his.

'The shoemaker will 'ave his shoes ready tomorrow,' he recited loudly in English.

Whenever I was there, one of his sisters brought in a tray of refreshments. This time it was the youngest, Marianne, who came in with two glasses of red wine (we always had wine) and a plate of the buttery little biscuits called *fougassons* that were a Vence specialty. My mother had only recently begun allowing me a thimbleful of wine with dinner, but I drank it here as if I were long accustomed to it, and as if I savored it, which I didn't. François, like most French children of the time, had undoubtedly been drinking it since he was seven or eight years old.

'*Allons, fiche le camp!*' François said to Marianne, meaning 'Beat it!'

She had put down the tray but showed no sign of leaving. She wanted, she said now, to hear him speak English. This time he told her, even less politely, to *foutre le camp*, causing her to flounce out with exaggerated indignation.

In the interim I had had time to pull myself reasonably well together and to assume the correct attitude. The new etiquette of Flaming Youth had not yet infiltrated the

Alpes-Maritimes, where a boy was not supposed to grab a pure, innocent girl and stick his tongue in her mouth even if he was in love with her.

'How could you dare . . !' I began, but François was ahead of me.

'Listen, don't you tell anybody,' he muttered, glaring at me. 'You'll be sorry if you do!'

'You can't threaten me. If I felt like telling anybody, I would. It so happens I don't.'

I intended to say that I would tell, however, unless he promised never to touch me again. Instead, I found myself asking him why he had done it.

'You don't even like me,' I said subtly.

He seized a handful of *fougassons*, stuffed them in his mouth, and washed them down with wine before he answered.

'I like you all right.' He did not, while he made this passionate declaration, look at me. 'You have nice *tétons*.'

It was not proper, either, for a boy to tell a pure, innocent girl that he admired her tits, but I decided to let it go.

'I like you, too,' I said. 'Only when I'm willing to come here and help you with your English, I don't think you ought to tell me I'm stupid.' Some wiliness, innate or learned at that moment, caused me to add, 'I'm not an experienced tutor, remember. The only reason I can help you at all is that English is my native language, and it isn't yours.'

I was tempted to add that in any other subject he would have had to help me, but I could not bring myself to go that far. It was probably true, since he was ahead of me in school but I thought he might believe it was because I was a girl. Though I was not sure girls in general were as smart as boys, I was sure I was.

In any event he seemed satisfied. He said, 'I don't really think you're stupid. That's just a way of speaking.'

He kissed me again before I left, leaving the tongue out of it this time but reaching inside the top of my dress. From then on, part of each tutoring session was devoted to our explorations. François, like any self-respecting French boy of seventeen, was fairly experienced. He knew all the things it was possible to do to me with his hand and taught me what to do to him with mine. Whether he would have tried anything further, or whether I would have let him, if we had not had to worry about interruptions from his family in the kitchen, I cannot say. As it was, we always had enough warning from approaching footsteps to get out from under each other's clothes and appear to be poring over the textbook, all four hands on top of the table.

I lived for those twice-a-week sessions. I thought about François all the time. I was obsessed with him. Nothing I knew had prepared me to feel as I felt when he touched me. The idea that a nice girl, or woman, had sexual feelings at all had not long been accepted. That the feelings could be anything like as strong as a boy's or a man's still was not. I could be in such a state only because of love. I invented a François who loved me – a fine, handsome, romantic François. That made everything all right.

My mother must have noticed. My schoolwork suffered. I went around in a daze, sometimes not hearing when she spoke to me. I got up at night and prowled through the house, unable to sleep for excitement because I had been with him that day or would be the next. Yet she said nothing. She would have considered it prying. If I needed her, I would come to her.

But she had never liked the idea of the tutoring. 'It's all right to help someone out,' she said, 'but you're giving up most of two afternoons a week, and I think that's too much. I think these Alberts are taking advantage of you. They'd have to pay plenty for a regular tutor.'

'They offered to pay me,' I said, 'but I told them I didn't want any money.'

'That must have seemed peculiar to them. Almost everybody wants money.'

I could have reminded her that she didn't seem to want much of it herself. According to the lawyer in Charlottesville, she was now a rich woman, but no one would have guessed it. She had bought out the man for whom she decorated china, and turned the place into a successful gift shop that attracted the increasing tourist trade, and she had bought a Daimler of her own so that she no longer had to borrow Madame Roche's, but nothing else had changed. We still lived in Madame Roche's villa. My mother wore the same nondescript clothes she always had worn. We ate well, and we had a girl from the village who cleaned for us three times a week, but we had had these comforts for as long as I could remember.

I did not, however, mention any of this. I was relieved that she dropped the subject of the Alberts. She said nothing more on the subject until late spring, when the letter came for her from my grandfather.

'Terrence has written to me about you,' she told me.

I had just come from a session with François and was as usual rearranging it to fit my fancy. I imagined he had whispered to me that he loved me, though all he ever whispered were instructions. We knew nothing about each other except the quickly accessible parts of our bodies, but I imagined that I understood his nature – strong, proud, secretly gentle – and that he knew mine as no one else ever could.

'Yes,' I said to my mother.

'Sit down, Megan, and listen to me. This is important.'

I sat in a rush-bottom chair and gazed dreamily at a still life that happened to be in my line of vision. It was a Matisse that Frank Gabriel had bought for my mother when the artist was relatively unknown. Now, priceless, it hung in an inexpensive frame on the white plaster wall of our modest apartment. The lopsided fruit made me think of the pear I had eaten that afternoon while François, with the casualness of familiarity (which I thought of as the intimacy of established love), pinched my nipples.

'Are you listening, Megan?'

The sharpness of her tone got through to me. This time when I said, 'Yes', I knew what I was saying.

'Your grandfather wants you to come to New York for the summer and work at the magazine office. He says it's time you began getting some experience. Evidently he's under the impression that you'll eventually live over there and make *McNally's* your life's work.' Her voice had an edge, a coldness, that I had not heard before. 'Do you know anything about this?'

'He's never written to me about coming for the summer.' The long summer of no studying, no tutoring; of picnics and fields and hidden hills beyond the reach of sisters with trays of wine and biscuits. 'I don't want to go,' I said.

'That's not what I'm asking you, Megan. I'm asking you whether you've known of his plans for you at *McNally's*.'

'Well, he's mentioned them. It all seemed so far off. I didn't really pay much attention.'

'You must have let him think you were interested, or he wouldn't have written me this letter.'

I was not used to this kind of inquisition. It was not my mother's style. It confused me, and when I was confused, I tended to react with anger.

'Suppose I did. Why shouldn't I? He wants me to be the editor of *Woman's World* when I'm old enough. What do *you* want me to do? Work in your shop and simper at the tourists?'

She looked for a moment as though she could not believe it was I who had talked to her like that. I could

413

hardly believe it myself. Then she turned away so that I could see only her clear, tight profile.

'I'm sorry, Maman.'

She shook her head. 'No. You're right. Why shouldn't you? I swore I'd never let you be forced into anybody's mold, so how can I try to force you into mine?' She said nothing for a time. Then she turned and looked at me again. 'Why don't you want to go over there this summer?'

'I just don't. I want to stay here.' Something in her face made me add in a louder, frantic voice, 'I won't go!'

She smiled and took my hands. 'It's because of the Albert boy, isn't it?'

'Oh, Maman!' The overload of new emotions came bursting through before I could stop it. I put my head down on our joined hands. 'Oh, Maman, I love him!'

She said nothing to this, only tightened her fingers around mine. I lifted my head. She was still smiling.

'His name is François, isn't it? Yes. The first boy I ever loved was called André. It was when I was about your age and at school near Nantes. He was the son of the cook, and all the girls were in love with him or thought they were. I was sure he loved only me because he kissed me and asked me to go to bed with him. I was so ignorant I thought he wouldn't do that unless he loved me.'

'What happened?'

'I found out he was kissing all the other girls and asking them all the same thing.'

'Maman, you must think I'm stupid,' I said. 'You just made that all up to show me—'

She laughed before I could finish. 'No, I didn't make it up. Really. But I admit I told it to you for a purpose,' she said, and then asked, all in the same tone and with the laugh still on her face, 'Have you been sleeping with François?'

I stared at her with honest outrage. 'Maman! How can

414

you think such a thing?'

'I think it because it's written all over you, though it's taken me long enough to recognize it. I suppose I've wanted to see you as still a child.'

'I don't know what you're talking about. Written all over me? How can it be when I haven't done it?'

She shrugged. 'If you haven't, it's only for lack of opportunity. In that case I'm sure you've been doing what you could.' She stood up. 'I'll write to Terrence before I start dinner. He wanted a prompt answer.'

I knew she meant she would tell him I was coming. I raged. I sobbed. I tore the notepaper out of her hand while she was writing. I shouted that I had confided in her, told her of my love, and she had dirtied it and turned it against me, and I hated her. I threatened to run away and become a prostitute in Paris. When she paid no attention to any of this, I finally went to my room, slammed the door, and fell asleep on the bed on my stomach with the pillow over my head.

When I awoke, she was sitting next to me with the pillow in her lap. She began talking right away, quickly, as if to get it in before I could gather myself together for another assault.

'Listen to me, Megan, I'm not angry or sitting in judgement. I'm not trying to punish you. I may advise you, but you know I don't interfere with you unless it's to keep you from danger. That's all I'm doing now.'

I hadn't much fight left in me. The idea of going off somewhere with François drifted into my mind and out again. I knew my mother too well to think I could win this one. Still, I couldn't simply collapse into acquiescence.

'Danger? What danger?' I sat up against the headboard, away from her. 'I suppose, no matter how many times I tell you we haven't done it, you're afraid I'll have a baby.'

'It's always a possibility. If you haven't "done it", as

415

you put it, all right, but that wasn't the only danger I meant.' She leaned her elbow on the pillow and looked at me as if trying to memorize my face. 'I don't want your heart broken. You're too young and too intense. If you leave him, you'll be sad, but it won't last when you're in a whole new life. If he ended it – and he'd probably be the one; that's how the odds go – you might be scarred. That doesn't have to happen to you yet.'

'Suppose I promise not to see him anymore. Couldn't I stay here then?'

'You wouldn't keep your promise. You might mean to, but you wouldn't.' I didn't even mean to. 'Believe me, Megan, I know the power of what you feel.'

I thought she was talking about love.

My parting with François was not the romantic tragedy I had envisioned. When I told him I was leaving, he was furious. I had promised to help him in English to prepare him for the *bachot*, and now I was going off before he was prepared, and if he flunked, it would be my fault.

'It would only have been a few more weeks anyway. If you're not prepared now, you never will be,' I told him, furious in my turn. 'Maybe if you'd done the exercises I gave you—'

'What good were your stupid exercises? All I needed was a little help in your *merdeuse* English grammar, but you were only hot to get me in your pants.' He saw what was in my mind and raised his voice, forgetting his family in the kitchen. 'If you throw that wine at me, I'll kill you.'

I would have thrown it at him anyway – it would have been worth the risk – but Jeannine appeared at that moment to ask what the trouble was. I ran past her and out of the room. She followed me.

'Why is he so angry?'

I managed, before I was convulsed by sobs of frustrated rage, to tell her it was because I couldn't finish tutoring him for the *bachot*. She put her arm around me, this girl who habitually kept space between herself and others.

'Never mind. Don't blame yourself,' she said. 'He won't pass the *bachot* anyway. It isn't only the English.'

This information stopped me in mid-sob. 'I thought you said he was so smart in everything else.'

'He is. He's very smart. But the teachers are against him.'

'*All* of them?'

'Yes.' I could tell she really believed this. 'He's smarter than they are, you see, and they don't like that. He says they do everything they can to keep him from learning.'

I understood, then, that François was a fool. I might have managed to redesign our final scene into a drama of disappointed love and forgivable bitterness and gone on sorrowing, but for a fool I could shed no tears. I was not wise enough to suffer one gladly. Not then or ever.

I thought I was going to stay with my grandfather and Aunt Fanny for the summer, but this turned out not to be so. I suppose my grandfather wrote the letter because he was thought to have more influence with my mother, who had always admired him, but it was in my father's house that I was to live. My father's and Angela's. I was apprehensive and agog about the whole venture, sometimes alternately, sometimes both at once. My favorite, most comforting, fantasy took me away from the ticklish house and household and installed me as editor of *Woman's World*, swept into that position (of whose function I knew nothing) in one summer, at not yet seventeen, by my precocious brilliance.

My mother closed the shop, though it was the height of the tourist season, put a sign on the door saying '*Fermeture annuelle*', and drove me to Le Havre, where I was to board the *Île de France* for New York. We went by way of Aix and Avignon and north through the Loire

Valley with its blur of châteaux, and I remember almost none of it. My mother talked. I had never heard her talk so much, so steadily. It was as if she meant to fill me with her voice, her words, and so herself.

'I want to tell you something about your father,' she said one day. We were on a road lined with plane trees. French roads everywhere are lined with plane trees. They say Napoleon had them planted so that when his troops bivouacked, they would have wood for their fires. 'It's something I think you should know to help you understand him,' my mother said. 'He's not an easy man to understand.' She drove, always, looking straight ahead through the windshield, never turning her head for an instant, no matter how wide or deserted the road. 'It had to do with Charles. His brother, Charles.'

'He killed himself, didn't he?'

I don't know how I knew this. I don't remember anyone's telling me. I don't think my mother had ever mentioned Charles to me before.

'Yes, he cut his wrists. He was about your age,' my mother said. 'Your father was devoted to him, and he worshipped your father.'

'You didn't know him, did you?'

'No, he died four years before I met your father. But I knew all about him. Terry used to tell me everything.' She was silent for a minute. All I could see was the side of her face. 'Charles was always on his mind. I think he probably still is, and that's why I'm telling you this. I wonder if Angela . . .' she began but she let that go.

'Do you know why he did it?' I asked. 'Charles, I mean?'

'Well, there's a question about it in your father's mind, and that's the point. Charles left a note saying he had discovered he had an incurable illness and didn't want to live with it, but your father thinks he would have lived with it. He thinks it's his fault he didn't. He thinks he, in effect, killed him.'

I shivered. 'But that's crazy, isn't it? If Charles couldn't be cured, and he was in terrible pain or something— What was the illness anyway?'

'He called it an illness. I don't know what it is. Nobody knows much about it. But he wasn't in pain. Not physical pain. He – light me a cigarette, will you, Megan?'

I got the Gauloises and matches out of her bag, lit one for her, and put it in her mouth. She had let me try my first cigarette when I was fifteen, and I had sometimes smoked one with friends, pretending that my mother, too, would kill me if she found out, but I had no taste for it.

'Your father came home unexpectedly from a selling trip one night,' my mother went on, with the Gauloise in the corner of her mouth. 'He thought the house was empty. Charles was supposed to be in Atlantic City with his parents, but he had made some excuse or other and gone home. He was in the house with a friend, a boy he had traveled to Europe with that summer. Sidney Keller.' She paused and then said the name again, as if she wanted to remember it. 'Sidney Keller. He and Charles were in Charles's room, but Terry didn't know it. He went to bed – it was late at night – and when some noise they made woke him, he thought it was a burglar and went tiptoeing down to the room with a cane to hit him over the head with.'

I could not imagine what to expect. All I could think of was that my father had killed Charles with the cane by mistake, but I knew that was not right. Charles had killed himself.

'They didn't hear him coming,' my mother said. 'When he turned on the light, he saw them in bed together, and he said something – he doesn't remember exactly what – something that expressed his loathing. Then he left the house, and he never saw Charles alive again. So he blames himself. He believes that when he let

419

Charles, who idolized him, know how vile he thought he was, it was more than Charles could bear.'

Once again my mother assumed I had knowledge that she either thought she had given me or that she supposed I must have acquired elsewhere. But I was totally bewildered. What, I asked my mother, was vile or loathsome about two friends sharing a bed?

'Oh, for heaven's sake, Megan, you can't be that dense,' she said impatiently. 'They were naked in each other's arms. They were—' She broke off, drove on in silence for a minute or two, and then said slowly, 'You do know, don't you, that some men and women are attracted to their own sex?' She saw that I did not. 'Well, it isn't uncommon, but the idea is horrifying to some people. It was horrifying to your father. As far as I'm concerned, what anyone does in bed, and with whom, is his own business and has no bearing on whether he's admirable or detestable.'

The last part of this filtered through to me in time, but at the moment I was far more interested in what seemed to me the insurmountable problem of logistics. How, with the limited equipment at their disposal, could two people of the same sex make love?

'They just use what they have,' my mother explained in her offhand way. 'Unless the object is to produce babies, I can't see that it matters what goes into which orifice, as long as it's pleasing to the couple involved.' She paused. 'Your father looked at it differently. He probably still does. I'm sure he'd give anything he owns not to have let Charles know how revolted he was, but that doesn't mean the revulsion went away.'

She said nothing for a while, nor did I. My imagination was busily contemplating the various anatomical possibilities my mother's rather vague explanation had suggested, and rejecting most of them in favor of my own limited experience. François had receded into a kind of void, as though he had died or

420

had never been born, but the things we had done together were vividly present. I was a little disturbed that they had not faded right along with my perception of the boy, that they existed independent of love.

After a time my reflections returned to the subject of Charles. 'I think it was crazy to kill himself because his brother thought he was horrible,' I said. 'Maybe he would have changed his mind later. If not, it seems to me that Charles could have got over it. At least he'd have been alive.' I shook my head. 'I'd never want to kill myself, whatever happened. I'd just go somewhere else, do something else – I don't know. Something. You can't do anything if you're dead.'

My mother laughed a little. 'I'm sure you would do something. You're too stubborn to give up.'

We passed a car going the other way. The driver, who looked like an American, stuck his head out of the window and waved, but my mother did not wave back. She never took her hands off the wheel for any reason other than to shift gears. No doubt the American driver would have comments to make about the unfriendly French.

'As a matter of fact, I don't believe Charles killed himself simply because of your father,' my mother said. 'I think there was more to it than that. You know about the McNally mystery, don't you? The first Terrence McNally, your grandfather's grandfather, who was repudiated by the family?'

I may have known about it once. If so, I had forgotten it. I asked why he had been repudiated.

'That's the mystery,' my mother said. 'Apparently it intrigued Charles enough so that when he was in Europe, he went to Ireland to try to find out. He and Sidney Keller went to the place the McNallys came from, and Charles told your father they actually found an old man who knew the story, had heard it from his father. But Charles never said what the story was. He said he couldn't talk about it just then, but he would later on.' She leaned her head slightly toward me, without turning it, and I took the stub of the cigarette from her mouth and threw it away. 'Later on he was dead.'

I was intrigued now, too. 'Sidney Keller must have known about it, though, didn't he? You said he went along.'

'Yes, but for a long time your father couldn't bring himself to face Sidney Keller. When he finally did go to see him, it was – a disaster.' Her clear voice clogged on the last words. She coughed, twitched her shoulders impatiently. 'Keller wouldn't let him in. He stood in the doorway and cursed your father, called him a murderer, slammed the door in his face. That was all Terry needed – to hear somebody else call him what he had been calling himself. When he told me, I said I was sure there were reasons that had nothing to do with him. I said if Charles was so upset by what he had heard in Ireland that he couldn't talk about it, that might have been part of his trouble. But no matter what I said, Terry only answered, over and over, "Yes, maybe, but I pushed him over the edge."' She took a deep breath or sighed; I couldn't tell which. 'After a while I stopped trying. He wasn't listening anymore. To that or anything else that wasn't connected to the magazines.'

A wisp of memory floated by me. My father standing near my bed, saying he didn't want us to go. *I love you both very much* . . .

'But he loved you,' I said. 'He didn't want you to leave. You said he wrote and asked you to come back.'

It was several seconds before she answered. 'I wasn't enough for him, though. He needed to be consumed, filled, diverted, with no time or room for guilt. No one woman could serve his purpose for long. He wanted me there to serve part of it, part of the time. And that wasn't enough for me.' She paused. 'It may be for Angela. There are women like that, with no real existence of their

422

own.'

We had turned off the main road and were bumping along an unpaved side road built for horses. I remember that we stopped at a small white inn with a swinging sign that creaked in the wind and said 'Auberge de la Madeleine', but I don't know where it was. It may be that my mother talked as much to take my mind, and hers, off our imminent parting as to help me to understand my father.

'Don't let them overwhelm you. Be your own person, no matter what.'

This was the last thing she said to me before the ship sailed. Neither of us shed tears. I seldom cried except in anger. My mother seldom cried for any reason. But she held me as if, at the last minute, she were not going to let me go. She knew, as I did not, that I wasn't coming back.

5

For six years I had lived alone with my mother and had no other genuinely intimate association. All at once I was surrounded, enveloped, embraced by hazily remembered people who regarded me as one of them. It would have been much harder for me without Angela. Angela, who was intuitive as far more intellectual people often are not, smoothed the way. She said to me on the pier, 'They wanted to come, of course, your father and grandfather, but they're pretty overpowering if you're not used to them. I thought it would be easier for you to see me first. I'm an easy person.'

My mother had called her sappy, but she managed all the business of getting my luggage from the ship to a taxicab with what struck me as effortless efficiency. She asked me about the crossing and agreed that all those days and days of ocean were a bore.

'And the silly entertainments they think up to try to distract the passengers.'

'Yes, and the silly men. The attractive ones are always spoken for.'

I laughed, delighted. 'Always.'

This was what she did from the beginning. In small, inconsequential ways she constructed a bond between us. She was, as she had said, an easy person. I was not, but she made me feel that I was, and with her I became so.

My father was as nervous with me at first as I was with him. He looked at me as if I were the wrong person, come to the wrong house.

'You're all grown up,' he said.

Angela put her arm around me. 'Of course she is. Did you think she had stayed eleven years old?'

I didn't know what to call him. It was one thing to write 'Dear Daddy', but I could not get my tongue around it. A child's name, I felt, unsuitable. My mother and I had always referred to him as my father, but I could not call him Father either. It was what he called my grandfather. For the first few weeks I managed without using any name at all.

'I don't know French,' Angela said to me one day. 'How do French children address their parents?'

I told her 'Maman' and 'Papa' ('Papa' with the accent on the second syllable) before I saw what she was up to. She seemed so incapable of cunning, even when I knew that she was not. It was like her look of fragility, her fluttery air, the faintly startled expression that resulted from the huge size of her gray eyes. All deceptive.

'Papa' came easily to my French-oriented tongue – a new name for an unaccustomed parent. Later, much later, I shortened it and Americanized it to 'Pa'.

Grandpa was no problem. His letters had prepared me for him. Unlike my father, he made me feel that we were taking up where, after a brief separation, we had left off.

424

It seemed to me that I had remembered him exactly, and my father scarcely at all. Yet they were much alike, two large men with bright blue eyes and prominent noses, my father better-looking, his hair less orangey, unstreaked with gray, and his nose less beaky. I could see that I resembled both of them, though my hair had as much blond in it as red, and my nose was almost straight, except for a little bump just below the bridge that distressed me. Angela insisted from time to time that I was pretty, but I was not persuaded. *She* was pretty, all soft, curving delicacy, of which I had none. It was Grandpa who knew the right, reassuring word.

'You're turning into a handsome young woman, Megan.'

I could have a bump on my nose, and angles in my face where pretty girls had curves, and yet be handsome. My mother would have wondered why I cared.

I missed her as desperately as a small child separated from her mother for the first time. I was so homesick that although I rarely cried, and never easily, the tears would gush from my eyes at the table, or in the street, or anywhere, with no warning. Once at dinner, before I could rush away, my father leaned toward me to say something, his face red and troubled, but Angela put her hand on his arm and stopped him. She knew I would have been humiliated if anyone had tried to comfort me.

It was more than a week before I started at the magazine. They wanted to give me time to get acclimated before putting me to work. Angela devoted herself to entertaining me with museums, matinees, and shopping on Fifth Avenue for clothes to replenish my meager and unfashionable wardrobe, and I took no interest in any of it. The museums recalled my mother's Matisse that hung on our wall in St-Paul. The theater reminded me of seeing *Abie's Irish Rose* with my mother. The clothes made me think of that evening at the Waldorf, when she had worn my dress to show her scorn for appearances.

They tried to arrange a date for me with the son of some people they knew. I refused to go to the phone when he called, but Angela looked so disappointed in me that finally I went.

I said, 'Hello, this is Megan. I'm sure you were forced to call me up, and I was forced to talk to you, but I don't want a date with you any more than you want one with me, and of course there's nothing personal in it because I don't know you from Adam. Good-bye.' He didn't have a chance to say a word.

I had talked loud enough for them to hear me in the living room. When I went back in, my father was laughing.

'You look like a McNally. You sound like a McNally. If I ever had any doubt before, now I know you are a McNally,' he said. It was the beginning of a beginning between us.

My grandfather and Fanny came for dinner every Thursday night. I remembered that he had always come on Thursday nights and played casino with me. I could see him at the table with a shadowy, faceless little girl, but I could not place my father or my mother in the scene. They played bridge now, the new contract bridge developed by Harold Vanderbilt. Fanny would have taught it to me – she was the expert – but I preferred to watch or go upstairs to my room and read.

I had called her Aunt Fanny before she and Grandpa were married. She was entitled to Grandma now, but she said it reminded her of an old lady in a shawl.

'Plain Fanny is fine,' she said. 'You can't tell it by looking at me, but under all this wrinkled, sagging flesh I'm as young as you are.'

A long time later my father told me he had first been attracted to my mother because she reminded him of Fanny. The only resemblance I could see was that they both had quantities of untidy dark hair. Fanny was plump and girlishly pink-cheeked, even then, in her early

426

sixties. She was shrewd but cheerful, outspoken but kind. At odd moments, for no particular reason, she would hug me. I liked her, but I missed my mother's understated, undemonstrative affection.

In my long letters to St-Paul, I did not say how I felt – my mother and I were not much given to outpourings – but it must have been obvious. I told her I did not care for the 'fancy' furniture with which Angela had filled the house (and felt a twinge of disloyalty to Angela) and was glad she had not touched my room, leaving it with the simple bird's-eye maple pieces that had been my mother's taste and were mine. I said it was the only place where I felt really at home. I did not say that I lay in bed at night, in that spacious room, listening to the ceaseless noise of the city streets, and counted the days until I would be back in my tiny, quiet room in St-Paul, in my real life with my mother.

It was the magazine that worked the cure. I had lost interest in it, as, in the throes of homesickness, I had lost interest in everything, but the night before I was to begin, a little of my earlier excitement began to stir in me.

'We're going to start you right in at *Woman's World*', my grandfather said. 'You might as well get the feel of it at once.'

'I've agreed to that,' my father said, 'on condition that you do a stint on the other magazines, too, and in all departments. Observing, for the most part. Maybe making yourself useful in small ways. That's how I started.'

'Yes, well, your father was only twelve when he started. You're almost seventeen. I'm sure you're capable of more than simply finding your way around and sharpening pencils.'

They were, I realized, talking to each other, not to me. We were in a taxi on the way downtown. I remembered, though I had not thought of it since, that my father and I

427

used to pick up my grandfather at the Dakota every morning, as we had this morning. Now I was going to the office with them. Fanny was along, too. She was supposed to have retired when she married grandfather. He brought her manuscripts home to read, so she still had some say in the business, but she also kept thinking up reasons to go to the office. That morning it was to show me around; she had more time to do it than anyone else.

'Why don't you two carry on this running argument by yourselves,' she suggested to my father and grandfather, 'and let us know when it's settled? They're only happy when they have something to disagree about,' she told me. 'You'll get used to it.'

I got used to it, but it never amused me, as it seemed to amuse Fanny. I could not feel, as Angela did, or pretended she did, that it was of no concern to anyone but the two of them. The first time I heard them go at it in earnest, fury swelling my grandfather's voice to a roar and shaking and choking my father's, I thought they must hate each other. My serene, unimpassioned years with my mother had given me no inkling that love could be at the eye of such storms. I thought it was only the magazines that held the two of them together. I imagined that everything else was put on because I was there.

It was not always my grandfather who won the confrontation, but he invariably assumed the guise of victor. I had spent a month at *Woman's World* when he told me he had been thinking I ought to get a sense of how the rest of the organization operated.

Neither my mother nor my grandfather in his letters had given me any notion of the size of the McNally enterprise. The offices had not moved from the original lower Broadway building, but now it was the McNally Building. We owned it all and occupied a substantial part of it. *Woman's World* alone had two floors of offices and one that housed a battery of stoves and ovens, washing machines and sewing machines, and a staff of women who cooked, baked, laundered, sewed, knitted, and embroidered samples of items to be featured in the

428

magazine. Two new magazines had been inaugurated since my mother and I had moved to France – *Lilliput* and *Country Squire* – one a competitor of *St Nicholas*, but for somewhat younger children, and the other for gentlemen farmers. *McNally's Monthly* was what Fanny called the seat of the kingdom.

My grandfather was both president of the McNally Corporation and editor-in-chief of *McNally's Monthly*. My father's title on the masthead of the magazine was Managing Editor, and Jacob Stern's was Coeditor. None of the titles seemed to me to have any exact definition except Grandpa's. He was the head of everything. Jake, at the other extreme, did not appear to be the head of anything.

The first time I met Jake – or the first time in what I thought of as my new incarnation – was when my grandfather brought me to him the day I started work. I took him for some poor old man who had wandered into the office by mistake and sat down to rest. He looked shriveled and stooped, with watery eyes incongruously magnified by the thickest lenses I had ever seen.

'You remember Uncle Jake, don't you, Megan?' Grandpa said.

Jake saw that I did not. He said quickly, 'I certainly don't remember *her*. I knew a cute little freckle-faced Megan. This stunning person must be another Megan.'

He was transformed by the depth and resonance of his voice and the liveliness of his smile. The moment before I would have had trouble enduring his touch without recoiling, but now it seemed natural that he should get up from his desk and give me a hug. He was Uncle Jake, Grandpa's oldest, closest friend, practically a McNally. I was beginning not to mind all the McNally hugging. My father was the only who was sparing with it.

I spent a little time on every magazine and in every department. I saw how contributions were handled, why some were tossed aside after a reading of one page and others went up the scale of assistants and associates to the desk of the top editor. I watched the art director

429

select magazine covers and illustrations for stories and articles, and when one of them asked me which of two photographs I would choose for a piece in *Country Squire* on small fruit orchards, he agreed with my choice. I helped with a paste-up of *Lilliput*, and I helped arrange a table for a photograph of food to appear in *Woman's World*. I learned proofreaders' marks such as carets, the symbol for a paragraph, and the meaning of mysterious instructions like 'stet', 'wf', and 'lc'. I sat in on a few monthly staff meetings of *McNally's Monthly* and listened to the editors of the different departments outline to my grandfather and, when he was in town, my father, the fiction, science features, business and political pieces that were planned for an issue several months ahead.

Finally I returned to *Woman's World*. I would have liked to attend a staff meeting there, but the editor-in-chief, a man named Howard Prescott, told me he did not admit anyone but editors to his staff meetings. I could have said something to my father or my grandfather, but I didn't. It was, I felt, between Prescott and me.

He was a man in his late forties, built like a bull, with a broad, high-colored, thick-featured face. He looked like a bartender or a wrestler gone soft. He looked mean, and he was. But he was a good editor. Grandpa had lured him away from another magazine, and if things did not go to his liking at *Woman's World*, there was no question that he would be lured away from us. This gave him the freedom to say what he liked.

'Why don't you go to a movie or something with your friends, instead of hanging around here playing magazine?' he asked me one day.

'I'm not playing, Mr Prescott. I'm training to take over your job.' I smiled into his inflamed little eyes. 'After you're dead, of course.'

It was not wise. As long as I worked under him, he did everything he could to make me miserable. I think that it became a game with him and that he could not imagine losing any game to any female.

But he did lose it. He made me hate him. At times he made me sick with rage. None of it mattered. I was enthralled with the magazine business. I *was* in training for Prescott's job, and there was no way he could drive me out.

I no longer thought with yearning of September. I scarcely thought of it at all, and when it crossed my mind, I pushed it away. I still missed my mother, but I had some half-formed notion that she would come to New York if I asked her to, and we would be together while I went on working at *Woman's World* and soon became its editor. But I did not dwell on this. I had plenty of time. The summers of the young are without end.

I really love it on the magazine [I wrote to her]. It's funny when you think of it, because when Grandpa used to ask me if I'd like to be the editor of *Woman's World* some day, and I said I would, I didn't really know anything about it. I was just saying words, and for all I knew I might not have liked magazine work at all. Do you suppose the way I've taken to it could be hereditary?

She answered that she was glad I liked what I was doing and that she thought work was more important for a woman than most women realized.

It isn't only a matter of financial independence. A German woman was once introduced to me as 'Frau Doktor Schmidt.' I thought this was the German title for a woman doctor, but it meant 'the wife of Doctor Schmidt'. That's what I'm talking about. You won't have to be known by what your husband does.

431

On a Thursday in August we were sitting at the table after dinner, drinking iced coffee. My father had just returned from one of his trips to see an author. It was hot outside, but our high-ceilinged dining room was relatively cool. On occasion, during a bad hot spell, Grandpa and Papa took off their jackets, but never at dinner, no matter what the weather. Annabel, the colored maid who cooked on Thursdays when the regular cook was off, looked in through the swinging door to see if she should clear away, but Angela shook her head. It would have been better if Grandpa and Fanny had come to dinner another time because Annabel was not much of a cook, but Thursday had always been Grandpa's night, and I suppose nobody wanted to suggest changing it.

'We have a proposition to put to you, Megan,' my father said.

'May I just say something first, before you begin?' Angela looked at Grandpa, not at Papa, and did not wait for an answer from either of them. 'Megan, this has been such a happy summer for me.' She was looking at me now. 'For all of us, of course, but I want to speak especially for myself. It's been wonderful to have you here. I don't know whether you know it or not, but I can't have any children of my own. Now I have a daughter. That's how I feel.' She gave me a smile of the purest affection. 'This doesn't at all mean that I expect you to regard me as a mother. I know you couldn't possibly when you have a fine mother of your own. If you can think of me as – well, maybe an aunt?'

She turned away and nodded to my father, not waiting for me to respond to all this. She must have known it would embarrass me. I had not learned how to deal with sentiment.

My father cleared his throat. 'Yes, as Angela says, we've enjoyed having you here. Your room was empty a long time. Now the house seems complete again. I—'

432

'Don't forget me,' Grandpa broke in. 'I used to feel sad because you were my only grandchild and I'd dreamed of a pack of them, but you're all those dreamed-of grand-children in one. All those young, redheaded McNally's, bright and feisty and with magazine work in their blood.'

'Bravo!' Fanny said, but without the tone she used when she was making fun of Grandpa's eloquence.

I was not one to diminish myself, but I thought they were exaggerating my importance to them. I thought this was their way of saying good-bye to me, making a ceremony of it. But why now, when I wasn't to leave for several weeks? *Leave*. My chest began to ache.

'We'd like you to stay, Megan,' my father said.

'Stay?' The word was as much of a shock to me as 'leave'.

'You'd be going away next year in any case,' Angela said. 'To Paris? To the university?' She sometimes made herself sound uncertain when she wasn't. 'And you'd have no chance, over there, to work on the magazine.'

'You can probably get into college here this year. I've been looking into it,' my father said. 'The French schools are far ahead of ours, and you've had top grades. If you pass its exam, Barnard will take you in the fall.'

It was too much for me to handle all at once. I didn't know what I thought or felt or what I wanted to say. I resented their waiting, expectant faces.

'You've been writing to Maman, haven't you? That's how you know about my grades.' It infuriated me that I could not keep my voice from shaking and that I could look no closer to my father's eyes than his forehead. 'You had no right to do that without asking me. You can't make plans for me behind my back as if I'm a child or a – a moron. Barnard! How do you know I'd even consider going to Barnard? I'm perfectly capable of making my own decisions, thank you!'

I started to get up from the table, but Fanny said, 'She's right, you know,' and that calmed me down a little. 'I didn't realize you'd written to Meg, Terry. You shouldn't have done that before discussing it with Megan.'

'He didn't write to her,' Grandpa said. 'I did.' He turned to me. 'I think that was proper, Megan. If we had discussed it with you first, and you had been agreeable, and then your mother had opposed the idea, we would have put you in the position of deciding between your mother and your father.'

'You are, anyway,' I said, but with less heat.

My grandfather shook his head. 'No, I don't think so. Your mother wholly approves of your staying here unless it would make you unhappy. This leaves you free to choose between two courses of action, rather than two parents.'

'I made the inquiries about Barnard and the rest,' my father said, 'so that I could give you an idea of your choices. If you go to Barnard, you can keep on living here with us and working at *Woman's World* on Saturdays and vacations. But of course, the decision's yours. We had no idea of making it for you, Megan.'

'She needn't decide right away either, need she?' Angela said. 'It's a big thing. She has to have time to think it over.'

I looked at my grandfather. 'What did Maman say?'

'She's writing to you. I'd rather you heard it directly from her.'

My mother's letter came two days later. She said what Angela had said, that I would have been leaving her soon, anyway, to go to the Sorbonne. It would have been easier, of course, to see each other if I stayed in France, but there was no reason why I could not come to St-Paul once a year. She said she had known when she let me go that I would probably not come back.

I realized that the life I have here, much as it suits me, has nothing to offer you. That business with the

434

boy pointed it up. You're certainly not cut out to be the wife of some dull, small-town Frenchman, keeping warm around the stove. I suppose if you went to Paris, to the university, you wouldn't end up that way. You might make some kind of career for yourself there, and you might marry some suitable Parisian, but there's no sense to it. You are, after all, an American, and you have a family in New York, and a career waiting for you, something you're happy doing. Of course, we'll miss each other, but I'll be much more content to have you away from me there than in the uncertainty of Paris.

6

That first summer had prepared me not at all for life as a college student in New York. I had been almost as sheltered as in St-Paul, my time largely divided between home and office. When I went anywhere else, it was with someone in my family. I knew no people my own age and had felt no need to know any. I was busy all day and content to spend my evenings with my newfound family or alone. It seemed to me it was not worthwhile to look for friends when I was to leave at the end of the summer.

But out there beyond my orbit, America in 1926 was on a spree. The young were in a frenzy of joyous rebellion against restrictions on behaviour, dress, language, and the interaction between the sexes. An entire social structure had been built around the sport of flouting Prohibition, complete with a system of organized crime to provide illegal liquor that college boys carried in their hip pockets. A girl who drank this 'hooch' with the boys, smoked cigarettes, wore short skirts with stockings rolled below her knees, and willingly 'necked' in her date's 'struggle buggy' was the 'bee's knees', while a girl who did not do all these things was a 'flat tire'.

Suddenly I was plunged wide-eyed into this strange, wild country. But I did not stay wide-eyed long. It soon became clear to me that the primary purpose of most Barnard girls was not to get an education but to be popular with boys. I understood that the girls who achieved this were attractive, daring, always ready for a good time, and had an indefinable appeal, like an estrous scent, known as 'It'. Some popular girls lacked most of these qualities but would 'go the limit'. The girls in the first group drew the line just short of that, and tended to explain the superior popularity of anyone else on her probable willingness to cross it in a desperate effort to attract boys. It was taken for granted that no boy who found out a girl was 'fast' would ever think of marrying her. It was also assumed that boys did not care for girls who were independent, intelligent, or taller than they.

I was convinced that the girls who knew the way to be had a wonderful time. Their phones rang day and night. They were cut in on at dances. They were taken to football games. They were driven around in fast sports cars. Handsome college boys fell in love with them. I made up my mind to become one of those girls.

If my studies had given me trouble, I might have been sidetracked. As it was, the work was a repetition of much that I had learned at the lycée, and I had plenty of time for other occupations. I spent only Saturday mornings at *Woman's World* – the editorial offices were no longer open all day on Saturday – and went there during vacations on a voluntary basis.

'She needs time off for fun,' Fanny had said to my father. 'I never thought you got enough of it when you were young. Terrence had you working at the magazine every spare minute.'

'That's what he wanted. He loved it,' Grandpa had retorted.

'Oh, Father drove me all right.' This was said in one of Papa's lighter moods. He did not have many. 'When I got to college and saw the other students enjoying themselves, I didn't know what they were doing. I thought it was some secret rite.'

'I don't know any better way to enjoy yourself than to do the work you love,' Grandpa said. 'Not that I don't think a young girl should have time for fun. In fact, I insist on it, Megan. From now on, when you have a vacation, it will be strictly up to you to decide what hours you want to spend at the office.'

'You always have a good solution, Father,' Angela said.

I often found it infuriating that almost anything any of us did, or proposed to do, was discussed by everybody else – sometimes even including Jake – but in this instance I was tickled with the system. They all approved of my doing what I was going to do anyway, and they were giving me more latitude to do it, with little notion of what was involved. The fun of my day was not the fun of theirs.

I had several odds to work against. The ideal college beauty was a boyish, flat-chested little thing who did not take up much room in a rumble seat. I was comparatively ample and well developed and could do little, even with painfully tight brassieres, to conceal it. I was too tall for a number of otherwise suitable boys. I did not like the taste of liquor, and sometimes tipped up a flask or a teacup in a speakeasy without taking any of the contents into my mouth. When I could not avoid swallowing a drink or two, I was quickly affected and often forgot to act helpless or stupid. I also had trouble convincing some of my dates that there were bounds to my obvious enthusiasm for necking. When one Columbia junior kept trying to force his penis between my legs, I finally grabbed hold of it and twisted it so hard he shrieked. He called me much worse names than François

437

had when I threw the book at him and cut his lip. After that nobody else in the junior class ever asked me for a date.

Still, my phone did ring often and I was cut in on at dances. I rode around in a number of jalopies, but I also went out once or twice with a Yale man who drove an old but fast and sporty Pierce Arrow runabout. I was invited to the Columbia-Syracuse football game at Baker Field on Thanksgiving Day by a sleek-haired, raccoon-coated sophomore who drank steadily from two silver flasks, one in each pocket, and passed out between the halves. In spite of my limitations, I thought I had become the kind of girl I had planned to be. I thought I was having the wonderful time I had expected to have.

In the spring of my freshman year Bill King, a Columbia sophomore, gave me his fraternity pin. He was named for William R. King, a distant ancestor who had been Vice President of the United States in Franklin Pierce's administration and died after six weeks in office. Bill's father had once run for the United States Senate, unsuccessfully.

I had taken to him because he was funny about these things. He called them his credentials and claimed they were what had got him into Delta Kappa Epsilon, known as 'Deke,' one of the most prestigious fraternities on the campus. I had also taken to him because he was nearly six feet tall and looked a little like John Gilbert, my favourite movie star that year.

When an older girl was pinned to an older fellow, it was supposed to mean they were 'engaged to be engaged'. In a case like ours it was assumed that we were in love with each other, might get serious when we were older, in the meantime would not date anyone else, and could now properly engage in 'heavy' necking. I tried to convince myself I was in love with Bill so that I could in good conscience accept his Deke pin and display it on my blouse or dress wherever I went. He tried to convince

438

me that since we had been doing heavy necking all along, it was now only natural, and due remuneration for the pin, to go all the way. But I held out. I knew that no matter what he said, if I gave in he would lose all respect for me and probably take his pin back besides.

The boys I went out with could not sit at the curb in their cars and honk for me. They had to come in and be greeted by at least one member of the family. This was one of the rules decided on at a family conclave to take up the matter of my social life. Others were that I must not get into a car with a boy who had been drinking, that I must get out of it as soon as the car stopped in front of the house, that I could not date on school nights, and that I had to be home by midnight unless an exception was negotiated for some special reason.

'If any of these restrictions seem unreasonable to you, Megan, please say so now,' my father said.

I think it was hard for him to get used to the idea that he was responsible for the behavior of a seventeen-year-old. Later he grew into it, but this was at the beginning. I think if I had said then that what I did was none of his business, he might have agreed. But I did not mind the restrictions. They dissolved any lingering sense I had of being a guest in the house, an outsider. They gave me something to exchange complaints about with other girls. Something to be skillfully circumvented if necessary.

The only objection came from Fanny. 'To my mind, the midnight business is ridiculous. If she's going to turn into a pumpkin, or do anything else foolish, she can do it just as well before midnight as after.'

'I think it's more a matter of health,' Angela said. 'Getting enough sleep?'

'If I was with a girl who could stay out as late as she pleased,' Grandpa said, 'I'd infer that she was not altogether respectable. I realize times have changed, but I doubt that young men have given up any inferences that

439

can advance their cause.'

Fanny said fondly that he was a dirty old man, and Papa said I had not had a chance to say anything. I told them it was 'jake by me', deliberately irritating a family that valued the English language. This was as much rebellion as I cared to express at the time.

One Saturday evening in May, at the end of my freshman year, Bill came to call for me. A crowd of us were going out together, but Bill picked me up first, before he had a drink, so my father would not smell it on him. He came in briskly and gave Papa his firm handshake, looking him in the eye and calling him sir. Papa liked Bill. All adults liked him.

'The way I see it,' he had told me once, 'there's no sense giving the show away just for the fun of shocking 'em. Let them think you're nice and polite and you'd never do anything they wouldn't approve of. It doesn't cost you, and it keeps 'em off your neck.'

I pretended to agree that 'they' were our opponents, but my family was still too new to me to be cast in that fashionable role.

We were calling for three other couples that May night and then driving up to Riverdale, on the rural outskirts of the city, to Ben Riley's Arrowhead Inn. There were much rowdier roadhouses that were popular with the college crowd, but Ben Riley's was a good place for a boy to take a girl who wore his fraternity pin and whom he respected. It was lively, and it had a hot dance band, but even married couples went there.

Bill drove a Ford jalopy that seated four people. Eight of us piled into it, sitting on each other's laps, arms and heads hanging out of windows. We rattled up Broadway, yelling and laughing and singing 'Runnin' Wild' and 'Ukulele Lady' at the tops of our voices. Flasks were distributed to everyone with free hands, so he or she could help those too crowded to move. From my perch on someone's knee, I kept pouring hooch into Bill's

440

mouth, at his instruction.

'You're going to get drunk,' I objected once. 'You won't be able to drive.'

'Don't be an old lady. You know I can drive fine when I'm ossified. Anyhow, you're getting half of it down my chin.'

In Ben Riley's we were seated at a table well away from the more decorous customers. I ordered a club sandwich.

'That's all she ever eats,' Bill announced. He was very drunk. 'It's what Irish girls are fed from the time they're babies. The bacon comes from special Irish pigs.'

Bill had never before made any reference to my Irish blood. The virulence Grandpa had told me he had encountered when he was young had barely touched me. I knew that there were certain cliques at Barnard from which I was automatically excluded, but there were others in which the name McNally, the connection with the McNally publications, was regarded with awe. Bill's remark could have been innocent of objectionable meaning, his drunken notion of innocent fun, but I didn't like it.

'That's not exactly right,' I said. 'The pigs are actually Durocs from the United States. My great-grandmother used to swim across the ocean once a month to get one. Then she'd swim back again with the pig on her shoulders. Durocs are red, of course, and that's how I got this color hair.'

Everybody thought this was hilarious except Bill, who muttered, 'Ha, ha! Very funny!'

I don't know whether he was annoyed because I got more of a laugh than he had, or because I knew about Durocs from *Country Squire* and he had never heard of them. Either way, I had deliberately broken two precepts of acceptable female behavior.

But Bill did not hold it against me long. He couldn't, and still neck with me. Necking was on the menu as

441

immutably as club sandwiches, and dancing was part of the foreplay. We danced with our hot cheeks pasted together and his hardness pressing against my belly. After a time he led me outside to the car. Two of the other couples in our party were ahead of us, one in the back seat and one in the front, but Bill shooed them out. As hard as I tried to be like all other successful girls, I could not overcome certain peculiarities. One of them was an insistence on privacy for necking.

We got into the back seat. It was a narrow space for our purpose, but we were experts. Even with his drunken fumbling, in only a few minutes my brassiere was unhooked, his fly was unbuttoned, and my dress was up above my thighs.

'Come on, baby, lemme,' he whispered, getting down to it faster than usual. 'Come on, you know you want it.'

I was too busy warding him off to know any such thing. 'Stop it, Bill, please. Why can't we just— *Stop* it, I said. You wouldn't like me to scream, would you?'

'Ah, come on! We love each other, don't we? Pinned to me, aren't you? What if I shaid I'd marry you when I graduate? Do it then, wouldn't you?'

'No. I wouldn't believe you anyway.'

'That'sh how much you know. Will marry you. Shwear I will. There! Now come on . . . Lishen. Lishen. Want to tell you something. If you won't, going to take my pin away. I know plenty of girls who—'

Before he could finish I had shoved him away, aided by my rage, his surprise, and his alcoholic unsteadiness.

'You can have it.' I unpinned the little pearl-encrusted emblem from my dress and flung it at him. 'Here! Give it to some dumb Dora who doesn't care what she does to get it!'

He began scrabbling around in the dark, looking for the pin, muttering to himself furiously. 'If it's losht, gonna pay for it – 'at's what you're gonna do . . . shtupid li'l mick . . . think I'd marry you? Me? William R. King, deshended from Vice Preshident, marry shtupid li'l mick . . .'

It was not, as I had thought, funny to him at all. He had pretended to laugh at his 'credentials', but he really thought they made him somebody. I got out of the car and slammed the door. He was as much of a fool as François. I was through with him for that, as much as for any of the rest of it.

On the way home I sat in the back. Another girl sat next to Bill, and he drove with his arm around her. The boy whose lap I was on kissed the back of my neck from time to time and rubbed my breasts through my dress. Nobody said anything, but this was an acknowledgment of what they all had noticed – that I was no longer wearing Bill's pin. I don't know whether it was ever found.

They said afterward that he must have lost control of the car. I don't know exactly what that means. I didn't see it happening. They said he drove head-on and at high speed into the telegraph pole 'while intoxicated'. Even his descent from a man who had been Vice President of the United States for six weeks could not keep that phrase out of the paper.

I mean that to be sad, pathetic, not humorous. Bill was killed instantly. So was the girl he had his arm around. The other girl in the front was permanently paralyzed. The boy lost a leg.

No one in the back seat was seriously hurt. My only injury was a black eye, and I don't know how I got it. I don't know or remember much about any of it, except the sound of moaning and a glimpse – or a nightmare fragment – of something red, composed of Bill and the windshield and the steering wheel.

I lay curled up in bed, shivering, for a day and a night and would not eat or speak to anyone. Death was all right for the old. I could not stand its closeness. I could not stand the last way I had been to Bill, or that I could

443

not go back and change it all and keep Bill's pin so he would not drive out of control into a telephone pole. But I could not stand it, either, that if I had been different to him and he had driven into the pole anyway, I would have been the girl next to him who was killed. She was only eighteen. The paralyzed girl was eighteen, too, and the boy who lost a leg, nineteen. I had a black eye.

I think somebody came and gave me something to make me sleep. When I woke the next morning, Angela was sitting in my crewel wing chair, the sun shining on her coronet of blond braids.

'If you'd like breakfast in bed,' she said, 'I'll ring Annabel to bring it.'

I said all right, and she pushed a button on the wall. In a few minutes Annabel, who must have been told to bring the tray when Angela rang, came with a soft-boiled egg, hot rolls, and coffee. I did not ordinarily care for soft-boiled eggs, but this morning I didn't notice.

'Do you want to talk about it?' Angela asked me when I had finished.

I shook my head. 'I want to forget it. Or try anyhow.' I thought for a minute. 'There's one thing. There's no use letting you think I'm grief-stricken. It isn't that. I wasn't – we weren't in love, or anything. I – just before it happened, I gave him back his pin, so you see it isn't that. It's just that it's so – so awful—'

She made a move toward me, but I shook my head again. 'I'm all right. I don't want to say anything more about it. Tell them please not to ask me questions, Angela – Grandpa, and all of them – because I don't want to answer any questions.'

'They don't always do what I tell them.' She smiled a little. 'But I'll try.'

Papa came up about an hour later as I was deciding I might as well get up and do something to distract my mind. He smelled of cigars, so I knew he must have been with Grandpa because that was the only time he smoked

444

them.

'This reminds me of when you were a little girl,' he said, standing by the bed and looking down at me. 'I used to come up here to talk to you like this sometimes.' His eyes were sad. 'I wish I hadn't had to miss all the years between then and now.'

That, I think – that moment, in the midst of the storm inside me – was when I felt he was my father.

'Angela says you don't want to answer questions, but I have one I need an answer to,' he said. 'I promise no one else will ask you anything.' He did not wait for me to comment. 'Megan, did you know Bill was drunk?'

It was suddenly the most terrible question of all. I had to shut my eyes to answer it. 'He always got drunk, Papa. I said something that night, but I didn't really try to stop him. I poured it into him, Papa. He asked me to, and I did. I poured it into him. It was my fault. It wasn't only because of the other things. It was because I didn't try to stop him, and I got in the car with him when I knew he was drunk, the way I wasn't supposed to, and that girl, Ethel, was killed when it should have been me . . .'

I began sobbing, great heaving sobs without tears. Papa sat down on the bed and held me until I was quiet.

'You'll feel better now,' he said. He still had hold of my hand. It felt natural to me, and I think to him, too. 'You mustn't blame yourself for the accident, Megan. He'd have drunk too much whether you helped him or not. You couldn't have stopped him. I know a little about that. I used to be a champion drinker myself in college, though at least I had sense enough not to drive a car when I drank.' He let go of my hand and stood up. 'I'd have thought you had too much sense to ride with him, but I don't want to dwell on that. You won't do it again.'

'No,' I said.

'I don't think any of us could have stood it if you'd

been killed.' He said this sternly and went to the door and turned back again. 'But just keep in mind that you weren't responsible for the accident. I don't want you living with guilt.'

I thought there was a faint emphasis on 'you', but I might have imagined it because of what my mother had told me that day on the way to Le Havre. No matter how she had tried to convince my father that other things were responsible for his brother's suicide, he had kept repeating, 'Yes, maybe, but I pushed him over the edge.'

I understood something now that I hadn't then. I understood that no one can talk guilt out of a person.

I thought of becoming a Catholic. Of course, I was one nominally, but I thought of becoming a real one, going to confession and taking communion. My purpose was not exactly to find comfort, but to be uplifted and purified. I went to mass at a nearby church a few times and once at St Patrick's down on Fifth Avenue, hoping to experience some natural kinship with the other worshipers, some spiritual awakening. Instead, I was uncomfortable. The smells were strange to me. I did not even know how to genuflect or cross myself properly. Of course, I could have learned, but I began to feel I would always be an alien among those pale, hushed kneelers. I lost my eagerness to enter a little curtained booth and tell an invisible priestly ear what I had done with boys in the back seats of cars, and why I was alive and other people were dead or maimed. Evidently religion did not come naturally to a McNally.

I did not speak of this aborted piety to anyone. I did not speak of the accident again, and nobody brought it up. Except for my time at *Woman's World*, where I went every weekday when classes ended for the summer, I kept to myself as much as possible. I refused all dates, and soon the phone stopped ringing for me.

In August I sailed for France to spend a month with

my mother. I had forgotten how much I missed her until I saw her again. I had forgotten how much I had loved the beauty and peace of St-Paul. But a month of quiet, repetitious St-Paul days was too long for me now. After the joy and excitement subsided, I began to feel restless.

'It must be dull for you here, after New York,' my mother said. She always knew. 'We can go to Paris if you like. See a little night life.'

'I don't want any night life. I had enough—'

I was going to tell her about that night in Bill's car, but then I couldn't. I had to keep it from crowding back into my mind.

'It's only that I'm used to working,' I told her. 'When I'm at the magazine, I'm always busy. There's something going on every minute.'

She suggested that I cut my visit short. She said she would understand. I was sure she would have, but I couldn't do it. I longed to be back, but I didn't want to leave her. I stayed, and accepted her suggestion that I help her in the shop, where my energy was an asset and my fixed saleslady smile concealed my distaste for the tourists who spilled out of the buses, and clawed like vultures at the hand-embroidered skirts and hand-decorated plates and handmade *Santon* dolls.

'Why don't you come and live in New York, Maman?' I pleaded when the month was over. 'You could open a shop there. You could live any way you like.'

'The way I like to live is here. This is my home,' she said. 'If I came to New York, it would be only because of you, to bind my life to yours. Suppose you married, then, and moved across the continent. Would I follow you?' She smiled at me. 'Soon you'll be able to come over here by aeroplane. Now that Lindbergh has shown it can be done, they say in a few years we'll have transatlantic passenger planes, and they'll be powerful enough to cross the ocean in much less than the thirty-three hours it took him. Imagine! If you can get here so

447

quickly, you can come for short visits several times a year.'

But I never did go more than once a year. There was never time.

When I returned to Barnard in the fall, I avoided the crowd I had been part of as a freshman and made no other friends. I studied. I spent hours in the library. I saw myself now as a devout scholar, in lieu of a devout Catholic – a lonely seeker after knowledge to whom pleasure was immaterial and mind was all.

One day I slammed shut a book I was reading in the library on the relationship between Greek ontology and Kantian psychology, left my notes on the table, and walked out into the cold November sunshine.

The only reason I went to the tryout was that I wanted to go somewhere, and I remembered seeing the notice. It was a tryout for parts in a play two juniors had written and planned to produce on campus. I did not get a part, and as far as I know, the play was never produced, but I liked the girls involved. They belonged to a loosely knit group that those who were not in it called arty. It attracted not only girls who painted and sculpted and wrote, but also girls who had a penchant for causes and spent a great deal of time organizing meetings and getting up petitions. Several were ardent Marxists. At least one that I know of was to have her career on the stage blasted some twenty years later by a senator from Wisconsin named Joseph McCarthy.

We had endless impassioned discussions on everything from the significance of free will to the desirability of free love, especially as described in a new book by Judge Benjamin Lindsey, advocating what he called companionate marriage. Sometimes a few of us drifted into some girl's room in the dorms and talked there. Sometimes we went in a crowd to Greenwich Village, to the studio of a girl we knew, and sat talking on cushions on the floor, with candlelight to blur the dinginess.

One night a man I had never seen before came bursting into the studio to announce he had sold a novel and wanted to take us all to celebrate at Barney Gallant's, the rather elegant speakeasy around the corner on Washington Square. Soon he attached himself to me and spent most of the evening at the Club Gallant trying to persuade me to have a drink and to come home with him when the celebration was over.

'Come on, we'll have fun,' he said. 'Don't act as if you've never done it before. I know a hot number when I see one.'

I looked straight at him and said, 'The last man who wouldn't believe me when I said no ended up dead.'

I don't know what he thought. Before he could say anything, I got up and left and took a taxi home. I don't know what happened to his novel. He might have become famous, and I would not have been aware of it because I forgot his name. I'm not sure I ever knew it.

Afterwards I felt it was obscene to use Bill's awful death for my own purposes, but when I had more experience with death, I changed my mind. I saw it was the useless premature deaths, the ones serving no apparent purpose and doing no apparent good to anyone, that were obscene.

7

In October of my senior year at Barnard the stock market collapsed. Because of this, another death occurred that had an indirect effect on my life, and a profound one, though it was not evident at the time.

Grandpa had been too skeptical of what he saw as the artificial surge of the market to speculate. He had advised everyone at McNally's against it. Some, especially those to whom he was a kind of powerful and all-knowing god, took his advice. Others could not resist the gambling fever that swept the country during the prosperous twenties, and used whatever funds they had to play stocks that went up and up as if to infinity.

The advertising manager of *McNally's Monthly* lost most of his savings. So did the editor-in-chief of *Country Squire*. The editor of *Woman's World*, Howard Prescott, to my mean and guilty disappointment, had never owned a share of stock. Papa, who did as he pleased when Grandpa could not stop him, had taken a flyer in Auburn auto stocks, which plunged 60 points in one day, almost 300 from its high, but he could afford the loss. The disaster from which there was no possible recovery was Jake's. With every cent that was not involved in the McNally Corporation, he had evidently bought stocks. The crash wiped him out.

It wiped him out and killed him. He was in Grandpa's office when the switchboard operator put through the call from his broker. Grandpa told us he just dropped the telephone, said, 'Everything's gone . . . everything Papa worked for . . . everything . . . I wanted to—' and then stopped, grabbed at his chest with both hands, and fell dead.

Grandpa, that rock of a man, seemed to go a little crazy for a few days. He walked around as if he hardly knew where he was, sometimes with tears on his face that he did not wipe away. Every little while he would stop anybody who was near him and ask why Jake had not listened to him.

'He was closer than a friend, closer than a brother. We shared each other's thoughts, respected each other's opinions. I told him the economy was unsound. Why did he pay no attention? Why did he risk everything? Without telling me, asking me. He didn't need more money. The way he lived, he couldn't spend what he had. Why didn't he ask me? We asked each other everything. We were closer than brothers.'

Nobody could answer him. Papa told him Jake had been, after all, over seventy years old, and yes, Grandpa was also over seventy, but Jake had been an old man for a long time, a man who seemed near death, while Grandpa was still vigorous, comparatively youthful. But it did not comfort Grandpa to think that Jake would probably have died soon anyway. That was not really the point.

Fanny thought she had the answer. She told it to me long afterward. I was the only one she said she was sure would never, in a burst of anger, repeat it to Grandpa.

'Angela wouldn't either,' I said. 'She doesn't have bursts of anger.'

Fanny smiled. 'Of course she does. They just don't show. But watch her hands some time when she thinks Terrence is interfering in her life. It infuriates her as much as it did your mother.'

'Maman loves Grandpa.'

'Yes, well, it would be too bad if you could love only people who never infuriated you. Anyway, it wasn't really Terrence your mother blamed for interfering, but your father for letting him.' Then she told me about Jake. 'I think it was something he had to do. Something independent of Terrence. *Against* Terrence, in a way. If he had made a killing it would have given him a kind of – I don't know – mastery that he lost to Terrence, little by little, over the years. Terrence talked as though he relied on Jake as much as Jake relied on him. I think he believes it, but it isn't true. At the end Terrence no longer relied on Jake at all, for anything.'

Grandpa would have liked to manage Jake's funeral. He told Jake's sisters that Jake had wanted to be cremated, but they were sure Grandpa must have misunderstood him. Orthodox Jews did not permit cremation. They knew Jake had stopped wearing a yarmulke after their father died, but they insisted he had still been an Orthodox Jew. They also insisted on having

451

the funeral service in their own synagogue. Jake was an important man, they said, and they wanted to be sure everyone who came had a seat.

But the dignitaries his sisters must have expected had never heard of Jake. He had had, other than Grandpa, almost no personal friends. One man with whom he sometimes played chess was there. His housekeeper came and sat diffidently alone in the back. The entire staff of *McNally's Monthly* and several editors from the other magazines came, but even with all of them and Jake's sisters and their families, the large sanctuary was half empty.

'I thought Sam would be here,' my father whispered to me.

'Who's Sam?'

'Sam Bernbach, Jake's nephew, Bertha's son. We used to be friends, but he moved to California, and I haven't seen him in years. I certainly thought he'd be here.'

'Who's that, sitting next to Bertha?'

All we could see, several rows ahead, was the man's back, but Papa said it was not Sam. This man was not as stocky as Sam, and he had light brown hair. Sam's hair was black. Or maybe, by now, black streaked with gray. The man next to Bertha looked young, even from the back.

I found out who he was at the burial in the Jewish Division of Kensico Cemetery. I saw him watching me and gave him a discreet smile, which he returned. We were recognizing each other as removed by years and years from what was going on. By degrees he managed to get close enough to whisper to me.

'Do you think there's a Jewish Division in heaven?'

For a minute I didn't make the connection, but then I did. 'If there is,' I whispered back, 'why don't we try crashing it when we get there?'

'Oh, I won't have to crash, but I hope you'll try. I'm against division, especially in heaven, aren't you?'

Somebody shushed us, and I felt like giggling, as at solemn moments in grade school. I was sorry Uncle Jake was dead, but I could not feel a real grief. Even Papa, who had loved him, said the Jake he had once been close to had died long ago.

I mouthed, without whispering, 'Who are you?' But I could not understand what he mouthed back. I liked his looks. He was not at all handsome, but I had had my fill of handsome men. He was about my height, maybe an inch taller, with large, irregular features. His eyes were pale blue under rather shaggy eyebrows. They might have been cold eyes except that they gleamed with fun. I thought he looked a little like a judge, a very young, humorous judge.

'Seth Bernbach,' he said as we walked away from the now inhabited grave. 'Bertha's grandson. My father, Sam, couldn't get here, so I was delegated to represent him. I'm at P and S, so it was handy.'

'P and S! We're practically schoolmates.' The College of Physicians and Surgeons was the Columbia University medical school. 'I'm a senior at Barnard.'

'I know, Megan McNally,' he said. 'I saw you at the service and asked about you.'

A few years before, I would have said I was flattered. I did not say it now.

'Seth. I like it. I've never known a man named Seth.'

'It's all right, but the reason for it is too cute. Saul, the grandfather; Samuel, the son; Seth, the grandson. My sister is Sharon. All *S*'s, and all biblical. I don't care what you name our first child as long as it doesn't begin with *S*.'

'That,' I said, missing only about half a beat, 'must be the fastest proposal since Adam and Eve.'

He waved at his grandmother, who had her head out of one of the limousines, signaling him to hurry, and said to me, 'I wouldn't be surprised if I meant it. If I do, I'll mention it again in a couple of years, when I'm in

453

practice on Fifth Avenue.'

'We don't have to wait for Fifth Avenue. We'll get a ground-floor apartment in Flatbush and you can use part of it for an office. As long as it's far enough from the kitchen so the patients don't smell the cabbage.'

'I don't like cabbage.'

By then we had reached the limousine where his grandmother waited. 'I see you two have gotten acquainted,' she said.

'Oh, yes,' Seth said. 'We've just been planning where we'll live when we get married.'

This was received with the kind of laughter that follows a strained and not very funny joke. I laughed, too. Seth did not.

I never did find out how much of a joke he meant it to be. I don't think he knew himself. It was some time before I heard from him again.

During the Christmas holidays I went to Vienna with Papa. Howard Prescott took the prospect as an occasion for some of his snide remarks.

'Maybe if you spent more time here, you might be of some conceivable use to me,' he said. 'Good men are selling apples in the street, and you dance in and out of here whenever you please because you're related to the boss.'

He knew I was still in school and not free to be there regularly, but he refused to recognize this, and I would not remind him of it. I would not remind him either that Papa was going to Vienna to get an article for *McNally's Monthly* and taking me along for the experience. It was a matter of pride with me not to make excuses to Prescott.

'You couldn't get anybody full time to accomplish as much for the magazine as I do in a few hours,' I said. 'The only reason you don't know it is that you're blinded by outrage.'

He must not have wanted to ask me what I meant, but

he couldn't resist it. 'Outrage?'

'Sure. You can't stand the idea that a woman can be brainy and competent, so you just shut your eyes to it.'

He had me reading proof for the next few days before we went to Vienna. Somehow he knew I hated to read proof, though I had certainly never told him so. It requires a kind of intense, mechanical concentration that I could maintain for only a short while. Determined not to give Prescott the satisfaction of letting a single error slip by, I had to read every galley at least three times.

I talked to Papa about Prescott on the train from Paris to Vienna. My mother had come to meet me in Paris for a brief reunion while Papa went to see a friend there. I did not complain about Prescott's attitude toward me, but I said I thought he was no longer the right editor for *Woman's World*. I had thought this for some time.

'He's old-fashioned, Papa. He still believes recipes and patterns and articles on the duties and pleasures of homemaking are all that interest women. A fine short story came in last week from a promising new writer, but he wouldn't buy it because the heroine was a lawyer, and she wouldn't give up her profession to marry.'

'Well, I don't know that he was wrong about that. How much popular appeal would such a story have? There aren't many women lawyers, and certainly not many who would choose it over marriage.'

'There will be, though, and I think we need an editor who can see ahead. Prescott's too old to change with the times.'

Papa smiled. 'A woman's magazine must reflect the times, Megan, not leap ahead of them. You're too impatient. When you've had more experience—'

'Oh, Papa, please don't patronize me. I've been around the magazine since I was sixteen. I think if I had to, I could run it right now.'

He looked out of the train window and said in a tight voice, 'I suppose your grandfather encourages you to believe that.'

I knew he did not agree with Grandpa that in time I should replace Prescott. He loved me and was proud of me, and we had grown as close as I think anyone could get to Papa, but he had a few fogyish ideas that incensed me. He had no objection to women editors or, in fact, to women in any capacity on any of the magazines, as long as a man was over them, in charge of them. The idea that a woman, even I, should be an editor-in-chief was unthinkable to him.

But I did not want to do battle with him now. I was too pleased to be there with him, too excited about going to Vienna. He had never taken me along on one of his trips before. He had never taken anyone. My mother would have gone if he had asked her, but he never had. I don't believe he asked Angela either, but she had no desire to go. She was happy in New York, busy with her charities, attending matinees, and concerts and entertaining or being entertained by her large circle of friends.

'To a woman like me, brought up in a small midwestern town,' she told me once, 'New York is heaven.'

I said to Papa now, 'You're a fine one to tell me I'm impatient. Who could be more impatient than you?'

'It's not impatience.' He turned from the window. 'I can't stay in one place long. I get restless. I've been like that since I was young. Your mother never understood it. She thought I wanted to get away from her.'

'She understood more than you know.'

'What does that mean?'

My heart began to pound. He had given me an opening to say something I was not sure I ought to say, but I was going to say it.

'Before I came to live with you, she told me things she thought I ought to know to help me understand you. She told me all about your brother, Charles, and the effect it had on you.'

456

His face turned as red as his hair and then paled. I thought he was angry. I thought he was not going to answer me.

But he asked me quietly, 'What effect?'

'She said you felt guilty for his death, and it has made you – well, difficult.'

He smiled. 'Do you find me difficult, Megan?'

'Sometimes. But I know what it's like to feel guilty. It can change everything.'

He seemed deaf to this, locked in his own thoughts. For several minutes he did not speak.

'I wish you could have known him. He had faults, of course, but I can't remember them.' It took me a moment to realize he was talking about Charles. 'He wasn't an intellectual, but he was everything else. Generous, loving, sweet-tempered, and as agile and beautiful as a fawn.' He paused. 'Just the one fatal flaw.'

'Like a birthmark,' I said, though I was not sure Papa meant it that way. 'And only fatal because he thought it was.'

'Or because I made him think so.'

I wished now that I had not brought it all up, reminded him, but I could not leave it there.

'Do you know what ever happened to his friend? The one who went with him to Ireland.'

'Sidney Keller. Yes. Sidney Keller is still alive,' Papa said. 'Alive and well and evidently prospering. He's an architect. I see his name in the paper from time to time.'

'But you've never tried to see him again? Maybe he'd talk to you now, after all these years, and tell you—'

'Tell me I'm a murderer? Do you think I'd care to hear that again?'

His voice was frightening, though he had not raised it. I said, 'I'm sorry, Papa. I've been stupid.'

He sighed. 'No, it's all right.' He put his hand over mine. 'I don't want any closed subjects between us. I can't always talk comfortably about what I feel, but that

457

doesn't mean you must shy away from asking.'

We stayed at the Krantz-Ambassador in Vienna, a hotel on the Kärtnerstrasse, the principal avenue, lined with fine shops. My bed was in an alcove, and all the walls in the room were hung with dark red damask. We ate wonderful, rich meals with desserts buried under mounds of *Schlag*, a whipped cream like no other I had tasted. We heard *Aida* in the great opera house and saw the ornate statuary in the courtyard of Franz Josef's palace, where the emperor himself was carved wearing the toga of a Caesar.

We stayed in Vienna a week and spent less than an hour on the specific business for which Papa had come. He proposed to have Dr Sigmund Freud write a piece for *McNally's Monthly*, explaining in popular language the theory of psychoanalysis that he had founded. He must have known that Freud would consider the idea preposterous, but Papa was challenged by preposterous ideas and often put them over. If anyone could have succeeded with Freud, Papa would have.

'Dr Freud, you would be doing a great service,' he said. 'There is so much misunderstanding of your theories that the American public is thoroughly confused.'

Freud was a grave, courtly man with a white beard. He sat behind a desk of dark wood in a dark, cluttered office. He said he wrote not for the American public but for students and professionals. He said, in his heavily accented English, that he was far too busy with that and with his own patients to write for a popular magazine.

I had heard how good Papa was at this kind of thing, but I had never seen him in action before. 'What is most troubling, sir, is that your theories are being distorted and misused,' he said. 'Especially among the young. If a girl describes a dream to a friend, more likely than not the friend will tell her she has a sex complex, without the slightest idea what a sex complex really is.'

458

They talked awhile longer. In the end Freud said he regretted having to refuse. I think he did. I think he was charmed with Papa. I had never before thought of Papa as a charming man, but in that office I saw that he could be.

'Well, I'll get a piece out of it anyway,' he said when we had left.

'How? He didn't tell you anything.'

'Yes, he did. His devotion to his writing and his patients. I can use his appearance, his manner, what his office looks like. Others have written explanations of his theories that our readers can understand. If they're paraphrased and worked in skillfully, they can seem to be his own explanations, given during the course of the interview. We won't actually say this is so, but our readers will enjoy the piece more if they think it is.'

It came to me that I still had something to learn about the magazine business, but I did not admit this to Papa.

It had begun to snow. We took a taxi to a café on the Platz Schwarzenberg, where Papa ordered wine for me (I had acquired something of a taste for wine) and *Schnaps* for himself.

'Speaking of guilt,' he said suddenly, 'I often wish I had been brought up in the faith. A person accumulates so much guilt in a lifetime. What a wise idea the Catholics have – to offer believers a way to shed it as they go along, and be free of it.'

'Oh, yes, I know. I had exactly the same—'

But he was not listening. He was turning his glass around and around in his hands and watching the motion as if fascinated.

'I've done the penances. For all the suffering I've caused, I've suffered, too. It doesn't work, though. I haven't been – what's the word? – shriven.'

He spoke quietly, conversationally, and that wrenched me all the more.

'Papa, you must try to believe that Charles—'

'Charles. Yes. But Father, too, when I was only a boy.'
I didn't know what he meant about Grandpa, but I
didn't ask. 'Meg. Your mother,' he said, and glanced up
at me and down at the glass again. 'Of course, we were
wrong for each other. I need a wife who can put up with
my ways. Meg is too strong, too—' He sat up, signaled
to the waiter for another glass, and then faced me. 'I still
love her, you know.'

I was going to say that I thought she still loved him,
but there would have been no use in it.'

'What about Angela?'

He smiled. 'Sweet, lovely Angela. The cleverest
moment of my existence was when I saw her across the
table at a dinner party and knew – knew with absolute
certainty – that she was gentle and malleable and that
she would fit her life into mine, as Meg never could or
would, and that she'd be happy doing it. I'm thankful
every day I live for Angela.'

But he left me that evening, saying he had to see an
author who would bore me, and went to some woman. I
knew because I was still up reading when he came back,
and I opened my door to say goodnight to him and
smelled her perfume on him. And I was sure, from his
total lack of confusion at seeing me, that he was an old
hand. I think Angela knew, too. If Papa had been clever
to marry her, she was cleverer. She had made a life that
had nothing to do with Papa, full of friends he had not
even met. In her gentle, inexorable way she got exactly
what she wanted. Grandpa, on the verge of selling the
large summer home he had bought on Long Island
Sound because we all were too busy to give it substantial
use, was persuaded by Angela to keep it for her. She
spent a month there in the summer and often went down
for weekends, filling the six bedrooms with her coterie.
She loved entertaining, which Papa did not, and did it
without him and with a flair. I was fairly certain that
none of this involved intimacy with men. She could have

used Papa's womanizing to excuse it, but I thought it unlikely. I thought she was almost sexless – something she could have easily disguised from Papa. But she was capable of giving me this impression deliberately.

'It's too bad she couldn't have children,' I said to Papa now, with a deviousness of my own. 'I know you were terribly upset and sad when my baby brother died. The last McNally. I remember you saying that.'

The waiter brought his drink, but he pushed it away. 'One recovers from sadness.' He smiled at me. 'Is that what I said? The last McNally? I didn't know what I was talking about. You're a McNally. No name you may ever have later can change that.'

We never talked this way again, Papa and I. On the ship going back I began calling him Pa. I don't know why or what it had to do with anything. It just happened.

8

When we got home, Angela told me Seth Bernbach had telephoned. He had left no message except to say he had called. I hoped he would call again. I had liked him, thought of him occasionally, chuckled over the nonsense we had fallen into as readily as if we had known each other for years. When I did not hear from him, I was disappointed. I even thought of calling his grandmother to get his number, but of course I didn't. Only *in extremis*, or if they were engaged, was it acceptable for a girl to phone a man.

Before long, he faded from my mind. It was a busy time. The last months of college were filled with preparations for final exams, for graduation, for parting with out-of-town friends who now seemed closer, more cherished than they had ever actually been.

At the office, and consequently at home in the family, we were going through a difficult period. Circulation of all the magazines was slipping, *Woman's World* more than the others, and we could not agree on the principal cause. My father and grandfather argued continually. Grandpa blamed the Depression. He said people had little money to buy magazines, and the solution was to cut our newsstand and subscription prices. Pa was against cutting prices. He thought people might be in temporary shock, but they would soon turn in ever greater numbers to magazines as the cheapest available form of entertainment. When Grandpa reminded him that radio was cheaper still, being free, Pa attacked the advertising manager of *McNally's Monthly* – a man Grandpa had brought into the company – saying he had allowed the ratio of advertising pages to editorial pages to decline steadily.

'You're talking nonsense,' Grandpa said. 'You're forgetting your ABCs. When circulation declines, of course advertising declines.'

'I don't know about the other mags,' I said, 'but I know what's wrong with *Woman's World*. It got bogged down somewhere back before the twenties and never caught up. I've been saying so for a long time.'

I had picked the wrong time to speak. Pa, still raw from his argument with Grandpa, told me to shut up.

'That was no way to talk to you. I apologize,' he said afterward. 'But try to remember, Megan, that you're still very young and very much of an amateur in the business, and when you purport to know what Father and I are racking our brains to figure out—'

'I'm sorry I sounded cocky, Pa. It must be the approach of graduation that's gone to my head.'

I don't think he noticed that I did not retract what I had said. I still believed I was right about *Woman's World*, and later Grandpa told me he thought I might be.

'Let's wait and see what can be done now that you'll

be working full time,' he said. 'Maybe you can feel out Prescott, make a little suggestion here and there.

Of course, I should have told him then about the impossibility of any such dealing between Prescott and me, but I did not. I wanted to handle it myself. I wanted to go in there and turn everything around single-handed, make a success of *Woman's World* in spite of Howard Prescott. I had Grandpa's backing. It did not matter to him that I was only twenty years old.

Seth Bernbach telephoned again one Sunday in June, shortly after graduation, six months after his first call.

'It's a nice day. What about taking a walk in the park?' he said as if we had talked the day before and were old friends. 'We could do something else later. If you're not busy, that is,' he added.

I knew I should not allow him to think I was available on such short notice, particularly not after all that time.

'I'm not busy,' I said. 'What time are you coming?'

'Right now. Well, as soon as I can get there. Say, twenty minutes.'

I ran upstairs to change into a yellow sleeveless dress and put on lipstick. For some reason I could not have explained, I was as excited as if I had never been out with a man before, though I scarcely remembered what Seth Bernbach looked like.

He had on a light gray suit. He was carrying a Panama hat that he did not put on. As soon as I saw him, he seemed familiar. The big, irregular features, the shaggy eyebrows, the pale blue eyes that were too full of humor to be cold.

'I called you back in December,' he said. 'Did you get the message?'

We were walking down Central Park West to the Seventy-second street entrance to the park. He had a tall man's stride, though his head was barely above my own.

'I got the message. It was just to say you'd called.'

463

'Yes.' He cupped my elbow as we crossed over to the park side of the avenue. 'I wasn't sure about calling you in the first place, and then, when I'd done it, I thought I might let it go. Until now.'

He was different this time. Serious. I had liked his humor. I liked him this way, too, but I didn't know what he was talking about.

'I don't know what you're talking about,' I said.

'No, of course you don't.'

He said nothing more for a while. I did not feel, as I had felt with men when I was younger, responsible for the silence, a compulsion to fill it up. We went down into the park and watched the men bowling on the Sheep Meadow. It reminded me of St-Paul, where the workmen and store-keepers played *pétanque* every day after lunch on a stretch of bare ground, but that seemed in another life.

'You're a tranquil girl,' Seth said finally.

I laughed. 'Oh, no.'

'No. Not tranquil. That isn't what I meant at all.' He frowned and shook his head. 'I don't know why this is so hard. Words generally don't give me trouble.'

We moved on, shunned the benches as if by voiced agreement, and went to sit up on the rocks in the sun. I could feel their warmth through my dress. He took off his jacket and folded it inside out.

'I used to climb these rocks when I was a child.' I said.

He nodded as though he had known that or had expected it of me. 'Contained was the word I was looking for.' He leaned back on his elbows, his face to the sky. 'I'm not sure yet what's under the containment. The day we met I saw this tall, slender, calm, elegant girl, and I thought, *She's containing something deep inside, some fiery essence . . .*' He laughed and rolled over onto his stomach. 'Oh, God, I sound like such an ass!'

I felt the strongest urge to touch his shoulder, but I kept my hands together in my lap. 'You don't sound that way to me. I'm lapping it up. It's the most enthralling subject I can imagine.'

There was another long silence. I could see the bulk of his shoulders through his shirt and the back of his neck above his collar, with a shallow hollow near the hairline. I had not noticed whether other men had it.

'You see, everything was all mapped out.' He was talking down into the rock so that I had to strain to hear him. 'Another year of med school, then the intern year, then a residency, then private practice. Sometime in there, during the residency probably, marriage to a nice Jewish girl. One was even picked out. Nothing definite, but a possibility. Let's say a strong possibility. A girl I've known a long time and considered myself in love with. Considered us in love with each other.' He tilted his head a little, as if listening to what he had said. 'It was all so simple. Then my father lost a lot of money in the crash, and I'm not even sure I can finish med school. That's the first complication.'

This time he said nothing for so long that I had to prompt him. 'What are the other complications?'

'You.' The word exploded from his lips. He sat up, hugged his knees, and looked off to where two little girls were playing hopscotch on the paved walk below us. 'If I fall in love with you, it will snarl everything up even more. That's why I didn't call you again. I decided it wasn't safe.'

'Then why did you call this morning?'

'I fooled myself. I told myself it was ridiculous, a first impression built up in my mind, and if I saw you again, I'd realize you were just another pleasant, attractive girl.' He paused. 'I'm sorry. I'm talking as if the way you feel has nothing to do with it. Maybe you can't see yourself ever, by any stretch of the imagination, caring anything about me. That would solve the whole thing.'

'Or when you really know me, you might not be able to stand me. That would solve it, too. Oh, Seth, this is a

465

crazy conversation. We're practically strangers. If we—'

'That has nothing to do with it. I'm not saying I'm in love with you now. Deeply in love, I mean, the way – you're right about that – strangers can't be. Even if they don't feel like strangers. But if I go on seeing you, I think I may fall deeply in love with you. That's the danger.'

'You'll have to explain why it's dangerous.'

'Because I'll have nothing. No profession, nothing. My family won't even try to help me. My mother is a very religious woman. My father isn't so religious, but he'd draw the line at this.' Seth was looking at me now with a pale blue glare. His voice grew rough. 'You go to bed with Gentile girls. You don't marry them.'

'But your father and mine were friends. Your uncle – great-uncle – Jake and my grandfather were like brothers. Jake's father and mother – Grandpa says they were parents to him, grandparents to his sons. How can—?'

'Believe me, Megan, if one of them had wanted to marry into the other one's family, it would have been different. Marriage and death. Remember the Jewish Division of the Kensico Cemetery? I hate it, but I can't change it. My parents would pretend they didn't have a son.'

'Then you'd better not see me again.'

'Is that what you want?'

'No, it's not what I want. I wouldn't have any trouble with my family. If it ever got to that point, but it's really crazy to start thinking—'

He was on his feet as soon as I said no, taking my hands to pull me up to mine,

'Let's go somewhere.' All at once he seemed exhilarated. 'Let's go dancing. I'm a good dancer. Are you? You must be. You move as if you are. Let's go tea dancing at the Lorraine.'

'Can you afford it?'

'Oh, God, you sound like a wife already!' he said.

No one on the staff of *Woman's World* cared for Howard Prescott, and as far as I could tell, he disliked everybody, only some more than others. His only use for people seemed to be as vehicles for doing what he wanted done. I wondered how he had found anyone he disliked little enough to marry and what kind of woman would have married him, with his thick, bull-like body and thick, mean face.

One day during my first month as a permanent full-time member of the staff I found one of the associate fashion editors sobbing in the ladies' room. She was a plain, dowdy woman in her early thirties named Ursula Charney. She had not been with the magazine long.

I asked her what the matter was and if there was anything I could do. She shook her head. She was standing over one of the washbasins, clutching its sides, as if about to vomit, dripping tears and perspiration. It was a hot July day.

'Miss Charney, if you're sick, let me call someone,' I said. 'If something has happened to upset you in the office, you may want to tell me. Maybe I can help. Or if you want, I'll just get out and leave you to it.'

She said something in a constricted voice that I could not decipher, but I was pretty sure she was not telling me to leave. I stood waiting while she blew her nose and washed her face. She looked terrible when she turned around, all puffy and red-eyed.

'It's that man.' She did not have to tell me what man she meant. 'He said he didn't understand how I was ever hired for the fashion department. He said I looked like something the cat dragged in. When I told him I was hired to write about fashion, not to look fashionable, he said if I didn't see the connection, I didn't belong here.'

'Do you mean he fired you? Oh, come on now, don't cry anymore.' Her eyes had started to brim again. 'Go on back to your department. I'll see what can be done.'

'I hope something can.' Her voice was much calmer. 'This is no time to be looking for another job.' She started out and then turned around again and peered at me with red-rimmed eyes. 'You know, I forgot you were only a kid. You talk as if you're forty years old.' She gave a little laugh. 'As if you own the place.'

I resisted telling her that I was going to own it. As soon as she had gone, I went out and took the elevator to the *McNally's Monthly* floor and marched into Grandpa's office. I was so angry that I forgot to find out first whether he was too busy to see me. Luckily no one was with him, and if he was too busy, he did not say so.

'I can't interfere with Prescott's decision, Megan,' he said when I had finished telling him. 'In the first place, I never undermine an editor's authority; it would be disastrous. In the second place, we can't be sure of the facts. You've heard only Miss Charney's side of it.'

'But, Grandpa, if it's true – if it's only because he doesn't like the way she looks – can we just let her be thrown out in the street and maybe have to go on a breadline?'

'You make it sound like *East Lynne*.' He swiveled his chair around and looked out the window. 'Even if it's as Miss Charney says, Prescott has a point. Outsiders come to the magazine. Advertisers, for instance. A fashion editor who looks as if she doesn't believe in what she writes makes a bad impression.'

'He didn't have to fire her. He could have—'

'All right, Megan. Let's drop it now,' he said sharply. 'The person to handle this is Katherine Dolson, her superior, not you. If Miss Dolson feels the Charney woman is valuable as one of her associates and has been unfairly treated, she'll speak to Prescott.' He turned and looked at me. 'In general, Megan, I don't think it's a good idea for you to go over the heads of your superiors and appeal to me. While you're in the office, you're an employee like any other.'

'But I know that very well. I've always kept it in mind. This is the first time I've ever come to you like this, and it wasn't for myself. I'd never come complaining or pleading for myself.'

'Yes, all right.' His voice was gentler, but not much. 'Aside from anything else, there's no surer way to make yourself disliked than to throw your weight around because you're the boss's granddaughter.'

I had tried to be so careful not to do what he said I had done that I felt as if he had stabbed me. He had never spoken to me in anger before.

A few days later I met Ursula Charney in the elevator. She was a rouged, lipsticked, bleached fashion plate, made over, I heard later, by the staff. I almost did not recognize her, and her mascara-fringed eyes swept past my face as though they had never encountered it before.

'I see you've kept your job,' I said.

She looked at me icily. 'What on earth are you talking about?'

'Well, I hope you think it was worth it,' I said. 'You looked a lot better as a human being.'

The way I wrote it in my weekly letter to Maman, it was a funny story about the kind of toadying fakery she despised. I left out what I had said to Miss Charney, for whose sake I had been humiliated by Grandpa. My mother would not have enjoyed that part. She did not believe in making enemies for any such trivial reason as a moment of satisfaction. I did not believe in it myself, but I sometimes had a way of doing it anyhow.

I made enemies, too, through no fault of my own. I did not have to throw my weight around, as Grandpa put it. It was enough that I was there, invulnerable, at a time when almost everyone else in the organization felt endangered. I had taken a cut in salary, like all the others, but my job was secure. No one had been fired yet, but only a few top editors were sure that if things got worse, they would not be. Every few days there was a rumor that the staff of the Art Department would be reduced, or that fiction and poetry were going to be handled by the editor of features, or that the Home Decorating Department was to be eliminated.

Most of this did not happen, but the danger was always there. Several magazines had folded altogether. Someone in Fiction came in one day with a report about a magazine that had let half its staff go and was buying inexpensive periodicals in England and employing low-salaried rewrite men to change the characters and situations to fit the American scene. The issues, unnumbered and undated, were sold in one region, and when the unsold ones were returned, any yellow edges were trimmed and the magazines sold in another region.

Even Howard Prescott was affected. It may not have occurred to him that he would lose his job, but he was no longer in a position to walk out any time he felt like it. Editors-in-chief were holding on to their chairs. Nobody was trying to woo them away with higher salaries, and much more pressure was on them to produce.

Prescott was no pleasanter to me, but he had to use me. He knew I had ability, and he could not excuse wasting it on routine jobs that less able people could do for lower pay. He handed me over to Fran Werner, the fiction editor – partly, I think, because she was one of the few women who headed a department, and he thought a woman might be more demanding of me.

'Keep her reined in,' he said to Fran in front of me. 'She thinks she was born knowing the magazine business because her name is McNally, but you're to treat her exactly as you would any other half-baked girl with more pretension than talent.'

, Fran was about thirty-five, a lean, athletic-looking woman with close-cropped, startling silver hair that gave distinction to her hawkish face. She was one of the best fiction editors in New York. He salary was high, but if

470

she had been a man, it would have been much higher. She made it a point to tell anyone who would listen that this was a disgraceful state of affairs, but not many agreed. After all, women did not have families to support. In fact, in these hard times they should not be working at all, taking jobs away from men.

During my part-time years on *Woman's World* I had worked in the Fiction Department, as I had everywhere else, at the most tiresome jobs Prescott could suggest. In Fiction I had been a first reader of the so-called slush pile – the unsolicited stories that came directly from unknown writers, not through an agent. A first reader had to go through hundreds of these stories, most of them awful, and pick out the occasional one that was at least worth sending on to a second reader for further consideration. I had been sustained in this deadly job by the hope that I might find buried in the garbage a brilliant new talent, but it never happened.

I had had no contact with Fran Werner, but I had seen her going in and out of her office with her loping walk, a cigarette always in her mouth, and I had heard her talking in her tough, husky-voiced way. I thought I would like working for her.

'Do you know how I'd treat that half-baked girl he was talking about?' she said to me when Prescott had left. 'I'd toss her out on her bum.' She looked me over with narrowed eyes. 'You I'm stuck with.'

'The girl he was talking about is his fantasy,' I said. 'Substitute "boy", and I think it would fade away, even if the name were still McNally.'

She grinned. 'Well, that's one way to get around me. You can't be a complete damn fool.'

I knew right then that we were going to be friends.

When Pa was away, and neither Angela nor I had other plans, we often went to the movies together. We both loved the movies and had similar tastes in stars, preferring enigmatic Greta Garbo to sugary Janet

Gaynor and sensual Clark Gable to wholesome Dick Powell. We would select a bag of assorted chocolates in the candy shop next door to the movie theater and sit munching happily in the dark, united by our enchantment with the story on the screen.

It was after one of these outings that I told Angela about Seth. We had just seen a gangster film called *Little Caesar*, starring Edward G. Robinson, and were walking down Broadway. It was an unseasonably mild March evening, eight months after Seth and I sat on the rocks in Central Park.

'That was too realistic. I don't think I care for believable characters on the screen,' Angela said. 'Nobody Clark Gable plays is believable. I love watching some heroine in a movie yearn to marry him, but I can't imagine marrying any such man myself, can you?'

It was an opening I must have been waiting for.

'I can't imagine marrying anybody but Seth Bernbach,' I said.

Angela was chewing a chocolate-covered caramel. A daub of chocolate smeared her upper lip, a jaunty blemish on her ethereal daintiness. I had to wait until she swallowed the candy, meanwhile wondering why I had spoken. Nobody knew anything about Seth and me.

'Yes, I remember now,' she said. 'He's Jake's nephew, the one who came to the funeral. Have you been seeing him or is this—?'

'I've been seeing him. More or less. On and off.'

Seth had planned to go back to California in the summer to put distance between us, 'so I can think straight'. Instead, he had stayed in New York, lived with his grandmother, and worked for one of his great-uncles, selling clothing in a Madison Avenue haberdashery. He had saved almost every dollar he made and had enough by the end of the summer to take care of all his expenses for his final year at P&S except the tuition, which his mother had paid for from some mysterous personal

472

source.

'She probably sold her soul,' Seth had told me. 'The dearest wish of her kind of Jewish mother is to have a doctor for a son.'

He was driving me crazy. We would see each other for a while, and then he would decide all over again that it was no use, it would never work out; no matter what I thought, my family would disapprove, too; it would be years anyway before he could support a wife; it was not fair to me. After an anguished parting and an agonized few weeks or a month, during which I was sure this time I would never hear from him again, he would reappear, saying he could not get along without me. If I told him to stay away, that I refused to go through it all another time, he kept after me with phone calls and letters or waited for me on street corners, and I was never able to hold out.

'I don't see how I could marry a man I couldn't count on anyhow,' I said to him once. 'You don't know your own mind.'

'That isn't true. Ordinarily I'm very stable. You can't judge a man by when he's in love.'

'Well, I'm in love, too, but I don't decide one minute that I'll die if I can't marry you, and the next that marrying you is out of the question.'

'You don't have the responsibilities or the problem. It isn't up to you to earn enough money so we can live decently. Your family won't like it, but it won't break your mother's heart.'

We spent considerable time arguing about all this. On the days we were definitely going to get married, we argued about my working, which I, of course, intended to do but which Seth thought was all right only if he was making enough money so we would not need my salary. We argued our way uptown, downtown, crosstown, and all around Central and Riverside parks. For some reason I did not understand – something obscurely connected in

Seth's mind with honor – he would not come to the house while our situation was so unsettled. We sat on park benches, making strictly limited love, and kissed good night in strange doorways.

'Maybe it's all just physical,' I suggested one night, 'and if you got that out of your system, you could get rid of me.'

He was furious. I was talking like a slut. I was belittling his love. He had, I learned, a temper that could spring from almost nothing, build to a high, icy peak, and disintegrate, all in a few minutes.

'I was only fooling,' I said, though in substance I had not been. 'You're losing your sense of humor. I'm not sure love is good for you.'

'That's nothing to fool about. We're not a couple of wild kids, out for a thrill. We're thinking of spending our lives together.'

'If we keep on thinking of it, our lives will be over before we get started doing it.'

That made him laugh. He had a funny, chuckling laugh that shook his shoulders but stayed in his throat. I loved his laugh.

'I love everything about him,' I said to Angela, 'and I never know from day to day whether I'll ever hear from him again.'

'Could that be part of the charm?' she asked me.

'Oh, God, I don't think so.' Seth said 'Oh, God' a lot. I was even beginning to talk like him. 'The most wonderful thing I can imagine is to be sure of him, to know I'll have him for the rest of my life.' I sighed. 'And then, what if we do get married, and his family disowns him and his mother's heart really does break? What if he feels terribly guilty about it and starts blaming me, hating me—?'

'I don't know, Megan. I really don't understand this intense family business. My childhood was pleasant. My parents got along all right, and I got along all right with

474

them and with my brothers and sisters, but when I married your father, I left them for another life. I keep in touch with them, but we haven't tried to hang on to each other. They don't try to tell me how to live.'

'I left my mother, didn't I? She doesn't tell me how to live.'

Angela did not answer this. I think she sometimes forgot about Maman. 'Suppose your grandfather disapproved of Seth and told you if you married him, he never wanted to see you again?' she said.

It was strange that she had made it my grandfather instead of my father. 'I can't imagine such a thing. He wouldn't tell me that. If he did, he wouldn't mean it. He'd change his mind.'

We stopped while I looked at a dress in the lighted storefront of one of Broadway's innumerable dress shops. It was a beige crepe with a velvet bolero in a shade of golden brown that appealed to me. I saw Seth admiring the way it went with my coloring. I saw Seth in everything.

'But I think I'd marry him anyway,' I said as we walked on. 'I don't see how I could give him up. It would be terrible, but I think I'd marry him.'

We crossed Broadway at Seventy-fourth Street and began walking west. A well-dressed middle-aged man came along, glanced at Angela, and then stared at me. Angela, in her early forties, was still beautiful, but it was outmoded beauty, too fragile and delicate for an age of Joan Crawfords and Marlene Dietrichs. Instead of modifying the effect, she emphasized it with filmy dresses and unbobbed hair. I suppose it was her disguise.

She said, 'Wouldn't it be better if his family knew about you? That would bring it to a head. They might not be as upset as he expects. If they are, he'd have to confront it and decide once and for all?'

'It might be better, but Seth won't do it. He'd never just try them out. He'd never tell them until he was ready to marry me no matter what.'

'I don't understand it,' Angela said again. 'They live a continent away. Why should they care as much as he thinks they will? How much will they ever see of him, whether he married you or somebody else?'

'It's a tribal thing, Seth says. If they take in strangers, they have a kind of atavistic fear that the tribe will be so diluted it will disappear. He says that's one reason Jewish families tend to be so close.'

'Closer than the McNally's?' The way she said it reminded me of what Fanny had told me about watching Angela's hands when she thought Grandpa was interfering in her life. 'Does Seth go along with all that?'

'Oh, he doesn't. He hates anything that divides people. But I think he's honestly afraid it might kill his mother.' I sighed again. 'And we have all the other problems besides.'

'If this one was solved, I think you could handle those?'

We had reached the house by then. No one was there. Annabel had left the year before to get married, and we had not replaced her. Instead, we had a woman who did the cooking and the light cleaning, and a man who came twice a week to do the heavy cleaning. The woman was a Negro named Mrs Evans. She had made it clear that she was not to be referred to as 'colored', since we were colored the same as she was ('Everybody is some color'), or by her first name, which she never told us.

'I've come on hard times like most people. I need the work,' she said, 'and I don't think housekeeping is beneath my dignity. But I'd like to be treated as a valuable employee, not a subhuman servant. I happen to be an educated woman.'

It was Mrs Evans's influence that had caused me a few months before to make one of my ill-considered comments to a strange white woman in the street. She was walking ahead of me, holding a small child's hand,

476

when a young Negro woman approached in the opposite direction, wheeling a baby in a carriage. The white child peered in at the baby and then looked up at her mother.

'Oh, Mommy,' she said, 'did you see the little maid in the carriage?'

I hurried to catch up with them and spoke in a loud voice as I passed by. 'Oh, Mommy, did you see the little bigot on the sidewalk?'

Mrs Evans lived in, but she often went out at night when her work was finished. She was out now. A note in her large, Spencerian writing was stuck in the hall mirror where we could not miss it.

> Mrs McNally, Senior, has been taken ill. She is at the Park West Hospital. I trust it is not serious.
>
> Mrs Evans

The Park West Hospital was a small private sanitarium a few blocks from the house. Nothing could be done for Fanny there or at the Columbia Presbyterian Hospital, where she was moved the next day and where I found myself hoping guiltily that I might see Seth. Fourth-year P&S students often had duties in the hospital, but he never appeared when I was there.

Fanny had had a massive stroke. She had had a minor one some months before, with no obvious aftereffects, but Grandpa, at her insistence, had kept it secret. She did not want us worrying over her, he said, or treating her like an invalid or a poor old woman. He had tried not to let her see how it worried him.

Pa took the *Twentieth Century* home from Chicago, where he had gone to interview an ex-gangster who was willing to write a story about the underworld, provided he was well enough paid and could be assured of anonymity. Pa told us afterward that it was too dangerous. He could not absolutely guarantee that the man's identity would not leak out somehow. The man had a great story to tell, and he was eager to tell it, but every time Pa was tempted to let him go ahead he saw in his mind one of those photographs of bullet-ridden bodies that were always in the tabloids.

He could not believe Fanny was so sick. Grandpa, in the beginning, was in a kind of frenzy of mingled hope and despair, but Pa was dazed.

'She was always so healthy – her color – like a girl—'

Grandpa kept talking. He was normally a great talker – he once told me his mother, Aggie, used to say he talked as if his words were on wheels – but this was like delirium.

'We thought that, yes. We thought it was good health, but it wasn't. It was high blood pressure. She never went to a doctor. A doctor would have told her, but she thought she was so healthy. She had such good color. Of course, now that we know, it will be different. When she gets better we'll know what to do . . .'

Pa spoke of Papa Stern, Jake's father, Seth's great-grandfather, who had had a stroke when Pa was a boy.

'Father told us about it at the dinner table,' he said to Angela and me when Grandpa was not in the waiting room. 'My mother said it was nothing for children to hear. She meant Charles, of course. I didn't matter.'

I thought how awful it was that he was thinking of this now, remembering it now, here in a hospital waiting room, after all those years.

'Papa Stern died of his stroke. I think he lived only a day or two, and then he died,' Pa said. 'The doctors don't know whether Fanny will live. I can't seem to take it in. Fanny!'

She lived. It was hard to think of it as life, but she might have felt it, somewhere inside. Nobody knew. She could not move or speak. If she heard, if she understood, she gave no sign of it. Her eyes did not look blank, but although she was able to blink her eyelashes, she did not respond when asked to blink them once for no and twice

478

for yes. She did not respond to anything. Only her hair, springing wild on her pillow no matter how often the nurses brushed it, seemed still alive.

Grandpa sat at her bedside, holding her hand all the time, except when he was prodded to go and eat or sleep. He said he had to be there in case she 'awoke' and tried to communicate. Once he insisted he felt a faint pressure from her hand, but the doctors said he had imagined it.

He took her home finally. He hired nurses because the doctors said she should have professional care, but he sat with her as he had in the hospital, hardly leaving his chair next to her bed. He did not go to the office. For the first time since he had founded *McNally's Monthly*, he let the organization run without either his presence or his instructions.

9

Every evening on my way home from the office I stopped at the Dakota apartment, went into the bedroom where Fanny lay in a rented hospital bed and talked to her. I didn't believe she was aware of it. Her body was there, but I believed Fanny had gone. I went, as people visit graves, on the off chance that she knew. And, of course, for Grandpa.

Otherwise, I went on with my usual life. We all did, except Grandpa. At first I felt heartless, callous, but there was nothing else to do, and before long I got used to it.

At work I was so happy that I forgot my sorrow. I even forgot Seth sometimes. Fran Werner gave me a chance to show my ability. She had me reading stories that had been weeded out by other readers, and soon took my opinion into serious consideration before sending a story to Prescott for final decision.

She let me work on revisions and cuts. Sometimes these had to be made at the last minute and without the author's permission because of a space shortage. Authors tended to scream about this, but there was no help for it. Advertising was what paid the bills, and it took top priority. The trick was to revise and cut so skillfully that the authors, who had written the stories many months before they were published, would not notice. I was good at this. I could copy an author's style so well that when I made changes in a story, wrote a new ending, for instance, the author often thought it was the original version. In time Fran began giving most of this work to me, and much less to Marjorie Sweetman, the assistant to whom she had usually assigned it.

All the fiction people were women. No man wanted to work under a woman chief. Miss Sweetman was one of three assistant editors, a small, plump woman with dreamy, watery eyes and hennaed hair. She had been with *Woman's World* since its first week. She spoke in a sweet, trembly voice and called everybody dear, like an unctuous saleswoman.

Howard Prescott summoned Fran into his office one day to direct her to put Miss Sweetman back on revisions. Fran told me all about it later; not exactly *de rigueur*, but Fran made her own rules.

'Sweet Marjorie Sweetman complained to him that I was favoring you because you're a McNally.' Fran was sitting on a corner of her desk, unconsciously blowing cigarette smoke in my face until my eyes were as watery as Miss Sweetman's. 'I told him to go fly a kite.'

'You didn't. Not Prescott.'

'Oh, well, I did the equivalent. I showed him one of Sweetman's revisions that the author wanted to tear somebody's hair out over – something like "He thought he had lost her forever in the living death of the convent" – and then I showed him one of yours. What could he say?'

'Oh, God, she must have been hating me the whole time she was calling me dear. Now she'll hate me even more. So will Prescott for proving him wrong. I'm not exactly the most popular girl in the office.'

'Do you care?'

'Sure I care. Who wants to be hated? But I'm not going to be stopped by it.'

'No. Don't be. You're going to make a fine fiction editor one of these days.'

I stared at her. I thought she was probing, trying to find out if I was after her job. It did not seem to be her style, but how did I know? Everybody suspected everybody else of wanting his job and stepping on his face to get it, and I was the most suspect of all because they all thought I could get any job I fancied.

'*You're* the fiction editor, Fran,' I said.

She waved her cigarette, dropping ashes in my lap. 'I'm not talking about now. I said some day. By the time I leave you'll be ready.'

'Leave? Why would you leave?'

'To get married.' Now she brought the cigarette close to her eyes and examined the burning tip. 'Did you think I was just going to rot here in this office the rest of my life? Old maid Werner?'

I had sense enough not to say that I thought she loved her work, that I thought it was important to her, that I thought she was the last one who would be doing what men always said working women did – just marking time until they found someone to marry. I don't know what I did say, but it wasn't any of that.

'She was my idea of a strong, independent, modern woman,' I said to Angela that evening. 'She's had a lover for years – it's no secret; everybody knows about it – an executive with the company that supplies the paper for our magazines. I assumed she didn't want marriage.' I pushed away my empty wineglass. We had just finished one of our solitary dinners. 'How can she delude herself

481

like this? She's almost forty years old. If he hasn't married her in all this time, he's not going to do it now.'

Angela smiled her lovely, tentative smile. 'I wonder if that doesn't happen to the strong, independent ones? They're used to being in control of things, and they think it carries over in the same way with men. But men—'

The phone rang at that moment, and I jumped up to answer it. It might be Seth. I had not heard from him in more than a week, meaning he was having doubts again. Otherwise, he called me every day. My heart was banging away with anticipation as I lifted the receiver, but when I heard his voice, I was suddenly, unexpectedly furious.

I suppose it was triggered by what Fran had told me. Tough, capable, talented Fran, waiting meekly around for years for a man to decide to marry her. All the other bright, attractive unmarried women on the staff who were past their twenties, hoping anxiously that it was not too late to be considered prospective wives by some of the lords of the earth. And me, I, Megan McNally, putting up with Seth.

'I'm through, Seth. The on-again off-again dance is over,' I said, before he could get past, 'Hello.' 'I don't want to see you or hear from you again. This time it's final.'

I hung up. The phone kept ringing for a while, but I ignored it.

Somewhere around two in the morning I got out of bed and read a problem story that Fran had given me to take home. It was beautifully written and had a good central idea, but the conflict was solved by having the heroine all at once, for no reason growing out of the plot, see the light – what we called a come-to-realize ending. I worked on it until nearly five before I got a stronger solution to suggest to the author. By then I was finally exhausted enough to fall asleep until after eight.

When I left the office for lunch with Joan Kastenbaum

482

from Sewing and Needlework, Seth was waiting on the sidewalk near the entrance. I tried to walk past him, but he grabbed my arm. Joan instantly smiled understandingly and walked on.

'I told you I didn't want to see you again, and I meant it,' I said. 'Let me go or I'll scream.'

He looked around deliberately at the lunchtime crowds pouring out of the McNally Building. 'Scream away. They're your colleagues, not mine.' He gave my arm a little shake. 'Listen, Megan, I have to talk to you. Something's happened.'

'I don't care what—'

'Megan, they know. My parents know. They got an anonymous letter.'

'What kind of anonymous letter? What are you talking about?'

'I'll tell you at lunch. This is no place – I took the day off from school to talk to you. It's the first day I've ever cut except once when I had the flu.'

'Well, I didn't tell you to cut. And I'm not having lunch with you.'

But he had started to walk away, and although he had loosened his hold on my arm, I was walking with him. I had to hear about the anonymous letter. After that I could still send him packing.

He took me to a restaurant where the lunch cost seventy-five cents, more than he could afford to spend, but the tables were not too squeezed together for any hope of privacy. He told me his father had telephoned from California the previous night, just before Seth called me. His mother had talked to him, too.

'All the letter said was that I was seeing a girl named Megan McNally. Just that one sentence. But they both started in on me as if the wedding was tomorrow. After all they'd done for me, my father said. My mother got hysterical. Her wonderful, brilliant, beautiful son was going to throw his life away on "an Irish *shiksa*".'

483

'Did she say it would break her heart?' I asked him coldly.

He glared at me from under his unbeautiful shaggy eyebrows. 'What she said finally, when she had calmed down, was that if you would convert, she might in time bring herself to accept you.'

'Convert?' I repeated inanely.

'That's right. Take instruction from a rabbi, take a ritual bath to cleanse you of your impurities, promise to bring up our children in the Jewish faith—'

I glared back at him. 'I suppose you want to know if I'll do it. If I will, you'll consider marrying me. This week anyway. Next week you may change your mind again.' I pushed my Yankee pot roast viciously around on my plate. 'What do you think I am, Seth Bernbach? Do you think I'll submit to anything – go through any kind of hypocrisy, submit to anything, lie, cheat – anything to marry you? Impurities! If I don't suit you or your father or your hysterical mother the way I am, to hell with the whole—'

'Megan, darling, shut up!' Now he was grinning at me, and in a minute I understood that the glare had not been for me at all. 'The more they talked, the more I realized what obnoxious, prejudiced tommyrot it all was and what an ass I'd be to let it affect my life. When you said last night you never wanted to see me again, I wasn't sure you meant it, but I knew if we kept on like this, sooner or later you would mean it.' His voice got very soft. 'I tried to imagine what that would really be like, and I couldn't stand it.'

I began to dissolve, but I was not ready to let him know it. 'So now what?'

'Now, if you're willing, I'd like to be engaged. Make it public. Announce it ourselves, if your family objects.'

'And get married when?'

'As soon as I'm out in practice and can make enough money to—'

484

'No. That would be two or three years. I won't wait that long.'

'But, Megan, I can't—'

'You can't, but I can. We can get along on what I make for a few years.'

'Live off my wife? What do you think I—?'

'Take it or leave it.'

We were married after lunch that day by the city clerk in City Hall. We used a ring from Woolworth's five-and-ten for the ceremony. I wore it even after I had a real gold band. I wore it until my finger under it turned greenish black.

'I wonder who could have written that letter?' Seth said on the way to City Hall. 'Who knew about us? Who knew where to write my parents?'

'I have no idea,' I lied.

'Well, I hope whoever it was will know how their spite backfired.'

'It might not have been spite.'

'What else could it have been?'

'I can't imagine,' I lied again.

Grandpa was delighted. Or would have been if his normal feelings had not been buried under the weight of Fanny's unchanging illness. The doctor told him there was no longer any hope of change, that she would probably have a second stroke that would kill her, that it was remarkable she had lived this long, but he went on thinking the doctor might be wrong. He had begun coming to the office again, but always after a few hours he had to go home and see for himself that she still had not moved and did not know or need him.

He hugged Seth. 'I wish Jake were here. And Mama and Papa Stern. They were the only family I had, you know, after my mother died. I wish they could know we're really one family now.' He released Seth and hugged me. 'This nice, smart, handsome girl you've married may be a handful. I'm warning you,' he said. 'She's a genuine McNally.'

He gave us a large check, with which we started a savings account. Pa gave us our furniture. He was not as enthusiastic about the marriage as Grandpa. He did not like the idea that I was supporting Seth, who thought Pa's coolness to him was because he was Jewish. I let him think so. He was used to being treated coolly because he was Jewish. I felt it was preferable to having him encouraged in his own feeling that it was unmanly to live on my money. I could always tell him the truth later, when everything had changed.

Maman sent us a beautiful set of hand-decorated porcelain from the shop. She wrote an entertaining letter, saying the two families had been so close that our marriage seemed almost incestuous. Nothing in the letter was sad, but it made me sad. I wanted her to know Seth. She would meet him in time, but it seemed unlikely that they would ever get to know each other.

Angela gave us a catered party for fifty of our guests. She kept wandering into the kitchen to see that everything was going smoothly, yet she did not seem to be supervising anyone.

'That's a lovely salad,' she said to a waitress. 'It will look like a floral decoration when you set it on one end of the table.'

I followed her and caught her for a moment as she came into the hall. We had not been alone since Seth and I were married.

'Well, the letter worked,' I said, 'but you took a chance with my life. It might have had the opposite result.'

She didn't pretend not to know what I meant. 'Not much of a chance. I usually get the result I'm after.' She smiled. 'It's a matter of experience.'

Woman's World declined steadily, but it was nearly five years before Grandpa was convinced it was Prescott's fault. Part of his blindness was his stubborn confidence in his own choices. He had brought Prescott into the organization, lured him away from another magazine because he was one of the best editors in the business. How could the man he had chosen be undesirable now?

The other factor was the loss of Fanny. She had been lost to him for months, but when she finally had another stroke and died, it hit him as if he had never dreamed it could happen. He had been miserable before, but now he seemed in agony. Sometimes he actually doubled over as if something had rammed him in the belly. He came to the office every day, held staff meetings, directed the business as he had always done, but with no gusto, no joy. He never laughed. He never roared. He was somebody else, some strange, tortured man inside the shell of Terence McNally the First.

Whatever remnants of genuine interest and energy he had left, he devoted to *McNally's Monthly*. This was his baby. If it had been up to him alone, he might never have started the other magazines. Through *McNally's Monthly* he had exposed corruption, influenced presidents, helped affect the course of history. One magazine could not have made him rich, but riches were of secondary importance to him. He had consented to the launching of *Woman's World* at a time when women's magazines were dominating the field, and had conceived of it as an opportunity for me, but he felt no personal involvement in it. He felt even less, I think, in *Lilliput*, though it was almost as successful in the children's magazine field as *McNally's Monthly* was among general magazines. These two periodicals now carried *Woman's World*. Grandpa talked of selling *Country Squire* – urbanization was eroding its readership – but it was some time before he regained the force to do it.

Pa with Fanny's support, had been largely responsible for the expansion of the business. He told us he could not have succeeded without her. Grandpa automatically opposed anything Pa suggested, but he had always listened to Fanny. She had known how to encourage his natural tendency to believe any important idea had originated with him. With Fanny gone, Pa had no way to influence him. I think he had long ago given up hope anyway of becoming a power in the organization while Grandpa was there. He was satisfied to be away from the office half the time, running around the country and to Europe, appeasing his restlessness, using his talent for nosing out stories for *McNally's Monthly* and persuading authors to write them.

'Don't worry about it,' he told me. 'We'll keep *Woman's World* going. It's probably just a phase. Even *Ladies' Home Journal* is having trouble right now.'

'Yes, for the same reason. Outmoded ideas about women's interests. If we don't—'

'Megan, Howard Prescott has been in this business for more than twenty years. You're still learning. Can you seriously believe your judgment is better than his?'

Sometimes I had to walk away from Pa before I said something I would regret.

'He wants to think of you as a child,' Seth said, 'so he can keep you under his thumb. I'm glad my parents are a continent away.'

Seth would not have admitted that about his parents before we were married. He had convinced himself that he was torn between his love for them and his love for me. That he was afraid to marry me for fear of its effect on them. But it was marriage he had been afraid of, marriage itself, the big step, the ultimate commitment that most women longed for as soon as possible and most men hoped to postpone as long as they could.

'I despise everything they stand for,' he told me one night in bed. 'My father's only standard is money. He admires anyone who has it and is contemptuous of anyone without it. My mother is a silly, possessive woman who feeds on her prejudices. Sharon caught some of them from her, but I was always too contrary. If Mama believed something, I made up my mind to believe the opposite.'

'Still, you became a doctor, the way she wanted.'

'The way *I* wanted. I had the idea first. By the time she mentioned it I was too far gone to switch. I bought a stethoscope with my allowance when I was in the fifth grade and hid it in my Erector Set box. I wore it when nobody was around. It hung down to my knees.'

The picture was so comical and so endearing that I laughed and kissed him. In return he kissed my hair in an absentminded, married way that I also found endearing.

'Didn't you ever wonder how I got into P and S? Not many Jewish boys make it.'

'Of course I didn't wonder. A brilliant fellow like you—'

'You know I'm not brilliant.'

'All right, how's highly intelligent?'

'Whatever you say. But I worked my butt off, I can tell you, for the marks to get me in on the quota. Not only because it was a top medical school. I was crazy to come east, to get as far from home as I could before I suffocated.'

'You kept giving me all these reasons why Jewish families are so close and your mother's heart was going to break.'

'Preserving the myth. Some are close, and some aren't.'

'Preserving the myth, my foot! You were looking for

excuses not to marry me.'

'Oh, God, shut up. Even the thought of not marrying you turns me to stone. I mean it.' He rolled toward me and pulled my hand down. 'Feel that!'

We were young for marriage. Girls had once, habitually, married younger, but they had married much older men. Wise, experienced men to protect them in their innocence, guide them, mold their limited feminine capacities, teach them to be wives. Seth and I learned together and taught each other. We grew up together.

It was not an easygoing marriage. We had impassioned arguments, often about something as inconsequential as the placement of a piece of furniture. But we could laugh at ourselves. We laughed a lot, even when making love. And there was this:

'One thing I never want to do, no matter how angry I am, is belittle you, even in private.' We had just been visiting friends who sniped at each other all evening, and I thought no marriage could survive such ugliness. 'I may say you did a foolish thing, but I never want to tell you you're a foolish man.'

'Even if I am?'

'Even if you are.'

'I suppose you never want me to belittle you either.'

'Suit yourself. Of course, if you do, I may—'

'No threats. I surrender. Knowing your fiendish temper. Should we cut our fingers and seal the bargain with our mingled blood?'

Once, over something like a missing button from a shirt, I hotly yanked out his dresser drawer and spilled all the shirts on the floor. Once at dinner, when I disputed his taste in wine, he coldly poured the few drops left in his glass over my head.

But we kept our bargain. I did not demean him. He did not diminish me.

'Oh, God, when I think how much depends on luck!' Seth

said a few days after Mac was born. 'If my father had gone to Jake's funeral and I hadn't—'

Seth interned at Mount Sinai. That was a hellish year for him. He loved the practice of medicine, but there was so much of it, of its dreariest aspects, so many sick and injured people to care for all at once. He had hardly any time at home. He never got enough sleep. The pittance he was paid barely covered his carfare and the socks he went through daily. All this made him irritable and unreasonable. I tried to be patient, knowing it had nothing to do with me, even when it seemed to. But I was not really good at this kind of patience. We had some rousing battles, each of them ending in a fierce embrace and a competition for the most culpable. Seth liked to whip himself with the fact that we were living mainly on my salary, but I think this no longer horrified him as much as he made out. I think the idea I kept repeating was getting through to him – that we had to support each other as needed, and it made no difference which of us was doing it at any given time or whether it involved money or something else. Still, it must have helped him to protest.

He was more concerned with money, anyway, than I was, even if he was only fighting against it. Nobody in my family was preoccupied with either amassing it or spending it. I had lived simply with my mother, less simply, though not lavishly, with my father and Angela, and now, with Seth, more simply than ever.

My salary at *Woman's World*, though no one on the staff believed it, was exactly what other female editorial assistants were getting. We managed to live in a pleasant neighborhood on Eighty-seventh Street near Broadway, but our apartment was small and cramped. Our bedroom, a former maid's room, could accommodate only the bed, a highboy that we both used, a tiny night table, and a straight chair. The kitchen was about the same size. It held a gas stove and oven, a porcelain sink, a small refrigerator with part of the mechanism sitting on top of it, and, as in many old New York apartments, roaches. The living room was relatively large, but it had only one window facing a courtyard and, except for a few hours in the morning, gave no appreciable daylight.

Seth kept telling me he wished he could get me out of this 'dump'.

'I'm happy here. As happy as I would be anywhere else.'

'You're just saying that to make me feel better.'

But I was not just saying it. The apartment was unbeautiful and inconvenient, but it made no difference in my happiness. Seth was there. Sometimes when he was not there, I frightened myself with phantom accidents and thought I could imagine how Grandpa felt without Fanny. Of course I could not. It was unimaginable.

Right after Seth started in practice, we moved to a ground-floor apartment in the same building. It had three additional rooms. We made one into a nursery and partitioned another into a waiting room and a consulting room. The third became an examining room. We bribed the landlord to install a separate entrance to the street, with a brass plaque that said SETH BERNBACH. MD. The bribe was modest, but labor was so cheap in that third year of the Depression that the landlord probably made a profit on it.

Mac's name was Seth McNally Bernbach, but he was never called anything but Mac. One of the nurses in the hospital started it because he looked so Irish – a large, lusty baby with a tuft of red hair and the red, snub-nosed, wrinkled, toothless face of an old gaffer in Mooney's pub. He grew out of that look, got darker hair, a nose more like Sam's, and the blue McNally eyes – a handsome boy, or so I always thought, with a good American face. By then Mac was his name.

It never occurred to us not to have children.

Everybody had children. But I wanted them early, before I had larger responsibilities on the magazine, and Seth thought we should wait until he was well established in his practice. Grandpa settled this for us.

He came for dinner one night when Seth was off duty. I was not much of a cook. I did not bother for myself, and Seth seldom got home for meals. When he did, he was too exhausted to know what he was eating. But Grandpa was used to fine food, and I wanted him to think I was as capable of preparing a fine dinner as of editing a story.

Two days before he was to come, I went downstairs to the *Woman's World* Food and Equipment Department and asked Mildred Grabe, the director to suggest a menu and show me how to prepare it. She wrote me out a menu that coincided with the recipes the cooks were testing at a row of stoves and ovens along one wall. I watched them grill a marinated boned leg of lamb, bake tomatoes stuffed with rice, bake and frost a chocolate cake. After they had finished, one of Mildred's assistants arranged the food on a table set with a yellow and white printed cloth with a basket of hothouse daffodils and white hyacinths in the center, and the photographer took the picture for the April issue, to appear three months later.

I went home that evening and marinated the lamb according to the recipe. I followed the other recipes, and everything came out beautifully. Grandpa was as admiring as I hoped he would be. Even Seth noticed the chocolate cake.

'Well, sure it's delicious,' he said. 'She can do anything. Why do you think I married her?'

I could afford to be modest. 'All I did was follow a recipe. Anybody who can read directions and do what they say can cook. Maman never told me that.' I looked at Seth, whose eyelids were beginning to droop. 'Remind me to tell it to our daughter.'

He said, 'What?'

Grandpa said, 'Are you making an announcement, Megan?'

'Not yet. Maybe soon.' Seth seemed to be asleep. He had learned to sleep sitting or standing, a few minutes at a time, with everybody talking around him. 'I hope very soon,' I said to Grandpa.

'I hope not, much as I'd love great-grandchildren. You're still very young,' Grandpa said. 'You should wait until you can afford an efficient housekeeper, capable of taking good care of your children while you're at the office.'

Seth opened his eyes. 'Don't you think that should be our decision, Grandpa, sir?'

'Yes, of course, but surely you can profit by advice.'

'If we needed advice, I think we'd come to you before anyone else,' Seth said. 'In this case Megan and I have been discussing it and considering it very carefully for a long while, and we've made up our minds. We plan to have our children while Megan can still take time off when necessary, without causing too much disruption at the office.'

'And who will look after these children at other times?'

'You can be sure we'll be as concerned about that as you are, Grandpa,' Seth said. 'We'll find someone.'

Grandpa never mentioned the subject again. That may have been partly because he still lacked the spirit, but it was not all of it. Even when he was once more himself, he did not try to run our marriage, as he tried to run everything else.

Sheila was born in 1934. There is no Sheila in the Bible, but I looked it up and found a Shelah. Thus, in spite of Seth's scorn for such 'cuteness', expressed the day we met at Jake's funeral, both our children had biblical names beginning with S. I chose to name our son Seth, but Seth chose Sheila. He said it was because it went well with Bernbach and yet was Irish. Maybe. But I

494

believe it was also a sop to his conscience, which had a way of taking off on odd tangents. He had little contact with his parents, though they had finally forgiven him for marrying me, but by following their system for naming children, I think he felt he was maintaining some kind of tie with them.

Mac was an easy, amiable baby. Sheila was a hellion from her first screaming day. I took a six-month leave of absence after Mac was born, but I went back to the office when Sheila was less than four months old. Of course, we had Julia Dunwoodie by that time. She had lost her job selling baby's furnishings in a speciality shop that had not survived the lean times, and she could not get another. She was in her middle forties and had no experience apart from layettes and teddy bears and carriage covers.

'I know you meant someone who's had a position taking care of babies,' she said when she came to answer the ad. 'I haven't, but I do know how to take care of them. I have two much younger sisters. My mother was a working woman, and I practically brought them up.' She looked at Mac, who was sitting in my lap, staring at her. 'I think you and I would get along just fine,' she said to him, and he smiled and held out his arms to her.

She suited me, too. She was a small, neat, no-nonsense woman with gray hair, cut short, and a calm, pleasantly seamed face. She spoke to a baby as she spoke to everyone else, in a quiet, crisp voice that could not be induced to rise or waver. Sentimentality was foreign to her, but she hugged when hugs were needed and soothed by means of her own unruffled manner. As far as we knew, she had no one, no family, no acquaintances except the nursemaids with whom she wheeled the baby carriage and sat in the park. When the children were old enough, she often took them with her on her Thursdays off, gave them a ride on the Fifth Avenue bus or the Staten Island ferry, treated them to ice cream or lollipops, and brought them home early. We paid her the going rate to begin with and raised her to fifty dollars a month when Sheila was born. Seth had begun to do well enough so that we could afford it.

'Oh, God, we're so lucky it scares me,' I said to him.

'Why? Do you think somebody's up there deciding it's time we paid for it with an allotment of misery? You sound like an old Jewish mama.'

It did scare me, though. So many people had nothing. There was a man I passed on my way to the office. He stood on the corner, every morning, week after week, in a shabby but clean suit and a ragged cap, holding a hand-lettered sign that said: 'I Need Work, Not Charity. Who Will Help Me Get a Job? I Will Do Anything Honest. I Have Good References.' I thought there might be something for him at the office, cleaning or something, but I was told men came in asking for work all through the day, every day. It was a terrible time to have so much.

Other people's luck ran out in other ways. Fran Werner came in late one morning, looking as if she had been on a drunken binge, though I knew she scarcely drank at all. Her eyes were bloodshot, sunk in purplish caverns, and the skin seemed to have loosened on her bones. She had a smear of lipstick on her mouth, but she had forgotten to comb her hair.

I got as far as 'Fran – what—' when she wagged her hand at me and sagged into her desk chair.

'I know, I know. I'm a mess. God!' she said. 'God! God! God!' She let her head fall back, so that she was staring up at me as I stood over her. 'A woman ought to have tenure after fourteen years, don't you think so, Megan? Don't you think a woman ought to have tenure?' She did not wait for whatever I might have answered. 'He's left me after fourteen years. He's gone. Nothing I can do, Megan. No hope at all. He told me last night

496

he's getting married. Nice while it lasted, Fran. Nice fourteen years. Now I'm ready for marriage – getting on, you know – and for that I need somebody new and young to perk me up, not old-shoe Fran. For that—'

'Stop it now.' I took her face between my hands. 'Please stop it and go comb your hair and put your lipstick on straight. I'll get you some coffee.'

'Coffee!' she said, but she got to her feet, staggering, and started toward the ladies' room. 'No use eyeing my desk any more, Megan. I'll be sitting there the rest of my life. They'll bring sightseers in to look at me. Fran, the fiction editor – a genuine antique.'

When she came back with her hair and mouth fixed, I thought she looked better. But then she leaned against the wall, facing me, and there was something so defeated and bleak about her expression, and about what she said next, that if the bastard who had done it to her had been there, I think I would have tried to strangle him.

'I don't know if I can stand it, Megan. He's what I lived for. I don't know. Even if I could get over this, I'm a woman who needs sex. Some people think only men really need sex, but it isn't so. The trouble is it's no good for me without love, and I'm too old to start all over again loving somebody else.'

'What are you talking about, too old? People twenty years older than you fall in love. My grandfather—'

But she was not listening. 'God, I envy you. You have everything I ever wanted.' She said it between her teeth, so that it sounded vicious, and then she shook her head and looked at me with what was supposed to be a smile. 'I'm sorry. I can't blame you, can I? It's not you who took it away from me.'

I said some of the useless things people say because it seems necessary to say something, and left her trying to get down to work. Early in the afternoon she called me back into her office.

'I'm going home,' she said. 'Anybody wants to know, I

felt the flu coming on.' She slid a thick manuscript across the desk to me. 'Take care of this. I haven't finished reading it yet, but there may be a serial in it. New author. Send it up to Prescott if you think so.'

'Before you finish it?'

'That's right.'

I felt uneasy about her all the rest of the day. When I got home, I called her number, but she didn't answer. She did not come in the next morning, and there was still no answer at her apartment. Howard Prescott came looking for her as I hung up.

'Do you know where Miss Werner is? She's not in her office, and she hasn't called in.' He sounded as if it were my fault. He always sounded like that with me. 'Did she say anything to you yesterday?'

'She said she thought she was getting the flu.'

'Why didn't she say something to me? Call her apartment and find out when she intends to show up here.'

A few years earlier I might have told him to call her himself or suggested that he say 'please', but I no longer indulged myself in these small ways. It was not worth it. I had to work with him. At least now he resented me only a little more than he did anyone else.

'I just called her apartment. There's no answer,' I told him.

'Ha! I thought she was sick. What's she doing out if she's sick?'

'She might have gone to the doctor. Maybe she's in the hospital. Maybe she's on her way here. I'm sure there's some—'

'Well, find out,' he said, talking as he left. 'I can't run a magazine without a fiction editor.'

I waited, hoping she would arrive. I closed my eyes and said to myself, *Please let her get here*, the way, as a child, I used to say *Please let me pass the test*, not knowing any more now than I did then with whom I was pleading.

At eleven o'clock I called the superintendent of her building and told him to go into her apartment with his passkey. I held on until he came back to the phone. *Please let her be all right.*

But she was not all right. She was dead in her kitchen, with the door and window shut and neatly sealed with newspaper and all the gas jets open on the stove.

Seth held me and stayed awake with me nearly the whole night. He listened to me and said almost nothing except 'I know, I know.' It didn't matter to me that he could not know. He was there, holding me, murmuring to me. For the first time I had to talk to him about those deaths in college, when Bill King smashed up his car. I had never told him all about Charles either, and now I had to tell him. It was as if by describing the other terrible deaths I knew of I could make Fran's death more ordinary, more bearable.

'I know, I know.'

In the morning, at breakfast, he kept me away from the subject of Fran. He began discussing Charles and how backward he believed our society was to stigmatize anyone for a predisposition he had not chosen and could not change.

'If your father reacted violently, it was because he's a product of his time. I feel sorry for him,' Seth said, which I considered magnanimous. Pa was cordial to Seth, as one is cordial to a stranger. 'Do you think he's still plagued by guilt?'

Julia brought the children in before I could answer. She fed them in the kitchen, so that we could eat in peace, but we always spent some time with them before I left for the office and Seth started on his rounds. Mac, nearly three, was in love with the sound of his own voice and chattered without pause and almost as fluently as his great-grandfather. Sheila, who was eleven months old and had been walking for a month, fancied herself an

499

expert at it and went tearing around the room, falling and shrieking with outrage every few minutes. I was delighted to see them and delighted when Julia took them away. Not every mother is a good one at every stage of her children's life. I got better as they got older.

'I was thinking about that business in Ireland,' Seth said when they had gone. 'The old man who told Charles about the first Terrence McNally. Even if it turned out not to explain anything or to help anybody, aren't you curious to know what it was? I am.'

'But the only one who knows is this Sidney Keller, and I told you how he reacted when Pa went to see him.'

'That was a long time ago. He may see things differently by now.'

'Pa would never risk it.'

'You could, though. He's not going to call you a murderer.' Seth looked at his watch. 'I have to go. I've got four patients in the hospital, and I told them all I'd see them before ten.'

He kissed me and went out, leaving me with the new and titillating idea of talking to Sidney Keller myself. It kept me thinking of something besides Fran's suicide, which was, of course, Seth's purpose. I was not overwhelmed by the tragedy again until I got to the office and saw her empty desk.

11

Seth asked me once or twice whether I had given any more thought to his suggestion about Sidney Keller. I had. I had even made a few plans of approach. But I always decided they were not feasible. I kept putting the whole thing off, telling myself I was too busy and had too many other things on my mind. It took me a long time to recognize that I was afraid to confront Keller –

afraid of his reaction, of what he might tell me, of the man himself, I don't know, but anyway, afraid. As soon as I realized that, I went to see him. The only way I ever found to stop being afraid of doing something was to do it.

In the meanwhile, I certainly did have other things to think about and cope with. Howard Prescott called me into his office the day after Fran's funeral and told me he wanted me to take over her duties temporarily.

'Until I get hold of a new fiction editor,' he said. 'It won't be long. I've got a man in mind.'

'A man?'

'Yes, a man. One trouble with this magazine is too many women. They're all right in departments like Beauty and Fashion and Crafts, but we need more men in key slots to put us on top again.'

He was baiting me, watching me with his mean little eyes. I was pleased, when I spoke, not to sound the way I felt.

'How is it you're asking me to take over, instead of Winifred Mann?' Winnie was the associate fiction editor. 'She isn't going to like it or me.'

'I don't run this magazine on the basis of who likes what or whom. That's a woman's way of running things.' He began scribbling at something on his desk, dismissing me. 'Let's hope you don't let everything fall apart before I get the man I want in here.'

Winnie was, of course, enraged. She was excitable anyhow, a short, chunky woman in her early thirties, married to a dramatically handsome man. I had a theory that she could not imagine why he had married her – any more than anyone else could – and that the uncertainty kept her permanently on edge.

'I went to him *immediately*. I asked him for the job – at least a *chance* at it,' she said, hurling her accusing italics in a penetrating voice. 'Six months I asked him for. A six-month trial to prove myself. I was Fran's *associate*, for

501

God's sake! What are *you?* An *assistant.* If you weren't a *McNally*—'

I reminded her that Prescott couldn't stand me and had certainly never favored me. I told her it was only temporary and Prescott was using me because he did not mind yanking me out again when he got the man he wanted, but if he put her in there, he would feel guilty about replacing her. I doubted that Prescott ever felt guilty about anything in his life, but Winnie accepted this. It was easier than accepting the suggestion that she was not up to the job, even temporarily, as she was not.

One of the first things I did as fiction editor pro tem was approve the manuscript Fran had given me to read her last day in the office. It was a remarkable story, beautifully written except for a few rough spots, about a housewife who takes charge of her husband's lumber business after his death and struggles, with eventual success, to make a go of it. To my mind it was the find every editor dreams of – the rare gem, hidden in the pile of junk submitted by unknown authors. I sent it to Prescott with a note strongly recommending that we buy it as a three-part serial.

He sent it back a month later, with his own note written in red pencil. It said: 'No! Absolutely no reader identification. How many women do, can, or want to run a business? Very poor judgment on your part.'

I waited a few days, until I had cooled down from full boil. This time I made an appointment with Grandpa and went up to his office in an all-or-nothing mood, my briefcase full of recent issues of *Woman's World* and the manuscript Prescott had rejected.

'Grandpa, I want to talk to you. To *you*, Terrence McNally the First,' I said, 'not this watered-down version that's been walking around in your skin for five years.' I plopped the briefcase down on his desk, sat in the chair opposite him, and looked into his astonished face. 'Five years is long enough. It's time somebody told you so. If you're not ready to take hold now, in your old way, maybe you ought to retire altogether and let—'

I had to stop because he was roaring. Not, as I thought for an instant, in one of his furies, but with laughter. He threw his big head back, his mane of hair still showing strands of red among the white, and laughed until he cried. He sounded and looked like a lion, the way I loved him.

'Oh, Grandpa . . .' I began, but he stopped me with a motion of his hand.

'No, no, don't soften up.' He wiped his eyes with his handkerchief, blew a trumpet blast into it, and leaned toward me across the desk. 'You take me back to when I was a boy and needed a switching from Aggie, my ma, to bring me to my senses. You're like her, you know. Not in looks – she and I were cut from the same ugly mold – but you've got her spirit. She knew, and so do you, that love isn't all to do with kisses and sweet words. Megan, after she died, I had only a spinster schoolteacher to love me, and all I could ever feel for her in return was gratitude. Then I had Sylvia, who loved no one but herself. Imagine what it meant to me to find Fanny. And to lose her when—' He broke off, jerking his shoulders impatiently. 'Excuses. Aggie never wanted to hear excuses. What's on your mind?'

I took the manuscript and the magazines out of the briefcase and shoved them across to him. 'Please look at these issues of *Woman's World*. Really look at them, Grandpa, and see if you think they're in tune with the times. Then read this story that I strongly recommended to Prescott we run as a serial and that he turned down as having no reader identification. I'd like you to see if you can find a connection between these things and the way *Woman's World* has gone downhill.'

His eyes were dancing. He was seventy-seven years old, but his eyes could still dance. It was a long time, though, since I had seen them do it.

'And if I find a connection, what then?'

'Then I'd like you to get Prescott out before he carries through his plan to bring in a man with his own ideas as fiction editor. He's too old to find a job somewhere else, so I hope you can use him in some other capacity, but if he stays where he is, *Woman's World* is going down the drain. Then' – I took a deep breath and sat up straight – 'then I'd like you to appoint me editor-in-chief and let me put *Woman's World* back on its feet.'

He said nothing, just kept looking at me as if I were entertaining him, and I thought any minute he might tell me to run along and play. I knew I would get no support from Pa. He was appalled that I had gone back to work at all after I had had children. We had had dreadful arguments over it, the only time I can remember that such painful things were said between us.

'You belong home with your children. They need you.'

'They don't need me all the time. They have Julia. She's marvelous with them, and they adore her.'

'She's not their mother. I don't know what it is with mothers in this family. They all run away from their children.'

'My children have not only a mother who is with them every morning and evening and weekend but a father who stays around, too.'

'Yes, well, some fathers are busy earning enough money so their wives don't have to work in order to live decently.'

We had both apologized later, but that had not changed anything. I don't think Pa believed most of the things he had said. He must have known Seth was working hard, not playing at doctor while I supported the family. But he certainly believed I belonged at home, not at *Woman's World*. He had to find reasons to stick to, even reasons that had no truth in them. He was a stubborn man.

And he made me feel guilty. I resented his doing that. He made me wonder whether perhaps I *was* depriving my children, warping them in some way, by leaving them with Julia most of the day. She was not, as he said, their mother.

Seth thought this was nonsense. 'How much more love and attention could they possibly get?' he said. 'They have you; they have Julia; they have me. In between they have Grandpa and Angela and your father. Do you think it doesn't count if it isn't labeled "Mother"? Your father thinks this way because his mother didn't love him, but that's a different story.'

Just the same I felt guilty, on and off. Not guilty enough, however, to stay home. I sat there now, opposite Grandpa, waiting for him to say something, and I thought if he made a joke of what I had asked him for, I might never be able to forgive him.

What he finally said, his powerful voice turned on low, was: '*Chutzpah*. Jake taught me that word. I can't say it the way he did, somewhere in the back of his throat, but even mispronounced, it's more expressive than any approximation in English. Do you know it?'

'I not only know it but I can pronounce it,' I said coldly. 'I gather you're telling me I have it.'

He still looked amused. 'Well, wouldn't you agree? You're – what? Twenty-five years old?'

'Twenty-six.'

'All right, twenty-six. You've been working in Fiction for five years, primarily as an assistant editor, until just lately, when you've been filling in as editor. A month or so in that temporary slot, and you come marching in here, *not* to say you think you could do it as a regular job – that might be an understandable notion – but no, you want to skip fiction editor and go right to the top. You assure me that you, a youngster of twenty-six with no experience except in Fiction, can put *Woman's World* on its feet. If that isn't *chutzpah*, can you tell what is?'

'I think you have your facts wrong. I've been on the magazine for five years full time, yes, but I've worked here for ten years. I've grown up here. It's part of me. Do you suppose I've just been sitting at a desk in Fiction, with my eyes and ears closed to the rest? I know how everything operates, in every department, and who everybody is and how well or poorly they're handling their jobs. I've made it my business to know because you promised me long ago, while I was still in France, that someday I was going to be editor-in-chief, and I wanted to be prepared.' He looked about to interrupt me, but I went straight on. 'If things were different, I'd have waited awhile. I'd have been satisfied to progress to fiction editor first. But there's no chance of that. Prescott wouldn't have me. He wants a man. He wants somebody who thinks, as he does, that the women who read our magazine have no interest in anything outside their homes and families, no capacity for anything else, not even any hopes or dreams beyond that. He's back in the Victorian age, and he's keeping *Woman's World* there with him. I've heard you say that any magazine that doesn't keep up with public taste is sure to decline. Well, *Woman's World* hasn't, and it's declining. If it's *chutzpah* to tell you I can change that, then so be it.' I pushed back my chair and stood up. 'But however incapable you may think I am, Grandpa, unless you're ready to say goodbye to *Woman's World*, you'd better get somebody in there with more vision than Howard Prescott.'

He waved his hand at me. 'Sit down, sit down. What are you flying off the handle about? You underestimate me, Megan. Some people, in some circumstances, have found that a dangerous thing to do.' Now he was openly grinning, and I had no idea what was in his mind. 'It's true I haven't had the same zest for things, the business or anything else, since Fanny died, but I haven't been quite so blind as you imagine. I've planned for some while to shift Prescott to *Country Squire*, where he might do very well until I sell it in a few years, by which time he'll be old enough to retire with an adequate pension. I've only been

506

waiting until I could find a suitable replacement. I had considered Frances Werner, but—' The grin was gone. He shook his head. 'I wasn't sure about her anyway. I wasn't sure her heart was in her work. She might have made a good editor-in-chief, but never a great one.'

He opened the humidor on his desk, took out a cigar, and went through his customary ritual, sniffing it, slicing the tip with the cutter on the end of his watch chain, lighting it with a long match that he struck on the sole of his shoe. As I waited, I wondered whether he had really had all those ideas for 'some while' or had just thought them up. He was quite capable of convincing himself that nothing I had told him about Prescott or *Woman's World* was new to him, even if none of it had entered his mind.

'I hear Lorimer is getting rid of the *Ladies' Home Journal* editor-in-chief,' he said now. 'He's giving the job to his associate editor on the *Saturday Evening Post*, Bruce Gould. To him and his wife, Beatrice. A husband-and-wife team, like Fanny and me, though with us it wasn't official.' He was looking out the window now, blowing smoke toward the ceiling. 'I've considered that, too. I mean, taking somebody from one of our other magazines or bringing in somebody from outside—' He was silent for a moment. Then he said, '*Chutzpah.* I didn't mean it as an insult, you know, Megan. At the right time and place it's a good thing to have. Good McNally *chutzpah.*' He turned around and pushed the manuscript and the issues of *Woman's World* back across the desk to me. 'I don't have to look at these. I'll give you six months.'

'Six months,' I repeated stupidly.

'I don't expect to see the magazine in the black by that time. It will take longer. But six months is long enough to tell me whether or not you can handle the job. We'll put it out that it's temporary, like your Fiction job now, until I find the right person. If you're capable, there would be no reason for me to continue looking. If not—'

I was around the desk before he could finish. 'Can the

editor-in-chief of *Woman's World* hug the editor-in-chief of the whole shebang?"

When I had emerged from his bone-crushing, tobacco-smelling embrace, he said, 'Don't forget the "temporary". Your age will make it hard for you to establish your authority. Being temporary will make it harder still. Like a substitute teacher. You may wish I had refused to let you try it.'

I never wished that. But there were times when I came close.

The day he left to move upstairs to *Country Squire*, Prescott called me into the office that would now be mine. He had cleaned out the desk and opened the windows, letting in a crisp October breeze that had already blown away any identifiable personal aroma. As I came in, he shut it.

'Well, it's all yours.' He was standing in the middle of the floor, his hands in the pockets of one of his baggy suits. 'Believe me. I'm glad to see the last of it. Poetry and embroidered pillows and creamed mushrooms on toast. I've been angling a long time for *Country Squire*.'

I wanted to believe, so I could go on detesting him, that he was trying to diminish the job because I was stepping into it. But I was afraid it had nothing to do with me. I was afraid he knew the truth about *Country Squire*'s future and had to pretend he didn't.

'I hope you'll be happy there.'

It sounded unnatural to me. We did not exchange such courteous clichés. But he only nodded and picked up the carryall in which I suppose he had his things from the desk.

'You may get along here. You've got a good head on your shoulders,' he said as he went out the door. 'For a woman.'

I did not like feeling sorry for him. He had once been a fine editor, but he had not kept up with the times, and he

508

had almost ruined my magazine. Besides, he was an unpleasant person. It would have been easier if he had not been just a little less unpleasant at the end.

His office – my office now – had two windows, one looking out on Fifth Avenue where horses and carriages had once clopped by, outnumbering the automobiles. Now, in spite of the Depression, the avenue was clogged with cars of every description and price, from a used Ford for sixty dollars to a new Packard for two thousand dollars. Even through the closed windows I could hear the squealing brakes and the honking horns, but soon I got used to it and noticed only when, for a few rare minutes, the sounds stopped.

I changed the drab brown draperies at the windows to a cheerful green and then turned the desk around, so I had my back to them and could not be distracted by the scene outside. I also brought a vase from home and kept it filled with fresh flowers that I bought from a street peddler who looked as if he might once have been a merchant prince. Otherwise, for the time being, I left everything as it was.

My first executive action was to hire my own private secretary. Prescott had taken his with him to *Country Squire*. I wanted someone new to the organization anyway, someone who had formed no partisan ideas and would be totally loyal to me. Dora Horvath was exactly it. She was a pale, bespectacled wisp of a girl, twenty-three years old, with a bad complexion and a slight limp from a childhood attack of polio. In an employers' market, where most of the employers were men, her intelligence and her first-rate skills as a secretary were overshadowed by her appearance. She supported an ailing foreign-born mother, and she had been out of a job for more than a year. When I told her she could start the next morning, she ran out of my office sobbing.

Next, I called a staff meeting to which I asked not only editors and other department heads but associates. When he began running out of chairs, Ralph Barnhard, the art director, went outside and brought in more. From the cheerful way he did it I felt he was going to be no trouble to me. I knew which of them would be difficult, and which impossible, but I was not sure of my allies. Some who had been friendly when I was only one of the staff would be likely to resent me as a boss.

I sat behind my desk and looked at all those waiting faces, knowing what was behind several of them and seeing it unconcealed on several others, and for an instant I had such stage fright that I thought I would not be able to speak. But I did speak, and as soon as I began, I felt fine.

'Some of you may be unwilling for various reasons to work under me as editor-in-chief, even temporarily,' I said to the staff. 'If so, let's get it out in the open right now, and if you want me to, I'll do what I can to have you transferred to one of our other magazines.'

Bob Thurston, the production manager, a small man with a military-looking stubble of gray and black hair on a squarish head, said. 'I'm going over to *Scribner's*, starting next month. I guess I'm a little too old to get used to working for a woman.' He gave me an indulgent smile. 'Don't take it personally.'

'This is not the place to take anything personally,' I said. 'This is a business office. Anyone else?'

'I don't know whether I can work for you or not until I try it.' Ralph Barnhard looked more like a football player than anybody's idea of an art director, but under his direction the staff artists, letterers, and photographers turned out some of the most elegant work in the field. 'But my feeling is,' he said, 'that if I could stand Howard Prescott as a boss, I can stand anybody.'

I heard a few laughs. One or two people applauded, but I couldn't see who they were. Then Winifred Mann, the associate fiction editor, spoke. I had been waiting for Winnie.

'I just want to know one thing. Am I going to be the

510

fiction editor? I certainly *assume* I am, but I would really appreciate being *told*.'

It would have been kinder, of course, to talk to her privately, but I could not afford to be kind. I knew Winnie. She would distort whatever I said to make herself look good and, in vengeance, to vilify me.

'We're going to do some new things in Fiction and Articles. We're bringing in someone who has worked under Cheney at *Collier's*. For the time being, for reasons of economy, this editor will handle both.' I looked from Winnie's incipient fury to the stricken face of the articles editor, Sarah Dorfman. She was a tall, skinny, dark-haired, capable woman, a few years older than I was, unmarried, devoted to her work, and probably my best friend on the magazine now that Fran was gone. 'Miss Dorfman will work directly under me,' I said, 'in the new post of executive editor. This will—'

'I'm giving my *notice*,' Winnie broke in. 'This is an *outrage*. If things were done *fairly* in this place, instead of on the basis of the most flagrant *nepotism*—'

'I'll be sorry to lose you, Mrs Mann,' I said. 'I'll be sorry to lose any of you. But my main concern is to put the book back where it belongs, on top.' To outsiders, *Woman's World* was a magazine. It was 'the book' here, among the staff. 'Those of you who are staying must make it your concern, too. It's in your own interest. Obviously the better *Woman's World* does, the better you'll do. We've all had a taste of that. When things were bad, we took a cut in salary. When things improve, everybody who has helped improve it will get a raise.'

Winnie, who had stood up as if to leave, was back in her chair. Somebody asked me about the new things I had said we were going to do in Fiction and Articles.

'We've stagnated,' I said. 'We're still printing the kind of stuff that appealed to women before the war. If it weren't for the fine artwork and the modern service features, the latest issue could be mistaken for the first one ever published. That's all going to change. We'll still publish romantic fluff – some of our readers want it – but we'll buy fiction of substance, too, starting with a three-part serial that came in a few weeks ago. We'll still print articles on how to handle an unemployed husband, but we'll also deal with such modern problems as divorce, mental illness, venereal disease, alcoholism—'

'Excuse *me*, Megan,' Winnie interrupted again, 'I'd just like to know what will happen if you buy all these *radical* pieces, and the person who takes your place doesn't consider any of it at *all* suitable for the book? Wouldn't it be better to *wait* and find out what the *permanent* editor-in-chief wants instead of building up a costly inventory that may never be *used?*'

'I appreciate your interest, Mrs Mann, but I think it's unlikely any such reversal will occur. My proposals have all been submitted to the head of the McNally Corporation and approved.' I heard an unidentifiable voice murmur, and I said, 'Yes, it's convenient to have my grandfather for a boss. If you know him at all, though, you know nobody on earth, granddaughter or son or closest friend, can persuade him to do anything he doesn't want to do or to approve anything he doesn't believe is good for a McNally publication.' I looked around at them. 'Incidentally, as you're aware, I use my maiden name in the office. It has a certain cachet.' That got a few laughs. 'Some of you who have known me a long time have been accustomed to calling me by my first name, and of course, I have no objection to it in private. In public, however – at staff meetings, for instance – I'd like you to address me as Mrs McNally.' I waited a minute and then smiled. Somebody told me years later that my timing was always expert, but if so, it was not conscious. 'It will remind me, as well as you,' I said, 'that I'm running the outfit now.'

After this I conducted my first bimonthly staff meeting, with each editor giving a précis of the material on fashion or food or whatever that would appear in the issue to be published three months later. Sarah Dorfman summarized her four articles, and Winnie sullenly but competently gave a synopsis of four short stories. I made a few comments, most of them favorable. There was not much I could do about this issue. It would be full of the same old stuff, bought months before. I had nothing yet to replace any of it. But I would have. The new fiction and articles editor would bring us some *Collier's* authors. I myself would find others who could write for women of the thirties; take them to lunch, suggest ideas, as I had watched Pa do.

'I'm going to bring it off,' I said to Seth. 'I know I am!'

'Of course you are,' he said.

'I'm the editor-in-chief of *Woman's World*. I really am. Sometimes I can't believe it.'

It was probably the most exciting, challenging, frustrating, miserable, triumphant period of my life.

Everyone stayed except Bob Thurston. Winnie Mann stayed. She kept forgetting not to call me Megan. She lost the only revised copy of a story by a temperamental author I had been cultivating, and there was no way to prove it was deliberate. We ran a piece about a woman's prison, and somebody sued us because the fictitious name we had used for one of the prisoners was the same as hers. The new head of Production wanted to walk out because I had to make an important change in an issue after she had the whole dummy pasted up.

The hardest thing I had to learn in six fast months was to delegate authority. It was not a natural McNally skill. But I learned it.

'What am I supposed to be doing here?' Sarah Dorfman asked me. 'Executive editor. It's five weeks now, and I have yet to execute or edit anything. Meanwhile, you're so swamped that you haven't time to say "please". You're beginning to sound like Captain Bligh.'

After that I had everything sifted through her to me –

copy, problems, complaints, ideas, changes in personnel. I still worked a full eight-hour day and frequently took copy home to read at night, but I was no longer overwhelmed. My disposition improved.

I began telling Dora what I wanted to say and letting her write my letters. She wrote them so they sounded like me, only better, often more diplomatic. She protected me, too; turned from pallid little lamb to implacable tiger against anyone, however importunate, that she knew I did not want to see or talk to on the phone.

The new fiction and articles editor from *Collier's* was a man. Grandpa had recruited him. I did not want a man, but Grandpa had approved everything else I wanted, and I felt I had to give in to him on this.

His name was Timothy Dugan. 'That's why you've foisted him on me,' I said to Grandpa. 'I suppose you think it's time we had another Irishman around.'

What I actually believed was that Grandpa thought he had to have this experienced editor, this man, there to keep an eye on things, on me. I resented Timothy Dugan before I ever saw him.

He came to my office in January, three months after he started on the job, with a manuscript in his hand.

'This story, Mrs McNally,' he said. '"Harvest of Love"? You remember it?'

He was a tall, bony, black-haired thirty-seven-year-old man with the greenest eyes I ever saw and a curve to his mouth that made him look always about to smile. His voice was soft and had a faint Irish lilt, though he had never set foot in Ireland. I was sure it was deliberate, part of a carefully cultivated Irish charm.

'I remember it,' I said. 'I turned it down.'

'Yes.' He read my comments on the manuscript in his hand. '"Crudely written. Not for our readers." Was it the language you objected to, Mrs McNally? We can fix that easily enough. I'd be happy to discuss revisions with the author.' The smile came on now. He had creases in his cheeks that resembled dimples. 'I think we have something exceptional here. A new talent. It came in cold, you know. Over the transom. Miss Dorfman was as excited about it as I was.'

'If I had wanted you to discuss revisions with the author. Mr Dugan. I would have said so. I turned the story down.'

He abandoned his smile and pulled up a chair, though I had not asked him to sit down. 'It isn't just this story, Mrs McNally. It's almost anything I particularly recommend.' he said. 'Now this is an interesting place to work. You're a remarkable woman, and I respect you. I'd like to stay. But if you have so little faith in my judgment, you can see that I can't.'

He was holding the manuscript with my rejection in red pencil clipped to it. Except that it was thinner, it might have been the story I had recommended to Howard Prescott, with Prescott's red-penciled 'NO!' attached. I think Prescott had at least acted from conviction, however mistaken, not to brandish or protect his authority. It took me awhile to castigate myself. I was out of practice.

'I want you to stay, Mr Dugan,' I said finally. 'You're the best editor on the staff. I should rely more on your judgment, and in the future I will – starting with this story you're so enthusiastic about.' I smiled at him. 'Go ahead with the revisions.'

He said, 'Good!' and went to the door.

'Of course. I'll want to see it again after it's been revised.'

He looked around at me. 'Of course.'

He looked around at me. 'Of course.'

A few days after that confrontation with Dugan I went to see Sidney Keller. Earlier I had read a piece about him in *The New York Times*, in connection with a church he had designed in Connecticut, and it gave me an idea.

'I'd like to interview him in the relaxed atmosphere of his own home,' I told his secretary. I thought it would be much easier for him to eject me from his office. 'It's for a book I'm writing on modern American architecture. I've already interviewed Frank Lloyd Wright. I know the *Times* has compared Mr Keller to Mr Wright.' My name, I said, was Mrs Seth Bernbach.

He had an apartment in the city and a house in Southampton. I suppose he had me come to the house because he had designed it and wanted to show it off. Ordinarily I read in trains, but now I was too nervous to do anything but stare out the window and repeat my lines. Apart from what he might say or do when he found out who I was and what I wanted, I was nervous about the man himself. I did not know what to expect. As far as I knew, I had never met a homosexual. I had seen boys do imitations, flopping their wrists and lisping, and I had passed an occasional man in the street who walked peculiarly or looked as if he had rouge on. But Keller could not be like that. If he were, or if Charles had been, Pa would have known it before he discovered them that night and said whatever awful thing he had lived with ever since.

The house was built into the side of a hill and looked as if it had grown there. An elderly housekeeper showed me into a large room with three walls of windows facing woods and, in the center, a tree going through the roof. The furniture was sparse and simple, low to the floor, and thickly cushioned. A Miró painting and a Picasso sketch hung on the remaining wall. I was looking at these, too tense to sit, when he spoke behind me.

'Mrs Bernbach?'

I knew he was a few years younger than my father, but he looked older. His hair was white, and his face was deeply lined. He was not tall, and he had a middle-aged paunch, but his finely modeled features and his dark skin against the white hair were striking.

'Your house is beautiful,' I said.

'I'm glad you like it.' His voice was deep and pleasant. 'It isn't everybody's taste. But then, of course, I don't

516

design houses for everybody's taste.'

It sounded like something he wanted me to quote. We sat on a sofa that curved in such a way that we were not next to each other but facing. I wrote down what he said in the notebook I had brought for authenticity.

'Do you live here alone?' I asked him.

'Except when I have guests.'

I went on with my prepared questions. He answered them all courteously and easily. I could not imagine him flying into a fury and calling anyone a murderer, but I was seeing him only as he wanted me to see him. I had no idea what he was capable of saying or doing.

When I ran out of the questions in my notebook, I began to invent others. I was stalling. The silence between questions grew longer and longer and more awkward as I improvised.

'I understand you interviewed Frank Wright,' Keller said, speaking into one of the pauses. He smiled. 'Did you find him as formidable as you seem to be finding me?'

I closed the notebook and put it and the pencil away in my bag. 'Mr Keller,' I said in what I felt was an unnaturally loud voice, 'I'm here under false pretenses.' The minute this was out of my mouth, I was so struck by its absurd staginess that I had to laugh, and most of my tension fell away. 'Well, I am,' I said, 'but I didn't intend to sound so melodramatic about it. Let me take a deep breath.' I took it. 'My maiden name is McNally, Megan McNally. I'm Terrence McNally's daughter.'

He was no longer smiling. 'That's melodramatic enough,' he said. He looked away from me for a moment, toward the woods outside, and then back again. 'What is it you want?'

'Nothing that can possibly harm you. Information, that's all. Information about my family that you have and that isn't available anywhere else.' I leaned toward him, wondering why I had been so frightened of him. He was only an ordinary, aging man – no, not ordinary; he was a

517

gifted architect, but only a man all the same.

'I want to know what Charles found out in Ireland about the first Terrence McNally. My father came to you after Charles's death to ask you, but—'

'Is that what he came for?' Keller was watching me intently, with an expression I could not read. 'That's all? Curiosity? I doubt it. He came to accuse me—' He broke off. 'Mrs Bernbach, or McNally, or whatever your name is, it was over thirty years ago. Before you were born. You could never have known Charles. You couldn't—' He stopped again and closed his eyes. 'Why in God's name are you raking it all up now?'

He was beginning to sound angry, but I was used to angry men. I said, 'Because my father could never come to you again – how could he? – and I never thought of approaching you myself until my husband suggested it. Then it took me awhile to work up the courage. I thought you *might* be formidable. After all, you threw my father out once. I couldn't be sure you wouldn't throw me out, too.' I had been speaking rather lightly, but now I changed my tone. 'My father came to you full of guilt for his brother's death, hoping you could tell him something to relieve it. You called him a murderer and threw him out. He's been living with that all the thirty years, Mr Keller, but you're no longer the boy who meant him to suffer. That's why I'm here. To ask you please to tell me anything you know that might help him to feel less responsible.'

I tried to watch Keller's face, but he had turned toward the windows again, and I could see only his profile. I thought maybe I had bungled it. It might have been better not to tell him Pa had suffered. For all I knew, Keller did still want him to.

It was several moments before he spoke. 'I can't tell you who or what was responsible.' His voice sounded heavy. 'Perhaps your father was. Perhaps I was. Or what the old man told Charles in Ireland. Or Charles's parents. Or society. Or—'

'You lived in the same society.' I said.

'I'm tough. Charles wasn't. Besides. I knew what my orientation was when I was very young. I grew up knowing. It hit Charles suddenly, like the proverbial ton of bricks. I knew about him before he knew himself. I knew he loved me just as I loved him, but I didn't want to push him into anything.' Keller turned around and looked at me again, as if he had forgotten I was there. 'Perhaps you find talk of love in this context revolting?'

'How can love be revolting?'

Keller's face warmed. 'He was so innocent. I've never known anyone like him. Of course, such innocence couldn't exist today. He worried about his lack of interest in girls, but he thought it was because he was slow to mature. When he began to realize it wasn't that, he thought perhaps he had some kind of illness. I understand now what a trap innocence can be, but then I felt that to tell him would be to seduce him, and I didn't want it to happen that way. I was very young myself.'

'Then you went to Ireland together.' I prodded him.

'Yes. Ireland. I'm rambling like an old man, but you've brought so much back.' He got up and began walking around the room as he talked, touching things, picking them up and putting them down again. 'I've never known why Charles was so wild to find out about this ancestor of his. He said it was a family mystery and he'd always been intrigued by it. Perhaps it was no more than that, but it seemed to obsess him. We must have covered every inch of that place – Lis-something-or-other – and talked to everybody who lived there before we found this ancient relic – he looked at least a hundred – who said he'd overheard his father or great-grandfather or whoever tell the story.'

Keller paused so long that I had to prod him again. 'What was the story?'

'Story's the wrong word. The old fellow looked up at

519

Charles – he was sitting on a stone in front of his house – and spoke one short, ugly sentence.' Keller stopped prowling. 'Shall I paraphrase it for you? It isn't really fit for a lady's ears.'

'I'm like you,' I said. 'I'm tough. Give it to me in the original.'

'He buggered little boys.'

I had imagined other horrors – everything from hatchet killings to incest – but not this one. It took me a minute to speak.

'That's all the old man told you?' I asked then, with more aplomb than I felt.

'It's all he knew. But you can fill in the rest. Think what it must have been like in that remote little community where everybody knew everybody else and they all depended on each other. A respectable married man with children. Perhaps a pillar of the church. Perhaps a friendly, likable fellow with what seemed to be a fatherly interest in small boys. Instead, he turns out to be a dangerous creature who preys on those boys. Nobody knows what was done to him after he was discovered, but probably the only way his family could go on living among their neighbors was to pretend he had never existed.'

'But he was sick . . .' I began, and knew the answer to that before Keller gave it.

'So are all the mentally disturbed, but in those days they were treated like animals.' He was watching my face. 'I think a cup of coffee or tea would be advisable at this point. Which will you have?'

I asked for coffee. He rang for the housekeeper and murmured something to her at the door. She actually curtsied, elderly as she was, and I heard her call him Mr Sidney.

'She was my mother's parlormaid,' he said when she had gone. 'She's worked for Kellers most of her life.' He sat down on the curved sofa again. 'Tell me about

520

yourself. The book on modern architecture was obviously fictitious, but I think you must do something else. You don't strike me as an ordinary housewife.'

'You're perceptive. I'm the editor of a magazine called *Woman's World*.'

'Yes, I know it, of course.' He had an attractive smile, his teeth brilliantly white in the dark face. 'You're a handsome young woman besides. As I remember your father, you don't resemble him.'

'My husband says I look a little like my father, a little like my mother, and a little like neither of them.'

'What does your husband do?'

'He's a doctor. Do you mind if we get back to the subject, Mr Keller? You haven't told me how Charles reacted when—'

'Shall we have our coffee first? This has waited thirty-odd years. Surely it can wait until we've had our coffee.'

He spoke in the same easy, pleasant manner, but now I realized he was not easy at all. He was a singularly controlled man under great tension. '*I can't tell you who or what was responsible. Perhaps I was,*' he had said. What my father had lived with for so long, Keller had lived with, too.

The housekeeper brought a platter of moist little cucumber and watercress sandwiches with the coffee, and we talked about nothing of consequence until she came to take the tray away again. I had been prepared to find him threatening, unpleasant, repellent, but instead, I liked him very much.

'Well, now, about Charles,' he said when the tray was gone. 'I told you how innocent he was. He had no idea what the old man meant. I had to explain to him what his – great-grandfather was it? – had done to the little boys. We sat on the grass in a wide empty green field, and I told him. I was so young myself.' Keller said for the second time, 'but I told him as gently as I knew how about men who are attracted to little boys. He got paler and paler as I

521

talked.' Keller put his head back and closed his eyes. He seemed to be seeing and hearing it all again, and I felt such pity for him that I almost wished I had not come. 'When I'd finished, he asked me if I thought a person could inherit anything like that, and then it all came out – the feelings he didn't understand, his response to me . . . Of course, he had no desire whatever to abuse little boys, but I don't believe I convinced him that it was an altogether different tendency and couldn't be inherited in any case. He kept saying he wasn't fit to live among decent people either. I told him if he wasn't, I wasn't. "Do you think I'm not?" I asked him, and he said – he said, "Oh, Sid, except for my brother you're the decentest boy I know."'

Keller said nothing more for some time. I imagined him crying tearlessly behind his closed eyes. When he spoke again, his voice was so soft that I had to lean close to hear him.

'We made love once. Only once. That was the time your father walked in on us and called us filth. But it was my fault Charles was there. It was I who thought it was time we were together.' He opened his eyes and looked at me. 'I called your father a murderer because I was afraid I was one. I'll leave it to you to decide whether it was he or I or neither of us.'

Words of meaningless reassurance came into my mind, but I did not say them. They would have been an insult to his dignity. He had showed me his wounds, and all I could do for him was leave him alone with them. I knew I would never see him again.

I should have gone back to the office. My desk was piled with work. Instead, I called and told Dora I would not be in until the following morning. I did not make up a reason. One of the advantages of my position was that I did not have to give reasons. I wondered why, when it was so easy for the powerful or the rich to be honest, they so often were not.

I went straight from the train to Angela. I wanted to ask

522

her how she thought I should approach my father with what Sidney Keller had told me – whether I should keep any of it back or even not repeat it to him at all. She knew Pa far better than I did. He and I were on shaky terms. He disapproved of my working at all and thought it outrageous that Grandpa had let me 'attempt', as he put it, to be an editor-in-chief. He alternated between telling me I neglected my children and saying that I spoiled them or spoiled Mac and neglected Sheila. He was hostile to Seth. That time on the way to Vienna when he had talked to me about Charles, and I had felt so close to him, was like a dream.

'I want him to believe Charles would have killed himself no matter what Pa said or did,' I told Angela. 'That's why I went to see Keller. But now I'm not sure what to do with what I know. If I hit the wrong note with Pa, I could make it worse than if I said nothing.'

We were in Angela's bedroom in the Seventy-fourth Street house. It was a big house for two people. Pa had wanted to move to an apartment, but Angela had not. She managed always to get her way and still make Pa believe that she deferred to him. It was fortunate that there was no evil in her. She could as easily have manipulated him, or anyone, for wicked ends.

She was getting ready now for one of her dinner parties, sitting at her dressing table and brushing her long, still fair hair. I often caught myself thinking that Sheila, who had similar coloring, might grow up to look like her, as though they were related. Angela would have been delighted to know about that slip of the mind. Whatever little malice she was capable of was directed at Maman, who was my mother and who despised her. I'm sure Maman was jealous of her because she was so important in my life and Pa's, but Angela had no way of knowing that.

'Why don't you let me tell him?' Angela said.

'Wouldn't he think it was strange? That I'd do it

523

through you instead of going to him directly?'

'Why don't you leave that to me?'

A few days later Pa came down to my office. where he had not set foot before. and sat on a corner of my desk. He didn't ask me if I was busy. Grandpa would have. but not Pa.

'That was a brave thing you did for me. going to see that appalling Sid Keller,' he said. 'It's a great relief finally to know the truth.' He took my face between his hands and kissed me. 'Thank you. kitten.'

He had not called me kitten since I was ten years old. He must have meant it affectionately, but it seemed to me to diminish the entire episode. I had wanted it to change his life, and he had reduced it to a girlish favor that had corrected a mildly troubling misconception.

'What difference does it make?' Angela said when I asked her what she had told him. 'It accomplished what you wanted accomplished.'

'Did it? He doesn't act as if he's dropped a load of guilt. He's the same as he always was.'

She said, 'Maybe he has other guilts? Maybe guilt is a habit with him? I don't know. I don't waste much energy myself on feeling guilty.'

At least I had the answer to the mystery of the first Terrence McNally, but I could not even share it with Grandpa. I could not explain how I had discovered it without letting him know about Charles and Sidney Keller, and it was not my place to tell him that. I wished I had not disturbed Keller for such questionable results.

12

When my six months were up, I found an envelope on my desk addressed to Megan McNally, Editor-in-Chief, *Woman's World*. Inside was a letter to Grandpa, dated two months earlier, requesting that I be kept on permanently in that capacity. It was signed by Sarah Dorfman, Ralph Barnhard, Mildred Grabo in Food and Equipment, and Timothy Dugan. Uncharacteristically, I dripped tears all over the page.

It took more than two years to put the book back up there with the *Ladies' Home Journal*. We tried to give our readers a definite perspective, a sense of women's place in a changing world. We offered a variety of subject matter, in both articles and fiction. We gave women a forum for a wide range of ideas. In time we developed a mass audience of loyal readers who believed in the book and regarded it as a friend and counselor.

This was the vision I had had long before I had the skill or the experience to make it real. But skill and experience were not all I needed. I had to be strong enough to contend with the struggles that went on constantly in the various departments for more say in the content of the book, more space in its pages, more importance, more power. I had to be stronger because I was young and a woman and a McNally. And I had to have a first-rate staff that knew I was the boss.

I had expected Timothy Dugan to give me trouble. He was an expert editor, eleven years older than I, and male. But he surprised me. He was no pushover, as he had made clear that day he questioned my rejection of his recommendations, but he did not once, in any way, challenge my position as his superior. He was an interesting man. Eventually he and his wife, Willa, became personal friends, close to both Seth and me. When Willa died of cancer under Seth's care, Tim came and stayed with us for three weeks, and even in his sorrow he was a charming guest.

Seth's practice grew much too large for the makeshift quarters attached to the apartment. We moved into six spacious rooms on Seventy-third Street, overlooking the Hudson, and Seth made a giant leap to an impressive office in the Apthorp, an elegant apartment building covering an entire block, Seventy-eighth to Seventy-ninth streets, Broadway to West End Avenue. It paid off. A doctor surely had to be topnotch if he could afford such an office. Some possible patients avoided him because his name was Bernbach, but others came to him believing that Jews, though one might not accept them socially, were smarter than anybody else. In a few years his practice nearly doubled.

He came home as tired, sometimes, as when he had been interning at Mount Sinai. I came home tired, too. We argued as much as we always had, only more quietly because of Julia and the children. But when a page in one of the issues of *Woman's World* came out blank, or when Tim discovered just before we went to press that a top story had been copied word for word from an old *Good Housekeeping* story, Seth listened to me groan. And when he lost a patient and thought of all the ways he might have saved the person, even when there was no known way – something he went through every time – I listened to him. And no matter how often we talked about the other things, the triumphs, relishing them, we listened to each other, too.

We had separate vocations, separate interests, but we had grown so tightly together that it was as if his blood were flowing in my veins, and mine in his. Whenever anything happened and he was not there – whenever I saw something beautiful or read something that impressed me – all my circuits began to click, storing it to tell him. It seemed incredible that I had ever not known him.

When Mac started kindergarten, going off the first day as if he were an old, experienced schoolboy, I wanted to send Sheila to nursery school. Seth and Pa said she was just a baby and still needed individual attention. Grandpa agreed with me that what she needed was to be knocked around a little. I don't know whether I kept her home in the end because she was so small and so pretty and it seemed awful to think of anyone's pulling her hair or pushing her down in the sandbox, or perhaps it was the first time Seth and Pa had ever been on the same side and I thought they ought to win together.

'She's just willful,' Seth said. 'Inside, you know, she's all soft and sweet.'

She was, but even at three she hid it. Mac was as open as a toy he had, a mechanical man with all its works visible. If a child in the park refused to let him play when asked, he would stand and watch for a while with big, sad eyes and then, the equivalent of a shrug plain on his face, go off and do something else. Sheila never asked. 'I'll play with you,' she would say regally, and was seldom turned down. Once when she was, by two older little boys, she swung at one of them and hit him square in the nose. It was what I might have done myself at her age.

We spent all day with them Sundays, when Julia was off. In the beginning Seth called his answering service every hour and often had to leave to attend a patient. By the time the children were eight and six, he had enlarged his offices and taken in a younger doctor with a growing practice of his own. They covered for each other. Seth's family Sundays were uninterrupted unless he had someone so sick that he would not leave him or her to anyone else. Some of his patients complained at first when he was not always available. One or two left him. He pretended he didn't mind.

'I have too many patients as it is,' he said. 'What am I supposed to do, work twenty-four hours a day, three hundred sixty-five days a year? That's what I've damn near done since I got out of school. That's what kills so many doctors before their time. If I dropped dead of a heart attack, they'd have to go to another doctor anyway.'

'*I'm* convinced. Now if you could only convince yourself—'

'What do you mean? I've taken the step, haven't I? If I weren't convinced it was the thing to do—'

'That's not how it works with you. Usually, because you're a very bright, sensible fellow, you choose the best course. Then you begin worrying about all the possible consequences. If one of those patients who've left you dies under another doctor's care, you'll feel guilty.'

'Don't be ridiculous,' he said, but he grinned at me, knowing it was true.

We were at the Central Park Zoo, watching the performing seals for the third Sunday in a row. The seals were Sheila's latest passion. I would have preferred a change of scene, but Mac had a new Brownie camera, a birthday present from Julia, and was happily snapping pictures of the animals, and Seth professed to be as enthralled as Sheila.

'You're not. You can't be. It's because you think she must have everything her heart desires,' I said. 'You and Pa.'

On the subject of Sheila, Seth and Pa had had a meeting of minds. They defended themselves and each other against Grandpa and me when we said they spoiled her. Pa had more respect for Seth, now that it was obvious I was no longer working to support him, but it was their mutual delight in Sheila that had softened his antagonism.

'Don't expect him ever to be crazy about Seth, though,' Angela had told me. 'Remember he had you back for only a few years when Seth came along and took you away again, before he was ready to let you go.'

'But Pa didn't see much of me anyhow. He was constantly off somewhere.'

'He thought he'd see more of you the next month or the next year. He thought he had plenty of time. That's why he doesn't change his ways. He always thinks he has plenty of time.'

Angela's insights no longer surprised me. Maman, who

came over to New York for a week twice a year, now that I was too busy to go to her, still insisted Angela was 'sappy' and stayed away from her. Seth thought so, too, until I told him she had written the anonymous letter to his parents that precipitated our marriage. Sappiness was one of her masquerades.

'Next week I am positively not coming to see the seals,' I said to Seth now. 'There's a limit to how much of your spoiling I'll be a party to.'

'Do you think you don't spoil Mac?'

'Mac is unspoilable.'

We argued about this a little, but it was an old, light-hearted argument. The things we became impassioned about were rarely of such consequence.

'Sheila's a lot like you,' Seth said. 'That's why you clash.'

'Mac isn't like anybody. Do you suppose he got mixed up in the hospital?'

'Have you taken a good look at him? He may not be mine, of course, but he's as McNallyish a looking eight-year-old as ever harked back to the Auld Sod.'

We did not go to see the seals the following Sunday. Sheila begged, sobbed, screamed, stamped her feet, and tried to bite me when I carried her to her room and locked the door. Then she shrieked through it that she hated me. She might as well have stabbed me. But it was the first of many times, and eventually I knew it was the defeat she hated, not me.

'I'm always the bad guy with her. I wish you'd be it just once,' I raged at Seth, 'and let me be the good guy.'

I knew, though, that it was not his fault. She could provoke him to fury, at times, but no matter how severe he was with her, she did not lash out at him as she did at me. When he would not let her near the radio for a week because she had listened to a program he had forbidden her, she wrote him a note in uneven but clear block letters that said: 'I WILL NOT LIV UNDER A ROOL

529

Pa accused me of preferring Mac, but it was not so. Mac was easier. He was sweet-tempered, readily amused, undemanding. At the end of a long day or a hard week I could simply enjoy him and not have to cope with bouts of temperament. He was a happy, responsive child. But he was not as interesting as Sheila. He was not as bright, except for a flair for language that Sheila wholly lacked. It was impossible not to love him, but it was just as impossible not to love a little girl who would not 'liv under a rool'.

Nothing was allowed to interfere with our family Sundays. I would not look at anything I had brought home from the office. I pretended that *Woman's World* did not exist. All day I was a devoted mother. I prepared the children's meals. While they were still young enough, I bathed them. After they were in bed, I cooked dinner for Seth and myself – something elaborate and special, for adult palates only. Afterwards we made what we called Sunday love. I wore my honeymoon nightgown so that Seth could take it off, instead of starting, as I did during the week, without a nightgown. We tried a variety of locations other than the bed – the rug, the sofa, the bathtub. Usually I was as inventive as Seth, but Sundays I left it all to him. He called me tootsie, and cookie, and little mother, and sometimes we rolled on the floor, laughing.

'If only Monday would never come,' I said, but I didn't mean it. I loved playing Standard Woman once a week, but I could not have stood it every day. Whenever I wondered if this was freakish, unfeminine, Seth laughed at me. But he was biased. It took a conversation with Tim Dugan to settle the question for me.

He and Seth and I were having dinner at the Plaza, where Seth had met Tim and me after a late staff meeting. It was a winter evening, shortly after World War II. Tim's wife, Willa, had been dead for six years.

He could talk about her now, as he presently did, with a little objectivity.

Seth had stalked out of the apartment in icy silence that morning, following an argument about what to do with Julia, who was no longer needed as a nursemaid. Now he was holding my hand under the table. The night before, I had listened to him, murmured to him, as he went through the litany of his latest *mea culpa* . . .

'I should have gone. I should have been there. What was I doing, hiding behind my age? I should have been there, fighting the sons of bitches, I should have known . . .'

'You did your part here. You were needed here. How could you have known? None of us knew . . .'

'We knew. We didn't believe it. I thought it was like the stories they told in the other war, Germans bayoneting babies. Sensible people don't believe such horrors. All right, harassment, internment camps – we were that shameful ourselves to the Japanese – but not the rest of it. After all, the Germans aren't animals; they're human beings. Animals? No animal does what they did. I should have gone and found out for myself.'

'No, Seth, no. You did more here than you could have done there.'

We had made love in the end, and in the morning we had argued about Julia.

He looked at peace now. Tired – he always looked tired – but at peace. He was nearly forty-one years old. He had lines around his eyes and a few gray hairs at his temples and among his shaggy brows. I was thirty-six. I had a few little lines myself, a little softening around the waist from long hours sitting at a desk. We had been married for more than fifteen years. Nothing would change us now, I thought, as Tim passed me the Palm Court's crisp warm rolls. We would always love and solace each other. We would always have flaming arguments, but we would always end in peace.

531

'It's interesting,' Tim said, 'how quickly Rosie the Riveter has reverted to Dolly the Dependent now that the war's over.'

'Well, she's had to, hasn't she?' Seth said. 'The returning veterans need her job.'

'I think there's more to it than that.' Tim smiled at me. He spoke in the lilting Irish voice that I had once believed was put on but now knew could not have been. He was much too straightforward. 'Megan, you're the only woman I've ever met who thrives on independence,' he said. 'The others, no matter how able or successful outside their homes, all seem to dream of someday returning to it. And it's not because they're needed or because they believe the life is preferable. They want dependence.'

I thought of Fran Werner, who had been so desperate to give up her important, challenging job and have a husband to support her. Even Fanny, restless as she was away from the office, had left it once she and Grandpa were legally married.

'Willa was an executive at Best's when I met her. I don't think you knew that. She never talked about it,' Tim said. 'She was making more money than I was. She had an almost unlimited future.' He speared a shrimp from his plate and then held it uneaten on the little fork while he spoke. 'I found that attractive, you see. Not the money. I don't mean the money. The kind of woman who could stand alone, without me to prop her up.'

'A battleship consort,' Seth said.

'Yes, if you like. Anyhow, a woman who didn't expect me to be always the strong, aggressive, dominant one, making decisions, responsible for her as well as for myself, while she stayed home the rest of her life and arranged the flowers.' He dipped the shrimp in cocktail sauce and chewed it meditatively. Seth gave my hand a what-do-you-know-about-this? squeeze. 'Willa quit her job as soon as we were married,' Tim went on. 'Nothing else had ever entered her head but to return to dependence the minute she could.'

'She thought she might have children,' I said. Willa had once told me what a disappointment it had been to her to discover she was unable to conceive. 'Wasn't that—?'

'I know she believed that was the reason. Afterwards she said it was too late – Best's wouldn't take her back, and she'd have to start way down the ladder again if she went somewhere else – but she never tried, you see. She never really wanted to share the maintenance or the command. That was up to me.' Tim stopped and looked at me, then at Seth, then back at me. 'I wasn't intending this to sound bitter or complaining. We had a good marriage. All I meant it for was to illustrate my point about Rosie the Riveter and you, Megan.'

'Megan's mother is another one,' Seth said. 'She lives alone in France. Nothing will induce her to live here, where her family is. When she comes over to visit, she won't even stay with us. She takes rooms at the Belnord. What is it she always says? "I must live to myself. I must have my own place."'

I took a sip of wine, wondering whether or not to say what was in my mind and then deciding I would say it.

'You know, Tim, I've always thought you must be wishing I'd go back home and leave *Woman's World* to you. Not that you've ever given me cause to think so, but it seems – well, natural, I suppose.'

'Natural.' Tim shook his head. He spoke to Seth. 'You see I'm probably as good a fiction editor as you'll find in the United States.' We had long ago separated fiction from articles again. 'The limit of my ambition and ability is to be the best. Megan is superb at her job, and I could no more do it than I could do Roosevelt's. Nor would I want to.'

'Megan could probably do Roosevelt's, too,' Seth said.

The only possible response to all that was to laugh. 'I

533

may be sitting with the only two men in the world,' I said, 'who have a preference for bossy women. How lucky can one woman be?'

13

Oh, I was so lucky. We were so lucky. When the Japanese attacked Pearl Harbor, Mac was nine years old and Seth, thirty-seven. Maman spent the war years in a country house in Scotland, looking after children evacuated from London. Seth practiced with a rescue squad that never had to rescue anyone. I stood on the roof of a school and watched the night sky for enemy planes that never came. Sheila and Mac collected scrap metal for armaments whose detonations they never heard. Angela rolled bandages for wounds she never saw.

Seth's young associate left all his patients in Seth's care and went to the Philippines, where he was killed in the shelling of a field hospital.

Pa was sixty-three and could have passed for fifty. He stayed around the office a little more, waiting, I suppose, for Grandpa to step down, but Grandpa still came in three days a week to run things. All through Roosevelt's administrations he had written a favorable editorial for *McNally's Monthly*, to every outraged one of George Horace Lorimer's for the *Saturday Evening Post*. The one that appeared when Roosevelt died was reprinted all over the world. Grandpa was eight-seven when he wrote it.

All periodicals did well in the expanding economy. In spite of competition from television, magazines entered another Golden Age. Two McNally books were launched – *Metropolis*, a magazine that focused on New York, and a weekly newsmagazine called *Now* – but *Woman's World* led the field.

Seth and I bought a house in Scarsdale. It was a handsome Colonial with nine rooms on two wooded acres. We spent weekends and vacations there, and the children and I lived there most of the summer. I got so much reading done on the train that I didn't mind commuting. Seth had an idea that someday he would give up his New York practice, buy a small and less demanding one in Westchester, and we would live in Scarsdale all year round. I could not imagine his doing it. He would only worry about the patients he had abandoned. But he liked to talk about it, and I listened.

The house solved the problem of Julia. She lived there, and looked after us when we came. She was a bumbling housekeeper and a terrible cook – her only skill was children – but she had been with us for thirteen years, and we could not possibly let her go. As things turned out, it was lucky we kept her.

By 1952 the new Golden Age of magazines was coming to an end. I saw it happening, but I felt nothing. I went to the office every day and read copy and held meetings and gave orders that must have been the right ones because I kept the book going. It was all mechanical, the automatic product of my long experience. My heart was somewhere else.

Mac was twenty in 1952. My heart was in Korea, where a sniper's bullet had cut him down.

Seth could not have got through it without me. I thought I could not have got through it without him. In only another year I knew I could have.

That was the year the large corporations, like Crowell-Collier, that controlled a number of periodicals among their other enterprises eliminated their magazine divisions. All magazines were losing money, but those without strong editors to prevent the corporations from meddling with editorial production were doomed. *Woman's World* survived. I knew I could keep it alive. I wanted to do more than that, though. I wanted it thriving again.

I was working on plans to enlarge the service features, one of several ideas I had for increasing readership. It was a mild April day, with a light rain spattering the windows. When Tim came in, I had stopped for a moment to watch it, thinking it would be good for the new grass the gardener had planted at the Scarsdale house.

'Megan—' Tim said, and stopped. I understood every shading in Seth's voice, but I heard nothing uncommon in Tim's. I was smiling when I turned around to him.

'Megan, a phone call has just come. Dora wouldn't put it through to you. She thought it would be easier for you if I told you about it.'

I knew then. I don't know how. It could have been any of the others, but I knew.

'Seth?'

'Yes, Megan. He was shot.'

'Shot?' The word made no sense to me. People were shot in a war. Mac was shot. Not Seth, here in New York City. 'What do you mean, shot?'

Tim had started to reach for my hands, but he saw not to do that. I had hard hold of my own hands.

'He had just left the hospital and was getting into his car. A nurse witnessed the whole thing, but there was nothing she—' He stopped to swallow. I could see his throat move. 'A man got out of a car parked behind Seth's. Apparently he tried to get Seth to go with him to treat another fellow who was lying in the car with a stomach wound. Seth must have said he wouldn't go; the wounded man would have to be brought into the hospital. The nurse saw them arguing, and then she heard the shot.'

'He's dead,' I said.

'He died instantly. He had no time to feel anything.' Tim bent down to me, not touching me. 'Shall I take you to him now?'

I shook my head. I had no wish to see him dead.

'Shall I call Sheila for you then?'

I said no and asked him to wait outside. I myself called Sheila at Vassar. I was very calm. I waited until she had quieted down a little, and then I told her to come down on the next train and take a taxi to the apartment.

536

I let Tim take me home. I think he stayed. I think it was he who called the rest and let them in when they came.

I went into our room and shut the door and pulled the shades. I got in on my side of the bed, with all my clothes on, and stayed there for two days. I think people came in and out, but I was too blind and deaf to know who they were.

At the end of the two days I got up and bathed and changed my clothes for Seth's funeral and went on living.

1958

His voice sounds stronger again. Is it true that the dying rally before the end? I think I have read this somewhere.

He is talking about Fanny. 'You were in love with her yourself as a boy,' he says to Pa.

'You never gave any sign of knowing that,' Pa says.

'I know a lot of things I never gave any sign of knowing.'

Pa leans close to the pillow as they talk, as if about to kiss the shriveled face. I think they have forgotten I am there. I whisper to Pa to call me if there is a change and slip out again, leaving them alone together.

Downstairs Sheila has set the food out on a table, but only Sam is eating. He has drawn a chair up near Maman and Angela, and he has a plate on his kees. His mouth is full, and he does not empty it completely before he speaks.

'If you would prefer to go back to the city tonight, I'd be happy to drive you,' he is saying to Maman as I come in.

'Thank you,' Maman answers. I wonder if he understands that she means 'No, thank you.'

Sheila is as far away as she can get, standing at the front windows and looking out at the greening lawn. When I join her there, she begins whispering to me fiercely.

'I wish he'd go. He doesn't belong here.'

'Well, he's your grandfather.'

She gives me the scornful look this deserves. Why do I say fatuous things to Sheila that I would not think of saying to anyone else? He is her grandfather, but he has barely spoken to her. Or to me, Seth's wife – widow. I don't know why he came, and I wish, too, that he would leave.

All at once he is beside me. He has put down his empty plate and is standing with us at the window, a thicker, coarser, older version of Seth that wrenches me with anger and sadness. Sheila starts to move away, but he steps in front of her.

'One minute.' He looks from me to her and adds, 'Please. I'm only staying until Terry comes back.' It's as if he had heard us, though he couldn't have. 'I have nothing against you. I wanted to say that. I thought if I came, maybe – but I'm an old man. I can't feel what I can't feel.' He looks at Sheila again. 'You're a beautiful young lady,' he says, and walks back across the room.

'What was that all about?' Sheila says, but the fierceness is gone.

She is beautiful. There is a small white scar high on one cheek, where the man she married at nineteen, a month after Seth's death, opened the flesh to the bone with his fist, but it doesn't diminish her beauty. She stayed with him stubbornly for four years. She is stubborn. She is sweet, tough, softhearted, independent, and beautiful. She is twenty-four years old, and I don't think she knows what to do with her life.

'I guess I'll clean up in the kitchen,' she says. 'I don't want to leave a mess for Julia.'

'She'll be glad if you leave it. She wants to feel useful.'

Poor Julia. She has been a godsend since I brought Grandpa here to live with me. She has tended him as she did the children, with a brisk, loving, unsentimental competence that he could accept. Now once again she will have no function that would not be better filled by someone else. No matter how I try to conceal this from her, she is too smart not to know. She left this morning for an emergency visit to her dentist in the city, but I'm not sure it was her tooth that ached.

I go to speak to Maman and Angela, making an effort, as I always do, to give them exactly equal attention. They both have a way of thwarting this, Angela by referring to some common experience that Maman has not shared; Maman, by talking to me in French. I wonder whether I will carry all my own foolish resentments and envies and prejudices with me into old age.

Sheila has not moved from the windows. She stands so straight, but I think if no one was looking, she would slump.

'Sheila,' I say, returning to her, 'why don't you come and live here with me? It will be a big, empty house for only Julia and me.'

She shakes her head. 'It wouldn't work.' Then she glances at me and says quickly, 'Unless you'll be too lonely. Then, of course—'

'I won't be lonely.' But I have been lonely for all the five years without Seth. Not alone, but lonely. 'I just had an idea you might like to come, at least for a while,' I say. 'It's a good place to relax and think things out.'

'I've thought things out.' She is not looking at me. 'I want to work for *Woman's World*. If you're willing to try me, that is. I know I've always sort of made fun of it,' she says before I can speak, 'but that's a whole complicated thing that has to do with you and Mac and you and – and Dad.' She takes a deep breath. 'I really admire you very much.'

She cannot say 'love'. It doesn't matter. 'If someone had come along this morning and offered me three wishes,' I tell her, 'I'd have wished that Great-Grandpa would live forever, that Grandpa would go home, where a man of seventy-six belongs, and leave the McNally organization to me, and that you would be there to carry it on after me.' I cannot help the little tremor in my voice, but she seems not to mind. She is smiling. 'Wait till I tell Great-Grandpa,' I say. 'He'll be as happy as I am.'

It is the first thing I tell him after Pa comes down and says he asked for me again. I hold his hand as I did before. I think it feels smaller and colder, but it has the strength to give mine the semblance of a squeeze.

'I knew,' he says. 'She told me.'

539

'When?'

'Old people don't remember when. Awhile back.'

I am not at all sure he knew. He has always been able to convince himself that he knows everything and thinks of everything before anyone else. But soon he startles me with knowledge I did not dream he had.

'Terry tells me lies about Charles,' he says. 'You know that's wrong, don't you? It says in the Bible that a man on his deathbed must be told the truth.'

I didn't believe it said that in the Bible or that he would have known, or cared, if it did.

'What lies did Pa tell you?'

He doesn't answer this. He says, 'A dying man does a lot of thinking. My mind has been full of Charles, and it came to me—' He has to stop for breath. He closes his eyes, so that the face on the pillow becomes the blank mask of a mummy. But when he speaks again, though his voice is weak, it is Grandpa's. 'He preferred his own sex, didn't he?'

'What do you—?'

'No, Megan, you mustn't lie. I'd have loved him anyway. I wish he'd known how much I loved him. It was only – I couldn't converse with him the way I could with Terry. He cared about such different things – sports—'

There is such a long pause that it frightens me, but then he opens his eyes, and his voice strengthens a little.

'That was the "illness" he said he had, wasn't it, Megan?'

'Yes.'

I waited, but he doesn't finish this. After a moment he goes on to something else.

'I believe he lied to me about Ireland. He said no one there had heard of the first Terrence McNally. Terry assures me that's so, as far as he knows. I've been thinking, and I believe they both lied.'

'Why should they, Grandpa?'

He opens his mouth and closes it. Finally he says, 'Because it's something disturbing. Something to do with the way Charles died.' His mouth moves soundlessly again. 'It will disturb me more to die not knowing. If you know,

Megan, tell me.'

I sense now what an effort of will this is, and I feel I must honor it with the truth. He is keeping himself alive for it.

'The first Terrence McNally was a pederast,' I tell him. 'Charles wasn't, of course, but he was too innocent to understand the difference. Apparently he thought that it *was* an illness and that he had inherited it. Whether that was the reason he killed himself or—'

'Inherited?' The word bursts from Grandpa's lips with something approaching normal vigor, but when he goes on, I have to lean close to hear him. 'I thought he knew . . . I thought she told him, out of spite . . . I thought that was why . . .'

'Grandpa?'

'If he knew, and believed I'd always hated him because of it . . . A father who loved his son would love him no less, but a man who hated him . . .'

I can't make out what he's talking about. I'm afraid that finally his mind is wandering. A kind of spasm crosses his face. It frightens me until I recognize it as a smile.

'He didn't know. He never knew.'

'He never knew what, Grandpa?'

He answers me with perfect clarity. 'That he wasn't my son. Hers but not mine. I loved him just the same. It wasn't his fault. I loved him very much.' The spasm-smile comes on his face again. 'I'm so glad he never knew he wasn't mine.'

He closes his eyes once more. I think he may have spoken for the last time, but his hand still holds mine, and so I wait. After a while he begins again.

I think he is saying, 'Marry,' but I can hardly hear him. I put my ear down next to his mouth.

Yes, that's what he is saying. 'Marry again, Megan . . . years still ahead of you . . . long-lived McNallys . . .' Then he makes a dry sound – a chuckle? – and I can hear him more clearly. 'Do you want to be lonely for fifty-one more years?'

'I'll be all right, Grandpa. I had a marriage. I had Seth.

That will last me a lifetime.'

'No . . . you'll be old and alone . . . marry Tim Dugan . . . good man . . . in love with you a long time . . .'

I can see he is going, and I don't want to cry. He would hate it if I cried.

'Stop trying to run my life,' I say. 'You know you can't do it.'

He looks pleased. No, I imagine it. He doesn't look anything anymore.

'You've mourned five years . . .' His voice is a whisper now. '. . . tell you what you told me. Five years is long enough.'

These were the last words he spoke.

'I feel privileged to have been in the world with him,' Tim said at the memorial service. 'He had a royal title – Terrence McNally the First – and it became him well.'

THE END

Golden Hill

SHIRLEY LORD

Set on the exotic island paradise of Trinidad, *Golden Hill* tells the story of three families whose destinies interweave to shape the history of the island. It is a passionate story of love and hate, lust and greed, malice and envy in which the members of the three families struggle and clash violently against the background of the depression, World War II, and the island's fight for independence.

"*Golden Hill* is indeed golden and glorious. I don't know when I've enjoyed a novel as much. It is insanely romantic and at the same time historically fascinating. It is as sensuous as a Caribbean night and the characters are memorable"

David Brown, co-producer of *Jaws*

0 552 12346 3   £2.50

CORGI BOOKS

A SELECTED LISTS OF TITLES AVAILABLE FROM CORGI BOOKS

☐ 12281 5	Jade	*Pat Barr*	£2.50
☐ 12142 8	A Woman of Two Continents	*Pixie Burger*	£2.50
☐ 08615 0	The Big Wind	*Beatrice Coogan*	£2.95
☐ 99019 1	Zemindar	*Valerie Fitzgerald*	£2.50
☐ 12387 0	Copper Kingdom	*Iris Gower*	£1.95
☐ 12066 9	Lady Susan	*Phyllis Ann Karr*	£1.95
☐ 12346 3	Golden Hill	*Shirley Lord*	£2.50
☐ 11959 8	The Chatelaine	*Claire Lorrimer*	£1.95
☐ 12182 7	The Wilderling	*Claire Lorrimer*	£1.95
☐ 12084 7	Echoing Yesterday	*Alexandra Manners*	£1.50
☐ 12206 8	Karran Kinrade	*Alexandra Manners*	£1.50
☐ 12311 0	The Red Bird	*Alexandra Manners*	£1.75
☐ 12384 6	The Gaming House	*Alexandra Manners*	£1.75
☐ 10375 6	Csardas	*Diane Pearson*	£2.95
☐ 10271 7	The Marigold Field	*Diane Pearson*	£1.95
☐ 09140 5	Sarah Whitman	*Diane Pearson*	£1.95
☐ 10249 0	Bride of Tancred	*Diane Pearson*	£1.50
☐ 12367 6	Opal	*Elvi Rhodes*	£1.75

ORDER FORM

All these books are available at your book shop or newsagent, or can be ordered direct from the publisher. Just tick the titles you want and fill in the form below.

CORGI BOOKS, Cash Sales Department, P.O. Box 11, Falmouth, Cornwall.

Please send cheque or postal order, no currency.

Please allow cost of book(s) plus the following for postage and packing:

U.K. Customers—Allow 45p for the first book, 20p for the second book and 14p for for each additional book ordered, to a maximum charge of £1.63.

B.F.P.O. and Eire—Allow 45p for the first book, 20p for the second book plus 14p per copy for the next seven books, thereafter 8p per book.

Overseas Customers—Allow 75p for the first book and 21p per copy for each additional book.

NAME (Block Letters) . . . .

ADDRESS . . . .

. . . .